Unforgettable Blues

Linda Holmes-Drew

Copyright © 2015 Linda Holmes-Drew
All rights reserved.

ISBN: 1508809291
ISBN 13: 9781508809296

Acknowledgement

Thank you to my children who always believed in me; the McLoud Writers Group who were there to encourage me; Lynn Jarrett, my editor and friend, whose help was immeasurable; Tanya Provines for the artistic expertise in designing my book cover, her priceless advice, and assistance; and special thank you to Glenda Kuhn, Debbie Walker, and Lura Chandler. Last, but certainly not least, thank you to Chelsea, my Maltese puppy, who never left my lap while I wrote and edited this book. Hugs and love to you all.

Dedication

To my beloved husband, David, who dared me. Thank you honey.

Introduction

She lay in complete wonderment at the icy coldness that surrounded her. Her inability to move or see was terrifying. What could have brought her into this black, soundless, paralyzing state of existence. Was this death? Was it a horrible nightmare? Her brain was racked with unbearable pain reminiscent of only a few months prior. Had she relapsed?

She tried to calm herself and use her sense of reasoning. Okay. That was a good sign. She could obviously still think. The fog seemed to lift in her mind as she attempted to move her hands once more. They were not paralyzed . . . they were bound, very tightly. She attempted to move her legs and found they were also tightly tied. It soon became apparent to her that her mouth had suffered the same fate and something had been put over her head. Why? Who?

Time passed in a series of fading from a relative state of reason to a semi-unconscious napping. During the times of reason, she searched her memory to try and put together what may have brought about this situation. Lilah had to know why, who and where she was. She came to the conclusion that she had to go back to the beginning. There was a time when life was relatively normal . . . before, the family moved . . . before, the trip to Lexington.

Unforgettable Blues

Chapter 1

Daddy was stompin' around the truck like a quarter horse at the gate. Mama was still carryin' out suitcases and tryin' to line up the little ones to make sure they was still clean and had used the toilet before loadin' up. If there was one thing Daddy hated, it was to have to stop ever 30 minutes for somebody to go pee. Truly, there wasn't a lot that didn't aggervate Daddy when he was travelin'. All he could think about was where he was goin' and how quick he could get there.

This trip was not a vacation.

This was a big move for the family. Daddy had quit his job and lined up a new one in northeast Arkansas with his brother, Uncle Deke Parker. Now, they had to get there and find a decent place to live so Daddy could start work in just a little over a week.

Mama got real upset when I told her that I wasn't goin'. I think she thought I'd be there to help her unpack and tend my five little brothers and sisters.

I had other plans.

Mama and Daddy was loaded up and about ready to pull out when Daddy motioned me closer. "Lilah, I don't like leavin' ya up on that mountain by yourself. I just don't feel right about it. Don't be rollin' them big green eyes at me neither. What if somethin' was to happen to ya?"

"I'll be just fine, now . . . they're supposed to come put the phone in sometime this week. Besides, I got ole Billy Boots to look out for me. Ya know as well as I do Daddy, that ole hound dog would fight a bear for me, let alone some danged ole trespasser. Now, ya'll get goin' so ya can get some miles passed before it gets too late in the day. Ya do know how much I love ya . . . Mama? . . . Daddy? Ya danged kids behave and write me lots of letters, 'cause I'm really gonna miss ya guys, too. Okay?"

And with lots of tears and hugs and cautions and wavin', my family headed out in Daddy's old Ford truck, pullin' that big old trailer he'd borrowed from Mama's brother, Uncle Rick. I stood there for a few minutes, wavin' and watchin' until I couldn't see 'em no more.

It was just a little after daybreak and there was still a heavy mist in the holler. The birds seemed to have just woke up and they filled the mornin' air with their songs.

Somehow . . . I never felt so alone in my entire life. Mama and Daddy's house was all closed up and the windows was boarded over. There's just not much sadder than a house without a family. I'd spent the night there so I could see 'em on their way.

And so they were. They was on their way. I patted Billy Boots on the head and turned toward the old house. I walked across the unpainted porch and opened the creaky screen door and stepped inside. Walkin' through the empty, quiet rooms, I remembered a poem I had read somewhere. It said somethin' like . . . "Couldn't they feel the laughter, taste the tears and see the footsteps that lingered there?" This was where I'd spent the very best years of my life. I remember helpin' Mama put up the wallpaper and watchin' Daddy when he put down the linoleum. My brothers and sisters and me had been born here. We'd laughed and cried and celebrated Christmas and many birthdays.

Now everything was changin'. I felt a heavy sorrow wrap itself around me.

"So . . . suck it up Lilah Marie." I could almost hear Nanny sayin', "There's sure nuff a better day a comin'."

I was sure that 1980 was gonna be a new beggin' for us all. It was just a feelin' in the air that I couldn't ignore.

I was 30 years old and my husband had done run off with some dimwitted carhop from the Jersey Dip over in Dover. Nanny felt real bad for me and she understood what I was goin' through. You see . . . her old man had left her for her own sister.

I walked out the front door and locked it tight and started to think of all that I had left to do at my own place. Wow! My own place. How I loved the sound of that. I knew that if Walt ever got wind of how well off I was now, he'd try to make a bee line back.

When Nanny'd passed away last winter, she had up and left her two mountain cabins, all her land, *about 200 acres, I was told*, and a pretty good chunk of cash . . . to me. She told her lawyer that since I spent most of my life seein' to her needs and takin' care of her, now she wanted to take care of me. I could only hope that there was no way Walt could lay claim to anything since our divorce had only been final for a few months.

Me and Boots climbed into my old Jeep and headed for home. It was close to a 30 minute drive back down the holler and 'round to the other side of the mountain where we turned off and made our climb up to the cabins.

The sun was up pretty good and it was gettin' nice and warm. I raced Boots across the yard and up the steps. Of course . . . he won! Billy Boots was a mixed breed German Shepherd and somethin' I hadn't yet been able to identify. Walt wanted to call him Billy and I was dead set on Boots. After a lot of bickerin' we compromised on Billy Boots. Since Walt left, Boots had become my best friend, next to Floy. She and I'd known each other all our lives. We'd went to school together up until I had quit in eighth grade to move up with Nanny and take care of her. Floy and I always went to church together and we were still as close as sisters. She was far more than just a friend. I called her my sister-by-choice.

Boots followed me inside and I stood in downright shock. What in heaven would I ever do with all this . . . stuff? There was boxes and baskets stacked almost to the ceilin'. Some was from me and Walt's place, some was stuff of mine from Mama's, and some was just stuff Mama didn't have room for or just didn't want no more. A lot of it was Nanny's things. Things I'd not brought myself to go through yet. It was more than I could think about at that minute. Maybe, I decided, I needed to regroup. I seated myself in Nanny's comfy chair on the porch and sat back to make a plan.

The trees was really gettin' pretty that spring. We'd had a lot of rain and everything was just peakin' out in those pretty shades of light green. The redbuds was really showin' off along with the dogwoods. The pond was full and the early spring "wild weeds" as Nanny called 'em, sure was pretty too.

Lookin' around, my thoughts wandered to the biggest of the two cabins I now owned. Nanny's Gran Pap had built 'em long before she was born. They said he wasn't very big but had a sturdy build and no sense at all. Nanny said he would fight a bear or an Indian . . . didn't matter to him. He was a good, God fearin' man who loved his family and respected his friends and neighbors. Accordin' to Nanny, he cut the trees for the house and built ever bit with his own two hands . . . well . . . and with some help from his kin. This one was a two-story with three bedrooms upstairs and one small one downstairs, a big ole kitchen and a front room, *or parlor as Nanny called it.* The big back porch was screened in later on so Nanny could do her laundry without the bugs haulin' her off. She used to say the skeeters was so big, they come with a knife and a fork. The front porch had rails and posts right out of the olden days. Everything had been made from hand-hewn wood. That included the mantle over the fireplace where, accordin' to Ole Granpap, the famous Marshall, Wyatt Earp had once leaned when he'd had to come in out of the weather while he was headin' back east to see some family. I don't know if Ole Granpap had a few nips too many or if it really happened. That was the story handed down for many, many years and nobody was gonna dispute Ole Granpap's word.

There was no bathrooms, only ancient outhouses. Ya could bet there'd be some changes made there within the next couple of weeks, too.

The smaller cabin was a little further up the hill and across a small pasture and nestled against the mountain. It was a cozy little one room place with a front porch to sit on and honeysuckle vines growin' off one side. Ole Grandpap's mama had lived there her last years and several had moved in and out since her passin'. Now it sat empty, dark, and quiet. I wasn't sure just what I planned on doin' with it, but I was certain somethin' would come to light.

I heard a racket down in the grove of trees just then and as I stood to see what was happenin', a little blue truck come flyin' up the road. I could hear Willie Nelson wailin' at the top of his lungs on the radio as my friend Floy made her unmistakable arrival. Boots ran down to meet her and place hisself right in front of her so, as usual, he could help her find her way.

"Hello, my friend!" She called before she even got out. "So how is the newest land baron in the mountains?"

I strutted around the porch makin' like I had a cigar and a big brimmed hat.

"My, my, if ain't Miss Floy, come to call. Get on out and come up here and I'll have the maid pour us a shot a lightnin'." I laughed while I acted the part of a big plantation owner. As she made her way up the steps, we greeted each other with a big hug.

Floy wasn't very tall, in fact ya might say she was pretty short. She had long dark hair and beautiful brown eyes and a gorgeous olive complexion. Most of all, she was as pretty on the inside as she was on the outside.

"I'm sure glad you're here, my friend . . . I was just gittin' ready to start a little project, and I could sure use some advice".

"Hmmm." Floy's eyebrows pulled together. "Now that sounds a little suspicious to me. What ya got up your sleeve?"

I never could fool Floy. She could see through me like a window pane.

"Well, let's go in and I'll make us some tea and I'll tell ya all about it."

We sat at Nanny's antique kitchen table while the tea brewed for awhile. We talked about my folks' move and about me decidin' to stay. Then the talk turned to Walt and what he might up and try to do when he heard about my good fortune.

"So Lilah, how much ya reckon you'll end up with? That is, if ya don't mind me askin'?"

"Well, accordin' to Nanny's lawyer, I don't suppose I never need to worry about a job. I gave Mama and Daddy enough to buy 'em a decent place to live, and I still got plenty."

"Can I ask a personal question, Lilah?"

"Sure, we got no secrets."

"How did your Nanny come by all that money?"

"Ya know, Floy, I really ain't sure. I heard stories how it's been in the family for generations. There was somethin' about Ole Granpap's daddy hittin' big gold out west. Then, somethin' else about ole Granpap havin' a very good buisness in the liquor trade back in Prohibition. The one I like best is some wild story about some family member stealin' a huge gold shipment from the Yanks durin' the Civil War! So, I don't know what's true and what ain't. I can say for a fact that Nanny always helped all the family and gave to the church regular. And she still had way more'n plenty."

"Wow! So what ya gonna do now? Just sit back here in the mountains and do nothin'?"

"Shoot no . . . first I gotta clean this mess up and get it organized. Then I will have two bathrooms in this house and one in the little cabin, too." I scratched my head and thought for a minute. "After all that . . . well . . . ya know how much I always loved horses. I might just take me a trip down to Lexington and maybe see a horse race or two . . . better yet, I might just buy me a couple of them fancy horses for my own. I'm thinkin' that I most likely will need a friend to go with me, just to keep me on the straight and narrow. Do ya know anybody who would maybe be interested and wanna go?" I winked at her as she nodded a definite yes.

After we finished our tea, we walked around the house and tried to make some sense of all the mess that had been tossed here and there in the move.

"Let's take all the kitchen stuff back there and then your stuff up to your bedroom." Floy indicated. "Then we'll take the parlor stuff to the front . . . everything else, we can store in the empty bedrooms upstairs and use them like kind of an organization center. What do ya think?"

"Well, Miss Floy, I think we have a plan." I was so happy she had agreed to spend the weekend and help me get myself together. Who knows, I might've just sat on that porch till I grew moss.

We jumped into the plan like there was no tomorrow. We plum forgot about lunch and worked tirelessly until the late afternoon.

"Floy, I got to go pen the cows up, feed the hens, and I'll be right back."

"No problem, I think I can find a couple things to keep me busy. I might even dig up somethin' for us to eat!" she answered.

I returned to the house to find she had made some sandwiches and fried taters and, of course, iced tea.

After supper, we went back to work. By bedtime, we had the kitchen and my bedroom pretty much under control. Shoot, we'd even hung up some pretty lace curtains. It may sound kinda silly, but even though ya know there's nobody for miles and miles, ya just feel better when there's curtains to give ya a little privacy. We was both amazed at how much we'd done in just one day.

Mornin' comes early on a farm, especially if you're on the northeast side of the mountain. There's nothin' in the world more beautiful than a spring mornin' in the Appalachian Mountains. I think it's about as close to God's own Garden of Eden as a human can ever hope to get and still be livin'. Seemed like no matter how early I tend to rise, them dang hens and that ole rooster was always up and about before me.

We had a litlle breakfast and about a pot of coffee, before we got back to business. It was really startin' to look like home and everything smelled so clean and fresh, just like the mountain air breezes blowin' through Nannys white lace curtains on the windows.

It began to warm up about noon and we was startin' to drag. After dinner we stretched out on the old hand made rag rug in the parlor floor and relaxed.

"When do ya think we'll be headin' for Lexington?" Floy asked.

"As fast as this job is goin', I figure the only thing that'll be holdin' us up will be gettin' a phone in and at least two bathrooms done. I don't know about you, but I'm right tired of that night pot and that rickity ole outhouse. I don't care how many ancestors used it . . . it's nasty, it stinks and I hate spiders.

I know the phone company's supposed to come Monday to do the phone, and I expect them Timpson boys and their daddy to be here middle of the week to start them baths. I guess we can plan on goin' in . . . about 2 weeks . . . if they're done. Can you get off that week?"

"I'll just put in for my vacation time. Grandad usually lets me come and go as I please so long as I'm there when it comes time to stock, do inventory, and figger taxes."

"Then we're set. Two weeks from now . . . and we're off to see them thoroughbreds. I can hardly wait." I told her. "It's somethin' I always dreamed of doin', but I never felt right about leavin' Nanny here alone."

Sunday, we made our way to church in my Jeep. It had begun to rain durin' the night and the roads were a little on the muddy side. It was a good 40 minutes or more into the little community we called town. Mason wasn't much more than a chug hole with a post office and a few little houses around it. We did have a small general store called Millers. Floy's Grandad owned it and it had about everything you might really need. If it didn't have it there, ya could drive a hour or more to the bigger town and get it or just have Grandad Miller order it, and it would be there in 2 days. Grandad Miller even had a little corner of his store turned into a tiny pharmacy that his nephew ran since graduatin' pharmacy school. We was all real proud when he put that in.

Across the road from the store was a little café owned by Miss Shoemaker. When they was bakin' dinner rolls, ya could smell 'em all over town. They was just as good as they smelled. The rest of the food was real good, too, and everbody went there after Sunday sermon for dinner. Mason also had a little gas station that may or may not have gasoline.

There was a very small elementary school at the end of Main Street, but the high school kids had to ride a bus over to Bigby and back.

We had two churches, however, a Baptist, and a Methodist. There was also rumor of a snake handlin' church up on one of them mountains. I was sure that anytime there was a poisonous snake bein' put in your hands . . . right near anybody'd get religion.

No more people than was in the area, ya could always find a pew somewhere to have a sit and pray.

The town wasn't much, but it was just the way we loved it. I had never spent much time in town, only on Sundays with Nanny until her health had got so bad the last several years that we just stayed isolated on the mountain. Floy had always kept me updated on the goin's on in town.

Sunday led to Monday and a flurry of activity as the phone company arrived early in the mornin'. They said they was wonderin' when somebody was gonna want service up here. There'd been a line over the mountain that they'd put in years before, but Nanny always told 'em she didn't need no such thing to pester her.

An hour later, Mr. Timpson and his three red-headed sons showed up.

"I'm surprised to see ya, Mr. Timpson. I didn't think ya was comin' 'til later in the week."

"Well, they decided to hold off on that other job, so I figgered we'd come on up and get started. Three baths'll take a little doin'."

"Ya just go right ahead . . . the sooner the better. I want to go ahead with the plans we drew up and decided on last month . . . so just go on and get right after it."

By dinner I had two new princess phones in the big cabin and a line and outlet in the little cabin. I got right on the phone and called Uncle Deke to see if Mama and Daddy'd got there yet. Sure enough Mama answered. It was so great to hear her voice. Even though it'd been only two and a half days . . . it seemed like forever. She said everything had been fine and they thought they'd found a house. I gave her my number and sent my love to all, and I started to feel better about their move.

I was beginnin' to feel much better about my move, too. Floy'd gone home on Sunday night, so Billy Boots and I had spent our first night alone in our new home.

Two weeks later, I was admirin' my indoor ceramic toilet. They'd also installed one downstairs in a small room under the stairs, complete with sink and small shower.

Mr. Timpson and his boys had got so much done in such a short time. I was real pleased. So, come that next Monday mornin', Floy and me was on our way to Lexington.

"It sure is pretty here, huh?" I asked as we sped along the mountain roads.

"Yeah, it is. Did ya see those great ole plantations back there? Someday, I want to belong to one of them." Floy laughed. "I can just see it all now . . . the gracious hostess of Tara, or Twelve Oaks, or Graceland, or maybe I'll call it Beulah Land. Sittin' on the front veranda sippin' mint juleps, whatever them are, and enjoyin' the delicate scent of lilacs and honeysuckle."

"Boy, ya paint a beautiful picture, but I think I'll be real happy with my own little piece of God's country."

"Lilah, it needs a name . . . let me think a minute."

"Well, it's always been called 'Parker's Mountain'." I offered.

"No . . . ya have a new start . . . like . . . a new beginin' and your place needs one, too. Maybe somthin' about the people that lived there and what they left of theirselves there . . . maybe . . . Ghost Mountain."

"No! Hell no, Floy, that's creepy as hell. No way! Besides...it's more valley than just that one mountain."

"How about Spirit Mountain?" She asked.

"Are ya nuts? No! Nothin' spooky soundin'. Okay?"

"Okay, I'll work on it and let ya know what I come up with."

We rode for quite awhile in silence while Floy worked her brain over tryin' to come up with a name for my new home. It was a good idea. I liked the thought of my home with an identity.

We checked into our hotel room, ate some supper, and I settled down for the night.

Floy was still frettin' about that name.

Mornin' come with a wake-up call from the front desk. As soon as we was up and dressed, we went in search of directions to some horse races or maybe a horse dealer. We was highly disappointed to find there was no races to be held there for awhile yet. I guessed I should have researched it a little better or maybe just researched it period. Still, the man we talked to at our hotel, told us about a horse sale to be held that afternoon on the other side of the city. Accordin' to him, it was a big production and a big "to do" that was a yearly, well-attended charity event to help elderly and disabled jockeys. However, he was quick to mention that it was "By Invitation ONLY."

We were both disappointed as we entered the downstairs restraunt.

"Okay . . . so I should've checked . . . I didn't know they had seasons and schedules. I thought Lexington always had horse races." I apologized for bein' so stupid . . . but, after all . . . this was the farthest I had ever driven without Mama and Daddy.

A friendly waitress took our order but I found it impossible to hide my irritation.

"Heck, that's okay." Floy perked up. "Who cares...we're havin' fun. Right? Hey, how about this name for your place . . . 'Horse Holler'?"

"Floy, that sounds like somebody with a sore throat!" I was surprised at some of the things she kept comin' up with. It was funny but it didn't help my mood.

"Yeah, you're right. Hadn't thought of that. Sorry." She sighed.

"Ma'am?" A man sittin' at the next table interrupted.

"Yes Sir?" I answered.

"I'm sorry to interrupt, but I couldn't help over hearing your conversation. I know the charity event you were talking about. My wife and I have an invitation to it, however we aren't going to be able to attend. We thought perhaps you and your friend might like to have it."

"Are ya'll serious? That would be wonderful!" I couldn't hold in the excitement. "Yes, of course. We'll be willin' to pay you for it."

"No . . . no. We will just be happy to see someone use it. I would just ask that you would not tell anyone where you got them. They might frown on my having given it away." He little more than whispered.

"Yes, yes of course. I can't thank you enough," I all but giggled.

His wife took the invitation out of her purse and graciously handed it to me and they left.

I looked at Floy, "Can you believe the luck? What do ya reckon the ods of that happenin' are?"

We headed out to the sale. The man at the hotel had given us pretty good directions. The sale was bein' held at a plantation on the far outskirts of Lexington. He warned we should have a loose pocket if we was goin' to that one. I wasn't all together sure what he meant, but I was thinkin' that if I wanted to get a horse . . . then I wanted a really nice one.

Sometime later we found ourselves turnin' up the beautiful azalea-lined drive that led to a breathtakin' beauty of a ole plantation home. The huge sign outside beckoned sayin', "Welcome to Ballantine Plantation . . . Home of Kentucky Derby Champion, 'Orion's Belt'."

"Look at that, Floy! I don't know who that Orion fella is but he must be pretty important."

"You're kiddin, right? He's a race horse, a famous race horse. Ya knew that. I know ya knew that."

We both laughed as we eased up the drive and to the back, as directed by men in . . . tuxedos. We were directed to park and very nicely helped from our car. I could tell by the expressions around us that my little Jeep didn't quite fit in with the Limos, Cadillacs and such that were parked around it. The gentleman escorted us around to the front of the stables and to a row of really cushy seats under billowy white canopies. As we was seated, we was served champagne, plates of little snacky things and given a list of the horses comin' up for sale. Those tuxedoed gents who served us even wore . . . white gloves.

"Wow! This is really somethin'." whispered Floy. "I feel like that ugly stepsister in the Cinderella story."

"Bull," I whispered back. "I got enough in my purse to say we have ever right to be here, too. Now ya hold your head up and make 'em wonder who in the hell YOU are!"

The sale began in grand style . . . at least I was impressed . . . and Floy . . . I think. The man was right. It was really a production and I wanted every horse that come in the ring. There was quarter horses, and Arabians and every single one was sired by so-and- so, and they all had a history I couldn't even start to understand. All I knew was how beautiful they was and that they had better manners than most of the people back in Mason.

After lookin' 'em all over, we was handed directions to where each owner or handler would entertain offers. I hardly new where to start.

"What do ya think, Floy?"

"Shoot, I have no idea . . . what is it I'm supposed to be thinkin' about?" she answered real seriously.

I shook my head and we wandered off in the direction most people was headin'. I had no idea how to go about this fancy way of horse tradin'. Hell, I was just a plain-ole-mountain-raised, Kentucky hillbilly. I approached a tuxedoed man who looked friendly and told him that this was my first time at such a event. Could he please give us a little advice. He assured us that this was not the regular sale procedure and a lot of people were also confused. It was to create a big show.

He smiled nicely and told us to simply walk through the viewin' areas and if we saw somethin' we was interested in . . . just walk up to the owner or handler seated at the shaded table and speak our intent. I thanked him graciously and off we went.

First we spotted the beautiful black Arabian that I'd had my eye on. There was seven or eight ahead of me to talk to the man at the table. I figgered I could come back later, so we walked on.

"Look at that!" Floy nearly pushed me down to get my attention.

I turned and saw two of the most beautiful horses I'd ever laid eyes on. They were both Arabians, one darker than the other. They stood majesticly as if they knew they were exceptional. It was easy to see that they had been brushed to a glossy sheen and their mane and tails were long and full. I'd never seen anything like 'em in my life.

"I don't remember those two comin' through. I think I'm fallin' in love with 'em." I whispered.

Floy looked confused, "Huh? What are ya talkin' about? I wasn't talkin' 'bout no horse!"

"What do ya mean? What are ya talkin' 'bout?" I asked her.

"Over there, back by that stable." She motioned across the way. I looked . . . real casual like, 'cause I didn't want to seem too interested in what ever it was that she had seen.

There stood an older man with thick, silver-blond hair and a close trimmed beard. He wore dark sunglasses, tight jeans, and a black shirt. He was leanin' casually against the wall, and I couldn't help but notice his lean, muscular body. The wind blew through his hair, and it glistened in the sunlight. I got the feelin' he might be much younger than he appeared at first glance. I also got the feelin' he might be goin' to try to buy my horses out from under me.

I moved up to the table where a truly older, mostly baldin', heavyset man was loungin'. I tried not to listen in, but it was pretty much impossible not to over hear what the man in front of me was sayin'.

"Now, that's horse shit and ya know it, Colonel. I been tryin' to buy that damn horse for two years now. He's gettin' older and still your price gets higher!"

"Well, sir," the bald man said, leanin' back and carefully pullin' a cigar out of his pocket. "Did ya ever stop to think that we'd rather shoot that damn horse than sell him to the likes of you!"

"Bastard!" Snapped the man tryin' to buy the horses, as he turned on his heel to go. "You don't wanna sell them horses. Ya just wanna show 'em off."

"Likewise, sir. I am more than sure." The bald, fat man chuckled and we heard a snicker from the edge of the stable.

I stepped up to the table, a little frightened.

"What can I do ya for, young lady?" The old man asked.

I cleared my throat and stretched myself up to my full 5'3" and firmly announced, "I, sir, would like to know what you're wantin' for them two horses?"

He sat there a full minute, starin' a hole right through me. I felt some of that new found confidence slip just a little.

Finally he spoke, "Ya mean ya don't wanna know nothin' about 'em? Don't wanna look 'em over, pet 'em . . . nothin'?"

"Well, yeah, course I do . . . if I can please."

"Go right on ahead missy . . . help yourself."

And so I did. Floy and I made our way over to the two horses. I noticed out of the corner of my eye that the blond haired man, who'd been eyein' my horses, had gone. I guess he could see I was serious. Them horses just plum took my heart, and I knew I could not leave without 'em. We petted, nuzzled, brushed, and whispered to 'em. We was answered with several soft nickers. Ready to do some serious horse tradin', I made my way back to the ole man to make him, what I thought, was a fair offer. For some reason he suddenly choked on his own cigar smoke. He stood up and staggered back to the stalls where I was sure he would probably choke and die.

However, he came out in a minute with a really puzzled look on his very red face, held out his hand and said simply, "Deal."

"Sir, can I ask what their names are?"

"Sure can . . . the lighter Arabian there is General Patton and the darker Arabian is Vern's Pride. Ya got ya a hell of a deal there . . . could probably get twenty times that for 'em . . . but, the owner said deal..and a deal is a deal. Let's go make it legal."

And so we did.

They was to be delivered in 5 days. I left feelin' very proud of my purchase and my new found horse tradin' abilities.

"How 'bout General Vern's Valley?" Floy asked.

"What are ya talkin' about?"

"Ya know . . . the name of your place."

"Sounds too much like a Chinese food restraunt. No!"

We stayed in Lexington a couple more days. But after our horse buyin' adventure, everthing else was like a second thought. We got invited back to Ballentine's for a buyer's banquet but we didn't feel like we really wanted to go. Fact was, I think we both was ready to get back to our own quiet country lives even though we'd had a fun trip. Most of the time was spent just ridin', talkin' and a whole bunch of laughin'. We'd done some shopin' in town and bought some new summer clothes. I got a few things for my house. Then we headed on home and late that night we pulled up to the door of the cabin.

"Ya should just go ahead and stay the night, Floy. Ya can leave at first light."

"Ya talked me in to it. I'm wore out anyhow." We went inside, climbed the stairs, and called it another day.

Floy was up and gone before daylight. It didn't surprise me much since she had a job she had to tend to, but I slept in 'til about six thirty. I got around to go feed the hens, let the cows out and Billy Boots was eager for some chow, too. I got done, finished my breakfast and mornin' coffee, and I headed back to the stable to get goin' on some stalls that would befit my very expensive, but beautiful, new horses. I wanted ever thing to be just perfect for their arrival. I knew there was a lot a work to do and I didn't have very long to get it done.

After dinner time, Mr. Timpson and his boys arrived to get started on the bathroom in the little cabin.

"So, your cleanin' up the stable?" Asked Mr Timpson.

"Yes sir, I found me two horses that wanted to come home with me. I got to make the place decent enough so they might want to stay." I laughed.

"Well, Red here, now he can help ya out if ya need it." He indicated his younger, very red-headed son who was standin' a little behind him. He seemed to be the shyest one. "J.D. and Sonny gonna have to help me with gittin' ya a bathroom built."

"No, that's okay Mr. Timpson. I think I ' bout got all I need to get done for today. But surely do appreciate your offer. And yours too, Red."

"Okay, then we're gonna get up to the little cabin and get busy. We got to make us a list of all that we're gonna need." They all headed up the hill.

By midafternoon, I was really tired of hearin' all that beatin', and bangin'. To be honest, I was just plum tired. Come sundown, everybody was gone and the animals was all tended. I sunk myself into my new tub and relaxed. All I could think about was them two beautiful horses that was comin' in just a few days. I made myself a mental note to try and find someone who could teach me to ride, along with all the details of tendin' to such fancy animals.

The days seemed to drag on forever, especially with the Timpsons and all their racket.

At last the day arrived. It was all I could do to slow down enough to get clothes on. I went out to sit on the porch with my second cup of coffee just as Billy Boots began to announce at the top of his lungs that somebody was comin' up the road. When I looked, sure enough, a big black pickup truck pullin' a matchin' black horse trailer was comin' out of the trees. I was so excited I could hardly stay on the porch. Afer a few of the longest minutes I could remember, the visitors come to a halt in front of my cabin.

Three rather unusual lookin' characters climbed out. They all looked way overdressed for horse deliverers.

"You Miss Lilah M. Cullwell?" One asked as he glanced at his clip board.

"Yeah, well, since my divorce come through, I'm back to Parker, again. Ya deliverin' my horses?"

"Yes Ma'am, that we are. Sure are pretty too. Almost as pretty as their new owner." The older of the three commented with a grin.

"Watch it Charlie. You're lettin' your mouth overload your you know what . . . again!'" One of the slightly younger men joked.

They walked around and opened the trailer. As they worked the horses down the ramp, I was amazed again at the absolute beauty of 'em.

"Where ya want 'em, ma'am?" asked one of the men.

"Over in the barn . . . I have stalls ready for 'em. Thank ya. Umm . . . I didn't ask Mr. Colonel, but are them ridable . . . I mean are they broke to ride?"

"Yes ma'm, I understand they've had the best trainers money can buy. I wouldn't be afraid to put any of my kids on 'em. They're gentle as lambs."

Before long they was headed down the road and I was left in peace and quiet with Patton and Pride, my two gorgeous horses.

I'd just left the stable and was walkin' in the house when the phone rang. It was Floy callin' from work.

"Hey, what's goin' on?"

"Not much, just finished sweepin' and gettin' ready to lock up. I was wonderin' if ya want to come into town and have some supper with me? I'll pay. I'm just . . . well . . . really depressed."

That just didn't sound like my dear friend.

"Whats a botherin' ya?" I asked her.

"I don't know . . . just bored . . . lonely . . . tired of listenin' to my mom and dad argue about stupid stuff. I just need to go do somethin', anything. What do ya think?"

"I think we need to go do somethin'. Let's wear our new outfits we bought in Lexington over to that new eatin' place in Dover. I heard its pretty good. Okay?"

"Sounds great. How long 'til ya can be here?" She asked.

"Give me an hour. I been lovin' on them horses and right now somebody might mistake me for one of 'em. I need a bath and then the drive down will take a little while. Make it 'bout a hour and a half."

"See ya then, Lilah".

An hour later, I was decked out in my sexy new jeans, mint green and navy silk shirt and mint green belt to match. My nearly black hair looked pretty good for a change. I simply let it hang down my back and considered again that I might need a good trim. It was past my bra strap and had a few split ends. Maybe I was just bein' vain . . . but I felt like I looked a little . . . sexy.

I locked up and headed for Mason with my Jeep radio blairin' that new Johnny Lee song.

Thirty to forty- five minutes later Floy and I was slowly makin' our way over to Dover. Since the trip to Lexington, I was gainin' more and more confidence in drivin'.

"I can't believe ya wore that dress." I scolded her "I thought we got the dresses for church."

"Well, Hell. Ya didn't say to wear the jean outfits."

"Well, Hell, Ya make me feel way underdressed. Ya look geat . . . for a depressed person . . . ya look awesome." I teased.

"I feel way overdressed and you just look cute as a button . . . I wonder why we always say . . . 'cute as a button' . . . I've never in my life seen a 'cute' button."

We broke into comfortable laughter as we drove in to Dover and found the café. It looked nice enough. It was just a really clean little place that lived up to its new reputation. It served a really good meal for a decent price.

"So are ya feelin' a little better now?" I asked her.

"Yeah, I just needed to go somewhere. I haven't been any place since our trip. Maybe I was just feelin' sorta trapped or somethin'. Could be, I just need a life. Somethin' besides work and livin' in my parents' basement."

"I always thought ya liked the basement? It's fixed up so cute. It's a regular little doll house." I tried to sound encouragin'.

"It's still in my parents' basement. They're always there, always watchin', listenin' and questionin' everything I do. I need space away from 'em."

"I see what ya mean. Ya need to look 'round for another place." I suggested.

"Sure, and where else can I live for the great price of 'free'?"

"Maybe ya need to find a better job?"

"I've thought on that too. But I'd have to move to Bigby or Dover to do that."

"Well, If ya want to get away . . . I'd give it some serious thought."

We ordered dessert and another glass of tea and were enjoyin' the comfortable atmosphere when the door opened and several rowdy men come in. We didn't look up and just continued with our tea and private conversation. We finished and stood up to leave when suddenly a strong hand grabbed my arm. I was jerked around to stand face-to-face with Walter. Stunned, I was pretty much speechless. It 'd been almost two years since I 'd laid eyes on him. He was still handsome with his touseled dark hair and liquid black eyes that spoke of both danger and deceit.

"Liler, *He'd always always put an 'r' on the end of my name. I hated it!* Damn sugar, ya sure are lookin' sweet. Hey guys! Look who's here . . . MY WIFE!" he yelled across the room.

I jerked away, "Go to hell, Walt! Go home to your girlfriend." We headed for the door.

"Way ya look sugar booger . . . I may just come back home!"

"Over my dead body!" I snapped as I slammed the door and we got into the Jeep.

" I can't believe that just happened" Floy was as caught off guard as I'd been.

"Me neither, who would've thought that jerk would be there. I'm just shakin' all over." We cussed and discussed Walt all the way back to Bigby.

On a sudden whim, I whipped the car into the parkin' lot of King's Klub. It was a local dance club where everyone had been goin' since the two-step country craze had started. It was a nice place to go have a few drinks and forget what ya wanted to forget. Nick King had owned the place as long as I could remember. His son Nicky was in charge now and had upgraded it a great deal. He'd added a large dance floor and a live band on weekends. Nicky'd been a friend of Floy and me most all our lives.

It was hard to believe how many people was there. The place was jam packed. Most everbody seemed pretty shocked to see us. I hadn't been out since Walt and me split and I had moved back to Nanny's.

We finally found a table off to the side and set down.

"I sure feel special." Stated Floy firmly. "I look really stupid in this dress in a country bar."

"Hey, ya look cute as anything so shut up and LOOK cute damn it." I teased. We was havin' fun just sittin' and watchin' all the flirtin', dancin', and horseplay that was goin' on.

Out of nowhere, this really good-lookin' guy appeared at our table.

"Would ya like to dance, Floy?" He asked politely. For some reason she looked at me like a trapped rabbit. I gently kicked her under the table and she quickly answered. "Ow! . . . I mean, sure . . . yes, I would."

He was tall and thin with a thatch of blonde hair peekin' from under his cowboy hat. They looked good together. But, from where I sat, he was gonna have to spend some time helpin' my friend get the hang of that two-step. They danced at a couple of songs and came back to the table.

"Thank ya, Floy." He said "Do ya want to try again in a little while?"

"Yeah, I would. Thank you, Toby." She answered sweetly.

"That seemed to go well." I teased again.

"Oh sure, it's not you that stepped all over that man's feet!" She laughed. "Is he not just the cutest thing you ever saw?"

"Not bad . . . not bad at all!"

They danced a couple more times and before long they was a fixture on the dance floor. I'd danced a few times with different ones, but I really enjoyed just sittin' and listenin' to the band. After a couple more drinks, I made my way to the little girls' room. When I came back out, I noticed that Floy and Toby was still workin' that two-step over. I stepped toward the bar and got one more drink when the man sittin' at the corner suddenly turned and like a klutz, I just walked right over him. My eyes locked with vivid blue ones for just a brief moment as his drink went flyin' out of his hand and out across the dance floor. One of the dancers stepped on the glass and went tumblin' over his partner causin' two more couples to end up in a major pile up. I didn't know whether to laugh or hide but opted to laugh with the rest of the crowd, seven or eight of whom was just layin' in the floor in hysterics. I turned to the man I'd bumped in to just in time to see him go out the door. He was extremely handsome and seemed slightly familiar, but at the same time I knew I didn't know him. I wanted to apologize for spillin' his drink, but I guessed from the way he left that he was pretty mad about it.

As the evenin' come to an end and they made their last call, Floy, Toby, and I headed for the door. Toby walked with us to the car and I couldn't help but notice that Floy allowed him a little kiss before she told him good night and got in the car.

"So just how well do you know this . . . Toby fella?" I asked. "Well enough to give him a little kiss I noticed."

"Oh stop . . . I 've known Toby Ellis since school, don't ya remember him? He was in our history class in eighth grade . . . before you dropped out and moved up the mountain. He was really heavy and really smart."

"You've gotta be kiddin' me . . . That's not the same Toby Ellis." I was just dumbfounded. "My God, he's so good lookin'! What happened?"

"Military and divorce . . . I understand they can work wonders some times." replied Floy. "He joined the army right after graduation in 1966 and then spent some time in Viet Nam, but was sent home after he was wounded only to find his wife had found somebody else. I guess he's had a pretty bad time of it and he's so sweet. It just don't seem right."

The weekend and the rest of the next week flew by. I had no idea that horses took so much time. Between them and the cows and chickens . . . I was short several hours of ever day. Billy Boots was my constant companion since the bathroom was now finished and the Timpsons no longer needed his help. I'd spent some time in my garden but there wasn't much to do since it was still early in the spring. I'd just finished plantin' the last few onions and a few other early vegetables and I'd just come in the back door as the phone rang.

"Hello?" I answered a little winded.

"Uh . . . yeah . . . is . . . uh . . . this . . . Miss Cullwell?" the soft voice at the other end asked.

"It's Parker now . . . but it was Cullwell. Can I help ya with somethin'?"

"Uh . . . yes ma'am . . . I . . . I was just checkin' to be sure the horses got there okay. No . . . uh . . . problems or anything?"

"Oh, no sir . . . they got here just fine. No problems at all."

"Are they . . . uh . . . workin' out for ya okay? They're really great horses. I just wanted to be sure everything was okay."

"Just great . . . is this Mr. Colonel?" I questioned.

There was a soft chuckle. "No ma'am . . . I . . . I . . . uh . . . I just help out some and I really was close to those particular fellas. So, I'll just let ya get back to whatever ya was busy with. Nice talkin' to ya. Bye."

And just like that . . . he was gone.

That was really weird . . . I thought to myself . . . and he had such a sexy, deep south accent. Cheez, I must be gettin' lonely or somethin'.

On Saturday, I picked up Floy and we made our way to Bigby. We both had on our proper country dance wear. Again, the place was packed. People we hadn't seen in years were there and it turned out more like a class reunion than anything else. We was hardly seated when Toby made an appearance.

"I was hopin' ya'll would be here again. How ya doin' Lilah?"

"I'm great Toby . . . how was your week?"

"It's a whole lot better now. Want to dance, Floy?" His eyes sparkled as he reached for her hand.

"Sure." She smiled sweetly.

I still couldn't get over how much Toby had changed since I'd seen him last. If he wasn't so obvious about his attraction to Floy . . . well . . . I think I sure could've been attracted to him. I watched 'em dance for a little while and had a beer.

"Hey, ya wanna dance?" Somebody asked.

"Sure" I answered and followed him to the dance floor. It wasn't long before I knew he wasn't from around there.

"Where'd ya learn all this fancy dancin'?" I was impressed.

"Aw . . . I spent a little time down in Texas. Used to hang out at a place called 'Gilley's'. Ever hear of it? It's what ever body down that way's doin'."

"Well, no . . . but I like it. It's pretty fun once ya get the feel for it . . . and you're a really good dance partner."

The singer stopped the band and told us to get ready to, "Let go a what we had . . . we was gonna play a little get aquainted mixer." When he blew his whistle, we was all to switch to the next partner. So there we went . . . first one and then another. I had so many partners that my head was swimmin'. I even danced with Toby and I'm not sure but what I may have even danced with Floy! Some dancers was really smooth, some could hardly walk, and others was drunk as all get out. Some were really good-lookin' and some were . . . well . . . less good-lookin'. Some were even older than my Daddy, but we was all havin' a really good time.

Without warnin' the whistle blew and the music switched to a really nice slow tune and I was swept into yet another set of arms. Arms that were gentle, but firm. The cologne the guy was wearin' was like none I'd ever smelled before. It was fantastic . . . almost hypnotizin'. We moved gracefully to an old waltz and I felt like my feet weren't really touchin' the floor . . . he danced that smooth. We come around the floor and I glanced up to see exactly who this perfect dance partner might be. My eyes were met by the most beautiful crystal blue eyes I'd ever seen. I was captivated. He was very tan and had the fullest, pouty lips. He had a close trimmed beard that looked to be a mixture of blonde and silver, just like his hair. It made ya think at first that he was older . . . but up close ya could tell that he wasn't that old at all. In fact . . . he was quite young.

The song ended and I found myself just standin' there like a idiot. Our eyes were locked on each other and I just couldn't seem to make myself look away. People began to walk off the dance floor as the band announced its break. Yet there we stood. Still holdin' each other like we was froze or somethin'.

"Uh . . . thank ya ma'am." He mumbled softly with a strong southern drawl and backed away. Then, just like that . . . he was gone.

I'm not all together sure how I found our table. I guess I did since that was where I was sittin' when Floy and Toby come over to rest a minute.

"That was really fun." sighed Floy. "I even got to dance the last waltz with Toby. How about you? Did ya enjoy that?"

"I . . . I . . . sure . . . I mean . . . I guess . . . well . . . no . . . I mean, I really did enjoy that." I stammered like a teenager. I sat there while they went on about who they danced with and how many old friends were there. I listened but I couldn't seem to hear. My hearin' didn't seem to work when my eyes was so busy. I looked all around the bar, the dance floor and even the tables, but Mr. Blue Eyes seemed to have just disappeared. Maybe he'd gone to the restroom, I thought, or outside for a breath of fresh air.

"Floy, did ya see the man in the black hat and black jacket that I danced that last dance with?" I whispered.

"No . . . I wasn't payin' no attention . . . I was tryin' too hard to not step all over Toby's feet." She giggled. "Why, who was he? Do we know him?"

"I saw him but don't recall seein' him around before. A stranger to me." Toby commented.

"Me too, but it was so strange. I almost felt like I'd met him somewhere before. I can tell ya this . . . I definitely do want to know him. Yeah . . . there ain't no doubt . . . I intend on gettin' to know that cowboy a whole lots better. All I got to do now . . . is find him!"

Chapter 2

Sunday mornin' come, like always . . . right after Saturday night. It was really a chore to force myself out of that cozy bed and into the shower. I had a whole hour to get ready and get to church, so I thought once about just stayin' in bed. It sure sounded like a good idea . . . but I could hear my Mama like it was yesterday sayin', "Now, I'm more than sure Jesus didn't feel like gettin' up on that cross for ya neither! But he did and I think the very least ya owe him is a hour or so on Sundays. That's little enough ya can do in return." How I hated hearin' that little mini sermon. Probably 'cause it was true and it just made me feel so guilty. At any rate . . . it worked. I got up and got ready and drove down to church.

Afterwards, I went with Floy and Toby over to Dover to the little café where we'd run into Walter.

"Do ya think there's much of a chance we might run into Walter and his idiot friends?" I asked Floy.

"Are ya crazy . . . when did ya ever know Walt to get up before 2:00 p.m. on any Sunday?" she reminded. Of course, she was right.

Never a Saturday night passed that hadn't found Walter right in the middle of any drunken nonsense anybody started or suggested. Sure enough, we got there and there was not a sign of him anywhere. Dinner was really good and conversation was okay until out of the blue, Toby casually commented.

"Lilah . . . did ya notice your mystery man in church? I seen him in the back corner when I turned around to speak to Uncle Bud."

I was speechless.

"No, I didn't. Are ya sure it was him? I mean . . . why would he be in Mason and at our church?"

"Hell, I don't know, Lilah . . . I ain't, ya know . . . a . . . mind reader!"

"Are ya sure it was him?"

"Well, pretty sure . . . he looks like a old man to me. I don't know why you're so interested in him. There's a lotta young guys 'round who'll be knockin' down your door as soon as they find out you're single again."

"Yeah . . . well." I sighed "There's just somethin' about this guy that really gets to me. I mean . . . there's just somethin'."

"He must've left with the last amen 'cause I never saw him." chimed in Floy. "I sure would like to get a look at him . . . I ain't seen ya this set on gettin' to know anybody . . . not even Walter back when we was in school." She sat there a minute with a look of deep thought . . . then outta the blue "By the way, not to change the subject, but I been thinkin' on it some more . . . What do ya think of 'Double C Ranch'?" She asked me.

"What does the 'c' stand for?" I was almost afraid to ask.

"Cabin! Ya know, like two cabins." she beamed.

"No . . . that sounds like somebody has a problem with their eyes." I said. I shook my head at her persistence.

Later that afternoon, I decided to take Pride out for a ride. It was our first time to really get to spend some time alone with each other since I'd learned to ride.

All saddled, just the way the trainer and ridin' instructor I'd met with had taught me, I climbed aboard. It was a little scary at first since he was so tall. We started off at a slow walk and later moved into a light trot. He rode so great I could hardly believe how gentle and smooth he was. We ventured a little further from the ranch than I had planned. The meadow was so beautiful that I just had to take a slow ride through it. Me and Pride ended up spendin' most of the afternoon ridin'. I couldn't remember a more relaxin' or peaceful time. When it come time to go back and get chores done, I found myself sad to return to the real world. For several hours Pride and I'd become a part of an imaginary and unreal world. The only important thing to remember had been to avoid snakes and holes.

I done a lot of thinkin' about the early settlers and what it must've been like for 'em to have tried to make their way through these mountains. They didn't have a clue what was 'round the next curve in the trail. However, I knew most of this area like the back of my hand. Most all my life I'd explored these mountains and valleys. Of course there was still a lot of places I'd never ventured . . . at least . . . not yet.

We made our way back to the farm just in time to feed and bed everything down for the night. Patton seemed a little upset that we'd been gone so long and had left him behind.

"We'll ride tomorrow," I promised, as I finished brushin' down Pride and settled 'em into their stalls for the night. I'd just stepped in the front door as the phone rang.

"Hello" I answered. It was Mama. She wanted to check on me and see how everything was goin'. She told me Uncle Deke was down with a cold and the kids were all in school, but only for a few weeks before it would be out for the summer. She'd wanted 'em to at least get familiar with the school and maybe meet a few of the kids. We talked about runnin' into Walt over in Dover and about Floy's new beau. Mama had always loved Floy and was real pleased to hear about her and Toby. We chatted a while longer and finally got off the phone. It made me a little sad as I realized how much I missed 'em.

Sometime in the very early hours I woke up to Boots' insistant barkin'. I listened for about 10 minutes before I decided to check it out. I couldn't see nothin' out the bedroom window except Boots, standin' defensive-like, in front of the house barkin' into the dark shadows . Most likely it was a coon or somethin'. I yelled out the window for him to knock it off. Shortly afterward, he was restin' on the front porch where he usually slept. I fell back asleep and before long I was awakened by that danged rooster and the breakin' of daylight.

It was Monday again and I had a lot planned for the day. First there was the mornin' chores and then a trip into town.

I went to Miller's grocery where I found Floy hard at work.

"Hey girl." I called as I walked in.

"I was just talkin' about ya Lilah." she answered. "Miss Telley wanted to know how ya was doin' up there by yourself and, of course, how your Mama and Daddy was doin'".

"Sounds like you're workin' hard" I teased. "What ya doin' for dinner? Can ya get away for a hour or so?"

"Sure. What's up?"

"Nothin', I just wanted to spend a little time with ya and see how everything is goin'. Is that okay?"

"You bet. I'll be off in about 20 minutes."

I went ahead and did my grocery shoppin' so when we come back from dinner it would already be done. We left it bagged and in the cooler then went to eat.

"Ya want to eat at Shoemaker's or do ya want to drive to Dover or Bigby?" Floy asked.

"Shoemaker's will be good for me. There's a lot I gotta do this evenin', so I need to get home before too late."

"Then Shoemaker's it is."

We sat at the only available table in the café. It was pretty crowded since it was the only real place to eat in town.

"Have ya seen Toby lately?" I asked as I sipped my tea.

"Yeah, he came by the other night. Ya can probably guess how that went. My Mom was right down as soon as she heard someone open the basement door. I've got no privacy at all. Lilah, she sat there the entire time. At least 'til I said that we was just about to leave and winked at Toby. We had to actually leave to get a minute alone. It's just makin' me crazy. I got to find another place."

"Listen, ya could come stay in the little cabin at my place, Floy. It would be perfect." I offered. She thought a moment as she sipped her tea.

"You're my best friend Lilah and I appreciate the offer. But that's just too far to drive to work and I kind of like bein' in town. It's closer to Toby . . . ya know what I mean?"

"I do . . . but if ya change your mind . . . the offer stands . . . okay?"

"Okay . . . so . . . have ya seen or heard from your mystery man?" she asked.

"Well now, What makes ya think that could happen? This is the first time I've been in town since Sunday. How could I possibly see or hear from him?"

"I guess I thought he might've called ya or somethin'."

"He doesn't even know my name let alone my phone number."

"Yeah, you're right . . . it would be a little difficult."

We'd ordered dessert and coffee when suddenly, Floy says "Okay . . . new subject . . . have ya thought of Happy Hollow . . . or maybe Mystery Mountain?" I looked at her for a couple a seconds and wondered who the heck she was talkin' to.

"What in Aunt Martha's world are ya talkin' 'bout?"

"The name of your farm . . . I been givin' it a lot of serious thought . . . what do ya think? I was thinkin' what with all those old stories and legends that Mystery Mountain would be really fittin'. Or if ya wanted somethin' a little happier . . . then . . . Happy Hollow."

"I can't believe you're still thinkin' on that." I laughed at her and shook my head.

We finished dinner and went back to the store where I picked up my groceries and headed back home. I was still laughin' at Floy and her determination to find a name for my place when I pulled in to the yard. Right off I noticed tire tracks that hadn't been there before I left. I looked around and no one was there and everthing looked the same as when I'd left that mornin'. Boots jumped off the porch to greet me and I put the mystery of the tracks out of my mind as I began to unload the Jeep.

Several nights later I found myself awakened again by Boots' constant barkin'. This was becomin' a habit, I thought, as I made my way to the window and peeked out. Boots was in the same area that he'd been obsessed with a few nights ago. This time I didn't yell, I just watched discretely from behind the curtain. It was hard to be sure but I thought I saw a movement out by the corral. When I saw it a second time I was sure of it. Someone was sneekin' around the yard! I slipped back to my bed, felt beneath it, and located my shotgun. It was always loaded and ready, just in case. Back at the window, I watched again. Whoever it was must be watchin' the house. I slipped out of my room and into the converted bathroom and quietly opened the window and took aim about halfway into the treetops. Slowly I pulled the trigger, lettin' the shotgun roar. The recoil sent me rollin'. I pulled myself together, picked myself up off the floor and peeked to see if I'd accomplished anything to speak of. It was hard to tell . . . Boots was under the porch howlin' and I was sure I got a glimpse of someone high tailin' it through the trees and down the road. I stayed up until daylight to make sure nobody sneaked back. When it got light enough I reloaded my gun and went out to look around. There was no doubt . . . boot tracks were in the area where I thought I'd seen somebody. My first thought was that there just might be a damn horse thief prowlin' about. I went back to the house and called the sheriff. About a hour later, he showed up with a couple of deputies.

"Hey Lilah, what the hell's goin' on?"

"Hi Stanley . . . looks like I had a prowler last night and maybe one night here while back. I'm wonderin' if it might be my new horses they're after."

We started toward the barn.

"What kinda horses ya got?" the sheriff asked. "I never did hear about no new horses."

I opened the barn door and we walked in.

"Damn girl, ya sure do have some horses! Whew . . . them two must a cost ya a fortune. Where'd ya git em?"

"Me and Floy went down to Lexington here while back and I bought 'em from a old man at a sale they was havin'."

"Well, that could sure enough be your problem . . . depends on how many people know ya got 'em."

"That wouldn't be very many. I don't go 'round tellin' all my business."

"Yeah, well, ya never know." After he looked around and made some notes, Stanley left. I decided I had to make some plans of my own in case my visitor returned. Back to Mason I went and straight to Miller's grocery to find Floy. I told her all about what had been goin' on.

"What ya gonna do now?"

"Well I got a couple of things in mind. But I'm gonna need your help. Can ya come out tonight?"

"Sure, is it okay if Toby comes along?"

"Of course . . . the more ideas, the better."

Later that evenin', when Floy and Toby got there, we sat down at the kitchen table to make some definite plans. I had a few things in mind but needed their input. After a lengthy discussion, Toby got to work settin' up a hot wire on the inside of the barn along with some strands of rope with several cowbells attached. In the mean time Floy and I drove down the holler aways to see Edgar. He was a long time resident of the mountains. I think he was there at the beginnin' of time, or at least as long as I could recall. He was home and happy to be of help. I told him about the prowler.

"I heard tell that from time to time there's always somebody a wantin' to start up. Now back in the day, we had lots a problems with them revenuers. Always sneakin' around . . . hidin' in the dark . . . I always wondered . . . did they not have nothin' better to do? Hell, looks like they'd a had a home and kin to be tendin' to. But hell no! They'd rather be up snoopin' 'round! Say, ya ain't brewin' no shine up there are ya Lilah . . . ya know your old mama'd just shit a squeelin' worm, now."

"No, Edgar, I ain't brewin' anythin' at all! I think they're just snoopin'"

"Well now, I think ole Roz here'll fix any a that goin's on. Won't ya girl? Roslyn's as fine a watch dog as your ever gonna meet! She don't believe in no strangers and she don't bide by snoops."

"Okay, Edgar . . . I sure appreciate your kindness. I'll have her back in a couple a days."

"No! No . . . now ya just hang onto her a good month or two . . . might be awhile before they get brave enough to come 'round again since ya done give 'em a good scare. Yeah, ya just hang on to her for a while. I'll see ya when I see ya comin' up the trail." And just like that he went back into his little cabin, shut the door and locked it. There was times I found it really hard followin' a conversation with Edgar. However, there was no better friend than him.

By supper time we had the chores done and all our traps set. Floy and me cooked somethin' for us all to eat and I'd already begun to feel more at ease about things.

Roz had become acquainted with Boots and was restin' quietly on the porch. It wasn't that I didn't think Boots was capable of protectin' me . . . it was just that . . . I didn't think Boots was mean enough to scare nobody off. Roz, on the other hand was three quarter mountain wolf and Edgar said the other quarter was just pure Devil Dog. I'd known Roz since she was a puppy and I'd often played with her. I knew she would help Boots defend to the death. Floy and Toby, however, were not so sure they wanted anything to do with her.

"Lilah, don't ya realize that animal could tear your throat out? She's viscious. I'm just scared to death of her." Floy was quick to point out.

"Trust me, she knows you're my friends and she ain't gonna hurt nobody in this house. Believe me when I tell ya that we can get a good night's sleep tonight. You guys are gonna spend the night ain't ya? I figger ya can stay upstairs with me and Toby can sleep on the couch or in a chair. Just make yourself at home. There,s also a spare room upstairs if ya want to sleep up there."

"Oh, no, down here is fine. That way I can kinda keep a eye on things." he replied.

"Thanks Toby, I really appreciate it. I didn't get a bit a sleep last night."

"No problem . . . you get some rest." he said as he lay back on the couch.

I guess I fell asleep the second my head hit the pillow. All I can remember was daylight comin' in the window and that damn rooster carryin' on in the yard. I must a slept hard since the night seemed to pass in a flash. The coffee was brewed and breakfast was started when Toby woke up.

"I was hopin' that was you in here." he said. "I sure didn't want to have to confront nobody this early in the mornin'." He teased.

"I'm sorry I woke ya Toby, I was tryin' to be quiet."

"Oh, ya was quiet enough . . . it was the smell of that coffee that brought me straight outta bed. Did ya get any rest?" he asked as he took the cup I handed him.

"I slept like a log. I never heard a sound out of them dogs. Maybe Edgar was right about 'em not comin' 'round for a while since I scared 'em so bad."

"I think it might not be too bad of a idea for me or Floy, or maybe both of us to stick around at night for a while, at least until we kinda get a idea as to what this is all about." He suggested

"Would ya really do that for me Toby? To be honest, I am a little bit nervous. I never had to deal with anything like this before."

"Hey, what are friends for anyhow?"

The next several nights went by without a single incident, so when Saturday came and Toby and Floy wanted us all to go out dancin', I felt good about the idea of gettin' out for a while.

We got to King's a little early. That was good since we got to pick a table instead of settlin' for whatever was left. As the band began a two-step, some of the couples includin' Floy and Toby made their way on the floor. A friend of mine from school come by the table and we chatted for a few minutes. She said she'd heard that me and Walter had divorced.

"I never did like him. He was always such a smart ass! He wasn't good enough for you Lilah. Ya just deserve a lot better than that." She told me.

"Its been over for a long time. Ever since he run off with that little bimbo from Dover. I don't care if I never have to see his face again." She wished me luck and then took off to the dance floor.

I watched the couples slide around the floor and thought how happy most of them looked. Although, some had a strong look of concentration on their faces as they tried real hard to keep the rhythm and remember the steps.

"Uh . . . would ya like to dance?" I came out of my trance and looked up.

"Yes, I would." I answered as I stood up on tremblin' legs.

The stranger led me to the floor and slid his arm around me. I couldn't help the shiver that went through my entire body as he pulled me close and I looked up into those beautiful blue eyes. We danced two songs and I never heard a single word nor did I know when one song changed to another. We never spoke to each other. Every time I looked up he was still lookin' deep into my eyes. I'd never seen any man so beautiful. Everything about him seemed so . . . well . . . whoa . . . girl, I told myself, ya don't even know his name. . . . and yet he makes your heart forget to beat!

As if he could read my thoughts he spoke. "My name's . . . uh . . . Chad . . . what's yours?" he asked so softly I almost couldn't hear him. I cleared my throat to make sure I could still talk.

"I'm Lilah".

"It's a pleasure to meet ya, Lilah. You're . . . uh . . . a . . . a very good dancer."

"Thank ya." I answered more shyly than I had ever been in my entire life.

The song ended. He walked me back to the table still holdin' my hand. He pulled my chair out for me and then just like that . . . he was gone . . . again.

"So, ya found him?" Floy teased.

"No . . . he found me . . . I think . . . but where did he disappear to? He was right here and then he was gone."

"I don't know, Lilah, but I would be willin' to betcha he'll be back." I sat down, totally perplexed. He was like liquid . . . he just kept slippin' away.

I watched every couple on the dance floor thinkin' maybe he was dancin' with somebody else. I checked out every table and every group of men standin' around . . . but still no luck. Then . . . just like that . . . a hand took mine and pulled me to the floor. I couldn't speak. I was so caught off guard thinkin' that he was gone.

"I . . . uh . . . I . . . I just had to dance with ya again . . . I . . . uh . . . I hope ya don't mind." He said softly.

The song was very slow and Chad pulled me close. My face was so close to his neck I could hardly breathe. The very smell of his skin and that wonderful cologne became imbedded in my memory. Never in my life had anyone made me feel like that. I wasn't so sure that I liked it. I mumbled somethin' about being glad he'd come back and how much I liked the song. He pulled me in closer and that was about the last clear thought I had. The song ended and a fast two-step must've started because everybody began to pass us on the floor. We just kept dancin' that very slow . . . very close . . . almost intimate dance to the song that only we seemed to hear.

"Hey! Mind if I cut in, buddy." I was jerked away by a very rough hand. We were whirlin' out around the floor before I realized it was Walter who had interrupted.

"Whatcha doin' out here, Sugar Booger? And who was that ole man ya was all 'huggled' up with?"

We weren't dancin'. . . I was bein' shoved and slung all over the place.

"Let me go, Walt." I tried to pull away but he just tightened his grip. Walter was a big, strong man. Good-lookin', but mouthy, and with a real ugly attitude. Again, I tried to yank loose.

"Let go!" I pretty much yelled.

Out of nowhere we had a third partner.

"Uh . . . pardon me, sir . . . but, I think the lady asked ya to . . . uh . . . let her go." Chad had appeared out of nowhere. We was at a dead halt on the floor and so was everbody else.

"Who the hell are you?" boomed Walter.

"Umm . . . well . . . My name's Barrett, Chad Barrett . . . and . . . uh . . . 'I' was dancin' with the lady."

"Well . . . I'm dancin' with her now! So, run along ole man before ya bite off more'n ya can chew." And with that Walt yanked me back on the floor. He'd only drug me a couple a steps when Chad was back.

"I said . . . I was dancin' with the lady." His voice was low and very serious. I tried to pull away from Walt before things got too heated. We'd started to draw a pretty good crowd. I pulled, Walt yanked and I went tumblin' on the floor. He took a swing at Chad as I screamed for 'em to stop, but the next thing I saw was Walt flip across the floor like a rag doll. Just about as quick, Nicky and his crew was there and everything cooled pretty quick. Chad gently helped me up. I guess I'd sorta turned my ankle 'cause it didn't seem to want to hold me up. He scooped me up and carried me back to my table and sat me gently in my chair. He knelt down and took my foot in his lap and carefully removed my boot.

After he'd checked it over, he looked up "I'm . . . I . . . I'm really sorry, honey . . . I didn't mean to start nothin'. Is your ankle okay?"

"Yes, I think it'll be alright."

I noticed blood on his lip.

"Chad, you're bleedin'. He hit ya . . . God . . . this is all my fault."

"I'm fine." he smiled a little crooked smile that tugged at my heart. "He just caught me a little off guard's all. I think he might be the one hurtin'." he said as he glanced over to where Walt was half sittin' in a chair with a towel on the back of his neck and one on his bleedin' mouth. That was when Nicky come over.

"Nicky, it was Walt's fault. He started the whole thing. Chad's a friend of mine. Walt just wanted to start somethin' as usual."

"Whoa, tiger! I saw the whole thing. I just come over to see how ya'll are and make sure nobody needs a doctor or maybe a wet towel. Walt's a ass and we all know it, and he's outta here as soon as he gets his bearings . I told him before I wasn't gonna put up with his shit and I meant it. Sir?" he turned to Chad. "I'm sorry about all this. I seen ya in here a couple a times and ya seem like a nice fella. I don't wanna lose your business 'cause of this. Let me send ya'll some drinks over here and let's get on back to the party! Okay? Okay!" He shook Chad's hand and walked back to where Walt was and ordered his buddies to get him out and take him home.

"I don't wanna see him back in here for a long damn time. Ya make that clear to him . . . Ya hear me?" They hauled Walt out as the band started up again. Chad sat down in the chair next to me just as drinks arrived.

"I ain't much of a drinker, but I think I can use this one." He smiled then winced with pain. I took a napkin from the table and moistened it with a little beer and gently blotted his lip. He stared at me with those intense blue eyes and my hand began to tremble as I continued to blot.

"I'm so sorry this happened to ya."

"Aw . . . I . . . I can't complain now . . . look at all the attention I'm gettin'." Again the crooked little smile.

Floy and Toby came rushin' up.

"Ya alright, Lilah?" she asked. "We just found out that it was you involved in that ruckus. They said Walt was beatin' up some ole man and . . . " She stopped mid-sentence as she locked eyes with Chad.

"Floy . . . Floy? Hello? . . . Floy, Toby . . . this is my friend Chad . . . Barrett . . . did ya say?" I turned to him and asked. He nodded. "Chad . . . this is my best friend Floy Felton and this is her date, Toby Ellis." Toby extended his hand and they shook. Floy stood there like she was frozen. I nudged her and she looked at me like she hadn't heard a word I'd said.

"Oh . . . I . . . I'm pleased to meet ya . . . and . . . I am so sorry I called ya a ole man . . . I mean . . . that's just what they was sayin' and . . . well . . ."

Chad took her hand "It's okay . . . I seem to hear that quite a bit lately. It's a pleasure to meet ya, too." He flashed a gorgeous, breathtakin' smile.

We finished our drinks and before we knew it . . . it was last call.

"Can we dance one more dance?"

"Sure." I smiled. I'd forgotten all about my ankle.

I don't remember what the song was, but it was slow and beautiful . . . and all I do remember was the warmth of his body and hearin' him hum softly . . . then it was over. He stepped back a little, looked at me, then took the tip of his finger and gently lifted my chin.

"Good night, honey." He whispered as those incredible lips touched mine so softly and briefly that I wasn't sure it had really happened. I opened my eyes and he was gone.

On the way home, I sat in stunned silence. Who was he? Where'd he come from? And why did he make it so difficult for me to breathe. Floy turned and looked at me.

"I agree . . . I see what you're lookin' at. He's just . . . well . . . beautiful."

"Aw shit." laughed Toby, "Ain't no man beautiful or purty!"

"Well," I said "if ever one was to be . . . it'd be Chad Barrett. It's not that he's just gorgeous, there's just such a sweet, sweet spirit about him. He's so gentle and so soft-spoken."

" . . . and you're just plain whooped." teased Toby, again.

"Oh . . . just shut up and drive . . . ya . . . ya hillbilly!" I teased right back.

We rode the rest of the way home quietly listenin' to the radio. Floy and Toby stayed the night as agreed. I lay in my bed later and relived every moment of the night. He'd taken up for me. No one in my life had ever done that. Never.

Chapter 3

Next mornin' I woke to the phone ringin'. It was Mama. One of the twins was hit by a car when he wrecked his bicycle on the street. She couldn't be at the hospital and take care of the other kids, so, if there was any way, she needed me to come down. Of course I could. Nothin' was gonna stop me from bein' where I was needed, even more so when it was family. I arranged for Toby to stay at the farm while I was gone, but Floy was insistin' that she was goin' with me.

"Lilah, your Mama's always been like another mama to me . . . If she needs you . . . then she needs me . . . and I'm goin'."

We were loaded and ready to be on our way by noon. Toby was lined out on the horses and the dogs but he was still a little tense about Roslyn. I assured him she was a great pet and he had nothin' to worry about. Floy called her Gandpa and cleared everything on her job and we was gone. I was nervous about the longest trip I'd ever driven and a little worried about my old Jeep . . . but I was determined.

Forrest City, Arkansas wasn't a very big town, but it was where Uncle Deke had lived ever since I could recall. It was a long drive from Mason, Kentucky. We drove all day until dark and decided we better stop and get some rest. We found a motel along the interstate and finally got checked in and in our beds.

Later the next day we made it into Memphis. The traffic was really bad but we carefully made our way through. We was fascinated with the city, but neither one of us had ever drove through a place so big.

"Lilah, look at that." gasped Floy "That buildin' is shaped like a big gold pyramid. I think we went too far . . . we're in Egypt!" She laughed. "Hey, reckon where that Graceland is? Ain't it here in Memphis some where? I'd like to see that! They say it's a mansion. That's where Elvis Presley lived. The one that died two or three years back, but I'd still like to see what a real mansion looks like."

"Maybe we'll try to find it on the way back. I never seen no mansion either. Now, watch for them road signs." I answered.

It seemed like little enough after she'd been good enough to make the trip with me. We crossed the river and were officially in Arkansas.

As we drove along the scenic highway, my thoughts began to wonder and I thought about Chad. Things had happened so quick I'd forgot to . . . well . . . I don't know what I forgot. I had no idea how to get in touch with him to let him know I had to be gone for awhile. How stupid . . . it wasn't like we was really involved. I'd just learned his name the other night. He may have left himself . . . or hell . . . he might even be married. It'd seem likely that someone like him would be attached. He probably had a dozen girls just like me. I scolded myself for bein' so dumb and gullable. Nanny always said not to count your chicks afore they hatched. Damned if I didn't think I was startin' to do just that. Well, I had other things I needed to cast my mind on. Number one was my little brother Jess. Him and Javis, my sister, was twins. But of course not identical, as one was a boy and one a girl. They was seven and cute as anything. I admit I was a little partial to them two.

After I was born, Mama was told she probably couldn't have no more babies. Ya can just imagine her and Daddy's surprise when about 18 years later baby James come along. Then 2 years later, Jake and 2 years after that, the twins. They decided that was enough, but somewhere along the way they must've got careless 'cause a little over 3 years later we got Lindsay. I told Mama I sure hoped they was done 'cause they was runnin' outta beds. Those kids was a lot like mine, too. I sure had missed 'em these last few months and I could hardly wait to see 'em.

Forrest City was a pretty little town. The rollin' hills and tree lined streets were welcomin'. There was a small downtown area that reminded me a lot of Bigbie.

Pretty as it was, I still preferred my little mountain cabin. I didn't have much trouble findin' Uncle Deek and Aunt Minnies house and Mama and Daddy's was just four doors down from 'em.

We drove up and all the kids come runnin' out to greet us. It was so great to see 'em, but I felt the absence of Jess right off.

Aunt Minnie rushed out, "Ohhh . . . baby girl . . . I'm sure glad you're here. I was 'bout worried to death 'bout ya. I don't like the idea of two little girls out drivin' that far by theyselves." She gave us each a huge hug and pulled us in the house while the kids unloaded the car. My baby sister, Lindsay was asleep on the couch. She was so beautiful and I just had to steal a kiss from her little pink cheek.

"How's Jess, Aunt Minnie?" I asked.

"Well, I understand he's better today. They're pretty sure he's gonna be okay. But he's gonna be in the hospital for a while and your Mama sure does need ya. I been doin' best I can to help, but since that hip surgery a ways back, I just can't get around like I used to. It gets to hurtin' so bad I just can't hardly stand it. Anyhow, we're just so happy to see ya."

"Aunt Minnie, do ya remember Floy? She's my best friend ever and she offered to ride along so I wouldn't have to make the trip alone."

"Well, I'll be dang . . . Floy? I didn't recognize ya! Ya up and growed up when I wasn't lookin' didn't ya?" Aunt Minnie laughed as she grabbed Floy for another big hug.

We visited for a while, had a glass of tea and eventually Daddy come up the drive.

"Ya just don't know how happy I am to see ya, girls." said Daddy. "I done missed so much work, I'm just hopin' they don't let me go. Deke says they understand, but it still worries me. It's a good job and I sure don't want to lose it."

"Don't worry Daddy. We can stay 'til things get better. But, I really would like to go up to the hospital now if ya don't mind us leavin' for a bit?"

A little later we was walkin' into the hospital room where Mama was watchin' TV with a half asleep little Jess. She jumped up when we walked in.

"Oh honey . . . I'm so glad to see ya. Ya just don't know how we've missed ya." she hugged me so tight I couldn't breathe. ". . . and Floy . . . thank ya so much for comin' . . . it's so good to see ya, too." I rushed over to Jess who had both legs strung up in some kinda contraption that looked more like torture than medical care.

"Hey Ugly," I whispered.

"Hey . . . uglier-n-me." he weakly teased back. I ruffled his hair and then gave him a kiss on top of his head.

"I'm afraid to hug ya. I don't know where all you're hurt."

"I think ya picked . . . 'bout the only place . . . on me that ain't . . . when ya kissed me on the head." he tried to laugh. Mama and me talked about his injuries and what the doctor had told 'em so far.

"We'll know more when they get the latest test results back tomorrow." Mama said. I told her she should go on home and get a little rest and let me take the night watch. She argued, but in the end she went back with Floy. It wasn't long before supper was served and I helped Jess with the clear liquid diet he was to be on for awhile. The nurse gave him his medicine, a shot for pain, and it wasn't no time before he was sound asleep. It was early yet and I just wasn't all that sleepy, so I wandered down the hall and found some magazines and a Coke machine and went back to Jess's room. A doctor and a nurse were standin' by his bed when I walked in.

"Is somethin' wrong?" I was suddenly terrified. Jess had been fine when I went out just a few minutes before.

"No, Ma'am" the nurse answered. "Dr. O'Grady's just making his rounds. No need to worry."

"Oh, thank the Lord. I was only gone a couple a minutes . . . I thought . . . well . . . it just scared me." I sighed in relief. The doctor finished his notes and turned as he pushed his glasses on top of his head.

"I'm Scott O'Grady." He extended his hand.

"Hi, I'm Lilah Cullwell . . . uh . . . Parker . . . I'm Jess's sister. How's he doin'?"

"Better than I would've expected. He sure took a nasty hit. I'll know more when I get some of the test results tomorrow. All in all . . . I'm pretty optimistic. It could've been a whole lot worse." He stood starin' at me for an uncomfortable moment. I guess I was probably doin' a little starin' right back.

Dr. O'Grady was very tall and one of those types you see in magazines that's just too handsome. He had very dark hair, but it was them green eyes that caught my attention. It was just hard to believe he could really be a doctor when he looked more like one of the guys on them calendars.

The nurse finished her duties and walked between us and toward the door. He smiled and followed her out. Well, I thought, the scenery ain't too bad around here neither. I dimmed the lights and sat back in the recliner and tried to relax.

My mind wandered . . . "Chad" . . . where was he? Would he notice I was gone? Would he even care?

The next thing I was aware of was the lights bein' turned up bright and nurses comin' in with all kinds of equipment. I jumped up to see what was wrong. They was just checkin' Jess's blood pressure, temperature, and givin' him more meds and another pain shot. It wasn't long before he was out again. I reached over and took his warm little hand and I soon fell back to sleep myself.

Mornin' comes early in the hospitals, too. I had never heard so much racket in my life in a place full of sick and injured people. About eight o'clock, Mama and Floy come back and brought me food, which I was very grateful to get. Mama told me that Daddy had gone back to work but wanted us to call him as soon as we got any more news.

Like magic, Dr. O'Grady walked in. He checked Jess and read his chart. "I haven't gotten the test results back yet, but I expect them some time this mornin'. He seems to be doing remarkably well. I'll get with you as soon as I hear something."

"Thank ya, Doctor." Mama whispered so as not to disturb Jess.

"Yes," I added "thank ya so much."

He turned and gave me that sweet smile again and left the room. Mama suggested I should go on to the house and get a shower and maybe a nap before I come back. I was kinda hesitant to leave 'cause I wanted to be there when the results come in. Decidin' that I did need a bath, Floy and I left quickly so we would get back as soon as possible.

Within an hour and a half we walked back in the room . . . about two minutes before the doctor and nurse entered. He had the results and we was thrilled to death that everything was as good as we dared to hope for. The worst he had was the two broken legs, a bruised spleen, and a mild concussion . . . all of which would heal in time. Mama broke down and cried, and that broke me right down with her.

"I've never seen so many tears over good news!" Dr. O'Grady laughed.

"We was just so scared." Mama sobbed.

"We can't thank ya enough, Dr. O'Grady." I held out my hand to him.

"No, just Scott, please." He held my hand for a second longer than I felt was necessary.

He smiled as he started toward the door. The nurse went out and he turned back.

"Would you like to grab a bite of lunch with me after I finish rounds?"

"Well, yeah . . . sure."

"I'll meet you back here in a couple of hours." He smiled again and left the room.

"How about that?" Mama teased. "Looks like ya got a doctor flirtin' with ya, Lilah. He sure is a handsome man. Might make somebody a good husband."

"Mama! I just met the man and he only asked me to dinner . . . not to have his kids." I snapped. "Besides . . . I . . . I met somebody else that . . . I'm really interested in. I think he could be . . . well . . . very special. But, yeah . . . Scott is good lookin'."

I was watchin' the noon news when the door opened and Scott walked in.

"How we doing, buddy?" He asked Jess.

"Pretty good, just hurts is all. When can I have some real food?"

"Now that tells me right off that somebody's feeling better. It'll be another day or so...we need to make sure everything is back in working order. I'll see if I can't get you something with a little more flavor . . . like some Jell-o or pudding . . . okay?"

"Okay." answered Jess with a disappointed frown.

"How about you, Ma'am . . . would you like to join us for some lunch?" he asked my Mama.

"Oh, no . . . no . . . ya'll go on. I'm gonna stay here with my boy and keep him company. But ya'll go on now." I turned as we started out the door,

"I'll bring ya somethin' back Mama, Okay?"

"I wish I had time to take you to a nice place to eat . . . but the cafeteria is about all I can do right now. It's hard to get away in the middle of the day." He smiled again and surprisingly, I found him very charmin'.

"Oh, this is just fine. I'd rather not go too far from the room anyway."

We got our food and sat at a table in the back. It was pointedly away from everybody else. I couldn't help but notice the intense stares when we walked in. One group in particular seemed especially interested in our appearance. It was a group of nurses sittin' at a round table that was the most obvious. The elbows and whispers seemed to be flyin'. We sat down and started to eat when a young nurse made her way to our table.

"So where is Gail, Scott?" she asked sharply.

He looked up casually, carefully wiped his mouth and gave her a cold smile.

"I'm sure I don't know, Anne. You know . . . it isn't my day to watch her." He laughed softly.

The young girl turned on her heel and with a red face, marched back to the table she'd come from.

"Is there somethin' I ought to be aware of Doc . . . I mean Scott? It seems like I'm causin' some kind a ruckus."

"No, not at all. I was seeing one of the nurses for a while…but that all ended some time ago. You know how gossips are? Always trying to make something out of nothing."

"All the same" I answered "I don't want to cause problems or upset nobody."

"Not a problem, Lilah. Not a problem at all."

We finished lunch and got Mama somethin' to eat and started back up to the room.

"Thank ya for lunch."

"It was my pleasure. I would like to see you again. Outside the walls of this place. You know . . . a real date. What do you think?"

"Well . . . I'll be pretty busy 'til Jess gets to come home. After that, I might be here a couple a days before I head back home. Maybe then."

"That'll be great. I'll be counting on that. Alright?" He flashed that handsome smile as we reached Jess's room. I went inside as he continued his way down the hall.

The next few days was hectic. Sometimes I stayed at the hospital, but most time I stayed at the house with the kids and tried to keep things as normal as possible. Floy was a god send. She was always busy with somethin'. She and I kept the laundry done up, meals cooked, and the beds made. I don't know what Mama or me would've done without her.

Scott must have been really busy too, but I wasn't worried about it. He seemed really nice, however, my mind kept travelin' back to Mason, back to the dance hall, back to Chad and that sweet, short kiss.

Jess seemed to be doin' really good. He was eatin' better and startin' to grumble about goin' home. It was such a relief to see the color back in his sweet little face. However, a muzzle on his little mouth might've been worth its weight in gold at times.

I'd just sat down in Jess's room when the door opened. A nurse stepped in and looked around,

"Is Dr. O'Grady in here?" She asked shortly.

"No, I ain't seen him in a while." I answered. She glared at me for a brief second before she caught herself.

"Thanks." she mumbled and stepped back out. Two seconds later the door opened again and Scott walked in.

"Well, hello there. I was about to decide you had skipped the country. Where have you been?" he asked as he took the seat next to me.

"At home tryin' to help Mama with the other kids. I wonder how she does it. It's a full time job to just keep the laundry done." I shook my head.

"Well, I'm thinking that if everything goes well, and I do mean EVERYTHING! I may let our little daredevil go home . . . in a day or so, that is."

"That'd be wonderful! What do ya think about that, Jesse?"

"I'm ready." he mumbled.

"Let's not get too excited," Scott cautioned. "I said, it will be a couple of more days yet. I want him to start on solid food first and see how he does. If all goes well . . . then home it is."

"I'm ready to see that day. It sure gets tiresome sittin' around this place and I know Mama and Daddy are ready to get things a little more back to normal."

"I'm sure they are. So what will that mean for you?" he asked as he moved closer.

"I'll probably stay a couple a days after he gets home to help get everything settled and then we should be headin' back home, too."

"We?" he seemed extremely shocked.

"Yes, my friend Floy and I. She's got a job to get back to and I have a farm and some animals that I need to tend."

"You have a farm?" He seemed really surprised by that.

"Yeah, I got a pretty good size farm, Why?"

"You just don't see very many beautiful girls in overalls running a farm."

He sat back down for a minute. Jess had drifted off to sleep again. The room was dimly lit and the halls were quiet for a change.

"So, Lilah, can I still take you out for dinner after we get little Jess home?" He spoke almost in a whisper. "Yeah . . . sure. We can go to dinner."

Just then the door swung open.

"Dr. O'Grady? You're wanted at the nurses' desk." The nurse from earlier announced.

She stood there as if demandin' him to move.

"Tell them I'll be there in a moment." Scott answered in a matter of fact way.

She continued to stand firmly in place. "They said it was important!"

Scott stood up "And I said . . . tell them I'll be there in a moment. Is there any part of that you didn't understand?"

"Yes, sir," she spun around with a glare and left the room. Scott turned back to me.

"Sometimes you just have to let people know where they stand."

He stepped closer and spoke softly, almost in my ear, "I'll see you later, Lilah" and he kissed me lightly on the cheek.

I stood there a moment in thought. He was a very attractive man. He was polite and really sweet, yet there was somethin' about him that bothered me. I wasn't sure exactly what it was. Just somethin' in his voice that I didn't think I really cared for. It was late . . . maybe I was just tired.

Floy brought Mama early and I was glad. I was ready to go home. On the way to the house Floy told me she had talked to Toby.

"He said he thought that prowler was back at the farm night before last, but Roz and Boots helped 'em decide to leave."

"I think we need to get back there as soon as possible. I feel bad leavin' Toby out there by hisself."

"Oh, I think Toby can take care of hisself just fine. You know he learned self-defense in the military. Besides, he says him and Roz are gettin' along great. I guess Boots is likin' her pretty good, too. He thinks we might be havin' some pups before too long!" Floy was excited.

"Lord! Edgar is gonna kill me . . . and Boots!"

We got to the house and I headed straight for the shower, then to my bed for a short nap. I was more tired than I thought seein' as how I woke up three hours later. Comin' downstairs, I found Floy and some of the kids in a serious game of Monopoly. She jumped up.

"Come in the kitchen" she said excitedly. "Toby called back! Guess who he ran into at the café in town?"

"I'm pretty sure I got no idea. Who?" I asked still half asleep.

"Your handsome . . . mysterious, stranger!" she giggled.

Now she had my undivided, wide-awake, attention.

"Chad? He saw Chad in Mason?"

"Yeah! In Shoemaker's."

"What in the world would he be doin' in Mason?" I wondered out loud.

"I don't know, but Toby said he was talkin' to two guys and when he saw Toby he got up and come over to his table. He asked him if he'd seen ya lately. Toby told him where we was and why and he said Chad looked pretty relieved. Like maybe he'd been worried since we hadn't been out to King's in the last three weekends. Toby thinks he come to Mason lookin' for you."

The thought had crossed my mind more than once, that Chad had probably just moved on by now. I suddenly realized that I knew very little about him. The one thing I did know was that every time he got near me I could hardly breathe. He was always in my mind and just talkin' to Floy about him and hearin' that he might be lookin' for me had made my hands start to shake

"I am so ready to go home, Floy. I can hardly wait to see him."

"I know. I miss Toby like crazy. He's about all I can think about. I don't know Lilah, but I think I might be in love with him. Is that nuts or what?"

"No, it ain't at all. It looks to me like he just might be feelin' the same way."

Two days later, Jess was dismissed from the hospital. We made a big deal out of his homecomin'. I cooked and Floy decorated. Daddy was able to get the day off to go pick up Mama and Jess. There was so much excitement we could hardly stand the wait. Finally, they pulled in the drive and all the kids rushed out the door. Even the neighbors were over for a special homecomin'. We all ate and visited and ate some more, but we could tell Jesse was gettin' really tired. It'd been a big day for him. Daddy got him in bed and they gave him his medicine and before we knew it, he was sound asleep. The kids got quiet and finally settled down for the night.

"It'll sure be good to sleep at home with my boy right here with us." Mama sounded just plum wore out.

"It'll just be good to have us all home for a change." mumbled Daddy as he looked straight at me.

I think we all got the best night's sleep we'd had in a month.

Things was goin' real smooth the next mornin'. Everybody seemed to settle right into a schedule. Jess was so glad to be home and to be able to visit with his brothers and sisters.

For the first time, I felt like Floy and me was in the way. We was extra hands that was no longer needed. We was just discussin' our trip back to Kentucky when the phone rang.

"It's for you, Lilah." Mama called from the livin' room.

It wasn't who I'd hoped against hope it was. It was Scott. He wanted to take me out to some country club place for supper. I agreed since I'd told him I would, but I have to say, it just wasn't anything I was real excited about it.

I put on the best dress I had brung. It wasn't real fancy, but I wasn't thinkin' about any dates when I packed and left. It was a simple pink and white shirtwaist and Floy'd put my hair in a French twist. We thought that gave me a little dressier look.

Scott picked me up at seven and we drove to the outskirts of town to a country club that I had no idea even existed. It was really nice, with people to park your car and all that. We even had reservations. I'd never been anywhere that had reservations. Scott was a real gentleman when he pulled my chair out for me. He ordered some wine and even ordered my meal. It was probably best since I wasn't real sure what the menu even said. It was a good thing they brought the food 'cause Scott kept orderin' glasses of wine and on a empty stomach, I was gettin' a little swimmy-headed. The food was wonderful and even the conversation was nice.

After dinner, we left and went for a little drive. He showed me some of the new things goin' up and some of the old things comin' down. We laughed and talked and I really started to enjoy myself. Before long he pulled up in front of Mama and Daddy's and turned off the motor. Like a true gentleman he came 'round and opened my door and walked me to the front door.

"I had a great time, Lilah. You are a very beautiful woman and I really . . . really enjoyed the evening."

"So did I. Thank ya so much for askin' me to go." Before I knew it he pulled me up against him and kissed me in a way I'd never been kissed in my life. It was sweet at first, then became very . . . insistant . . . . demandin'. Way too passionate for a first date. It was when his hands slid down and grabbed my butt and pulled me so close that I could feel everything he had to offer that I pushed him firmly away. He tried to pull me back but I pushed away again and told him I had to go in. I quickly opened the door.

"I'm sorry, Lilah." He whispered, breathin' hard. "You're just so damn sexy and I want you so much. I have since the first time I laid eyes on you."

"I hardly know ya, Scott. I'm not ready for that kind of relationship. Good night." Turnin', I walked inside and firmly closed the door.

I went into the room Floy and I was sharin' and plopped down on the bed beside her.

"What's up?" she asked rollin' over. "Did ya have a good time?"

"Yeah, for a while. But I don't like bein' groped. I don't know . . . I liked him well enough at first. I just . . . well . . . he just does nothin' for me. It's hard to explain. I enjoyed his company okay . . . I just don't like for him to touch me." I groaned.

"Well, I have to confess . . . I saw that goodnight kiss from the window and . . ."

"Ya mean to tell me that ya was playin' peepin' Tom?"

"Yeah, and I can tell ya, I wouldn't a liked it neither. Pretty pushy, I thought."

"Yep, me too. I don't think I care to go out with him again." We talked and laughed for a while and finally fell asleep.

I woke to the phone ringin'.

"Lilah Marie? It's for you!" yelled one of the kids.

Still half asleep, I made my way into the hallway and took the phone.

"Hello?"

"Good Morning, beautiful". It was Scott. "Did you sleep well?"

"Yeah, I did, thank ya. And you?" I tried not to sound as irritated I was.

"It was okay . . . I just had very sexy dreams about you all night." he half whispered.

That was more information than I needed or wanted.

"Well, I'm sorry about that. Maybe you'll sleep better tonight."

"Only if I get to spend it with you." He whispered again.

He must've been at the office or the hospital 'cause he was talkin' so low I could hardly hear him.

"Scott, I don't want to be rude, but I'm leavin' day after tomorrow to go back home. This is never gonna be more than just a casual friendship."

"Yeah, right." He said, almost sarcasticly. "That wasn't the way you acted last night."

"What are ya talkin' about? I didn't act any way last night."

"The way you kissed me back told me exactly what I wanted to know. Now come on and admit it. You were as turned on by that kiss as I was!" His voice became a little gruff.

"Scott . . . I'm sorry . . . but, no . . . I wasn't." I answered as nicely as I could make myself.

"What? You were as into it as I was. If we had been somewhere besides your family's front porch . . . hell . . . you'd a been all for it! Admit it . . . you know it's true."

"You're so wrong and . . . so . . . so . . . just do not call me again!"

I hung up the phone.

I marched back into the bedroom. My anger was to the point that I couldn't even think. I smacked Floy on the butt.

"Get up girlfriend, what do ya think about leavin' tomorrow?"

She pulled her head out from under her pillow.

"Whenever you're ready. I miss my man." She answered with a quilty grin.

By nine o'clock the next mornin' we was packed and in the car. The hugs, kisses, and traditional tears had all been spread around and we waved as we pulled out of the driveway.

We talked for a while, sang for a while and then settled into a nice easy quiet as we sped down the highway. Jess was so much better now and Mama had things under control. It was definitely our time to leave. If I'd spent one more minute avoidin' Scott, I was sure I would've been sick. What did I ever see in him? Yeah, he was very good-lookin'. It seemed all the patients and staff thought so, too. But his attitude was about more than I could stomach. I think he was his own biggest fan. When I was married, I'd had enough of that from Walt to last a life time. There was a lot of things about the two that reminded me how much alike they were. They both seemed to think that if they even looked your way, that ya should just be so grateful and be willin' to jump right in their bed. I'd promised myself a long time ago to stay clear of any more Walters! Maybe that was why I was so attracted to Chad. He was so very polite, gentle, very soft-spoken and ready to jump to your defense in a flash. I missed him. The distance couldn't get less . . . fast enough.

Before long we rolled into Memphis. I remembered my promise to Floy, who'd fallen asleep in the passenger seat. Maybe I could just slide on through and tell her I was passed it before I remembered. No. I'd never do that to my sweet friend.

"Hey! Sleepy Head. Ya best wake up and help me find this place." I reached over and gave her a shake.

She sat up and looked a little puzzled "Where are we?"

"Memphis, Tennessee! Home of the big gold pyramid and the great Elvis Presley!" I announced. "Now, how do I find this . . . Graceland?"

"Well, I do know it's on Elvis Presley Boulevard. I bet if we find that, it'll lead us to it."

We drove around and searched until I was so lost I was sure I'd never find my way back to the highway. Finally, I had to stop at a gas station and fill my tank.

"Sir? Can ya tell us how to find Graceland?" I asked the clerk inside.

"Yep." the old man answered. "Ya a fan a Elvis?"

"No sir, not me. I'm a dyed in the wool country fan. Ya know . . . Hank and Waylon and old Willie? But my friend sort of likes his music. She wants to go by there, so I agreed to take her."

"Boy, that's a new one . . . I thought ever purty gal they ever was, was in love with Elvis. I knew him ya know? Yeah, he stopped here once in a while. 'Cause we're 'bout the only ones open real late. Ya know he couldn't go no where in the day . . . had to wait 'til late night. He was 'bout one a the nicest fellas I ever met. Real polite, kinda quiet most times. But sometimes he was a hoot now! Sure did like him. Real sad what happened . . . damn well a shame . . . not many left in this world with his manners and willin' to help folks the way he did."

I had to admire the old man's respect for someone who, accordin' to Floy, the papers and stuff seemed to trash ever chance they'd got. Maybe he was a lot different from what they wanted ya to think he was. At any rate, we got our directions and made our way back around the way we'd come and before long we was on Elvis Presley Boulevard. Next thing I knew, we passed the gates the old man had told us to watch for. We turned around and went back and found us a parkin' place.

"Now what?" I asked.

"I wanna go over and touch them gates and read the wall."

"Read the wall?"

"Yeah, read the wall. People from all over the world has wrote stuff on it. I wanna write somethin' too!" Floy said as she dug a marker out of her purse and got out of the car.

I jumped out and followed her across the street.

"Are we gonna get in trouble for this? What if the cops come? Floy wait !"

We got to the gate. It was pretty cool, with the white wrought Iron and the figger of a man, a guitar and music notes . . . it was very grand! I had to admit, there was somethin' about that place. It was peaceful, quiet, kinda sad like, even with the traffic passin' by.

"I never give much thought about it before." I mumbled.

"About what?" Floy asked as she ran her hand down the edge of the gate openin'.

"Well, about all this. It's peaceful . . . but it's like there's this sadness that comes all the way down to the gate. Can't ya feel it?"

"Maybe that's what I'm feelin'." she answered. "I just almost wanna . . . cry. It's like the whole place is still waitin', or maybe . . . just broken."

She walked down to the wall. "Look at this . . . 'The King is dead . . . take me too!' and . . . 'I will love you even into the next life' . . . love GM . . . here's one from Japan . . . I have no idea what it says . . . and one from England . . . 'But to see you just once more' . . . JL . . . Liverpool, England . . . this is so sad." We walked around and read so many notes that we lost track of time.

Sometime along the way, Floy found a space and wrote somethin' and signed it. I took the marker and found a place of my own.

"What are ya doin'?" she asked me.

"I don't know. I just feel like I want to leave somethin' too. There's so many beautiful messages here."

I thought a few minutes then wrote 'Never before and never again has anyone been so loved' . . . LMC . . . Mason, Kentucky.

"Damn!"

"What?" Floy asked.

She came over and read what I wrote. "That's beautiful, Lilah. Why did ya say 'damn'?"

"My initials are wrong. Remember, since I'm divorced . . . it's a 'P' not a 'C'."

"It's ok . . . just pretend ya wrote it before the divorce was final."

"Yeah, Okay . . . I guess that'll have to do . . . Floy?"

"Yeah?"

"Let's get outta here. I got such an ache in my heart I can hardly stand it and I don't even know why."

"I know" she answered "It's like ya can feel all the hearts that was shattered."

Just then it began to rain lightly. She looked up, then turned to me with tears, or rain, runnin' down her face. "I think even the angels might still be cryin'."

I nodded. With an unspoken reverence, we turned quietly and made our way across the street to our car.

As we left, I flipped on the radio. As luck would have it, a beautiful, sad song was playin'. Floy looked at me.

"That's him . . . that's Elvis . . . I love this song . . . it's called 'Sweet Memories', I think. How perfect to leave to." She smiled and we drove on.

We each had our own thoughts about the whole matter. I'd never heard the song before, but I have to say it was 'bout the most beautiful song I'd ever heard.

We drove 'til dark and found a place to spend the night.

The next mornin' we was up and gone, anxious to get back home. It seemed like we'd been gone for years. The trip had been an adventure but we was ready to end it.

Later that evenin' we came through the grove that led to my house. The first thing I saw was Boots high-tailin' it down the road. Not far behind him come Roz.

We was gettin' our bags out when the barn door opened and Toby come runnin' up across the yard.

"Hot damn, I thought I'd never see the day ya'll would finally get home!" He scooped Floy up and swung her around. Then he kissed her 'til I thought she was suffocated.

"Boy, did I miss ya, sweetheart!"

"I sure missed ya, too." she laughed and kissed him again.

"Well, I feel like a fifth wheel. Hi Toby. How's everthing goin'?" I snickered.

"Not bad." He answered. "I been runnin' back and forth from work and checkin' on my place and then comin' out here to spend the night, 'til I was sure I met myself comin' down the road once or twice."

He told us that nothin' much had happened at the ranch and it'd been really quiet the last few weeks.

"How're my horses?"

"Great! I been ridin' 'em some. Man, them's some nice ridin' horses." He shook his head.

"How about that prowler? Any signs of him?" I asked.

"No. Just that one time and I'm not sure it was really anythin' to worry on. It could a been just an animal or somethin' out here."

We had a cup of coffee and a sandwich and continued to visit for awhile.

"Oh." Toby said as he turned to face me. "I heard old Walter's been back out at Kings a stirin' up shit. They said Nicky threw him out again. He was in there tryin' to start up with Chad. They said Chad just sat there and ignored him, but that he looked like he was really startin' to get pissed! There'll be real trouble between them two before it's all over. You know how Walt is when he gets a bur under his saddle. He just won't let it go. Ya mark my words…big trouble."

Chapter 4

The rest of the week was spent tryin' to get things back to normal I'd really missed my private little piece of the world. I took Patton for a little ride early and Pride a little later in the mornin'. They seemed as glad to be with me as I was to spend time with them. Floy had gone home and was back at work. Toby, too, had went back home, leavin' me with words of caution about the past prowler. I assured him that Roz and Boots would alert me to anything suspicious.

Saturday night was takin' its sweet time arrivin'. Toby, Floy and me had made plans to go to King's, and I was so in hopes that Chad would be there. In the back of my mind, I was a little worried that Walt may've made him so uncomfortable that he'd decided not to hang out there any more. I figgered I'd find out the next night.

My jeans fit great and my new black shirt with the silver embroidery looked even better than I'd dared to hope. I added a silver scale stretch belt, black boots, and silver jewelry. I felt like I was ready to take on the world.

I picked up Floy and we headed out to King's. As usual, it was packed to the point that we had to really search for a parkin' spot. We was surprised when we got to the door and found bouncers standin' on each side.

"Hi Tony! What's goin' on?" I asked as he gave me a hug.

"Hey, gal. Nicky got us watchin' the door for that damn ex of yours. He keeps tryin' to stir up a fight everytime he comes in. You know how he is . . . don't know when to keep his damn trap shut."

"Yeah, I know just what you're talkin' about." I commented.

"Tony? Is Toby here yet?" Floy asked.

"I ain't seen him, Floy. But I bet he'll be here soon. He pouted around here the whole time ya'll was gone. We gave him a bad time about it." Tony laughed. "I'll tell him yall's here when he comes in."

We went on in and found a small table in the back. It was the only one open.

"He'll never find us back here," moaned Floy.

"Sure he will. Men can see in the dark when it comes to findin' a woman. We could hide in the bathroom and I promise he'd find us."

We'd just got our drinks and the band was in the middle of a good two-step when Toby appeared out of nowhere.

"What you beautiful women doin' hidin' back here?" he grinned. "Tony said ya'll was here but it took me nearly five minutes to locate ya." We both burst out laughin'.

"I told ya, didn't I . . . they can find ya in the dark."

"What the hell are ya'll talkin' 'bout? . . . Oh, hell . . . come on baby . . . let's scoot a boot." He said.

Off they went with the other hundred couples on the dance floor. I looked at every corner, searchin' for Chad. He was nowhere to be seen. I sat there through three or four songs and had another beer.

Eventually, I danced a couple of times, but not with anybody of interest.

Floy and Toby come back to the table and I asked 'em if they'd seen him anywhere. They looked at each other and then down at the floor.

"What?" I asked as they sat down.

"Yeah" answered Toby. "He's at the other end of the bar."

"Really?" I eagerly stood up.

"Wait, Lilah," Floy said as she grabbed my hand. "Don't go over there." I sat down.

"What's wrong?" For reasons beyond me, I suddenly became nauseated.

"He's not alone." she mumbled and looked to Toby.

"What? He has a date? Just tell me."

"Looks like it could be." replied Toby. "Do you wanna leave?"

I thought for a minute and tried to pull my insides together. This was somethin' I hadn't expected.

"No." I stated firmly. "We come to dance and by all that's holy, we will dance."

I snatched Toby before he could think and dragged him on the floor. We danced 'round the far side and I strained my eyes to try to see if he was really there. Sure enough, there he set, with some cowgirl who had hair down to her knees and a blouse open to her navel.

"Seen enough?" Toby asked as we danced by.

"More than enough." I whispered.

When the song ended we were back near our end.

"Sure ya don't wanna leave?" he asked. "We could go get somethin' to eat."

I didn't know what I'd expected. We'd never even been on a date. But, somehow I felt stupid, really stupid, for ever lettin' my guard down.

But he'd looked so unbelievably good. I thought to myself. With that red western shirt and that white Stetson hat, he'd have taken my breath . . . if I wasn't so damn . . . hurt.

"I don't wanna ruin everybody's night. Go ahead and dance and I'll just sit here for awhile." I tried to sound calm and under control.

"No. Hell, let's go . . . I'm hungry anyhow." Toby said as he started us toward the door.

We made our way through the heavy crowd, but just as we got to the door, a hand reached outta nowhere and grabbed mine.

"Lilah? Where ya goin' in such a hurry?" that soft, sexy voice asked.

I knew before I turned around who it was. The voice. The scent of that wonderful cologne. I jerked my hand away and rushed out the door.

"Wait!" was the last thing I heard him say before the door closed.

We went to the Jeep. As quickly as we could, we left the parkin' lot. We drove into Dover and went to the drive-in. It was the only eat'n place that was open that late.

"Do ya wanna talk about it?" Floy asked.

"Nope." There was no need to discuss it. I didn't even want to think about it. I just wanted to go home.

Sunday night the phone rang.

"Hello?"

"Ya didn't make it in to church. Why?" It was Floy.

"I just didn't get up in time." I offered.

"I ain't buyin' that. What'd ya do all day?"

"Nothin' much. Fed the animals and watched some TV. 'Bout it."

"Lilah, are ya ok? I mean after last night . . . I know ya was really disappointed. I wish we hadn't even went."

"No, I'm glad we did and I'm glad I found out now rather than later on. I guess it's just . . . outta sight, outta mind with him."

"Well, Lilah, now . . . ya got to remember . . . ya kinda did the same thing. Remember your date with Scott?" I sat there for a good bit thinkin'.

"Ya coulda went forever and not reminded me of that. It's not the same thing."

"How do ya figger?"

"Well, that was down there . . . not here . . . in OUR place. Well, I guess we don't really have a place,   but . . . oh hell . . . never mind. I gotta go."

I hung up.

The next few days seemed to stretch into forever. With no job and no close neighbors, there just seemed to be a big hole in my world. I rode the horses every day and played with Roz and Boots. I fed the chickens and gathered eggs and looked after the few cows that I owned. Now that the remodelin' and all had ended, there was just too much time on my hands. After some serious thought, I decided that maybe I'd go over to Bigby and see if the nursin' home needed any volunteers. It'd only be a day or two out of the week, but it'd give me somethin' to do when my work was done at home.

That afternoon I took off to town. It was a nice drive and I stopped by Mr. Miller's store to see Floy. She walked up to me with a pouty face that made me laugh.

"What's wrong with you?"

"I made ya mad and ya hung up on me." She poked her lip out even further. I hugged her.

"I'm not mad. Ya just made me feel guilty that I was mad at Chad for doin' the same thing that I'd done. That's all. You're my best friend and I could never be mad at ya. What time do ya get off today?"

"Whenever I ask. Why?"

"Want to ride to Bigby with me? I'll even buy ya supper."

"How can I pass up a deal like that." She went to talk to her Grandpa and then got her purse and away we went.

On the way, I told her my plan. She thought it sounded like a great idea.

"Maybe I'll get to see ya a little more," she beamed.

It didn't take long at the nursin' home. They needed help so bad that I hardly got the words out of my mouth before they accepted my offer. I'd come in two afternoons a week and spend time readin', writin' letters for those who couldn't and helpin' 'em eat. As well as anything else they needed. I was really excited about this idea 'cause I enjoyed older people and I liked listenin' to what they had to say. It would remind me a lot of the years I'd spent with Nanny.

Afterwards, we made our way over to the café. It was early and there wasn't that many there. We ordered and sat drinkin' our tea when the door opened.

"So ya thought ya could hide from me, huh? No such thing gonna happen little ladies."

It was Toby.

"What are ya doin' over here?" Floy said as she jumped up and gave him a big hug.

"Deliverin' some stuff over to Dover for the boss man. And what are ya girls doin' this far from home without me?" he teased as he pulled up a chair and joined us.

I told him all about my new job. He thought I was nuts and advised me that if he had all that security, the last thing he would do is go find a job.

"No, I think ya would be just as lost as I've been lately. I just need to do somethin'... productive."

"Well, maybe. I sure would like to try it for a while though." He laughed and I thought to myself how lucky Floy was to find someone so sweet and cheerful. They were definitely a good match. When we'd finished eatin', we started to the cars.

"Hey." said Toby. "It's ladies night at King's. Want to go try dancin' again? Maybe you'll meet somebody better to dance with than me."

I thought about it for a minute. It was the middle of the week and I was sure Chad wouldn't be out there. I just wasn't ready to see him again. I might never be ready.

"Yeah, I guess we could go for a little while, but not too late. I don't like goin' out to the farm that late by myself."

"Okay, let's go."

We walked up to the door and were greeted by Tony and some of his bouncers.

"You still guardin' the door?" I asked.

"Yep. Just tryin' to keep it safe so purty little gals like ya'll will keep comin' out here." He teased. " Did ya know some big ole feller is followin' ya?"

I turned around to see it was only Toby, bringin' up the rear.

"Yeah, he does that sometimes. I guess he can't find nothin' better to do." He laughed and we went on inside. There were quite a few people there, but nothin' like a Saturday when it was literally cheek-to-cheek. We got some beers and found a table. The music was good and it wasn't long before Floy and Toby hit the dance floor. They was gettin' pretty good and Toby sure did love to dance. I caught myself lookin' around and just hopin' against hope that Chad might be there.

Several guys had asked me to dance. One in particular seemed as though he might a took some lessons. He was pretty talented on the dance floor. He was one of those partners that make it so ya don't really have to know what you're doin'. They just sort of "dance ya" and make it "look" like ya know what you're doin'. I was impressed and found myself enjoyin' dancin' with him. He sure wasn't bad to look at eather. His name was James, but he said that most people called him, Jamie. He was a construction engineer workin' on a job in the mountains north of Bigby, but he was originally from El Paso, Texas. I'd thought for a little bit that he might be Mexican, but I later learned that he was Italian and Apache Indian. I didn't even ask how that come about. He was very dark with jet black hair and the blackest eyes I'd ever seen. He was very tall and well-built with a Hollywood smile that reminded me of someone . . . but I couldn't quite put my finger on it. It was surprisin' how much he talked as we danced. I liked him. We spent the rest of the night either dancin' or sittin' at the table talkin' and drinkin' with Floy and Toby. When we finally left, he asked me when I might be back.

"I can't say for sure, Jamie. Maybe in a week or two."

"I'll look for ya." he answered.

I waved good-bye as we pulled out of the parkin' lot. It was late and I was really tired. Toby had to drive the company truck back to town, so Floy and I were alone. I let her out at her Mama and Daddy's and headed for my little mountain home. It was a good night and I'd had a good time. Then, I started thinkin' again... about Chad. It was obvious how little I really knew about him. I didn't know where he lived, where he worked, or even where he was from. I'd learned all that and more in the few hours I'd spent with Jamie in one evenin'. No matter what, the one thing I couldn't explain was the way I felt every time Chad touched me. Even the brush of his sleeve took my breath. When he looked in my eyes, I became lost in the incredible blueness of his. My heart would almost forget to beat. Damn, I was even havin' a hard time rememberin' to breathe just thinkin' about him.

I turned off the main highway and took the road that led to my dirt road when I noticed headlights that turned too. It only caught my attention 'cause the lights had been behind me since I'd left Floy. It was probable that someone else was goin' my way since several people lived at the foot of the mountain. As I sped up a little, the lights came faster. When I slowed down they seemed to slow down too. There was a growin' sense of uneasiness. I come to my turn off and made the sudden decision to pull in at a neighbor's house and turned off my lights. The truck went slowly by. As soon as it was out of sight, I backed out and went back to my road and sped to my house. Just as I come out of the grove of trees, I saw the dogs runnin' to meet me. I was never afraid as long as they were there.

Inside the house, I relaxed for a minute then went upstairs, changed and crawled in my bed. I wondered if it'd just been my imagination or if I was really bein' followed. Decidin' that I had a really active imagination, I rolled over and curled up.

The next thing I heard was that damn rooster tellin' me I'd slept long enough. I was glad he thought so, 'cause I sure had a different opinion on the matter.

I rolled over and stretched and thought about what I might want for breakfast. It seemed dark for the hour, but as I started to get out of bed a rumblin' boom shook the house. The heavens opened up and it began to rain like crazy. This was sure goin' to ruin my day. It was so hard to get motivated when it was cloudy and rainin'. I went down-stairs and opened all the doors and pulled back the curtains. The light was nice and I really loved the sound of the rain hittin' the gravel outside. I made a cup of coffee and went out on tthe porch to enjoy the mornin' by rockin' in my chair. Boots and Roz realized I was outside and ran up to greet me. They laid down on the porch, one on each side, and watched the rain with me. It was really comin' down. I could hardly see the grove from where I was sitttin'. That was always a good way to gauge the heaviness of the rain or snow. I tried to remember how many times I'd sat out there with Nanny. Sometimes, when I was very young, I'd spend the whole week with her and most times I was never ready to head home. She used to wake me up with a cup of coffee in her hand. For no reason I'd just open my eyes and she'd be standin' in the doorway to my room with a cup of coffee, with cream and sugar, just the way I loved it. We'd go out on the porch and sip our coffee and talk. Nanny used to tell me stories about when Daddy was a little boy and some of the things that'd happened.

One of my favorites was the one about how they used to sleep out on the porch at night or in the yard on cots 'cause it was just too hot inside. She said that one night they was all asleep but her when she'd heard somethin' runnin' in the corn patch. She woke Gran pap and asked him what he reckoned was makin' all that racket. He said he had no idea and they should just be quiet and maybe it'd go on. So they laid there as it was comin' closer. They had all the little ones out with 'em, but the older ones was scattered all over the place. Whatever it was got really close. As they heard it come through the patch, she wasn't real sure but what it was a chargin' bull. It hit the barbed wire fence and let out a screamin' roar like nothin' she or Granpap had ever heard before. Then . . . nothin'. When they felt safe, they gathered up all the kids and moved 'em inside. She told me that the next day, when Grandpap went outside, there was no tracks nowhere, but there was a big thatch of hair and some blood caught up in the fence where it'd hit. Now, I've often wondered just what that could've been. I've never heard of such nowhere in these mountains. But I do know that Nanny was not one for makin' up or addin' to any story. I'd enjoyed lots of 'em over the years . . . I sure had missed them days.

After breakfast, I went up into the spare room where we'd put all Nanny's things. Maybe it was a good day to start goin' through some of that stuff and gettin' it sorted out. There was everythin' from her clothes to her keepsakes. I found a box of pictures . . . ya know the kind where everybody looked like they'd just attended their best friend's funeral. Nanny was a beautiful young woman and Granpap was really handsome, too. I could certainly understand why they'd had so many kids.

Not many in the family understood my relationship with Nanny. They all said she could be a real witch when she was younger, but I never saw that side of her. I wished she was still here so I could talk some things over with her. She didn't give much advice but she was a great listener. When she did voice her opinion, it was usually very sound and well thought out. I wondered what she would have thought of my feelin's for Chad. She was a great judge of character and I would've really valued her advice.

I picked through some of her clothes. The ones I remembered her wearin' most was especially hard to look at. Her little shoes was piled in a box and another held her little handbags. I picked up the black one that she always carried to church. Winter and summer, she always carried the black one. Openin' it up, I was surprised to find it exactly like I remembered it bein'. She had a pair of gloves, a little coin purse full of change, a ladys white hankie with her initials embroidered in the corner, and a package of Juicy Fruit gum. As far back as I could remember, whenever she opened her purse in church, I could always smell the perfume on her hankie and Juicy Fruit gum.

I still could.

There was also a box that held her hats. Nanny was a firm believer in wearin' hats on Sunday mornin' and to funerals. I remember once she didn't have a new hat to wear to her friend's funeral so me and her took three of her older hats apart and created one stylish, new hat for her. She was very proud of it, mostly 'cause we'd made it together. I found it in a separate hat box, carefully wrapped in tissue, as if it was high dollar. She must've loved that hat.

With tears streamin' down my face, I realized I wasn't ready to do this. I went back downstairs and curled up on the couch. Turnin' on the television, I found a good movie to watch and lost myself in their problems and tried to forget about my own misery.

The next day was Friday and I was excited about my first day at work. I dressed casual in slacks and a pullover and took off for Bigby. It was a beautiful day after the rain the day before and I enjoyed the drive. My nerves were a little on edge since I didn't really know what to expect on that first day.

Dora, the lady in charge, got me pretty well-informed and then took me to several rooms to meet different people that she thought I might be able to help. They was such sweet men and women. They were so excited that I would be comin' to see 'em on a regular basis and that made me pretty happy too. I spent some time with several different ones that afternoon and planned to spend some time with the others when I come back.

There was a couple that I hit it off with right away.

Mae was "older than dirt," she declared. She was totally white-headed with twinkly blue eyes and naturally rosy cheeks. The very last of her family, she had only had one son and he was killed in Viet Nam. She laughed and said that when it come her time to pass over, that all her family would be there to remind her that she was late as usual!

Then there was Lamar, an elderly man in his late eighties. He was totally blind, but insisted he could tell more about what was goin' on by listenin' and smellin' than he ever did by watchin'. I stayed all afternoon and even then, I wasn't really ready to go.

It was late when I left Bigby, and it was startin' to get dark. As I drove by King's, I noticed there was a pretty good crowd, but I wasn't goin' in there alone for nothin' in the world. I just kept drivin' toward Mason. I thought I would swing by Floy's and see what she was up to. When I turned on the main road that led to her street, I noticed lights behind me. There I was, bein' paranoid again. When I turned on her street and the truck behind me turned too, I 'bout panicked. I drove past her house and turned at the next corner. Sure enough, the truck turned too. I drove to the end of that street and made a block and went back to the main road . . . so did the truck. By that time I was gettin' reallly shook up, and I drove down by the sheriff's office. As luck would have it, Stanley and one of the deputies was standin' outside smokin' a cigarette when I pulled up.

"Hey Lilah, what ya doin' out this time of night?"

The dark truck slowly drove on by. The windows were tinted so dark I couldn't see anything.

"Stan, did you recognize that truck?"

"Didn't pay much attention . . . why?"

"It's been followin' me for a couple a nights now."

"You sure?" he asked as he stepped out in the street and looked around.

"I'm pretty sure, Stan. It seems to turn every time I do. Don't ya think that's a little odd?"

"Well, ya keep a eye out and let me know if it happens again."

"Okay," I warned " But if it tries to follow me home again, I'll get my shotgun out! And I do know how to use it, too!"

After Stan cautioned me about my gun, I left and went on over to Floy's. I tapped lightly on her door so her Mama wouldn't hear it. It took her a few minutes to open up. She was in her robe.

"Are ya already in bed?"

"Well, yeah, in a manner of speakin'." she giggled.

"Oh Lord! Is Toby here?" I whispered.

"Yeah." she whispered back as she looked at her feet.

I backed out the door.

"I'll call ya tomorrow." I said and headed back to the Jeep.

This whole deal had just been a mistake since the minute I decided to stop by. I was a little nervous about the drive up to my place. I watched carefully as I started out on the main road. Just before I reached the turn-off, I noticed lights coming up fast behind me. I turned quickly and then waited to see what happened. The car sped on by and I felt complete relief. The rest of the drive was no problem. It was comfortin' when I pulled up at the house, much to the delight of the dogs.

I changed and went out to feed all the animals and brush my horses. The booby trap set up was becomin' a pain to work around, but I still felt like my horses was a little safer with it there.

It was just as I left the barn that the dogs both turned to the brush and started to growl. The hair stood up on both of 'em as well as myself. I hesitated a second, then hurried to the house. They both stayed where they was as if they had somethin' tree'd. With the shotgun in hand, I stepped out on the porch and called the dogs.

They wouldn't budge.

I hadn't heard a car or a truck, so I concluded that maybe it was just a coon or 'possum. Whatever it was, it knew I was aware that it was there. It made me feel safer with the dogs on guard and after a considerable amount of time, I went back in to search for somethin' to eat.

I ate, but I was still uneasy, so I double-checked to make sure the doors was well-locked. I went upstairs, changed, then sat down near the window with my gun. My chair was back far enough that I could see out, but nobody could see me. I was surprised to see that the dogs was still near the bushes. They'd laid down, but was still watchin' the same spot. After an hour or more, I still saw nothin' move. Knowin' that whatever or whoever was out there was bein' carefully watched, I finally gave up and crawled in bed and tucked my shotgun in beside me.

I didn't sleep well at all and was sort of glad to see the daylight. It'd got to where I just felt much safer in the daytime and I'd started to develop a real dread of the dark.

Floy called later that mornin' and wanted to apologize for that night. I told her I didn't have a problem with it and would've probably done the same. She laughed and said that if she ever caught me in bed with Toby, she would have a real big problem with it. They was goin' to King's that night. It was becomin' a regular tradition on Saturday nights and they wanted to know if I'd go too.

"I always feel like a fifth wheel, Floy. You and Toby don't need me hangin' 'round all the time."

"Oh horse feathers. I thought we all had a great time together. Besides, Toby's the one who told me to call and ask ya." She answered. "So, be here about seven or seven thirty and we'll ride together."

"Okay. I'll see ya 'bout that time." I realized that would mean another night comin' home by myself in the dark. Maybe, I would put Boots inside the house and leave Roz in the yard just to be safe or maybe I might just see about spendin' the night with Floy.

When I got to her house that evenin', we sat there talkin' and waitin' on Toby. I told her about the truck that I thought had been followin' me lately.

"Are ya sure, Lilah? Who would do that?"

"I don't know. I didn't recognize the truck."

"Maybe it's Walter" she offered. "Or do ya think it could be Chad?"

"Why'd Chad be followin' me? All he has to do is pull up and talk to me. No, I don't think he's the type to do somethin' like that. Now Walter, that could be somethin' to consider. I hadn't thought of that. It's just the kind of stupid thing he'd do."

Toby pulled up and honked. We went out and got in just as Floy's Mama and Daddy came out to see who it was. We waved and took off.

We stopped to get a bite to eat first and then went on out to the club. It was crowded again and it took a while to find a parkin' place. We passed by the now regular patrol at the door and began to search out a table. Luckily we found one not too far from the bar. I was very tense about bein' there and I just didn't think I could handle seein' Chad with "Lady Godiva", again. Maybe I did go out with Scott one time. Okay, so now we were even, but I just didn't think I could see that again. Toby and Floy were already on the floor and into their second song.

I turned up my glass to take a sip and looked up over the rim. My gaze locked with those gorgeous blue eyes that I'd spent countless days and nights tryin' to remember to forget. In his black hat and black shirt, he was stunnin'. He started toward me and my heart literally pounded in my chest.

"Hi." he spoke low as he dropped to one knee by my table. "Would ya please dance with me?"

I sat starin' at him for a full minute and I knew in my head I should say "NO". But my heart made my mouth whisper "YES". I stood up and he took my hand and led me on to the floor. We danced a quick two-step and then it went into a slow ballad. He pulled my body close to his and it was all I could do to keep control. Why did I let him affect me like that? I wondered if his "Lady Godiva" had felt that way when he held her.

"I . . . uh . . . I . . . I think we need to talk." He whispered in my ear.

"About what?" I played dumb and as if I didn't have a care in the world.

"About what happened last weekend."

"I didn't know anything happened." I turned my head so he couldn't see the lie in my eyes.

The song ended and we started back to my table. Floy and Toby were there when we reached it. Everyone spoke and he pulled my chair out for me. I sat down and he leaned over me. I looked up just as his lips covered mine. This time it was a deep, passionate kiss that reached into my very soul. He knelt by my chair.

"I'm gonna go get a beer." He almost whispered.

"Okay." was all I could manage. I watched as he walked into the crowd and dissapeared.

When I turned around and looked at Toby and Floy, they were both givin' me that goofy look that people get when they have just seen somethin' that shocked the heck out of 'em.

"What was that all about?" asked Floy in amazement.

"I have no idea." I breathed through numb tinglin' lips and tried to pull myself together.

It was awhile later when I realized he hadn't returned. Floy and Toby were on the floor again. I sat there with the burnin' of his kiss still lingerin'. Floy come back to the table as Toby headed to the bathroom. I could tell at first glance that she was upset.

"What's wrong?"

"That bastard!" she fumed.

"Toby? What did he do?" I couldn't believe it.

"No! Not Toby. That damn, Chad! He's at the other end with that ole gal hangin' all over him!"

She had to be wrong. Would he be that cruel? I stood up.

"I can't believe that."

"Can't believe what?" I heard from behind me. I turned sharply and almost fell over Jamie, the Texan from the other night.

"I can't believe you're here." I lied.

"Well, I sure am and I'm ready to dance with ya, pretty lady."

We headed for the dance floor. As usual, Jamie was as smooth as glass on the floor. He made us look so good and I couldn't help but grin at him. He made dancin' such a pleasure. As we came 'round the other end of the floor I searched out of the corner of my eye to see if what Floy thought she saw was true. At first I didn't see anything and then...there they were. He was leanin' against a pole and she was all but wrapped around him. He looked up long enough to lock eyes with me again. Deliberately, I turned to Jamie and gave him my sweetest smile. He smiled back and pulled me in close. At that moment, the song ended and conveniently went into a very slow song. I let myself dance as close as I could without bein' obscene. Leanin' back, I looked square into Jamie's liquid black eyes and smiled, but before I could back away, he put his arm around my neck and kissed me. Not a short, quick kiss, but a long, slow kiss. Bein' honest, I'll have to admit . . . it was a very nice experience. If I hadn't been so hung up on Chad, I might've been very tempted by Jamie.

The thought went through my head that I might be better off if I just forgot about Chad Barrett all together and focused a little more on what was right in front of me. We danced to several more songs and each time we rounded that corner I watched out of the corner of my eye for Chad. I didn't see him anywhere. Finally, I was back at our table and I asked Floy if she'd seen him again.

"No, I ain't and I say good riddance. He's just one of them playboy types. I think Jamie is better for ya anyhow."

There was a sudden ache in my chest as I thought about him leavin' with that . . . that . . . whatever she was. I couldn't stand the thought of him holdin' her, kissin' her, and God only knows what else they'd be doin'. I was furious, I was hurt, but I think, mostly, I was more jealous than I'd ever been in my entire life. How I wanted to be in her shoes and I wanted to be in his arms. For the first time, I realized that I wanted to be in his bed!

The rest of the night was spent dancin' with Jamie or Toby and one or two other guys I'd known from Mason. We stayed until closin' time and danced the last dance of the night.

There wasn't much to say on the way home. Floy fell asleep wrapped in Toby's arm, while he hummed with the radio. I just looked out my window and wondered where Chad took her. What were they doin' right that minute? My imagination began to run wild as I let myself consider what might be happenin'. It was easy to picture 'em in a hotel room, drinkin' wine and Chad slippin' his shirt off as she slid out of . . . No! I had to stop it and accept that I was nothin' to him. He was just havin' a good time and I happened to be in his path. We didn't really have anything between us but a few dances and a couple a kisses. My biggest question though, was . . . why did my heart hurt so damn bad? I'd never felt anything like it in my life. One thing was for sure . . . I didn't ever want to feel anything like it again!

Chapter 5

We finally got back to Floy's and I decided to go back home. There was a deep need to be alone to think this all out. I told 'em I'd had a good time and I'd see 'em at church tomorrow. As I drove the long road back home, I kept a look out the back window to make sure nobody was followin' me. At last I turned on the dirt road that led up the mountain to my little cabin. I finally cleared the little grove of trees and all I could think about was curlin' up in my bed, havin' myself a good cry, and goin' to sleep. Sleep was a good thing. It was a place to escape the things you just didn't want to deal with.

I came up the hill to the cabin and was caught off guard by a big black truck parked in the yard. I stopped. I didn't know anyone who drove a black truck, but I was sure that the truck that had followed me had been very dark and maybe even black. It was hard to know whether to turn around and leave or see who it was. What if this was the truck that had been followin' me? Maybe it was the prowler I'd been worried about. Whoever, they'd be awful brave to just come up in my yard, but regardless, this was my place and they had no business here. My headlights immediately shown on someone sittin' on my porch . It was a man in a black hat and black shirt that sat there pettin' Roz like he knew her. I was sure I recognized him, but could not dare to think it was true. He looked up into the headlights, I would've known those unforgettable blue eyes anywhere. I got out and walked up to the steps. He just sat lookin' straight into my eyes.

"What're ya doin' here?" I asked shortly.

"I . . . uh . . . well . . . I . . . I was waitin' on you." Again I noticed that beautiful southern accent he had. Most people 'round abouts did . . . but his was a little different.

"I'm surprised. I thought ya had plenty to occupy your night." I walked around him and up to the door.

"Roz, you're fired!" I hissed. "Your job is to keep strangers away . . . not to entertain 'em."

Boots came barrelin' out the door as soon as I unlocked it. He ran right past me and straight to Chad.

"You sure have a way with charmin' dogs as well as women, don't ya?" I was pretty curt but I was havin' a hard time bein' nice. After all, he'd left with another woman. That was twice he'd chose her over me and I didn't take rejection very well. I started inside the door as he caught my arm.

"I gotta talk to ya, Lilah. I . . . I . . . I don't understand what's goin' on here."

"You don't understand! Exactly what is it that ya don't understand?"

"For starters . . . why did ya run out last weekend? I'd been out there every weekend lookin' for ya. Toby told me about your brother, so I understood why ya hadn't been out. But I sure didn't get it when ya went runnin' out the other night."

" Maybe I just thought three'd be a crowd." I snapped.

" What do ya mean, three?" He looked really puzzled.

"I mean your half-dressed "Lady Godiva" with the hair to her knees." Anger and jealousy boiled in my veins. " Looked to me like ya had your hands plenty full already!"

"Are ya talkin' about . . . Danna?" he asked.

"How the hell would I know what her name is? You were the one . . . wearin' her . . ." I tried to pull away.

"No. Honey, ya got it all wrong. I . . . I met Danna quite awhile back, the first night I got here. I danced with her a few times, we had a couple a drinks and that was all. She's just not my type." He tried to explain.

"She sure looked like your type tonight. She seemed to distract ya long enough for ya to forget I was even there. She's the one ya left with! So what the hell are ya doin' here?"

I didn't want to hear any lies. There was too many years that I'd spent hearin' Walt try to lie his way out of one thing after the other. He stepped back and dropped his head for a second then looked up and straight into my eyes.

"Lilah, I didn't leave with her. I was tellin' her as nice as I could that I wasn't interested in anything more than a casual friendship with her. I guess she . . . a . . . she . . . well, she's one of those kind that don't take rejection too good, ya know? She was determined that I needed to give it a chance. I . . . I . . . uh . . . I told her that . . . well, that there wasn't anything there to give a chance. Lilah . . . I don't like to hurt anybody. Then I looked up and saw ya with that guy. Ya looked like ya was havin' a . . . a real good time. I . . . I just decided I better leave."

"So, ya didn't leave with her?" I asked a little embarrassed.

"No. I left by myself. I rode around for a while, but I just couldn't stand the thought of ya leavin' with that guy. Later I drove back to the club and waited until ya'll come out. I was glad ya was alone, I mean . . . well . . . ya know . . . just with Toby and Floy. So, I followed ya until ya turned off at her street and I just came on out here. All I know is that I just had to talk to ya. I had to know if there's anything between us or if it's that other guy you're really interested in."

Standin' there, I looked him straight in the eyes and searched for a sign that would tell me if he was the man I prayed he was, or just another Walt. His eyes were soft, sexy with a hint of mystery in 'em. Those beautiful full lips seemed to promise so much more than I could even imagine. He was without a doubt the most gorgeous man I'd ever laid eyes on. What in the world did he want with me?

Before I could speak again, I found myself in his arms, full against his body, his lips covered mine in a kiss I would never forget. He had one arm around my waist and the other was behind my head, holdin' my lips to his as his tongue slipped gently into my open mouth. I quivered and thought for sure I would faint right there in his arms. He leaned me against the door facin' and let the entire length of his warm, lean, muscular body cover mine. Never had I felt such animal passion for anyone in my entire life. Somethin' inside told me I should resist, push him away, that things were movin' way too fast, but God how I wanted that man. My entire body ached for him. He seemed to be havin' a hard time breathin' and his kisses were becomin' deeper and I could definitely feel his need as he held me closer. When his hand slid gently up my side and cupped my breast, I knew I had to stop it now or go all the way. I didn't want to stop!

But I did.

I pulled away and met his heavy lidded eyes. They'd become a very dark blue.

"I really want ya, honey . . . I need ya like I . . . I've never needed anybody." He whispered so softly I could barely hear him.

"I . . . want ya too, Chad. But not yet, it's just too soon. I'm just not ready for that yet."

He dropped his head and took a deep ragged breath,

"Okay. . . I . . . I'm sorry . . . I . . . uh . . . I just got carried away . . . you're so . . . beautiful and I . . . I haven't been able to think of much else but you since the first time I saw ya . . . I'm sorry."

He stood up straight and pulled me to him. We just stood there and held each other.

"Would ya like to come in for a while?" I asked . . . 'cause I didn't know what else to say in the awkward silence that stood between us.

"Sure." he answered as he stepped inside.

"I have fresh lemonade in the ice box . . . I mean . . . fridge if ya want some." He nodded.

"Sit down and I'll be right back."

I could hardly think. It wasn't that long ago that I was ready to try and erase him from my memory and now here he was in my livin' room at three o'clock in the mornin'. It just didn't seem real and was more like one of my crazy dreams. One thing was for sure and certain, if it was a dream, I didn't ever want to wake up from this one.

We sat at the table and talked some, mostly just starin' at each other. I still couldn't believe that he was here . . . in my kitchen.

"Where ya from?" I asked, not bein' sure what to talk about.

"I . . . uh . . . I kinda lived in a lotta places. I been in California, Hawaii, Mississippi, Texas, Tennessee. I been all over." He answered quietly.

"So . . . what kind of work do ya do?" It seemed like I was interviewin' him, but I figgered the best way to find out what I wanted to know was to ask.

"Well, I . . . I'm retired now."

"You're not old enough to be retired." I laughed and the air seemed lighter.

"Ya don't have to be old to be retired." he replied. "Ya just have to work your ass off."

I had to agree with him.

"So what do you do?" he asked me.

"I'm . . . retired."

"You're certainly not old enough to be retired." He teased as he gently bit his bottom lip and winked at me.

"Well, like somebody once said, ya don't have to be old . . . ya just have to . . . inherit!"

I wished I hadn't said it as soon as the words slipped out. After all, I didn't know him all that well. He could be some . . . con man . . . or . . . gigolo . . . or Lord only knew what. I felt a little unnerved by the realization of what I'd just told him.

"There's nothin' wrong with that." he commented. "Ya know, there's one thing about money . . . no matter how hard ya try . . . ya just can't take it with ya. Ya might as well leave what ya can't spend for somebody else to enjoy. Whoever ya inherited from must a loved ya very much. And that's a great thing . . . to be loved that much." He smiled so sweetly that I began to relax.

"It was my Nanny. She left me this land and these cabins. They been in the family for . . . well . . . generations."

"That's somethin' to really be proud of. Nothin's more important than family. It's what life's all about. Ya know, people think it's all about success, and fame, and who ya are and who ya know . . . but it's not . . it's family." He looked sad.

"Where does your family live, Chad?"

He sat there for a long time before he answered. He spoke in little more than a whisper.

"Mama died more than twenty years ago. I . . . uh . . . I never went through anything so hard in my life. We was real close. She was my angel." He sat with his head down for some time.

Then he continued "Daddy went on with his life. He remarried. I see him from time to time. He's about the only family I see. I like to travel and see things I never seen before . . . meet people and just enjoy life. Anything else ya wanna know?" His smile nearly took my breath.

"Yeah." I answered nervously. "Are ya . . . married?"

He shook his head then looked me straight in the eyes .

"Naw honey, I . . . I was . . . once . . . but no . . . I ain't married."

Without meanin' to, I let out a big sigh of relief. All of a sudden he stood up.

"I just noticed the time . . . I better leave and let ya get some rest."

"No . . . wait." I stammered. "Stay. I mean . . . it's late . . . or . . . early. Stay . . . ya can sleep on the couch and leave in the mornin'. Ya shouldn't be drivin' this late."

"Ya mean . . . with all the lemonade I been drinkin'? Maybe you're right. I wouldn't wanna get picked up for drinkin' and drivin'."

I got him a blanket and a pillow then locked the doors and started to turn out the lights. He caught me in his arms.

"Where are you gonna sleep?" he whispered.

"Upstairs . . . in my room." I answered nervously.

"Will ya stay down here with me . . . on the couch? I promise I'll be nice. I'd just like to lay on the couch and hold ya. Nothin' else. Okay?"

I thought a long moment, it wasn't so much him I didn't trust as it was myself.

"Okay . . . but . . . nothin' else."

Chad took off his boots and stretched out the length of the couch. I was nervous as I eased down beside him and pulled the blanket over us. It felt so good when he put his arm around me and whispered in my ear, "Good night, honey." After a few quiet moments, I heard him sigh and I lay there listenin' to his steady breathin' as he drifted off to sleep.

I knew there was no way I would ever go to sleep, myself.

I awakened when that damn rooster let me know that day was breakin'. Chad didn't move, so I just lay still and before long, I guess I was back to sleep too, 'cause the next thing I heard was the phone ringin'. Who could be callin' this time of morning? It stopped, but not before it woke Chad. He stretched and then pulled me closer.

"Mornin', little girl." he mumbled in a sleepy voice.

"Mornin' " I whispered "Sorry about the phone. I don't know who it could've been. Nobody calls this early."

He raised his arm and looked at his watch. He chuckled.

"Honey . . . it's twelve thirty in the afternoon."

"Twelve thirty . . . are ya sure? I never sleep that late. Never." I sat straight up.

"Well, who cares . . . ya got somewhere to go?"

"No. But . . . " he pulled me back down beside him.

"There's only me and you and a couple a dogs. I love it right where we are . . . what about you?"

I laid there a minute and thought it over.

I'm an adult! And yes, I do love it right where I'm at! I thought to myself.

I looked up at him. There was that crooked little grin again.

"Yes, I love it right where we are."

He leaned toward me, again with that soft shadow of a kiss. I melted inside. His lips were soft and warm and I so loved his gentleness.

After a couple of tender kisses, I suggested some breakfast.

"Are ya hungry?"

"Yeah, I think I might be."

"Would ya like pancakes or bacon and eggs?"

He grinned.

"Yeah."

I had to laugh. He was like a little kid who wanted to try it all.

"Okay, then that's what we'll have."

I got up and ran upstairs to brush my teeth and wash my face. When I came down, Chad was foldin' the blanket.

"Here's ya a toothbrush." I offered. "I always keep extras and there are towels and wash cloths in that bathroom."

I pointed to the downstairs bath. He looked at me kinda funny and asked.

"Do ya have a lotta overnight guests?" I almost laughed again until I saw that he was quite serious.

"Not really. Sometimes Floy stays and I hope my family will come to visit sometime soon. Mostly I just buy everything in quantity 'cause I live so far out of town."

He looked strangely relieved. "Well, that makes good sense," he answered and took the toothbrush and went into the bath.

When he came out, I had bacon and eggs fryin', coffee brewin', and pancake batter mixed. He walked up behind me and slid his arms around me.

"Sure smells good, baby. I haven't had a good-home cooked meal in I don't know when." He nuzzled my neck and my knees went weak.

"I hate to tell ya this . . . but if ya don't stop that . . . ya ain't gonna have one now." He jumped back and put his hands behind him.

"Okay . . . okay . . . I don't want to interfere with the cook." He teased as he reached for the cup I'd set out and poured himself some coffee.

"Do ya want me to pour ya one too?" He asked me.

"Yes, please."

He handed it to me and walked over and opened the back door and stood lookin' outside.

"Looks like another beautiful Kentucky afternoon."

I turned and looked at him. He just stood there, leanin' against the door frame. The afternoon sun was shining in his face and his thick silver blonde hair glistened as it blew in the gentle breeze . He still had on the black shirt from the night before and those perfect, tight fittin' jeans. He turned just then and glanced at me. The light hit those amazin' bright blue eyes and I found it impossible to make myself look away. He smiled sweetly and looked back outside.

"It's nice out here. The wind in the trees and the birds singin'…it's… terra de gracia…. it's like a different world."

That was when the hot grease from the bacon popped on my hand and brought me back to what I was supposed to be doin'.

"Yeah, I'm in love with this place. Always have been. I spent a lot of time with my Nanny out here. I guess I pretty much grew up on this mountain."

"It'd be a great place to grow up." He said thoughtfully.

"Let's eat!" I changed the subject.

Chad sat down with his coffee and waited for me to sit. I was shocked when he took my hand and bowed his head.

"Lord," he began, "thank you for this wonderful meal prepared by these precious hands. Grant us Your blessin's this day and we'll give You eternal thanks. Amen".

"Amen" I shly echoed.

It was a beautiful moment, but it kinda took me by surprise.

After breakfast, we went for a walk around the place and soon found ourselves up at the little cabin.

"This is where my Great Grandma lived before she died. Some of the families moved in and out when they hit hard times. It's empty now, but I come up here sometimes just to check things out."

"It's nice . . . reminds me of another little place . . . I like it." He commented.

As we walked, we gained the company of Boots and Roz who were very excited that we were outside with 'em. We gradually made our way down to the little spring-fed creek. I sat down on a large bolder and watched Chad skip rocks across the water while the silly dogs jumped in to try and catch 'em. We had to laugh at 'em as they splashed in, got out and shook, then turned to jump right back in. We finally wandered across the pasture and then back up by the barn.

"Come on," I said. "I want to show ya something.'" We went inside. "These are my boys."

I pointed toward my gorgeous horses. They nickered and danced around like they knew what I was sayin'. Chad walked right up to 'em. It was funny how they each tried to push the other aside to get to him.

"They are definitely beautiful." He petted and talked to 'em and they acted like they'd known him for years.

I thought to myself, *Yeah, he does have a way about him that makes ya feel that way. I guess my horses and dogs are pretty good judges of character.*

"Do ya wanna go for a ride?" I asked him.

"No," he answered after a moment's thought. "I need to get back. I need a shower and I've got some business to tend to. But, I'd like to take a rain check on that if it's ok?"

"Sure. Any time ya want."

We walked back toward the house and stopped at his truck.

"I'm glad ya came out, Chad."

"So am I." He stared at me thoughtfully.

He pulled me into his arms as he reached up and pulled the tie from my ponytail. He ran his fingers through my hair then took my face gently into his strong hands. He kissed me gently at first, then his tongue slid between my lips and the kiss became more intense as I wrapped my arms around him. I loved the way his firm body felt, but was more amazed at the way his kisses made me feel. My head was whirlin' and my body was yearnin' for more. Much more. At last he stepped back.

". . . uh . . . I" he cleared his throat ". . . umm..can I call ya?" he murmured.

"Sure," I whispered.

He looked at me . . . shook his head . . . grinned that adorable crooked grin and got into his truck. I stepped back as he backed out and drove away.

Still dizzy when I reached the porch, I sat down for a few minutes in the rocker and thought about those last wonderful hours. I'd wanted 'em to last forever.

Chapter 6

It was gettin' a little late in the afternoon, but I decided I'd take Pride out for a short ride before I fed the animals and locked up for the night. Since I wouldn't be gone for long, I coaxed the dogs into one of the stalls and locked it. I saddled Pride and we headed out across the valley. The sun was a ways from settin' and I was sure we had plenty of time for a good gallop. I didn't know about Pride, but I sure needed to run off some steam. It was his nature to break into a full gallop and we raced across the pasture and over the hill. We'd gone a long way at top speed!

I loved to run those horses and they loved to run, but before long I realized how far we'd gone. We stopped by one of the ponds while I let Pride have a little drink. I could've used a drink myself but didn't think to bring anything along. It was never my intention to go that far.

As we rested awhile, I again relived the events of the day. My lips tingled at the thought of Chad's kisses. He certainly had that . . . that . . . country boy charm thing. I didn't see how he could've been married and she willingly let him go. Was she insane or just stupid? I knew for sure and certain, if I was to ever be in her shoes . . . no way would I let that man get away.

I don't know how long I'd sat there day dreamin' when I realized that it was getting' dark . . . fast!

"Come on boy, we gotta get home."

Back in the saddle, we hadn't gone very far when Pride stopped dead in his tracks, backed up and reared straight into the air. I tried to control him, but quickly realized that I didn't have enough experience to know what to do in that situation. Without warnin', he bolted off in the opposite direction. I had dropped the reins and all I could do was hold on to the saddle horn for dear life.

I don't know how far he ran. It had become dark in the hills. The valleys were even darker. Everything was pretty much a blur as Pride raced over the crest of another hill. There was a downed tree in his path. He jumped over it and must have caught his front foot enough that we went tumblin' end over end. The last thing I rememberd hearin' was a horrible, terrified scream from Pride.

A sudden noise brought me back to the present and the reality of my situation. Everything seemed to echo and the icy coldness began to creep into my very bones. How long had I been there? What time was it? Again the fog slowly began to clear from my head. My stomach rumbled and I shivered from the damp cold. I forced myself to go back to my memories . . . I knew that somethin' there had to hold a clue to my situation.

I tried to open my eyes, but the blindin' glare of the sun caused horrific pains to shoot through my head. I could barely move, but I could see the image of Pride standin' not too far away with his head down and his front foot lifted. It was difficult to focus. I could see a lot of blood runnin' down his leg. I tried to get up but a gut wrenchin'' pain made me cry out. I must've passed out again 'cause when I opened my eyes, it seemed much later in the day. There was still a horrific pain in my head and I needed a drink badly. My whole body was numb with pain.

Pride looked really bad as he hobbled over to me. His saddle was almost underneath of him. I knew he needed my help, but I couldn't even help myself. Once again, I tried to raise up on my elbow but nothin' would move and I feared that I had broken my back. I couldn't feel my legs or feet and it began to dawn on me that I was in a really dangerous situation. There was no way on earth that I could get up. Pride couldn't go very far and no one knew that we were out there. Tears started to roll down my cheeks as I tried to move again. The pain had become more than I could bare as I slilpped again into a painfree darkness.

Sometime in the night I awakened. I laid still and tried to remember all that had happened. Glancin' around I spotted Pride in the bright moonlight. He'd made his way painfully down to a small stream. He carefully started to make his way back to me. He put his nose down near my face and nuzzled my cheek.

The water from his mouth moistened my lips and I was grateful for what little relief there was. Every inch of my body was hurtin'...hurtin' so bad I wasn't sure that I could suvive it. I wanted to scream, but I knew that would do nothin' but scare Pride and alert every wild animal in the woods that we were there. I gritted my teeth and tried to relax.

I must have gone unconscious again 'cause the sun woke me up by shinin' in my face. I still couldn't move anything but my head slightly and my left hand.

Pride was still near and tryin' to graze while standin' on three legs. The one he hurt was still seepin' blood, but now it was very badly swollen. I was worried sick about him. He seriously needed to be tended. I would just die if anything happened to one of my boys. It was all my fault. I shouldn't a rode so far so late.

What if no one found us?

What if we died right there?

And Patton and the cows and the chickens and my dogs, what would happen to 'em? They needed to be fed and watered.

Tears rolled down my burnin' cheeks.

Extreme thirst began to make my mouth feel like cotton.

As the day went on, the sun got hotter. There was no doubt that I was in more trouble when I started to chill even in the hot sun. Pride come back to me. He must've been back to the water. He nuzzeled my face again and a few more drops of water dripped from his nose.

When at last the sun began to set and was out of my eyes, I started to cry again. I just didn't know how much more I could take. I laid there and watched as large birds had begun to circle overhead. They sat in the trees and called to each other. I was sure they was discussin' the odds that we would soon become a tasty meal for them. I had started to shake and couldn't control it. If I could just get up, I could get Pride's saddle blanket, but I was so weak now that I couldn't even turn my head.

Again I drifted off. I had dreams 'bout Mama and Daddy and the kids and a nightmare about Jesse getting' hit by that car. It was somehow mixed with a painful dream about Chad and that girl at the club. He was kissin' her and she was naked. He had his hands all over her body and I kept callin' to him. I cried out for him, but he wouldn't or couldn't hear me. Then at last . . . I slept.

I was startled awake by somethin' sniffin' at my face and when I opened my eyes I let out a scream. It was a large cat of some sort. I think my scream scared it as bad as it'd scared me. It jumped in the air and was gone. Pride come up from the spring in as much of a hurry as he could manage. He snorted and posted hisself there beside me. I guessed he'd been standin' in the creek to relieve his leg 'cause water splashed on me when he ran up.

The sun was comin' up yet again and I dreaded another agonizin' day of heat and thirst. My mouth had become so dry I could hardly move my tongue. If someone didn't find us, I was sure we wouldn't make it through another night. The daylight came anyway, but not the sun. Mercifully, it was very cloudy. Around what I thought was noon, it began to thunder. It started to sprinkle . . . then rain . . . wonderful rain. I opened my mouth and let the raindrops fill it. I could hardly swallow, but each time it got a little easier. The rain was cold and I started shiverin' even worse, but at least I was no longer thirsty. As the rain turned into a gentle mist, I drifted off into yet another restless sleep.

When I woke up, the sun had found its way to the horizon again and I'd started to make my peace with God. I prayed for my family and I prayed for my animals, especially Pride. He'd tried so hard to protect and save me. I prayed for my friends, especially Floy and Toby, that they would find great happiness together. I thanked God for lettin' me know Chad and getting' to experience that once in a lifetime feelin'. I begged his forgivness and resigned myself to what I believed was about to happen. I then surrendered and closed my eyes.

My dreams were even more tortuous that night. I heard a great, rollin' thunder and my dogs were there. Barkin' the way they did when I drove up. There were heartbreakin' dreams about Toby and Chad and yet they seemed so real. Chad was holdin' me and kissin' my sun-burned face. His lips felt so soft, so cool.

Great wrenchin' pain hit and I couldn't contain it any longer. I screamed. It had become impossible to open my swollen eyes and I couldn't move. Then mercifully, everthing ended and there was no pain, no sound, and the darkness wrapped itself around me as I accepted that death, cool, blissful death, had come at last.

I could hear faint sounds in the far off distance.

There was people talkin' and movin' around. I tried to open my eyes but I just couldn't do it. My mind wondered where this was and I tried again to open 'em.

From somewhere in that distance I heard a voice say, "Call the doctor . . . I think she's comin' around."

Someone touched my lips with a cool, wet cloth.

"Lilah? Open your eyes, honey." a voice urged.

I tried again, but I was just too weak. The cool cloth touched my lips again. I opened my mouth to speak, but nothin' would come out.

"What is it baby?" Was that Chad soundin' so upset? Why? He had made his choice. He was with the one he wanted.

"What do you want, honey?" I thought I heard him say.

Everything became black and peaceful again and I didn't hear anything else. I had no idea how long I was asleep, but I was at peace for at least a while.

I felt myself swimmin' back from a deep pool of black water. I could see a small light somewhere above me and I knew I had to make it to that light so that I could breathe. As I neared it, I began to hear voices. For just a brief moment, I thought that, just maybe, I didn't want to come up. There was no pain where I was, but it seemed that I had no choice. I kept gettin' closer and the voices became clearer until at last, I thought I heard a slightly familiar voice.

"She's comin' outta it now. Let's see how she's doing."

I wanted so bad to tell 'em to just leave me be in that peaceful, pain-free place. Slowly I became aware of the sickenin' feelin' of total confusion. It'd gotten very quiet, almost too quiet. I rested a little and then dared to try to open my eyes again. The light was very bright and I could barely see it through the slits of still very heavy eyelids. I blinked to try and clear the blurriness and a hand grasped mine.

"Baby . . . wake up and talk to Chad . . . please honey."

I knew that sweet gentle voice and I tried to speak, but words just weren't there. My lips moved to whisper . . . "Chad?"

"Yes honey, yes, it's me. Can you see me?" I tried to move my head, but the sudden pain made me whimper.

"Just rest baby, I'll be right here. Just close those pretty green eyes and rest." Chad kissed my forehead and then my cheek.

Yes, this was a beautiful dream . . . NOW I could rest.

One night . . . I thought I woke up. It seemed easier to open my eyes. I blinked a couple of times and I could focus a little, but I was afraid to move. I glanced around. There in a chair beside my bed, I thought I could see Chad, sleepin' on a pillow propped on the bed rail and I was sure I could feel his other hand holdin' mine. I tried to take a deep breath. The sudden pain that shot through my chest caused me to shudder. The figure sat bolt upright

"What is it, honey?" He was standin' over my bed.

I forced a smile of sorts and managed to whisper, "Water . . . please."

"You can have ice . . . they said only ice . . . wait . . . let me go get some." He left and I lay there a moment tryin' to determine if this was real or just another crazy dream. There was no way that it wasn't a dream. Chad was with that woman . . . he'd had no desire to be with me. I tried to turn over in my bed and before I could stop myself, I let out a cry and fell back in a breathtakin' pain.

The nurses came rushin' in. They turned the lights up bright and started checkin' my blood pressure, temperature, and all the stuff they do when you're at their mercy.

At some point, I heard someone tell me that I had a badly-bruised lung and some broken ribs, so I had to lay flat in the bed with no tryin' to turn over. The nurse told me the doctor would be in the next mornin' and would talk to me about everything. She gave me more medicine in the IV and I felt myself slip gently away.

I was in and out of reality for countless times. Sometimes, I imagined that I found Chad still sittin' there. Sometimes it was Toby and many times I thought

I found Floy there. Once, for whatever reason, I even imagined that I saw Scott there. I was so confused that I couldn't separate my dreams from reality.

Then one day, out of the blue, I was somewhat awake and fairly alert. Floy was sittin' beside my bed readin' a book.

"Hey." My voice cracked as I managed a weak whisper.

She jumped.

"Hey. How ya feel? Do you need anything, honey?"

I half smiled. "Don't . . . know. Chad . . . was he . . . ?"

"He went home to take a shower and get cleaned up. Honey, he ain't left your side since he found ya. He has slept here, ate here, and 'bout paced the tile off the floor when he had to go outside."

I was very confused about what she'd just said, but I smiled again. It seemed to be the only part of me that didn't hurt.

"What . . . happened?"

"Ya don't remember?" she asked me.

I managed to barely shake my head, no.

"We don't really know, Lilah. I'd called ya several times before Chad found Toby. I couldn't believe it when he said he'd been callin' and wondered if ya had gone out of town again. Me and Toby met him out at your place to be sure nothin' was wrong. He knew somethin' wasn't right when we first walked in. He said the breakfast dishes were still out . . . Ya can explain that when you're better. Toby came up from the barn and told us that Pride was missin' and nothin' looked like it had been fed or watered in a while and the dogs was locked in one of the stalls. That's when we really got worried. Besides, your car was still there and your purse was in the house. We called the Sheriff and Stanley and some of the deputies come right out. Ya know, when word got out, there was over a hundred people out there lookin' for ya."

"How . . . did . . . did ya . . . find me?"

"Edgar!" she said. "Edgar come up to help and told Chad that if ya was in a hundred miles of there and Roz and Boots caught your scent, they'd find ya. Chad saddled up Patton and several others had brung horses and they took the dogs and headed out. They told us that they had to go a long ways before the dogs picked up your scent and took off down the valley. They were all surprised when they turned and headed up into the mountains. I guess they followed them dogs all over hell's half acre, but ya know that Roz has enough wolf in her that she can smell blood for miles! When they come up over this hill, they could see Pride down below. He was just standin' there. When they got down to him, they could see ya on the ground by Pride's feet but, ya know, that horse wasn't gonna let nobody get near ya. He was protectin' ya. Toby said Pride's leg was swollen twice its size and he couldn't even begin to stand on it. He could hardly walk 'cause his saddle was hangin' underneath of him."

"Pride?" I began to panic as I started to remember some of what'd happened. "Pride? . . . is he . . . OK?"

"Yeah, he's a lot better . . . I think. They sent him to Lexington to some friends to make sure he healed right and then they'll bring him home." Floy told me. "Ya know . . . at first . . . they thought ya was dead, honey. Toby said Chad jumped off that horse and fell to his knees and that he even saw tears rollin' down his cheek. He said it was awful. But ya was bad hurt and really, it was touch-and-go for a while. We was all just scared to death and we knew we just couldn't bear to lose ya."

She squeezed my hand as I smiled at her and tried to nod my head. She had told me so much so fast that very little had registered in my dizzy, throbbin' head.

"Mama?" I managed to whisper.

"I called 'em and told 'em what happened. We been in touch every day since. Your Mama couldn't leave Jesse and your Daddy didn't have no time off. I told 'em that we wouldn't leave ya for a minute."

"Why can't I . . . I move?" I wanted to know.

"The doc said that ya had some broke ribs, and a dislocated shoulder" she paused for a second, and a broken wrist and left leg." She sighed.

"Is that . . . all?" I mumbled in shock.

"Well . . . no, there's also a bad broke foot. They think ya got hung up in the stirrup and couldn't get loose. Least not 'til the saddle turned and let your foot slide out. You're so lucky it didn't break that leg, too. If that ain't enough . . . ya got a really bad concussion, along with a major sun burn and extreme dehydration! Sweetie, we came so close to not havin' ya with us. I don't know what I would've done without ya in my life." Her voice broke and she choked up.

It was a lot for me to digest. I closed my eyes and tried to remember, but nothin' made sense. Why was I in the pasture to begin with? There was nothin' I could remember except leavin' King's. I could vivdly remember bein' at the club and how Chad had left with that woman. My heart ached as I clearly began to remember seein' him with her and I started to cry.

"Don't cry sweetie." pleaded Floy "You're gonna be alright. The doctor said it was just gonna take some time."

The door opened and the nurse came in.

"Time for your pain meds, Miss Lilah" She put somethin' in the IV and everything changed to warm black velvet. I closed my eyes and tried to tune out the incredible ache in my heart, that by far, surpassed the pain in my body.

The last thing I remembered was hearin' Floy say, "they just gave her some pain medicine. She'll sleep for a while. Do ya want to go have somethin' to eat?"

Then I heard someone answer, "Sure."

I opened my eyes. It was dark except for a dim light comin' from somewhere outside the room. A hand took mine so gently.

"Hi, beautiful." It was a slightly familiar voice. I forced a weak smile.

"Are you feeling better? When your Mother called me, I got the first plane up here. I was lucky they were short-staffed. I've been working since I arrived."

I blinked and tried to focus. I blinked again and the face became a little clearer.

"S . . . Scott? What . . . how?"

"Don't worry, beautiful, I'll take very good care of you. I promised your Mother." He whispered softly.

When I woke up the next mornin', I was alone. It was quiet and the room was still dark. The door opened and Toby walked in.

"Hey there, sunshine. Look who's wide awake." He said as he sat down a vase of beautiful pink flowers and took a chair.

"Hi . . . Toby." I managed a smile.

"Floy'll be up in a minute. She was talkin' to your doctor down the hall. Ya sure took a tumble, my little friend. Oh, and I heard yesterday that Pride's doin' well. There don't seem to be no permanent damage. It'll just take some time. I knew ya would be glad to hear that."

"Yeah," I nodded and released a sigh of relief.

It wasn't long before Floy came in. "Mornin', Sweetie. How ya doin' today?" she asked.

I nodded.

"I was talkin' to your doctor outside," she said and gave me an odd look.

She turned to Toby. "Baby, would ya go see if ya can find me a hot cup of coffee? I really need a pick-me-up this mornin'."

"I bet I can manage that" he answered as he gave her a quick kiss and went out.

As soon as the door closed, Floy turned to me, "I don't want to upset ya, Sweetie, but I gotta tell ya somethin'. Your Mama called Scott and asked him to come check on ya. He's here! He's workin' here temporarily and he's one of your doctors!"

It was easy to see that she was really upset. " I know . . . he . . . he came in last night . . . I thought I was dreamin'. I guess I . . . was sort of . . . awake"

"What should I do?" Floy looked terrified.

"About . . . what?"

"Lilah, Chad went to check on Pride. He'll be back tomorrow!"

"So what? It don't matter . . . I . . . I don't care what he does."

I felt sudden tears well up and roll unchecked, down my cheek.

"What do ya mean, 'ya don't care'. Lilah, he . . . " She stopped when the door opened.

"Mornin,' beautiful. How do you feel today?" It was Scott. "What are you upset about? There's no reason to cry. Everything is looking really good."

I shook my head.

"I don't know," and I continued to cry .

He took my hand and sweetly kissed it.

"It's normal with all the medication and trauma. It'll go away in time. Besides, I told you, I will be right here for as long as you need and want me."

I felt strangely comforted when he said he'd be back to see me later and left.

Floy walked over to the side of my bed. "Sweetie, I just don't trust him. Ya said yourself that he made ya uneasy. What should I do?"

I swallowed and took a deep breath. " Maybe I was wrong. Maybe, I just . . . didn't . . . didn't give him a fair . . . chance."

Toby came back with the coffee and they stayed a little while as I dozed on and off.

"I'll be back about one o'clock. I gotta help Grandpa 'til noon," Floy whispered as she turned toward the door.

I nodded and closed my eyes thinkin' that maybe if I went to sleep, everything would make more sense when I woke up.

Floy came back after lunch. "Everybody in town is askin' about ya. There are so many people that want to come up to see ya. They said at the nurses' station that they are gonna move ya to a regular room tomorrow. Wait 'til ya see all the flowers at the nurses' station that are for ya. Toby slipped those in this mornin'. Ya know ya ain't supposed to have flowers in intensive care. Are ya feelin' any better, sweetie?" She finally took a breath.

"Maybe a little. I been awake a little more . . . got broth for lunch," I sighed.

"Oh, and the nursin' home called. I told 'em what happened and the lady, Dora, said somebody named Mae got everybody together and they had a prayer circle for ya. She said they planned on doin' it every day until ya come home. Ain't that sweet?"

I nodded, "I only worked . . . one day."

"Well, ya must have made a great impression." She smiled.

Floy stayed 'til late in the evenin'. She left sometime after dark.

Later, I began to have a great deal of pain and when the nurse came in, I told her about it.

"It's because the doctor has started to cut back on the pain medication so that ya can stay awake a little more. It's time for another dose anyway," she smiled at me as she put the medicine in the IV. It only took seconds for it to take affect. I still didn't like the feelin', but I did like the relief it gave me as I dozed off peacefully.

It was very late in the night when Chad appeared. He was softly kissin' my lips and my neck. It felt so wonderful. He moved down to my chest and then I felt his tongue touch my breast. I tingled from head to toe as I wrapped my arm around his neck. Then . . . a loud slammin' door. I was startled awake! It wasn't a dream. And it wasn't Chad. It was Scott that I pushed away.

"What . . . what are ya doin'? STOP!"

He stood up and looked at me. "I'm sorry, but you just looked so beautiful laying there sleeping so peacefully. I shouldn't have done that. I am sorry." Then . . . he was gone.

Later I was awakened by nurses doin' the vital checks.

I realized then that it had all been a bad dream. It made me sick to think that I'd wanted it to be Chad so badly. After seein' him with that . . . woman, why did the thought of him still make me feel the way it did? And why in the world would I dream about Scott? Especially in that way.

The next day was tough. They started movin' me early and when we went into the new room, I was really surprised. There were flowers everywhere and it did look more like a flower shop than a hospital room.

"Look at this, Miss Lilah!" said my nurse "Isn't this just beautiful? I've never seen so many pretty flowers. You are truely loved. That's a great thing . . . to be loved that much."

Somehow, her words sounded so familiar. I'd heard that same sentence somewhere before. It made me feel sad, but I had no idea why.

Floy was there before lunch.

"I told ya that ya had a ton of flowers, didn't I?" She laughed. "Ya look better today. How do ya feel?"

I thought about tellin' her my stupid dream, but decided it was better off forgotten.

"Better." was all I said.

"Chad called first thing this mornin'. He said he was gonna stay in Lexington for a while. He wanted to keep an eye on Pride and he had some other business to tend to."

I kept lookin' at the TV in my room and just nodded.

"Seemed odd to me. He just didn't sound like hisself. He just said to take good care of ya. Then he said somethin' weird. He said it looked like ya was already bein' taken care of pretty damn well."

I didn't understand what that meant, but it was okay. I didn't need anyone to take care of me.

"Did he come by here last night?" she asked. "I know he came back to town last night 'cause Toby saw him at the gas station."

"No, I never saw him," I answered coldly.

Several days later, the door opened and in walked my Mama. I was so excited to see her.

"How's my baby?" She rushed to me and started to hug me. "I don't know where to hug ya, everything's in a cast." she sobbed.

"It's okay, Mama. I'm feelin' better ever day."

She kissed me on the forehead. "Oh baby, your little face is just peelin' like a snake. Are they puttin' anything on it?"

"Yes, ma'm. They're takin' real good care of me." "I knew when Dr. O'Grady got here that he would see to ya. He likes ya a lot ya know."

"He's nice," I answered as an uneasy chill made me shiver.

We visited for some time before Floy got there.

"Floy, ya done a real good job of lookin' after my baby," Mama told her.

"I wouldn't have it any other way, ma'am. Where ya stayin' while you're here?" Floy asked her.

"Out at Lilah's, I suppose. I can't stay but a day or two. I can't expect Minnie to watch all them kids for very long."

"No. No, you're comin' to my little place. It's not much, but there's plenty of room. That way ya can use my car or ride with me." Floy told her.

"Well, thank ya honey, I appreciate that. Tell me, is there anywhere's that I can get a cup of coffee?"

Floy told her where to go to get the coffee and as she left she asked her to bring her one, too.

"Floy, what about Toby? I thought he was stayin' with ya whenever he could sneak in? "

"No Sweetie, he's been stayin' at your place ever since they brought ya to the hospital. He said it was easier than drivin' back and forth all the time. He likes that ranch a lot. I expect him to dump me anyday and make a play for you and your ranch," she teased.

"Sure, I can just see that happenin'. He's head over heels for ya."

"How's it goin' with Scott?" she asked.

"He's just my doctor. I try to look at him with different eyes, but it's just not there," I shook my head.

"Good." she sounded relieved. " I don't like him anyway . . . he sneaks around like he's up to somethin'. I come in one night . . . well . . . never . . . "

The door opened about that time and Mama come in with two cups of coffee.

"Floy, I didn't know if ya wanted it with cream and sugar or just plain."

"I like it anyway ya brought it." They both laughed and I enjoyed watchin' my Mama and my best friend have a light-hearted conversation.

Mama decided to stay with me that night. I was glad 'cause I felt, for some reason, safer. It was the best I'd slept in what seemed like forever.

Over the next few days, I had more company than I could imagine. People I hadn't seen in ages come by to wish me well. It seemed that everyone in town had gone out of their way to come visit. Eveyone, except Chad. I decided he probably had his hands more than full with that hussy . . . that Danna girl. It suddenly dawned on me. How'd I know her name was Danna? Someone must've mentioned it somewhere. It didn't matter. He'd made his choice.

Scott was comin' 'round more than I felt was necessary. He was always makin' a production of his devoted dedication to my well-bein'. There was a lot of nights that I woke up to find him standin' by my bed. It'd started to really give me the creeps.

Mama'd gone home and they said that I could go home too . . . in another week. I was more than ready, but there was a lot to work on and a lot of arrangements to be made.

Since I had to have someone there 'round the clock, I hired a private nurse to stay in the daytime and Floy and Toby agreed to stay the nights. Scott, of course, volunteered to come out and check on me a couple a times a week.

When it got close to time to go home, Floy went to the house and cleaned everything. She fixed up the livin' room like a bedroom 'cause I had no way to get up the stairs. I could hardly wait to get back to my home.

Scott would have it no other way but to have an ambulance take me home. He said it was too far to sit in a car. I had to admit that it felt better to lay down than to sit. It was easy to tell when we started up my little dirt road. It was rough and I could feel it when we took the curve that went through the grove just before we reached the house. I was thrilled to tears when I heard Roz and Boots come running up to the ambulance with their loud welcome. When they took the bed out of the back, the two dogs nearly turned me over tryin' to get up to lick my face. I told 'em to stop a moment while I petted my babies. It already felt so good to be back home.

Chapter 7

We finally got in the house and I got settled on the couch. As I lay back on the pillow, I got a faint whiff of a very familiar cologne. I was surely losin' my mind since Chad had never set foot in my house. He didn't even know where I lived.

Floy and Toby were both there as well as my new nurse, Dee. After the ambulance was gone and everything quieted down, I took a deep breath and looked around.

"It seems like I've been gone for months." I sighed. Floy took my hand.

"Sweetie," she paused "Ya have. It's been over eight weeks since ya were home."

I just couldn't believe it. Eight weeks! How could that be? Stunned, I looked into her eyes. She nodded.

"Really?"

"Really." She answered.

"Really." Toby confirmed.

I sat there speechless. I'd missed eight whole weeks of my life.

It was two weeks since I'd gotten home. We'd developed a routine that worked pretty well and Scott had been out several times to check on me. Accordin' to him, my ribs were healin', even though it still hurt when I moved and he'd taken the cast off my wrist. He was to come out that day and see about takin' the cast off my leg. I was excited about bein' able to get around a whole lot easier.

It was just before lunch when Scott finally got there. Toby and Floy were both gone to work and I was alone with Dee.

"Hello, beautiful." He called as he came through the front door. "Are you ready to get that cast off?"

"Oh yeah, ya can be sure of that." I answered him.

Dee came in to assist Scott. I was really glad 'cause I still didn't feel comfortable when I was alone with him.

While he was removin' the cast, Scott's fingers continuously touched my skin. His touch gave me cold chills every time. When the cast was off, he ran his hands from my ankle to my thigh and back down. He said he was checkin' to make sure everything was in line but somehow, I doubted that was true and didn't really feel it was necessary. I made sure Dee stayed right in the room.

When he left, Dee asked "Ya don't feel very comfortable with Dr. O'Grady do ya?"

"Why do ya ask?"

"Because I don't either" she answered as she went into the other room.

When Floy and Toby come home from work, they was almost as excited as I was about the cast bein' gone.

"All ya need now is to get that one off your foot." said Floy excitedly.

I sat there a minute. "Yeah . . . that's all I need." I said as I wheeled my chair back into the livin' room.

"Toby, will ya take me out on the porch, please?"

Dee opened the door as Toby worked my chair outside. It was getting' late and the days were startin' to get shorter and a little cooler, especially at night after the sun went down. Somehow, the weather seemed different. It felt like fall might be early that year.

Floy came out and brought me a blanket. I wrapped it around me and suddenly that fragrance was back and I felt an overwhelmin' desire to burst into tears. I didn't know why, but holdin' the blanket to my nose, I inhaled and realized that it too smelled exactly like Chad. It left no doubt in my mind that I was losin' what little sanity I had left! I sat there with that blanket to my face for a long time.

I decided to go in about dark and was gettin' ready to call Toby when car lights come out of the grove. We wasn't expectin' nobody, at least not that late anyway. Boots and Roz made a mad dash down to greet the guests. The truck, pullin' a black horse trailer, drove down by the barn and parked.

"Toby! Toby!"

He came out the door " Yes ma'm?"

"There's somebody down to the barn".

He looked "Great! It's Pride comin' home. Chad said he'd be bringin' him sometime this week." he said as he ran out toward the barn.

My heart began to pound in my chest. I was very excited that Pride was home, but even though I was furious with Chad . . . I still desperately wanted to see him. I'd refused to discuss anything about him with anybody since all that had happened. Still, I just wanted to look at him one more time.

Toby turned the lights on outside the barn. I could see men movin' around but I couldn't tell who was who. I wanted so bad to go down there that I could've screamed!

"Do ya want me to tell him you'd like to see him?" Floy asked softly from behind me.

I sat there a few minutes then answered. "No, if he didn't care enough to come to see me when I needed him most . . . then the hell with him!"

"But Lilah, he . . ."

"No! I don't want to hear anything about him. Take me inside." I whirled the chair around and Floy opened the door while Dee come to help me into the house.

Later, I heard the truck pull up from the barn. It stopped outside the front door and I held my breath in anticipation.

He was just outside the door.

After a couple of minutes, it drove away. I felt like I had no more air to breathe. He probably had his woman with him, or he had to hurry and get back to her.

I was tired. I decided to go to bed.

Three days later, Floy and Toby were at work as usual, when the phone rang. Dee took it in the kitchen and when she came out she was very upset.

"Lilah, that was my sister, my Dad is very sick and they need me. Will ya be ok until the others get home?"

"Sure, they'll be home in three, maybe four hours. I can lay here and watch TV and maybe take a little nap. Ya go ahead and take care of your Daddy."

She brought any meds I might need and plenty of water.

"I'm set." I told her. "Now go."

It was very quiet after she was gone. I decided to read a book someone had brought me and of course it put me straight to sleep.

When the front door opened, I awoke and I was startled to see Scott standin' there.

"I didn't expect ya today." I said as an instant unease seemed to fill the room.

"I just decided to come out and check on my favorite patient. How do you feel today?" He came closer.

"I'm fine. There's really no reason for ya to waste your time drivin' all the way out here. Ya was just here the other day."

"It's my pleasure, believe me. There's nowhere else on this earth I'd rather be."

I scooted up so that I was close to sittin' up. He immediately sat down by my feet.

"Where's everyone at?" he asked as he glanced around.

"Well, Dee had an emergency and had to leave, but Toby will be home any minute."

I was suddenly very nervous.

"So, we're all alone here." His smile seemed to hold a wickedness I'd never seen before.

"Only for a few minutes . . . and Floy should be here, too." I stammered.

He looked at me and grinned again. "Why so nervous, beautiful? You know that I would never do anything to upset you, don't you?"

"Sure, yeah".

I'd forgotten to have Dee put the phone nearby and there was no way to get to it.

Please Floy . . . get home early . . . sometimes she does . . . please! I prayed to myself.

Scott put his clammy hand on my bare leg. With only a robe on and my blanket over me, I moved my leg quickly away. He reached again. This time he caught the one with the foot cast still on it. The one I could hardly move. He ran his hand up over my knee. As I tried to push it away, he scooted up between my knees.

"What are ya doin?" I could hear the shakiness in my own voice.

"Just getting a little closer to you." He whispered.

"Well, I don't like it . . . Please move."

"No, thank you." He whispered gruffly as he removed the blanket and moved even closer.

"Scott, this isn't funny. I don't feel like bein' aggravated."

"I'm not gonna aggravate you, baby. I'm gonna make love to you like you've never been made love to before. You're all I've been able to think about since we met."

"No!" I yelled. "You stop and leave now!"

Before I realized it, he had me pinned down on the couch. He grabbed my face and kissed me so roughly that I felt like his whiskers was rakin' my skin off. His hands were everywhere and his lips moved down my neck as he began to roughly bite at my shoulders and breast. I tried to push him away and he grabbed my hands. The wrist I'd broken throbbed with pain. He held 'em above my head with one hand and with the other he tore my underwear away. His knees were between my legs, which were still very weak, and my ribs shot pain throughout my body. He raised up and pulled his pants down to his knees.

"Please! Don't do this Scott! I'm beggin' ya . . . DON'T!" I screamed.

"Shut up!" He yelled as he slapped me across the face. "You know you want it. I knew you wanted it the first time I kissed you and by God, you're gonna get it!"

I screamed again and that time hit me with his fist. My head was spinnin' as I felt him roughly begin to enter me. He was abruptly lifted into the air as someone grabbed him by his shirt and flung him across the room.

"You son- of-a-bitch! I'll give ya somethin'," a familiar voice growled.

Scott tried to get up when a flyin' foot caught him upside his head. About all I saw after that was Scott being tossed out the door.

"Come back here again and they'll have to carry ya out in a box!"

I could hardly see, but I knew that voice. My head ached like I'd been hit with a rock and everything was just a blur. The door slammed shut and locked and I panicked for a moment as I thought maybe, somehow, Scott had made it back inside.

A hand reached out and touched my face. I jumped and threw up my arm to protect myself.

"No . . . no . . . please!" I begged.

"It's okay, honey. It's me . . . Chad."

I started to cry uncontrollably. He closed my robe and wrapped me in my blanket and held me close.

I don't know how long we'd sat there like that when Floy come burstin' in the back door. She stopped cold.

"Would someone mind tellin' me why Scott's in the front yard?"

"Is he still there?" demanded Chad as he leaned forward.

"Yeah. But he seems to be havin' some sort of a issue with his clothes." she looked confused.

"Is he movin'?" Chad asked again.

"Yeah. He's kinda crawlin' bare assed across the yard."

Chad chewed on his bottom lip and looked down at me. I looked away. It was next to impossible to look at him at all after what he'd witnessed.

"Chad? Tell me what happened!" Floy demanded.

"The bastard was tryin' to rape her when I walked in! I should a killed him!"

"What? Where's Dee? Why was she here alone?" she yelled as she came to me.

I told her what happened as best I could between sobs.

"Chad got here . . . just as . . . " I broke down again.

When Toby got there they called the Sheriff. Chad never left my side and I didn't want him to. It was the only place in the world that I felt really safe.

Stanley and his Deputy brought a doctor from the hospital. Everyone had to go out while he checked me. He did what he called a rape kit, but I told him that he'd only started to enter when Chad grabbed him. I had bite marks on my face, neck and breast and bruises on both my wrist and the beginnin' of a serious black eye. The doctor was more concerned about my wrist and the fact that I was still recoverin' from a concusion than the attempted rape. He wrapped my wrist in a bandage and told me to put ice packs on it and not to use it for awhile. The blow to my head had done it no good at all. I was ordered to stay in bed and he'd be back the next day to make sure that I was doin' better.

When everybody come back inside, he asked my permission to tell the sheriff everything. At that point I didn't feel like I had any secrets, so I told him to tell 'em all. It would save me from havin' to tell it over and over.

When he'd finished, Chad got up and walked outside. I felt sure he didn't want anything to do with me now. He probably thought of me as . . . damaged goods.

"What's wrong, Sweetie?" Floy knelt beside the couch.

"He . . . he left." The tears began again.

"Who?"

"Chad, he'll never come back now. Not after what he saw."

The door opened and he walked back in. He looked at me and come straight to me.

"Why ya cryin', honey? What's the matter?"

He took my hand and looked at the bruises. He kissed each one and whispered softly "Please don't cry, honey. I can't stand it when ya do that."

"Why did ya go out?" I sobbed.

"I . . . uh . . . I . . . I just needed a little air. I wish I'd killed that son-of-a-bitch." he said. "Im not leavin' here 'til they catch him."

He was very matter of fact and I loved the way it made me feel when he just stepped up and took charge.

The Sheriff finally left and headed back into town to see if they could locate Scott.

Toby and Chad went to feed and lock up my animals. Floy helped me get a bath, a fresh gown, and robe. She gasped when I took everything off and she saw all the bruises and bite marks.

"It's okay," I told her. "I just hope they catch him. Floy, what if he comes back?"

"He wouldn't dare come back with Toby and Chad both here." Floy reassured.

I finally got settled back on my couch while Floy made supper. The guys came back in and we ate in the living room. Toby and Floy went to the kitchen to do dishes and left me and Chad to talk.

"I don't want to talk right now," I told him, "I just want ya to come lay down with me and hold me like ya did earlier."

He grinned that little crooked grin "I'd love to do that."

He carefully crawled over behind me and wrapped his arms around me. I pulled the blanket over us and we closed our eyes and said nothin'. It felt so right, so strangely familiar as I laid there feelin' his heart beat against my back. I could still smell that wonderful cologne as I drifted off into a deep sleep.

Sometime in the night I woke up screamin' in a panic. I thought Chad was Scott and I'd dreamed that he had me chained in a dark room without windows. I began to fight and try frantically to get away.

"Honey, Honey! It's just a dream! It's me, it's Chad!"

He was tryin' to keep me from hurtin' myself, but I was scared to death and believed that I was fightin' for my very life. I finally opened my eyes and began to realize I'd had yet another terrible nightmare.

"Chad? Chad . . . I'm sorry. I . . . I thought ya . . . was . . ."

Toby and Floy came runnin' down stairs.

"What's wrong? What happened?" They was both askin'.

"It's . . . it's ok. She just had a bad dream. That's all . . . a bad dream."

I nodded and cuddled into his arms and went back to sleep.

Before I opened my eyes, I heard that damn rooster crowin' his little heart out. I laid there a couple of minutes and tried to remember what'd really happened and what I'd simply dreamed. When I opened my eyes, I looked straight into Chad's face. He was sleepin' so peacefully. I don't think he'd moved all night. His long eyelashes lay across his cheeks and his beautiful full lips were slightly parted just enough to see his perfectly even, white teeth. His skin was so tan, as smooth as velvet, and his hair fell down across his forehead into his eyes like silver blond satin. I prayed silently that he would forever be right there with me.

Quietly, I inhaled his breath and the scent of his skin. He moved slightly. I closed my eyes. I wanted to treasure every precious second.

Later that mornin', I heard Floy and Toby comin' down the stairs, so I pretended to be asleep hopin' maybe they'd let Chad sleep a little longer. I wasn't ready to be out of his arms. They tiptoed through the livin' room and into the kitchen. They were gettin' ready to cook Saturday mornin' breakfast when I heard the back door open. It was Dee. I hadn't expected her back for several days. She told Floy that her Dad was much better and that it wasn't as serious as they first thought. Everyone had just over reacted. I listened as Toby and Floy told her about the day before. Dee sounded horrified.

"It's my fault. If I hadn't left, none of it would have happened. Did they catch him yet?"

"We ain't heard. I hope they do and soon. I'm afraid Chad's goin' after him and I don't want him to get in trouble." Toby answered her.

"I'll never leave her alone again. I swear! Never!" promised Dee.

"No one's blamin' you, Dee. If you'd been here, ya might've gotten hurt too. He's insane." added Floy.

"I can tell ya this much" Toby said "There was somethin' weird goin' on at that hospital, too. Chad was tellin' me down at the barn the other night that the reason he left and stayed gone was 'cause of, as he put it 'some doctor' at the hospital. He told me the night he come back from takin' Pride to Lexington that he went straight up to Lilah's room. The door was slightly cracked open and he thought she was probably asleep, so he eased it open. He was shocked . . . and pissed when he saw some doctor leanin' over her with her gown untied and open. He saw him kissin' her breast! And . . . he said she was moanin' like she was enjoyin' it. I set him straight about that. I told him that, Hell, she was knocked out with heavy drugs all durin' that time and for some time after that. She wouldn't have even known what was goin' on let alone enjoy it. I think our doctor friend was up to a lot we weren't aware of!"

I was stunned. Dear Lord what else had he done that I didn't know about. I felt violated all over again.

Then, I heard Floy say, " I don't think she remembers everything. In fact, I'm sure of it. I tried to talk to her about some of it, but she just keeps shuttin' me down. Ya know, she thought that Chad left with that girl from the club the last time we was out there. I don't think she has a clue that Chad come out here and ended up spendin' the night."

"Yeah, he told me about that too," Toby added. " He was upset 'cause of Jamie and she was all pissed about that girl and all the time . . . Hell, they're crazy about each other. He told me that they slept on the couch that night . . . just like they are right now. Nothin' happened. Just like right now. I agree, she don't remember none of that."

I lay there and started to think about it all. That did explain a lot, like the pillow that smelled like him and the blanket, the same one we had over us right then. He really had been there that night . . . not with Danna. That's how I knew her name . . . Chad had been the one that told me. I opened my eyes, again. I was startled to look straight into those incredible blue eyes. He bit his bottom lip and then smiled that crooked little smile.

"Mornin', chica" he whispered.

"Mornin'" I whispered back.

He pulled me closer and we just lay there lookin' into each others eyes. Shortly the smell of fresh coffee and fryin' bacon and eggs was more than he could stand.

"Ya ready to eat, honey?" he whispered.

"In a little while. Go ahead."

He began to try to get up.

"My other arm's asleep. I don't know how I'm gonna get out of here and not hurt ya."

"Wait, I can get up."

When I sat up however, a great rush of dizziness and nausea overwhelmed me and I passed cold out. I was only out for a minute or so, but it was long enough to cause a small riot. Floy said he yelled like a crazy man for help. They all rushed in just as I was comin' out of it. Somehow, Chad was up and kneelin' on the floor. Dee said it was not uncommon after the trauma of the day before. She was a little concerned about the blow to my head and was glad when they told her that the doctor was comin back that mornin'.

"I'm sorry," I told everybody. " I . . . I didn't mean to scare ya."

I looked at Chad and those baby blues were wide as saucers.

"Don't do that again" he said " Ever!"

Just before noon, the doctor showed up.

"I don't see anything any different than before. I just wanted to be sure. However, I do want you to stay in bed for a couple of more days, then you can go back to what you were doin'. Oh, and keep that wrap on your wrist for a while. It's pretty swollen and I am concerned about the bruises. So, let's limit the use of that also. Anything else?" he asked.

"Yeah, uh . . . I . . . I wondered if ya heard anything about O'Grady? Have they caught him?" Chad wanted to know.

"I haven't heard anything this morning. I'm sure if they had, they would've called right away," the doctor said as he was packin' up his equipment. He started out the door, then turned.

"Take care of her . . . and don't leave her alone for awhile."

"Don't worry doc, that ain't gonna happen," answered Toby.

It felt so safe with everyone there. Floy, Toby, Dee, and most of all, Chad. The rest of the day was quiet.

That night Chad slept on the couch beside me again. This was somethin' that I could sure get used to. I slept unbelievably good that night and didn't wake up 'til that damn rooster decided everyone should be gettin' up.

Floy and Toby were up first and got ready for church, but Dee and Chad stayed there with me. The day seemed worse than the day before. My body ached all over. To make matters worse, the Sheriff called to let us know that they'd not found a trace of Scott. He'd cleaned out his hotel room and vanished. It made me very nervous to think that he might still be around. He was crazy enough to try anything. It made me feel guilty that I'd ever even given him the time of day. If I'd ignored him, none of this would've happened.

On Monday, Floy and Toby had to go to work, so Chad and I were alone except for Dee. Once she realized that Chad was takin' great care of me, she kept to her room a good deal. She did the cookin' and even some cleanin', although it wasn't really her job. She was becomin' more of a very dear friend than my hired nurse. She'd helped me with my bath that mornin' and Chad had surprised us both by cookin' breakfast. I wanted to eat at the table but they made me go back to bed. In all honesty, I was still a little dizzy.

Shortly after I laid down, I heard the front door open. I looked up and all I could see was the outline of someone standin' there with the sunlight shinnin' in around him. I blinked and looked again as he moved closer and I saw who it was. There stood Scott! I tried to scream for help, but pure fear froze in my throat as I looked around frantically for Chad or Dee or Floy, anybody! I finally managed a blood-curdlin' scream.

"Please!! Help me!" Then he grabbed me.

"Lilah? Lilah? Honey, wake up . . . wake up!" I opened my eyes . . . and it was Chad. "It was just a dream, Chiquita. It's okay. I'm right here and I ain't goin' nowhere." He grabbed me into his arms and I burst into tears again.

"It was him . . . it was Scott and . . . he looked so . . . angry and so dangerous. I couldn't find nobody and . . . and . . . I was afraid he would try to . . . to . . ." Chad held me close and kissed my face.

"I'll die before I ever let him near ya again."

"Is there anything I can do, Mr. Barrett?" Dee asked.

"No thank ya, Dee. She'll be okay. I'll sit here with her."

That evenin', after Floy and Toby got home, Chad left long enough to get his clothes and some of his things. Floy and Toby were stayin' in my bedroom and Dee had the guestroom. They all went upstairs to try to make enough space in the spare room where I had Nanny's stuff stored. Chad would then have enough room to put his belongin's.

Never in my wildest dreams did I ever imagine that Chad Barrett would be movin' into my house. Everything had just happened so fast that maybe, I thought, that was why I was so dizzy. Later when he returned, Toby helped him unload his truck, and they headed to the barn. Floy came in and sat down beside me.

"We haven't had much time to talk," she said quietly.

"I know, but it's been kinda crazy around here."

She looked me straight in the eye. "Are ya really okay, sweetie?"

"I think so. It's just . . . I . . . I can't believe all of it happened. Chad walked in and saw . . . he saw . . . what Scott was tryin' to . . . "

I knew I had to get a grip on my emotions, but I was so humiliated.

"The other mornin' I heard you and Toby talkin' about what Chad saw at the hospital, too! I don't remember any of it. How do I know that . . . that . . . he didn't . . . ya know . . . do more?"

She dropped her head "Ya don't. I should never've stepped out, even for a second."

"Ya had no way of knowin'."

"But we was both uneasy around him. I should've kept a better watch. You was kept sedated because of the pain and I should've been your eyes and ears," she mumbled as tears trickled down her cheeks.

"No. It was nobody's fault. He was the only one to blame." I tried to reassure her as well as myself.

Two weeks soon passed and I was feelin' a lot better. I'd only had one or two more nightmares and Chad stayed on the couch with me every night.

At last the day came when I got my last cast off. The doctor made the trip out to the ranch again.

"I bet you're ready for this?" he asked when he walked in.

I could hardly wait to be rid of all the casts and bandages. Before I could say much, it was gone. What a shriveled up little foot that was. I couldn't believe all the stitches. They went in every direction.

"Lots of surgery there," he said as he removed several of the tiny spider like knots.

"When can I walk on it?"

"Not for a while. It took a lot of sewin' to put that back together. We don't want to rush it."

I was disappointed, but I knew in my heart that he was right and I was very lucky to still have a foot. He carefully removed the rest of the stitches and gave Dee instructions on how he wanted her to care for it.

That night after supper, we decided to go sit on the front porch. Summer was turnin' into fall so fast I couldn't believe it. I'd missed most of the summer while I was in the hospital. It was so hard to accept that the beautiful things of summer had mostly slipped by. There wasn't but just a few of the lightenin' bugs still showin' off in the shadows.

I'd started to get in my wheelchair when Chad swept me up into his arms and carried me outside. He gently sat me in one of the rockin' chairs and Floy covered me with a blanket. We were all sittin' there sippin' on coffee when Chad got up and headed toward the barn.

"Where ya goin'?" I asked. He just kept walkin'.

I looked at Toby. "I thought you guys already shut everything down for the night?"

"We did." He answered as he took another sip of his coffee.

It was only a few minutes when the barn door opened and Chad rode out on Pride. I was so excited I could hardly contain myself. It was the first time I'd seen him since the day of the accident. It was a magnificent sight, both the horse and the man ridin' him. He rode him right up to the edge of the porch.

"Somebody wanted to see ya," Chad grinned as Pride stretched his neck 'til I could pet him. He nickered and nodded his head as if to say, "Yeah . . . we're okay."

"Is he completely healed?"

"Sugar, I wouldn't be ridin' him if he wasn't. He just doesn't have shoes on yet, but the ground's soft. He's done great."

I was so happy to know that he was home and well. It was such a huge relief and I still found it hard to let him go when Chad took him back to the barn and penned him up for the night.

Dee decided it was past her bed time since she was usually up long before any one else. Chad came back to the porch and we sat in the cool night air and talked for awhile.

Floy stood up, "I gotta get some sleep, too. I'm a workin' girl who needs her rest."

"Wait on me," said Toby standin' up. "I need my beauty rest too."

They said their good nights and headed upstairs hand-in-hand. We sat on the porch for a while longer and watched the fireflies off in the distance.

"Ya ready to go in?"

"I think so. It's been a long day." He carefully picked me up and carried me back inside. He put me on the couch and then locked all the doors and turned out all the lights but one small lamp. I already had my gown and robe on.

"Would ya help me out of this robe, please?"

"Sure," he said as he gently unbuttoned it. I started to protest that I could unbutton it, I just couldn't get it off my shoulders. But I decided that, on second thought, maybe I did need that extra help.

I laid down on the couch as Chad took his boots off and started to crawl over me.

"Aren't ya tired of sleepin' in your clothes?" I asked. "Ya could take 'em off and be a lot more comfortable."

I was a little emabarrassed at how that may have sounded.

"I mean . . . I hate to see ya . . . well . . . nobody sleeps in their clothes."

"Are ya sure ya won't mind? I'll admit . . . I don't usually sleep fully-dressed."

"I'm sure" I assured him with more confidence than I felt.

He turned out the lamp and took off his pants and shirt. He crawled over on the back side like always and slid under the cover. I hadn't given a thought to how it would affect me to feel his bare legs next to mine, let alone his bare chest and arms. My heart was poundin' in my chest yet again. We lay there like stick figures. Neither of us movin' and barely breathin'. I don't know how long we lay there like that... both of us pretendin' that it didn't make a difference. There was certainly no way I would ever go to sleep and I knew deep in my heart that Chad was as awake as I was.

"You asleep?" He whispered in my ear.

I waited a minute before whisperin', "No."

He put his arm around me and I just knew that he could feel my heart almost beatin' its way out of my chest. I could feel his warm breath on the side of my face. Against my better judgement, I turned my face toward him.

"What ya thinkin'?" He whispered.

I didn't dare tell him what I was really thinkin' about. I hadn't been with a man since Walter and I'd split years ago. Well, except what almost happened with Scott, but that didn't count 'cause that wasn't anything I'd wanted. What if Chad felt differently? Maybe, he really did consider me damaged goods. He'd been so wonderful the whole time he'd been there, but he'd never even tried to touch me. All those nights we'd slept in each others arms and he didn't even try. He was probably just bein' his noble, considerate self. Then his hand reached up to touch my face as his moved closer. I could hardly breathe as his lips softly touched mine. His kiss deepened and his tongue made it's way between my lips. I responded likewise. His hand slid down my back and pulled me closer to him. In my heart of hearts I knew that I would not, could not, push him away. It was the taste of him, the smell of him, the feel of his body that I couldn't resist. I didn't want to resist. He began to kiss my neck, my shoulders and his hands held me gently, but firmly, against him. I'd never even come close to wantin' any man the way I wanted Chad Barrett.

He kissed me softly then pushed back.

"Good night, baby girl," and he turned away. I was stunned.

What could I have done to turn him off so suddenly? I could barely get my breath, but now I was sure I'd been right. I WAS damaged goods! He couldn't get the image of Scott out of his mind. He'd never be able to look at me the same way again. When I turned my back to him, the tears rolled down my face. My lips still burned from the heat of his kiss as I heard him sigh and a little while later, he was asleep.

It must have been hours before I finally fell asleep. Even in my sleep, I still wanted him as I dreamed of makin' love to him. I dreamed of kissin' and laughin' and dancin' and just bein' a part of his life. Then it was daylight and the rooster began to crow.

Even before I opened my eyes, I knew that he was gone. My bed felt cold and empty. I didn't know when he got up or how he got up without wakin' me. Just the same, he was gone. Turnin' over to his pillow, I could still smell the scent of his cologne and the tears trickled down my cheeks again. He was probably gone for good this time, now that he'd realized how he really felt. I wanted to close my eyes and never wake up again.

Dee must have already come downstairs 'cause I could smell the coffee brewin'. I heard Toby and Floy comin' down as quietly as they could on old rickety stairs. They was whisperin' and gigglin' but they had no idea that I was awake and Chad had already left. I heard someone come back through the livin' room and I pretended I was still asleep.

"Ya awake, honey?"

My eyes popped open. "Yeah." I whispered.

"I brought ya coffee. Cream and sugar just like ya like it." He bit his bottom lip and raised his eyebrow. I sat up but I still couldn't believe it was Chad. There hadn't been a doubt in my mind that he had left. I didn't understand but I didn't really care. He was here for now and that was all that mattered. I gratefully took the coffee and sipped it.

"Ya cryin' again, baby? What's wrong? Did ya have another dream?"

I looked into those crystal blue eyes again and simply nodded

"It'll get better, honey, I promise. Just give it time. Okay?"

Chapter 8

Days turned into weeks and still Chad stayed. Even Floy and Toby refused to go home. They said they didn't feel right leavin' us out there when there'd been no word on Scott O'Grady. As far as anyone knew, he was still on the loose.

Dee just came out twice a week to visit with me. We all missed her. She'd become like family to us. I decided I would talk to her about a permanent position with me as housekeeper, cook *We all loved her cookin'*, and friend.

The leaves were startin' to turn colors and the hills and mountains were unusually beautiful. Fall had sure enough come early that year. It was only the middle of September and we'd already had a heavy frost.

Chad come bouncin' in the back door one evenin'. "Hey, baby, what do ya think about you and me goin' for a ride? Pride and Patton are ready to go if ya feel like it."

I thought about it for a long minute. Since the accident, ridin' had been the last thing on my mind. The thought made me a little nervous, but I felt fine, so I had no physical excuse for not goin'.

"Yeah . . . let's go ride."

Chad pulled my coat and ridin' gloves from behind his back and gave me that cute little curly lip smile.

"I thought ya might say yes," he said a little embarrassed.

He was strikin' in a green leather western jacket and his black shirt and black hat. Who in their right mind could resist any invitation from someone who looked like that? We climbed into the saddles. He turned and rode close. He buttoned my coat and wrapped the scarf that I'd grabbed around my neck.

"It's a little chilly this evenin'," he said smilin'.

Then he reached back and turned his collar up, secured his sunglasses, pulled his hat down in front, and away we went. I was surprised at how well he rode. He looked like he was born to it, or maybe like some western movie star. I couldn't help but enjoy the view of the horse, as well as the rider, as we went through the pasture and down the valley. When we got to the creek, Chad pulled up.

"Wanna take a break?"

"Sure" I said as I slid carefully from the saddle.

There was some beautiful trees growin' along the creek bed and the red and gold colors were just wonderful. I walked over and kicked my feet through the leaves as I admired 'em and turned to see where Chad was. He was just standin' by the horses watchin' me.

"What ya doin'?" I called to him.

"Watchin' you. Why?"

He turned to the horse and took a blanket off the back of the saddle. I watched him walk toward me. *Yeah, there was only one word for Mr. Barrett, or maybe four . . . just down right sexy!*

"I brought a blanket in case ya needed a break. I thought it would give us somethin' to sit on."

"Good thinkin', Cowboy. Where did ya learn to ride like that?"

"Aw . . . uh . . . I . . . I uh, I had some horses for awhile. I rode a lot back then." He smiled as he looked around for the perfect place to spread the blanket.

He took my hand and helped me sit down. I had a few tender spots here and there, but I was so much better. He sat down beside me then spun around and lay down with his head in my lap. Just at that moment, a breeze tumbled a ton of beautiful colored leaves right on top of us.

I laughed, "That reminds me a lot of a song I heard once. Me and Floy was leavin' Graceland in Memphis. I don't remember the exact words." I said, "but it was the most beautiful song I think I ever heard. Somethin' about . . . 'autumn leaves come fallin' down' and then somethin' about . . . 'you touch 'em and they burst apart like sweet memories.' Me and Floy heard it on the radio when we was comin' back from Arkansas. It was such a pretty song."

I looked at him thinkin' he probably thought I was nuts. He was just layin' there lookin' up through the tree tops.

"Yeah," he said " . . . 'and red bouquets and twilights trimmed in purple haze and quiet nights and gentle days . . . with you.' It was a great song."

"You know the song I'm talkin about?"

"Uh . . . yeah . . . I . . . I heard it before."

He sat up and stared into my eyes. Sometimes when he did that I felt like he could see through to my very soul, that he knew every secret I ever had or might ever have.

"Lilah, I . . . I . . . uh . . . " he suddenly took me into his arms and held me so tight it almost frightened me. It was almost a desperate cling. I pushed away slightly and I was almost sure that I knew what he was goin' to say. He liked me a lot but he just couldn't get over what had almost happened with Scott.

I swallowed hard and braced myself to hear it.

He raised up on his knees and pulled me up with him. With his hands on each side of my face, he slowly leaned in and kissed me. Very lightly he brushed his full soft lips across mine. His thumb was on my chin and he gently forced my mouth open as he slowly explored the inside of my mouth with his tongue. Slowly, gently and very senuously he moved it in and out. I felt myself begin to tremble as I melted hopelessly against him. He opened my coat and slowly slid it off my shoulders. Cautiously he began to unbutton my blouse, very slowly as if he expected me to protest. When he slipped it off my shoulders and I knelt there in my bra and jeans, I slowly raised my hand and removed the sunglasses from the top of his head . I stared into his eyes and searched for any trace of my own heart, the one I'd so freely given him. I pushed his jacket off his broad shoulders and began to unbutton his shirt. I could feel the heavy beat of his heart beneath my hand as each button was as carefully undone as he'd undone mine. It slid off his shoulders and down his tan muscular arms. I never looked away and neither did he. He nervously chewed on his bottom lip as he put one tremblin' hand to my waist and the other slid up my back to unsnap my bra. It slid down my arms and off my body and he gently cupped my breast. My body shuddered at the touch of his warm, gentle hand as he lowered his head and took it into his mouth. The sensation of his hot, sexy mouth took my breath as he suckled gently and his tongue made circles around the nipple. It became almost impossible to breathe and I thought I would surely never breathe normally again. He raised his head and looked up at me. My breath caught in my throat.

"Do ya want me to stop?" He whispered with that satiny, southern accent.

"Do ya want to?"

He looked at me a moment longer. "No, honey, I don't."

He carefully laid me back on the blanket he'd brought and removed the rest of our clothes. I desperately searched his eyes, lookin' again for any sign of the revulsion that I feared seein'. He gazed deeply into my eyes and I knew beyond any doubt that he would find the love and the need and the passion there, 'cause I could see it so clearly in his. I nodded and I knew it would give us full permission to do what we both had wanted and needed for so very long.

He gently rolled over and held his weight above me. Our kisses became more heated as his hands caressed my body, my face, and places where I hadn't been touched in so long. His knee slipped between my quiverin' thighs. He eased them gently apart as I slid my hands down his silken back muscles and pulled him to me. I needed him . . . wanted him in a way I'd never known existed. When he gently slid inside, I willingly became lost in a world of crystal blue eyes and fire-hot kisses. We moved with unabandoned passion, want, and need. Never had I dreamed it could be like that. I'd never experienced anything like it as I reached for more . . . although I didn't know what. Then suddenly, unexpectedly, somethin' miraculous happened. An explosion of senses, feelin's I didn't know I was capable of.

I cried out just as Chad tensed and moaned intensely in my ear. Then slow, gentle movements that completed and satisfied us both to the depth of our very beings!

The sun was goin' down and yet we lay there naked on the blanket. I didn't care. We were wrapped in each other and that was all we needed.

"I didn't . . . uh . . . I didn't hurt ya, did I?" He asked as he nuzzled my neck.

"Mmmm . . . wonderfully so. I never knew it could be like that, Chad." I whispered.

"What do ya mean? I don't understand."

"Well, I always wondered why people called it 'makin' love'. My ex husband was the only man I've ever been with like that. I always thought of it as a 'two-minute-waste-of-my-time', . . . but . . . now." I tried to explain as my face flushed with sudden embarrassment.

"And now?"

"Now . . . I think I understand . . . 'Makin' love'." I smiled up at him.

He grinned that adorable grin and winked. My heart missed another beat.

We washed off in the creek and swam a little in the cold, shallow water. It was gettin' dark and I sure didn't want nobody to come lookin' for us. We dried each other off with the blanket and got dressed. It was difficult seein' as how we kept steelin' kisses between every button.

"We better get home baby, or they might call out the Sheriff and his possee." Chad teased.

"I could stay right here for ever," I sighed.

"Yeah, me too . . . but they'd just come find us," He said thoughtfully and bit his lip and looked down at the ground.

"C'mon, baby. Let's go." He helped me up on my horse and climbed on his. We let 'em walk most of the way back to the barn.

We was late for supper and had to endure a five minute lecture on how we should pay more attention to time. We was told that it was too cold out there and didn't I remember the last time I rode that late? It was just too late to be ridin' in the dark! We also heard how worried they'd been.

However, we were very surprised to find that we'd been moved out . . . of the livin' room that is. Toby and Floy had taken the liberty to move into Dee's room and had moved all my stuff from downstairs back up to my room. They'd changed the bed and the whole room was perfect. Best of all, the livin' room was back to bein' a real livin' room and not the sick ward. Once again, we could sit around and watch TV or talk.

That night we opted to play some serious dominoes. It was girls against the guys. Chad kept lookin' across the coffee table at me and lightly lickin' his lips, nibbled his bottom lip, and then gave me the slightest hint of a smile. For obvious reasons, it just drove me crazy. I was pretty sure what he was thinkin' about and I was sure he knew that I was thinkin' about it, too. Toby cleared his throat, quite obviously, and when we looked up, they were both smilin' very knowin' smiles. I figgered they knew, too. I was a little embarrassed and I tried to ignore 'em, but I was too gloriously happy to really care what they thought or what they knew.

"Do ya think ya might feel like goin' out this weekend?" Toby finally asked.

"Where to?" I asked him as I glanced at Chad.

"Well, Floy and me was talkin' about goin' out to King's and doin' a little dancin'. Do ya think ya might be up to it? After all, ya spent all afternoon . . . ridin' a horse!" He gave me a devilish little wink.

I looked at Chad, Chad looked at the floor, then I looked at Floy, who had an impish little grin that said she knew way too much. Pullin' myself together and with a very red face, I simply said, "Sure, why not?" and immediately began to shuffle the dominoes.

We all ignored that very loud silence.

Later, after Floy and Toby had gone upstairs, Chad and I was still sittin' on our pillows on the floor. We leaned back against the couch and relaxed.

"I kinda liked our little couch bed." Pouted Chad.

"Yeah, me too. It was really cozy."

He sat there very quiet for a few minutes and I felt there was somethin' on his mind, somethin' he wanted to say, so I turned around, laid down and put my head in his lap.

"What ya thinkin'?"

"Hmm . . . well . . . I . . . I was thinkin' about somethin' ya said earlier. It's been on my mind all evenin'." He was runnin' his fingers absently through my hair.

"What is it?" I asked him. He closed his eyes for a second and rubbed his forehead. Then he looked into my eyes again.

"Ya said, earlier . . . ya know . . . after . . . after we . . . well . . . ya know. Ya said ya didn't know that it could be like that. What did ya mean?"

I thought about it for several minutes.

"I . . . I went to school in these mountains and I got to know Walter in the third grade. He was kind of a cut-up and always doin' somethin' to get attention. By junior high, all the girls thought he was somethin'. I guess I did too. When he asked me out, I was thrilled. All the girls wanted him and I was goin' steady with him. We was together from then on. He never dated nobody else and I didn't either. At least I didn't think he dated nobody else. I found out later just how wrong I was. When I would a been a junior and he was a senior, we went to the prom. Afterwards, he wanted to go park somewhere. That was my first time and he was so rough. He didn't care that it was my first time, he just took what he wanted and it was over. I was so terrified that someone would find out. That my parents would know what I'd done and that I wasn't a virgin no more. I didn't know if he'd used protection or not and I was scared to death I'd get pregnant. I was always taught that if ya slept with somebody, then ya ought to get married. It was a huge relief when a few months after he graduated he asked me to marry him. I was stupid enough to think it was 'cause he just loved me so much. It didn't take long before I heard that there was another girl over to Bigby who thought she was pregnant and her parents was gonna make Walt marry her. He decided if he was gonna get married, it might as well be to somebody he at least knew. We'd done it a couple more times since that first time and I thought that was just how it was supposed to be. We got married that summer and it was always the same thing. I figgered that sex was for men and that women just tolerated it. I've heard some of the girls talk about how they enjoyed it and how this one and that one was such great lovers. It was beyond me to understand how they got that idea . . . at least . . . until today. See, I never knew that it could be good for women, too. I didn't know that anybody could make a person feel so much, or enjoy sex with somebody so much. You're amazin' Chad." He looked shocked.

"So, you're tellin' me that was the first time ya ever . . . uh . . . ever . . . well . . . ya know . . . was totally satisfied?"

"Yeah, the very first time . . . ever."

"In my opinion" he spoke softly "ya were still a virgin. I'm so sorry that it's been that way for ya. I wish I'd been there . . . I promise ya . . . your first time would've been a lot different."

"Chad, as far as I'm concerned . . . today was the very first time. The first time I was ever 'made love' to. I'll never forget it. It was . . . beautiful."

He slipped his arms around me, pulled me close and kissed me so sweetly, "And if you'll let me . . . I'll show ya a lot of beautiful things about makin' love."

I didn't get a chance to answer. He drowned my words with his lips.

"Let's go upstairs." he whispered.

Just as we turned out the lights and started to the stairs, Boots and Roz began a frantic barkin'.

"What the hell is that all about?" Chad said as he started to the door.

"Wait! Let's go upstairs. We can see better from up there."

I grabbed his arm and we slipped quickly up the steps. We topped them just as Toby was hurryin' out of his room.

"I think there's somebody out there" he said.

"That's the same way they acted when that prowler was sneakin' around," I told 'em.

"What prowler?" Chad seemed to have no idea what'd been happenin'.

"From months ago, just before the time I met you, when somebody was prowlin' around. I thought they was after my horses. They just quit comin' around and I thought it was over."

We watched from my window. The dogs continued to bark at the bushes.

"I'll go check it out." Chad offered.

"I'll go with ya," Toby said as he started toward the door.

"No, you stay with the girls and be sure they're safe. Just in case it might be O'Grady. Okay?" Chad instructed.

"Ya got a gun, honey?" I handed him my shotgun and he slipped down the stairs.

He went out the back door and around the yard. After he was gone for awhile, we were startin' to get worried.

"Should I go check on him?" Toby asked me as he started to slip his boots on.

"Not yet . . . let's wait."

We were watchin' when he came out of the brush where the dogs were barkin'. He stopped long enough to pet 'em and lead 'em back to the house. We all rushed down the stairs to meet him at the front door.

"What did ya find?" Toby asked as soon as he stepped in.

Chad looked tense and just shook his head, "Aw . . . it was nothin' . . . couple a hunters got lost. I got 'em headed down the road and told 'em this was private property and no huntin' is allowed. That's right ain't it?"

"Well, yeah. But we never had no problem before and what about all the other times that somebody was sneakin' around up here?" I asked him. "Do ya believe 'em?"

"Yeah, they seemed sincere and they looked like they was out huntin' coons and stuff. They won't be back."

"But Chad . . ."

"I said they won't be back!" he snapped and went up the stairs.

Toby and Floy looked at me with the same puzzled look I probably was wearin' myself. We locked up and headed up stairs. Toby and Floy went back to their room as I headed down the hall to mine. Chad was sittin' at the window starin' out into the night. I didn't say anything as I quietly slipped between the sheets.

"Ya comin' to bed?" I asked.

"Yeah, in a little while."

"What's wrong, Chad?"

"Nothin', just go on to bed and I'll be there in a little while." He mumbled.

He was upset and I didn't understand, but I went on to bed. It was hard to fall asleep. Later Chad came to bed. He turned his back to me and stayed that way for the rest of the night. It was sure not what I expected for our first night in a real bedroom and in a real bed.

When I woke the next mornin', he was already up and gone. Floy and Toby'd already left for work, but someone had made coffee and I was ready for some. I poured a cup and had just sat down at the table when I heard some noise out back. Cautiously, I walked over to the back door and looked outside.

It was Chad.

It looked like he'd decided to split some wood. Even though it was pretty cool in the mornin's, he'd taken off his shirt and had worked up a good sweat. I stood and watched him swing the splittin' maul time after time. He already had a good stack, but he seemed to be enjoyin' the work. Most likely, he was tired of babysittin' me since he'd hardly ever left me there alone, usually only when the animals needed tendin' and lately he'd asked me to go down with him.

I'll admit that I was enjoyin' the view. Very muscular and very tan, the muscles in his back and arms rippled every time he took a swing. His silvery blonde hair that he usually kept perfectly styled, was tousled and hangin' in his face. It'd gotten quite long and was almost below his ears, but it was beautiful as it glistened in the mornin' sun.

I don't know what it was that made him turn around, but he looked back toward the house and wiped his forearm across his face. He saw me and waved, then went back to what he was doin'. I loved him bein' there. It felt like a real home and a real family with him, Toby, and Floy there. She was like my sister and Toby had become like my brother-in-law and with Chad, it'd become a perfect family. Deep in my heart, I was hopin' it would always be just like that.

I went back and poured myself another cup of coffee, one for Chad, and went out the back door. When I reached the wood pile, I sat down and waited until he reached a stoppin' point.

"Hey, good-lookin'? Want some coffee?" He turned and looked surprised.

"Sure." He said as he walked over to me. He took the hot cup and carefully sipped it.

"I probably should have brought somethin' cold instead. Huh?"

"Huh uh, this is fine. Tastes good."

He sat down beside me and looked over toward the barn as the sun lit his bright blue eyes.

He turned to me.

"Sorry about last night. I didn't mean to . . . well . . . I'm sorry."

"It's okay . . . but what upset ya so much?"

"I . . . I can't explain it. A lot of stuff that I just can't get into. It has nothin' to do with you really . . ." He paused. " . . . but in another way, I guess it does. Just please, don't question me about it. Okay? Let's just enjoy bein' together. I just wanna spend every minute makin' ya happy and lettin' ya know how I feel about ya."

He looked toward the mountains and it was as if he were thousands of miles away.

"Okay, Ya can tell me when you're ready. Just know that I'm here and I . . . I'm ready to listen any time." I stood up and walked back to the house.

On Saturday, we were all excited about goin' out. We'd been cooped up in that house for weeks and was ready to do just about anything. I spent extra time on my hair and make-up and had chosen a powder blue, silk shirt to wear with my perfectly-creased jeans. When I went downstairs, everyone was ready and waitin'. I was shocked when I saw Chad. I'd guessed he would be wearin' his usual black but instead, he was standin' there wearin' a powder blue western shirt with jeans and his black hat. He grinned that adorable, crooked grin.

"I cheated!" he said.

"What do ya mean, ya cheated?"

He pointed to his shirt " I peeked to see what ya had laid out to wear." He smiled sweetly.

As I walked over to him, I noticed that his initials was embroidered on his shirt pocket. I pointed at the first one, "What's the 'T' stand for?"

"Thomas." he answered.

"Hmm . . . Thomas Chad. I like it." I teased.

"No. Thomas Chadwick," he quickly corrected.

"I still like it," I said as I started toward the door.

" 'bout time," Toby complained as he opened the door.

"Yeah," Floy added, "I thought maybe we was gonna play the name game all night." She giggled as we locked up and left.

We got into Chad's truck. It was the first time I'd ridden in it.

"This is really nice," I told him.

"Thank you." he said as he turned and very slowly looked me over from head to toe . . . and by the way . . . you're absolutely beautiful tonight. I'm really proud to be your date."

I looked at him as tears welled up in my eyes.

"I'm thrilled to be your date, too. And I have to say that . . . you look very sexy tonight."

"Yeah?" He whispered as he started the motor. "Do ya think I might get lucky tonight?"

"Right now, I'd have to say . . . ya can probably count on it." I whispered back as I inhaled the fragrance of that wonderful cologne he wore.

He put his arm around me and pulled me as close as I could get without sittin' in his lap.

We'd already had a light supper so we went straight out to the club. It was really comfortin' when so many people rushed up to me and said how they was so glad to see me out again.

We laid claim to a table and went to the dance floor. It'd been so long that I didn't know if I could still remember how to dance. I didn't need to be too concerned. Chad was a great dancer. He held me close and breathed softly into my ear. The slow song only encouraged our close, intimate dancin'.

"Chad Barrett, you are bein' a tease. Ya gotta know how that turns me on."
"Is it workin'?"
I smiled at him, "Oh, yeah."
He bit his bottom lip and winked at me.
A couple of dances later, we went to our table.
"I don't want ya to overdo it. Okay?"
"I'm fine, really." I told him.
Toby and Floy finally came back to the table.
"We were about to decide that you two had run off somewhere." Chad teased 'em.
"Nope," said Toby, "Just tryin' to catch up on a lot of missed dancin'."
I sat there for a minute.
"I'm sorry guys, I didn't think about what all ya'll have sacrificed 'cause of me. For months, all of your lives have rotated around me and my problems. How can I ever make it up to ya? I feel really bad."
"Whoa!" said Toby, "Lilah, I known ya most all my life and ya gotta know I 'm madly in love with your best friend here. Hell girl, we'd do anything for ya. Anything to protect ya. Besides . . . I'd been sneakin' over to her house at night and prayin' we didn't get caught by her Mama and Daddy. Hell, we been livin' like we're all old married folks. Personally, I love it."

"I agree." declared Floy. "Mama and Daddy ain't none too happy that I ain't been home, and they don't know that Toby's been there the whole time. But ya know full well that I'm always here for ya. Always!"

Chad added, "Man, if this is bein' inconvenienced, just don't ever stop. Inconvenience me some more."

"Well, I got just one more thing on my mind," Toby shyly announced. "Like I said earlier, I do love the way it's been these last months."

He got out of his chair and knelt beside Floy. " Sweetheart, I've been in love with ya since junior high school. I'm still in love with ya. I want to know . . . would . . . would ya . . . ," He reached into his shirt pocket and pulled out a tiny box, "Would ya marry me, honey?"

Chad and me and probably fifteen other people who was watchin', held our breath and turned to Floy to see what she would say. She looked at me, I smiled at her, and then she looked back at Toby.

"I . . . I . . . uh . . . I . . . oh yes, Toby! Yes! I will marry you." She said as Toby grabbed her up and swung her around. Everyone was clappin' and whistlin'.

"Hell yeah! She said. Yes! She said yes!" Toby was beside himself.

I was so happy for her. She truly deserved a good man like Toby. At least she'd been smart enough to wait on someone special and not get mixed up with somebody like Walter. I went to 'em and hugged Toby and told him how happy I was. Then I hugged my best friend and congratulated her and, of course, we both cried.

"Why do women always cry . . . even when they're happy?" Toby asked.

Chad hugged Floy, congratulated her, and then he shook hands with Toby. "Congratulations son, ya got a great little woman there."

"I know," grinned Toby. "And I have some great friends, too. I know we haven't known each other all that long Chad, but I want to ask ya . . . will ya do me the honor of bein' my best man?" Chad looked seriously surprised and thought a moment.

"It would be my absolute pleasure. Yeah. I'll be your best man."

Floy turned to me. "Do I even have to ask?"

"Nope," I answered, "I'd be hurt if ya asked anybody else."

Her ring was a beautiful array of diamonds around a solitare, all in a nugget settin', and a perfect fit for her tiny finger.

"Well, that was a big surprise," I said to Chad as we went back to the dance floor.

"Yeah," he answered, "I don't think any of us saw that one comin'."

"I'm really happy for 'em. It'll be fun to plan the weddin'. I'm already thinkin' about the decorations."

The song ended and we returned to our table.

"Floy, I got to go to the little girls' room. Wanna go?"

She got up.

"I never did see a woman yet that didn't have to have help to go to the bathroom," he laughed "Chad, I gotta go to the little boys room. Wanna go?"

"Oh yeah, might be dangerous in there," teased Chad as he got up and took off with Toby.

Floy and I headed in the opposite direction.

"Men!" She said. "Gotta love 'em. It's a tough job but I guess somebody's gotta do it".

We were still laughin' as we got in line at the ladies' room. There was about ten women ahead of us. We was three away when a stall door opened near where we was standin'. Danna stepped out, stopped short, and glared at me.

"Bitch!" She muttered.

"Excuse me?" I shot back.

"I didn't stutter,'Bitch'," she repeated the insult as she walked out the door.

"I can't believe that," Floy looked at me in disbelief. I just shook my head and took my turn. Floy was still upset when we got back to our table.

"What's the matter with you two?" Toby asked as he stood up.

"Nothin', just Chad's old flame tryin' to start somethin' with Lilah," Floy told him.

Chad leaned forward, "What happened?"

"She called her a 'Bitch' that's what. I couldn't believe it!"

"It's okay, Floy, just ignore it," I told her.

Toby got her by the hand and pulled her toward the dance floor.

"Lilah's right baby, just ignore it."

I turned to Chad who hadn't said much. He was starin' at the dancers around the club.

"Ya ready to dance?"

"Sure," he got up still lookin' intently around.

As we danced, he continued to watch the tables.

"Are ya gonna dance with me or is there someone else ya would rather dance with?"

He looked at me strangely. "There's nobody else in this world that I'd rather dance with than you. I was just lookin' around."

The band went into one of their slower songs and Chad took the opportunity to pull me as close as he could. I clearly felt his heart beatin' against my breast. He was just sweaty enough to give off that wonderful aroma that drove me so crazy.

He buried his face in my neck.

"I want you." he whispered in that soft southern drawl that I'd so come to love.

At that moment, an elbow in my back knocked the breath completely out of me. I gasped and almost fell on top of Chad.

"Look out, Bitch!" someone yelled.

Chad caught me in mid-fall. "Are you okay, Honey?"

We were near our table and he helped me over to it so I could sit down.

"What . . . the . . . ?" I gasped as I still struggled to breathe.

Floy and Toby walked up as Chad turned and started toward the floor.

"Watch her for a moment . . . would ya, please?"

He stomped away.

"What happened? Where's he goin'?" asked Floy.

"Danna . . . she elbowed me . . . in the back." I finally managed to tell her between gasps for air.

"Oh shit!" Toby said as he hurried after Chad.

Toby told us later that he caught up with him just as he pulled "Godiva" away from the bar. He wasn't sure what to make of it until he heard Chad.

"What the hell do ya think you're doin'?"

"But baby . . . I met ya first," she whinned.

"I told ya that we were nothin' but friends."

"Well, what's she, your friend with benefits?"

He said Chad grabbed her by the wrist and pulled her over to a table.

"Correction," Chad told her firmly. "We're no longer friends! Don't go near her. Don't speak to her. If ya do . . . you'll answer to me. Do you understand?"

Toby said the look in his eyes was pure fury. Danna backed up .

"Okay . . . it's just that I really liked ya, Chad. I thought we had somethin' between us. You're all I been able to think about since I met ya. I was really, really hopin' we might . . . get together. Guess not? Huh?"

"Guess not, is absolutely correct. Now, go find somebody else . . . Leave me alone . . . and leave her alone."

Toby said that he shot her a look that would freeze fire. He started back to the table when he saw Toby.

"What ya doin'?"

"Thought ya might need some help." Answered Toby.

"Na, I think I got it under control," he laughed as he walked up to the bar and ordered us drinks. It was late, so we decided it was time to eat and go home.

We chose the little café in Dover. It was pretty busy when we got there and we had to wait a few minutes.

Standin' in line, I couldn't help but notice the admirin' glances of a number of pretty girls, aimed at my date. He stood out in a crowd to the point that when we was bein' seated one of the girls even had the nerve to flirt out loud.

"Hello gorgeous . . . ya want a late date?"

I glared at her as I felt the anger turn my face red. I couldn't believe the nerve of her.

"Naw, honey. This one has all my open dates. Sorry." He wasn't rude, but he got the point across

We ordered and were enjoyin' our meal and talkin' about Floy and Toby's weddin' plans, when a loud crowd came in. When I looked up, I immediately felt sick as I leaned my face into my hands.

"What's wrong, honey?" Chad asked with concern in his voice.

I glanced up and locked eyes with Toby. He'd seen 'em too.

"Nothin', I'm just tired. Are we ready to go?"

"Sure," everybody agreed.

It was my hope that we could slide out amoung the crowd without Walter and his rude friends seein' us.

"Hey Sugar Booger!! Where ya goin'? Is it Grandad's bed time?" Walter's voice boomed across the room. A heavy silence fell and only the song on the juke box was heard.

His friends all broke out laughin'. Chad and Toby stopped in their tracks. Chad slowly turned toward Walter. I knew that look. His eyes became a deep dark blue and the muscles in his jaw began to flinch.

"You talkin' to me, son?"

"No Grandad . . . I'm talkin' to my wife!"

Chad's fists clenched.

"I'm not your damn wife, Walter!" I yelled at him. "Now leave us the hell alone!"

"Well . . . okay . . . my EX-wife," he sneared. "Never was much of a wife anyhow. Didn't cook worth a damn. Didn't clean the house. And, I tell ya ole man. I never could get her pregnant, so if I was you, I wouldn't be countin' on no kids. Hell, if I couldn't get the job done, I know some old son-of-a-bitch like you can't do it!" He grinned.

Stunned, as well as mortified, I turned and ran out of the café with Floy close behind. By the time we got to the truck, Chad and Toby'd come outside, too. Walter and his crew was right behind 'em along with a large crowd of bystanders.

"What's the matter Grandad? Ya scared?" He taunted.

Chad turned back and glared at him. "I whooped your ass one time and I'll do it again if I have to. The best thing ya can do, son, is go back inside and finish your meal."

Walter stepped toward him.

"I ain't your damn, son! Ya didn't whoop my ass, ya just caught me off guard. I'll beat the hell outta ya!"

Chad took his hat off and tossed it to me about the same time that Toby threw his to Floy.

"Oh shit," Floy whispered, "There's five of 'em to our two."

"You mean . . . our four," I informed her as I reached in the back of Chad's truck for anything to help even the score.

There was a metal pipe that I threw to Floy and then I reached for somethin' else. I found a short piece of 2x4 that was just my size. Walter was still runnin' his mouth when Toby spoke up.

"Ya gonna fight or just give lip service? I got a lotta other things to do tonight!"

"Why ya even in this, Ellis?" Walter looked a little puzzled. "It ain't even none a your business!"

"Well, ya see Walt, it's like this. I never did care for ya anyhow and I ain't gonna leave my best man to fight alone. So, yeah, it does involve me. Now ya gonna fight or just paw the dirt?"

Walt let out a roar and charged at Chad. His gang of friends was right behind him.

Chad ducked and Walt flew right past him and into the gatherin' crowd. He tripped one of the others and Toby dove in with both fists flyin'. Walt made another run at Chad and met with his foot up'side the head. It was amazin' to watch him. It made me think of Bruce Lee, in the movies, the way he was so calm and exact and every move was so precise. He was so smooth and graceful and yet every blow that Walt took sounded like someone hit him with a baseball bat. Toby, however, had three on him and was gettin' the short end.

"Let's go." I urged Floy.

We grabbed our tools of destruction and started that way just as several guys from the crowd stepped forward and evened up the score. We stepped back and waited to see if we was gonna be needed. I was so proud of those guys for steppin' in, even when most of 'em didn't know Toby and Chad. They just didn't like the odds.

The whole thing didn't last long. Walt was out like a light and three of the others were barely able to move while one of Walt's brave crew had run like hell when the fight started.

The police pulled up just as it came to an end. Thank goodness, it was Stan and some others that I knew. They rushed in and started handcuffin' everbody, includin' Toby and Chad. The sight of Chad with his hands cuffed behind his back like a common criminal, broke my heart.

"Stanley! Wait!"

"Lilah? What ya doin' out here in this mess?"

"It wasn't Chad and Toby's fault . They was just defendin' theirselves." I pleaded.

"I thought they looked familiar. Got any witnesses?"

"Yeah, but ya got most of 'em handcuffed. They was just tryin' to stop the fight." I felt guilty as I lied.

Stan started questionin' everybody includin' the owner of the café. When all was said and done he agreed that Walt and his gang had started it and they put 'em all under arrest.

As he was takin' the handcuffs off Chad and Toby, he asked me, "Just one thing ladies. I'd like to know exactly what you two intended on doin' with that pipe and that 2x4?" Chad and Toby both looked at us in surprise. I still had the board in my hand.

"Well . . . um . . . Stan, its like this. It was layin' there and I picked it up so none of 'em could use it as a weapon." He looked me square in the eyes for a moment.

"And I guess ya found that pipe just layin' there too, huh Floy?"

"Oh, yes sir. Didn't want anybody to get hurt, so I just got it right outta the way."

He looked at us both intently as his tongue rolled in his mouth. I knew that he knew we was lyin' through our teeth.

"Ok . . . I guess we'll leave it at that. But in the future, if ya find anything like that layin' around. Just toss it in the back of the truck. We wouldn't wanna see nobody get hurt. Ya hear me?"

"Yes, yes . . . Of course," We both answered.

We got in the truck and started home. This time Chad didn't have a scratch on him.

"Ya okay back there, Toby?" he asked as he glanced in the rear view mirror.

"Oh yeah, that was better'n dessert. Nothin' like a good fight after supper!" Toby laughed.

Chad put his arm around me and tenderly pulled me close.

"You okay, baby girl?"

"I guess," I answered as I laid my head on his shoulder.

It was a relief when we got home. I was dog-tired and still feelin' the sting of Walter's words. He was mean, but I'd never known him to be so cruel. We got Toby in the kitchen so we could check out the damage. He had a cut above his eye, one on his chin, and a huge black eye.

"Do ya hurt anywhere else?" I asked him.

"Yeah, all over my damn body," he complained.

Floy patched up his cuts with stristrips and then put him to soak in Nanny's big tub upstairs. The rest of us took turns showerin' in the downstairs bath.

We finally got to bed.

Chad slid in beside me.

"You're awfully quiet. Want to talk about it?" He asked.

"Not really."

"Are ya mad 'cause we got in that fight?" He persisted.

"No way! We were ready to join right in. Walt and them bums asked for everything they got."

"That reminds me . . . just what were you two gonna do with those weapons? I happen to know that they was in the back of my truck, 'cause I put 'em there." I slid down in the bed and covered my head with the sheet

"We was gonna help you and Toby kick some butt!"

He busted out laughin'.

"Ya would've done that for us?"

I peeked out from under the edge, "Yes and I'd do it again if I thought ya needed me.

He laid there a minute then leaned over and whispered, "Well, get your 2x4, honey, cause I need ya! And I want ya. Lord, how I want ya."

He pulled the sheet down and I welcomed his lips on mine. This time was different. His kisses were slower and softer. He kissed my face, my neck, and then my ear. His hot breath was almost unbearable.

He teased my earlobe with his tongue and then worked his way back to my neck. With sweet kisses and gentle nibbles, he managed to send my senses reelin'. Clothes had disappeared. The only thing between us was our skin. He kissed my shoulders and moved down to my breast. From time to time he came back up for another kiss. Each time the kisses became a little more demandin'. He moved back to my breasts and kissed and nibbled until I thought I'd surely die. His hands were around my waist as he moved to my navel. His tongue darted in and out and his lips set me on fire. I slipped into ecstasy when his mouth covered mine and his tongue was persistent, searchin' and his teeth began to nibble on my lips. When his kisses covered my stomach, I was on fire with more passion and desire than I ever imagined existed in me. His lips moved down further and I gasped as they touched places no man's lips had ever touched before. The sensation was unbearable. I wanted to cry, scream, and beg for more, but I knew that Floy and Toby were just down the hall and I did still have some degree of modesty. Just as I thought I couldn't take any more I felt him lift my hips and slide inside. Deep inside. As he moved in and out and pulled me to him, I felt the same intense, wonderful feelin' from the day by the creek. Then suddenly it was there, that wonderful excruciatingly glorious peak. I felt him push and hold and then again I heard that deep groan of satisfaction and I knew he'd joined me in sheer heaven.

Chapter 9

The next mornin' we went to eat in Mason. On the way back we stopped by Floy's Mama and Daddy's so she and Toby could tell 'em the good news and she could show off her new ring. Chad and I let 'em out and we rode around for a while and decided to stop at a park near Bigby.

"Let's go for a walk," he suggested as he helped me out of the truck.

We walked over to the swings. I sat down and he began to push me. It was very relaxin' and I wondered why everyone didn't have a swing in their yard.

"I think I'd like to have a swing like this in the side yard, or maybe two. It makes me feel like a little girl again."

"You are a little girl, my little girl." Chad said as he pushed me again.

Finally I stopped the swing and got out. We walked over to a bench and sat down.

"Baby, tell me what's botherin' ya? You're so quiet today and . . . well . . . you're just not bein' yourself." He asked as he leaned over and rested his elbows on his knees.

The cool breeze blew around my feet as I sat there for a long time. He expected an answer and I knew I should give him one, but I just wasn't sure what to say. I didn't know how to bring it up.

"Honey, if ya don't talk to me . . . how can I know how to fix it?" He spoke softly.

"Ya can't fix it, Chad. Nobody can."

I tried not to cry, but the tears seemed to have a mind of their own. He turned and took my arms and made me face him.

"You can't keep me in the dark. I can't handle bein' shut out. Not by you."

I looked deep into his beautiful, concerned eyes. The last thing I wanted to see was disappointment in 'em. How could I know if he would understand, but he was right, I owed him an explanation. After several minutes of tryin' to decide where to start, I gave up and just started talkin'.

"It's somethin' Walter said last night. I'd pretty much pushed it out of my mind and I hadn't had any reason to give it any thought."

"Walter said a lot of stuff last night. Most of which didn't even make sense. What the hell did he say that upset ya so much?" I sat there a while longer before I continued.

"I was a good wife. I'd watched my Mama all my life and she was my example. Her and Daddy been married all these years and I ain't never heard 'em have a real fight. I knew that when I got married that I had certain responsibilities like cleanin', cookin', and laundry. I knew as a wife that there was certain . . . sexual obligations. So I rarely told him 'no' and I tolerated it. Then, after awhile, I . . . I . . . I wanted a baby. Mama had her first baby nine months after they got married . . . but in all that time . . . I never got pregnant. I had a hard time acceptin' that I couldn't have no babies. After we split up, Boots became my baby and then Pride and Patton. But last night, when he said that . . . it all come back to me and I felt like . . . a . . . a failure. He made me feel like less than a woman. If I could've got in that fight, the first one I wanted to get to was Walt! I think I could have killed him, Chad. That's not me . . . I'm not that way. He just brought out all the anger and hurt that I'd bottled up inside me for so long."

There. I'd told him. Now, if he wanted to walk away I'd understand. He was the type of man that would probably want lots of kids. Now . . . he knew that I could never give 'em to him. He sat there for a long time, lookin' at the ground.

"I'm so sorry, Lilah, I . . . I . . . uh . . . I heard him say that. But . . . I . . . I didn't pay no attention to it. He already had me so pissed off I could've ate lead. I didn't give it another thought. He was just blowin' off at the mouth and I never had a clue that it hurt ya like that, honey."

He stood up and wrapped his strong arms around me. The pain eased, I felt like I was safe and when Chad held me like that, nothin' could ever hurt me again.

We got back to Mason and went by to pick up Floy and Toby. It was pretty obvious that somethin' was wrong as soon as we saw 'em standin' by the front gate with several suitcases. They got in and I could tell that Floy was fit to be tied.

Turnin' to the back seat I asked, " What's up Sweetie? Were they not happy for you?"

"Well, to be honest, I think we just picked the wrong time to break the news," She answered sharply.

"Why?" I knew her Mama was anxious for her to find someone and raise a family.

"We walked in and the first thing they done was drop their jaws when they saw Toby," she fumed.

"I don't understand." It was hard to imagine that anybody wouldn't love Toby.

"Hell, Lilah, look at his face! He's got a black eye and two big bandages."

"I didn't think of that. We should've waited a week or two."

"Do ya think? I couldn't think fast enough to make somethin' up and dumbass here had to blurt out 'Aw, It was just a little scuffle last night. It's alright, we whooped their butts!' I thought Daddy was gonna have a stroke. Mama hauled me off to the kitchen actin' like we was gettin' some tea and tried to line me out 'bout how I wasn't gettin' involved with no thug like that. He wasn't no different than Walter Cullwell. And how did that turn out for Lilah? If that wasn't enough…Toby'd followed us into the kitchen and had to add, "Oh hell, Mrs. Felton, it's okay . . . that's whose butt we whooped last night!'"

Toby spoke up, "Yep, . . . and that's when she invited us to get the hell outta her house. So we did."

There was a sudden shocked silence.

Chad unexpectedly burst into laughter. We all looked at him in shock.

"My boy, my boy . . . I bet that made a lastin' impression on your future in-laws."

Again there was dead silence for only a few seconds before Floy started to laugh. Then Toby and I couldn't help but laugh, too.

"Do ya think they'll come to the weddin'?" Toby asked innocently.

Floy smacked him on the arm "That's enough out of you mister."

We continued to laugh and joke about it all the way back to the house.

A few days later, Floy set the date.

"I don't wanna wait any longer than we have to. I don't ever want to go back to that basement."

"Ya don't have to worry about it. Your home is here for as long as ya want it." I reassured her.

"I know, but the truth is, I just can't wait to be Mrs. Toby Ellis."

"So when are ya thinkin'?"

"I'm thinkin' the middle of November. A late fall weddin'. What do ya think?"

"It don't matter what I think . . . what's Toby think?" I continued.

"Shoot, Toby thinks we're already married. He asked me the other night if I was pregnant yet."

"Are ya?"

"I better not be. I gotta weddin' dress to find and I don't want it to be a maternity one."

I sat there lookin' out the window. Floy walked over and put her arm around me.

"I'm sorry, that was insensitive of me. I know how much ya wanted a baby when ya was married."

"It's alright. Ya know . . . life goes on. Sometimes ya don't get things you're expectin' and sometimes ya get thing's ya never did expect."

We sat there awhile and talked about where to have the ceremony, a definite day and where they planned to live. We decided on November 15 at our church. As far as where they'd live, that was Toby's decision.

"Ya do know that only gives us five weeks?" I told her.

"Then let's get busy."

Over the next three weeks everything was about the weddin'. We shopped in every spare minute we could find. We talked Chad and Toby into buildin' an arch for the church. She wanted a really rustic, mountain look. The guys'd just finished with it when Chad come in that evenin' with a very serious expression.

"Can we talk?" He sounded serious as he took my hand and led me upstairs to our room.

"What's wrong?"

"I know it'll be cuttin' it close, but I gotta go out of town for a week or so."

"But Chad, that'll barely put ya back in time for the weddin'."

"I know, but it's somethin' that can't be helped. I'll get back as soon as I can. I promise, chica. Ya know I don't wanna be away from ya any more than I have to."

"But where're ya goin'?"

"The Caribbean. I wouldn't go if it wasn't urgent."

I stood there and looked at him in complete shock.

"What's in the Caribbean?"

"Business, honey, just business. I'll try to get back even sooner. I've negelected this as long as I can. I really don't wanna leave ya…but I gotta go."

He left right after supper.

For the most part, I was so busy that next week that I didn't have much time to think about it. It was all about flowers and dresses, bridesmaids, flower girls, tuxes, cakes, and decorations. It was insanity.

"I'll never get married again," Floy said one afternoon as we both collapsed on the couch.

"Good. I don't think I could go through this again," I sighed

"Sure we will. I predict that your's will be next," she teased.

"Hush, you'll jinx it." I cautioned her.

The door opened and Toby bounced in.

"Good evenin' ladies. I come a bearin' news!"

"Yes, master?" teased Floy.

"I've found a new place for us to dwell after the weddin'," he announced proudly.

Floy jumped up, "Where?"

"I'm buyin' Lilah's Mama and Daddy's old house. The one down in the holler."

"Are ya really?" I was stunned. "When did ya talk to 'em?"

"Yesterday, but they had to think about it. They called me back at work today and we struck a deal."

He was so proud of himself and Floy was so happy. It'd be a lot closer for us to visit than it had been all the way into Mason.

"So when's Chad comin' in?" He asked excitedly.

"I don't know. I haven't heard a word from him. Did he get fitted for his tux before he left?"

"Yeah, we both went the same day. We got a head start."

The day of rehearsal, I still hadn't heard a word from Chad. I was really gettin' worried that somethin' had happened to him. We all gathered at the church and went through the rehearsal.

"What are ya gonna do if he don't show up?" I questioned Toby.

"Hell, I don't know . . . I ain't never had a formal weddin' before. I guess I'll just grab somebody outta the crowd and make 'em just stand there and nod their head." He teased. "He'll be here. He gave me his word and I believe him. Quit worryin'."

Just as we started to run through it one last time, the door opened and in rushed Chad.

"Sorry, I'm so late. Plane broke down."

He was out of breath, his shirt was half-unbuttoned and his hair was hangin' in his eyes. He was a mess, but thank God he was okay and he was home.

"I knew you'd be here, buddy," Toby grinned and shook hands with him.

Chad took his place beside Toby and the groomsmen as the music started. I was Floy's stand-in bride and she was the maid of honor in my place. As I started toward the altar, I found it impossible to take my eyes off of him. His blue eyes glowed as he watched me make my way slowly down the aisle. It'd been over a week since he left and I couldn't wait to be in his arms. As I got to the front, he bit his bottom lip and winked at me. That was all it took, I broke rank and flew into his arms. He grabbed me off my feet and kissed me so long and so hard that my head was spinnin'.

Someone tapped me on the shoulder.

"You're takin' up valuable time here. There's food a waitin' after we get through," teased Toby.

We got back in our places. The preacher just stood there until everyone was settled.

"May I make a suggestion to the real bride?" he said in a very serious tone.

"Yes, please do," Floy answered in a equally-serious voice.

"Tomorrow night, do not, and I repeat, DO NOT . . . run into the best man's arms at this point!"

There was silence for a second before everyone caught the joke and burst into laughter.

I made Toby go home that night, after all, it was bad luck for the groom to see the bride before the weddin'. Floy pouted all the way home. She started to her room and turned at the bottom of the stairs.

"Lilah . . . tomorrow's my weddin' day . . . I just can't believe it."

"I know sweetie . . . now get to bed and get some sleep . . . 'cause I bet ya ain't gonna get none tomorrow night."

She giggled, went up the stairs and shut her door.

As we stepped into our room, Chad swung me around to face him and whispered "They'll both be gone tomorrow night and I'll bet ya that YOU ain't gonna get no sleep either."

"And what makes ya think . . ." I taunted right back "that you're gonna get any sleep tonight?" He stood up straight and gave me that bad boy grin, "Who said I planned on it?"

He carried me to the bed and laid down beside me.

"I missed ya baby. I never missed any body that much. Every night when I stepped outside, I looked up at that moon and wondered if ya were lookin' at it too. I told it to watch over ya 'til I could get back." He rolled over and kissed me.

I was certainly right . . . there was no sleepin' that night!

The weddin' was perfect. From the very beginin' it started off great. Floy's Mama and Daddy showed up and that was a big reason to celebrate, especially when her Daddy walked her down the aisle. Bein' Floy, just as she reached the altar, she turned toward Chad and for a brief second, everyone wondered if she would really do it. She backed out.

Floy was beautiful with her hair up in curls and her dress was a vision in pearls and beads. Toby stood there like he was paralyzed. The reception went off without a hitch. When it came time to toss her bouquet, there were at least twelve young women waitin'. It was bad enough that Chad had already caught the bride's garter. I think the women somehow fely that if they got the bouquet then somehow it would pair 'em with Chad.

Only over my dead body!

When Floy threw it, it was like a straight shot into my hands. Someone shouted from the crowd

"Guess we all know who's next." I looked at Chad and he smiled sweetly.

It was already startin' to get cold and we'd had a little snow shower the week before. I was so excited for Floy when Toby told her that they'd be honeymoonin' on a Caribbean cruise. We were all a little jealous of the warm sunshine they'd be enjoyin'.

Chad and I'd already planned to take that two weeks and paint and do some work on their new home. I could hardly wait for 'em to get gone so we could start.

After all the pictures, cake, and punch, we sent 'em away in a shower of birdseed. We knew that that time of year, the winter birds would be very grateful.

When we got into Chad's truck, he turned and looked at me and I wondered what he was thinkin' so seriously about. His bright blue eyes spoke volumes to me and I noticed that they'd watered up. He swallowed hard. He turned back and started the truck and we went back to our little cottage on the mountain.

"Ya never did tell me why ya had to go away." I cautiously mentioned.

"Yes, I did. I said I had to go on business."

"What in the world kind of business do ya have in the Caribbean?" I wanted to know.

"Actually, it was the Dominican Republic, and I have business interests there. It has to do with some retirement investments, and I have to go check on 'em from time to time. Now quit worryin' about it. I'm back. And . . . I . . . I just want ya to know . . . how much I . . . I love ya, baby girl."

I didn't know quite what to say. It was the very first time that he'd ever said the words 'I love you'.

Floy'd let it slip often enough exactly what she'd planned for her house. I'd been takin' notes so that I'd have some idea of what would make her happy. The next week and a half was spent with painters, floorin' people and finally, some new furniture. I'd decided to give 'em new livin' and bedroom furniture as a weddin' gift. After all, she was my very best friend and was so much like a sister. Besides, I certainly had enough money and was happy to do it for 'em.

Chad was excited. He was determined to contribute to the gift by supplyin' 'em with all new kitchen appliances and a dinin' room set. We could hardly wait for 'em to get back and had just finished up two nights before they were due home. We'd hung curtains and tried to get as much done as we could with the decoratin'. I knew that they had a lot of weddin' gifts and personal things from their homes that they'd want to add in, but the house looked great. We locked it up and hung the card on the door that read,

"Welcome Home, Mr. & Mrs. Ellis. You're invited to Thanksgivin' Dinner on the mountain! Love, Lilah and Chad."

"Well, that should do it. Now let's go spend some private time up on that mountain" Chad whispered as he nuzzled my neck.

I woke up late. I could tell that Chad was already up by the smell of coffee and breakfast that had made it up to our room. I dressed and hurried downstairs.

"Mornin' sleepy head." He said as he kissed me. "Happy Thanksgivin'!"

I smiled and took the cup of coffee that he offered me.

"And Happy Thanksgivin' to you. What are ya doin' up so early?" I asked, just as lightnin' cracked and the thunder rolled.

It startled me and I dumped my coffee. I got another cup and walked over to see what he was doin'.

"What ya plannin' on doin' to that turkey?" I asked as I peeked over his shoulder.

"I . . . aw . . . I don't know." He glanced around. "I . . . uh . . . I thought about bastin' him with some of this here peanut butter and callin' it good." He laughed.

"What? Are you crazy?"

"Well, I've been called that more than once in my life. I think the peanut butter would make him look all nice and brown and nobody would know the difference."

"Honey, I don't wanna bust your bubble but, yeah, I think people would know the difference."

He stepped back. "I guess I better give up the kitchen and let a real professional take over."

I thought it was a sly way to get out of helpin' with the cookin' and it was very obvious that he'd put the peanut butter on his toast with jam. He got his cup of coffee and walked over to the back door and opened it.

"Feels a little chilly." I commented.

"Yep. But I tell ya, I sure love that cold Kentucky rain."

"Mmm . . . me too. Do ya suppose they got in last night? I'd love to have been a little bug on the wall."

He just stood there in the doorway. The rain began to spray through the screen and still he just stood there.

"Chad?" I called. "Honey?"

He still didn't move or answer. I walked over beside him and looked out the door. The rainy breeze that was blowin' was very cold. I looked up at him and was surprised, once again, to see tears in his eyes.

"Chad? Are ya alright?"

"Yeah, it's just cold. Early mornin' rain usually means an all day rain. I hope they get here alright." he spoke softly.

Somethin' in his voice sounded different. It was almost like a loneliness or great sadness. I could feel it so strong that I felt a shiver run over me and I knew it wasn't from the cold air.

I had everthing cooked and ready to serve at 12:10. I'd made pies, cakes, turkey and all the fixin's that go with it. At 12:40 I was gettin' a little nervous. By 1:20 I knew somethin' was wrong.

"I'll get Patton and go check it out." Chad put his coat and gloves on and hurried out the door.

He didn't have to go more than half way down the mountain, when he found 'em trudgin' up the road.

Toby said their truck had slid in the mud and got stuck so they decided to try it on foot. When they come in the back door, I was so relieved to see 'em that I grabbed Floy and gave her a big hug even though she was soakin' wet. Chad had let her ride Patton and he and Toby had walked beside 'em.

When everyone got dried off and seated with a cup of hot coffee, Toby stood up and took Floy by the hand and pulled her up.

"Lilah, Chad . . . we was so surprised when we got home. Our house had become a real home, a beautiful home." He said.

"It's absolutely perfect. We wouldn't change a single thing. But how in the world can we ever thank ya?" Floy added as tears began to flow. "We love ya both so much. Nobody ever had any better friends."

We spent a minute huggin' and bein' hugged.

"You're my best friend, Floy. Toby, I couldn't have created a better person for her than you. I love ya both and I just want ya to be as happy in that home as ya both deserve to be." I said. Chad spoke up "I . . . I gotta say that one of the best things that ever . . . uh . . . ever happened in my life was when I went to Lexington and saw Lilah and Floy for the first time. Then when she knocked a drink outta my hand at King's, I knew that followin' her had been the best thing I'd done in a long time. I had no idea that I would end up here on this mountain like this or that I'd find two of the best friends I've ever had, to go with it. I . . . I been a lotta places and I've known a lotta people, but this is the first time in my life that I've had friends that don't want nothin' from me, and what they say is for real . . . I . . . we . . . really enjoyed fixin' your place up for ya. I'm just glad you like it."

I was confused by the fact that he saw us in Lexington, 'til I thought about it for a minute. Then it dawned on me that he was the one that was standin' by the barn when we was talkin' to Mr. Colonel. I was even more surprised to learn that he was the man whose drink I'd knocked out on the dance floor. That was why he seemed so familiar to me. How funny that I'd never put it all together.

Floy and I got the meal on the table and we sat down. As usual, Chad took my hand, then reached and took Floy's. I took Toby's hand while he joined hands with Floy and we all bowed our heads. Chad gave a beautiful blessin' and we all shared our first Thanksgivin' meal. Like most people do on holidays, we thoroughly stuffed ourselves.

"That was some good eats, Lilah," Toby complimented. "That turkey was the best I ever had."

"Thank ya very much . . . but ya should be so glad that I come in when I did this mornin'. We come real close to gettin' a peanut butter-basted bird for dinner." I teased and elbowed Chad.

"What?" Toby asked in surprise.

"Hey, I always believed that anything is good with a little peanut butter," Chad laughed as we went to the livin' room with hopes to watch a Thanksgivin' Day football game.

It was decided that Toby and Floy should stay the night since the weather had changed from rain to snow and that the guys could pull the truck out in the mornin'.

"So, here we are again, just one big happy family." My heart overflowed with love as I took a mental picture of my precious little family.

We finally went upstairs to our rooms. I walked over to the window, sat down on the sill and looked outside. The yard and everything in it was covered in fresh fallin' snow. Huge flakes drifted down and began to pile up on the window ledge.

"Do ya think the horses are warm enough?" I asked Chad.

"Yep, I put blankets on 'em when I fed 'em."

"What about Boots and Roz?"

"Cuddled up in their dog house on their blankets, like we would be if ya would get over here in this bed," he teased.

I hesitated a minute and watched out the window. There was somethin' about the snow fall that made me sad, but I didn't really know why. I thought about how funny it was that snow hardly made any noise at all when it fell. It put me in mind of down feathers, so soft and goin' wherever the wind chose to blow 'em. I was sure that snow was one of God's best pieces of artwork.

Mornin' came and Chad took the tractor to help Toby and Floy to get the truck out. He hadn't been gone very long when he come in the back door, covered in snow.

"Is it snowin' again?"

"It just started up again when I was puttin' the tractor up."

"Did they get headed back home?"

"Yeah, it didn't take much to pull 'em out. We should call 'em in a little while and make sure they got there ok."

An hour later, we called and they were home safe and warm.

"Honey, why don't we go see if we can find that Christmas tree you wanted?" Chad suggested.

"In the snow?"

"Sure, it'll be fun!" He grinned.

Sometimes he was so much like a kid and I loved him for that. He made life so excitin'. I hadn't had that for years. I hurried up and got all my warmest clothes on, and we headed out to the barn.

"What're we goin' out here for?"

"To get a hatchet and a tarp."

"I get the hatchet part . . . but what do we need with a tarp?"

"To pull the tree back on, silly."

As he came out of the barn, I carefully scooped up a handful of snow, formed a ball, and threw it at him. It hit him in the back. I sensed that I'd best run for my life. I wasn't fast enough. His snowball popped me right in the back of my head. We both laughed and he took my hand as we went up the mountain to look for that perfect first tree.

We must've looked at about three dozen trees. They was either too tall, too short, too fat, too skinny, or just down-right ugly. We'd gotten pretty far around the side of the mountain and still hadn't found our tree. The snow was really comin' down by then.

"Let's take a break." Chad suggested.

He spread out the tarp under a rock ledge that gave us some shelter. Then he pulled out a thermos of hot coffee and a couple a turkey sandwiches.

"When did ya get that?" I asked him.

"When you were upstairs gettin' ready." He answered.

"That my love, was some really good thinkin'," I smiled.

He looked up from pourin' the lid full of coffee and handed it to me. I was once again struck captive by those incredible crystal blue eyes. I knew then what Nanny used to mean when she said a man had bedroom eyes. My stare must've made him a little nervous 'cause he started to bite on that bottom lip.

"I wish you wouldn't do that," I told him.

"What?" he asked me with a pure look of innocence that stole my heart. I didn't believe for a minute that he had any idea how totally irresistible he was.

"Bite on your lip like that."

"Why?"

" 'Cause I . . . well . . . just 'cause," I teased.

He grinned, looked down and shook his head. We quietly finished our coffee and sat watchin' it snow for the longest time.

"I love this weather," Chad spoke softly, " and I do love Christmas. It's the time where ya get to give every body ya care about gifts. I've always loved this time a year. Ya know, when I was just a kid, me and Mama and Daddy used to have snowball fights back at . . . home. When I got old enough and made some money, I always made sure we had a big Christmas!" He paused very deep in thought. "Big ole Christmas . . . " He sighed. "We'd already had more than our share of hard Christmas times. I swore it'd never be that way again. The first Christmas I had after Mama died was . . . was 'bout more than I . . . I could bear."

He crossed his arms over his knees and laid his head on 'em. I didn't say anything. It was a time for quiet memories. I gently put my arm across his shoulders and leaned my head against him and listened to the silence of the still fallin' snow.

It wasn't long before he raised his head and rested his chin on his thumb. I couldn't resist the temptation and grabbed him by the neck and pulled him backwards onto the tarp. This time it was my lips that took his by surprise. At first I showered his beautiful face with kisses, but before long I found those wonderful pouty lips. I kissed 'em softly at first, then gently slid my tongue into his mouth. His hand came up behind my head and pulled me into a harder, deeper kiss. Raisin' up on one elbow, I looked into his eyes.

"Chad, I love ya so much . . . more than I ever thought I could love anybody. Ya own my heart, my body, and my very spirit . . . I do love you."

"Don't . . . I . . . I . . . Don't . . . talk. Just kiss me like that again."

I did. Again and again until I wanted him so badly I couldn't think. Boots and pants disappeared and we made wonderful, careless, passionate love, right there in the snow. The cold didn't exist for us. We created enough heat to keep us warm for the rest of our lives. It seemed to be that way each and every time we was together. In the heat of passion, I sometimes felt as close to death as I did to the wonderful, exhilaration of life.

Afterward, Chad leaned over me and looked into my eyes. I felt a deep flutter of panic inside, mixed with anticipation and I was afraid of what he might be thinkin'.

"You're everything I ever dreamed of, honey. I . . . uh . . I . . . I need ya to know that no matter what might happen in our lives, whether we're together or if somethin' should happen . . . I do love ya, baby girl, and you and you alone . . . will always . . . own my heart."

He put his finger under my chin, lifted my lips to his and kissed me softly, just the way he'd done the very first time. We laid there, wrapped in the tarp until the cold started to creep through.

"I think we're doin' a pretty bad job of findin' a tree." Chad mumbled casually as he nuzzled my ear.

"Yeah," I said "but I got no complaints".

When we pulled the tarp from under the ledge, I couldn't help but notice that we'd left perfect imprints of our bodies, side by side, melted into the snow.

"It's us," he pointed out.

"We almost made snow angels!" I giggled.

" Honey," he grinned, "them ain't no angels."

I turned to look at him as he bit his lip and winked.

We spent another half hour lookin' for that tree and were about to give up when we walked over a small hill. The moment we saw it, we knew that it was to be our first Christmas tree. We walked all around it to make sure it was perfect from every direction.

"What do ya think, chiquita?"

"I think it's the most beautiful little tree I've ever seen."

We pulled the tarp up beside it and Chad began to chop. It didn't take long before it fell perfectly onto the waitin' tarp. I clapped my hands and cheered for him.

"Good job, Honey!"

"I didn't sweat this much when we were under that ledge awhile ago," He teased.

"Of course not," I snickered. "I was doin' all the work!"

"I was doin' all the work. Ha!" He mimicked in a funny little voice and tossed a loose snowball at me.

"Hey, look over there," He jumped up excitedly. "It looks like a . . . cave or somethin'." We both got up and headed toward another small, shaggy tree that seemed to cover the entrance to a small openin'.

"Did ya know this was here?"

"No, I never noticed it before. In fact I'm not sure I've ever been this far around the mountain."

"Cool, let's take a look," He crawled inside, "C'mon, baby, it's bigger inside."

I crawled through the openin' and he was right, it was a good deal bigger inside. It was very dark and smelled old and musty.

"Do ya wanna explore it?"

"NO! Honey, there could be a bear in here hyber . . . hyber . . . sleepin'! There are a lot of bears in these mountains ya know. Let's get out while we can."

I was uneasy about the place and couldn't get out fast enough. Somethin' about it gave me the creeps.

"We'll have to come back sometime and check that out. I wonder where it goes to?" he sounded determined.

"Probably to the end and back." I joked.

"Naw, probably to some hidden treasure or it's an old Indian ceremony cave or somethin'," he teased as we walked back to our tree.

"Sure. Okay." I told him as I picked up the side of the tarp and folded it over the tree. It didn't take us long to get it wrapped up and start haulin' it back to the ranch. It slid easily over the fresh snow. As we was walkin' along I started to sing "Jingle Bells" which led to "Rockin' 'round the Christmas Tree." Chad hummed along for awhile. When I stopped, he began to sing a beautiful version of "O Little Town of Bethlehem." When he finished, I was left speechless.

"Ya have an incredible voice, Chad. I think that's the first time I've heard ya sing?

"Aw . . . I . . . I used to sing a little here and there. Ya know, school choir and stuff."

Then he broke in to a horrible version of "White Christmas." I told him if anybody heard that . . . they'd probably shoot him to put him out of his misery!

Chapter 10

When we come down the side of the mountain, we walked by the little cabin.

"Who did ya say lived here?" He stopped to check it out.

"My Grandpap's Mama lived here her last years, and died here."

"It's a cool little pad," He said as he opened the door.

We entered the small livin' area. It was still partly furnished. Whoever had lived there last had left a sofa and a very small chair. In the little kitchen area, was the old wood stove Big Nana had cooked on. The tiny bedroom area still had an old iron bed and a huge armoire against the wall. That was the only thing that resembled a closet, in the place. Chad opened the new door that led to the new bath I'd had Mr. Timpson build.

"Damn," he said as he walked in. "This is really nice. It don't look like it even belongs with this cabin."

"It didn't," I told him. "I just had it built before we went to Lexington. I thought while I was buildin' bathrooms, I might as well put one everywhere I thought one would be handy. It was a heck of a job gettin' runnin' water up here, but someone might need to live up here some time. Now it's ready."

"Looks really nice. They did a good job," he complimented. "Just one thing? Where's the back door to this place?"

"I never even thought about it. I guess they didn't think they needed one. Probably easier to guard just one door!"

We left and continued down the hill to the house. Boots and Roz ran to meet us. They'd started out with us, but I guess they decided we was gettin' too far from home. They'd left us about halfway up to the trees.

I left Chad trimmin' the bad limbs off the tree and I went inside to clear a place to put it.

It was a tough decision . . . after all, it was our first Christmas and the placement had to be just right. I rearranged the end tables and moved a chair. It'd be perfect. When I sat on the couch, there was a great view of the fireplace, the television, as well as the spot where the tree would stand. I got the bucket off the front porch that we'd brought up from the barn, and headed back to the kitchen so Chad could put the tree in it and fill it with dirt.

As I walked into the kitchen, I was startled to find Chad standin' in the door leanin' heavily against the door frame.

"Are ya ready for the bucket already?" I asked him as I eagerly hurried to where he stood.

When he looked up at me, he was as white as a ghost and his lips had a slight blue tint.

"I . . . I . . . uh . . . I don't feel so good, hon," he mumbled as he wilted to his knees.

When I tried to catch him, I was suddenly aware of the pool of blood on the back porch and the trail of blood across the yard from where he'd been choppin' on the tree. Carefully, I laid him down in the kitchen floor and shut the door to keep the cold off him. I immediately noticed the tear in the leg of his jeans. The blood flowed steadily onto the floor.

"Chad! What happened, honey?"

"I . . . uh . . . I don't know . . . the hatchet slipped and . . . I . . . I," He passed out cold and went limp in my arms.

I had to think.

There was nobody for miles and this was really serious. I took off my belt and put it around his upper leg and tightened it so that it would stop the blood, then I took a kitchen knife and cut off the leg of his pants. There was a gapin' gash in his thigh and I could see the muscles, tendons, and what looked a lot like bone. My head began to spin and I thought I was for sure gonna be sick. As soon as it passed, I hurried to the phone and called Floy at her Granddad's store. I didn't have a clue if they'd be open so late and it was the day after Thanksgivin'. It surprised me when Granddad Miller answered the phone.

"Grandad, this is Lilah, is Floy there, please?"

She came to the phone. "Lilah? What's up?"

I told her what'd happened.

"I can't get him to town and I don't know what to do!" My voice broke and I tried to control the sobs.

She told me to keep pressure on the wound and loosen the belt ever so often and keep him layin' down with his leg up and cover him up in case he went into shock. She'd bring help right away.

As quick as I could, I got a heavy blanket from the couch, a pillow, and a cold wet rag and tried to keep hold of myself. I watched the clock like a hawk so I'd know when to loosen the belt. As soon as I would loosen it, the blood would start to flow without pause, then I would tighten it back and wipe his face with my rag. After what seemed like forever, he seemed to come around a little and tried to open his eyes.

"Wh . . . Where's Joe?" he mumbled.

"Who's Joe, honey?"

"T . . . t . . . tell daddy . . . I . . . I didn't mean it. I . . . I . . . " and he was out again.

"Chad? Baby, please wake up. Talk to me, honey. You're scarin' the hell out a me! Please!" I begged.

He lay there limp in my arms and all I could do was wait, wipe his face, and brush his hair out of his eyes. The only thing I wanted was for him to open those incredible blue eyes and look at me again and bite that beautiful lip and wink at me like he'd done so often. My small amount of control was slippin' away.

It seemed like days since I'd called Floy. I looked at the window and noticed that it was growin' dark outside.

"How damn long can it take!" I screamed.

Panic had long since passed and I was frozen with fear.

I continued loosenin' the belt and pullin' the blanket up around his neck. It wasn't long after dark that I came to the horrified conclusion that no one could get here 'cause of the snow. I was gonna sit right here and watch the love of my life die in my lap. It was all 'cause of a tree. A damn TREE!

When I heard a tractor comin' up the drive and the dogs barkin', I started to scream for help. By the time they got to the kitchen, I was totally hysterical again.

Toby rushed in first followed by Dr. Garron, from over at Bigby, Granddad Miller's nephew, Morris, was right behind with a large box. Then . . . Floy was there, tryin' to force me to let him go. I couldn't, I was sure that if I did, I'd never hold him again.

Finally, a sound slap across my face brought me back to reality.

"Ya gotta let the doctor get to him!" She screamed. "He's gonna die if ya don't get outta the way."

Realizin' then that she was right, I let 'em take him.

Floy covered the couch with some blankets and Toby helped the doctor carry Chad into the livin' room. He was ashen and completely limp. It was impossible to tell if he was still breathin' as I sat frozen in a chair and watched in horror.

"How'd this happen?" Doctor Garron asked.

"The tree . . . he . . . he . . . trimmed it . . . the hatchet," I went to pieces again.

It was easy to see that everytime he loosened the belt the blood would again flow freely. It gushed with every beat of his heart. How much blood could ya lose and still live?

When he started to insert the IV needle, Chad stirred and tried to take a swing at him, but Toby grabbed him and held him down.

"It's okay buddy, we're gonna help ya. Just try and relax," he spoke gently in Chad's ear.

As soon as the doctor got the IV going, he shot somethin' into it and told Toby it was okay to let him go, that he would rest. I felt sick to my stomach as I watched him clean and wash the wound. It seemed to me that he was bein' awful rough. He had Morris loosen the belt so he could find the artery that was doin' all the bleedin'.

"That's it." he said as he worked quickly.

He began to stitch the wound. I heard Morris as he counted over fifty stitches to close it.

"Is he gonna be okay, now" Toby was as worried as the rest of us.

Doctor Garron was takin' Chad's blood pressure again. He looked up at Toby.

"What's your blood type, son?"

"Hell, I think it's like B or somethin'.'"

"How about you, Morris?"

"Mine's O, but I'm diabetic. I don't think that'd be very good."

He turned to me and Floy. "Ladies, I need a donor and I really need it now. Do either one of you have type O?"

I stood up. "I do. What do I need to do?"

"This is a little primitive, but I have no choice. I'm gonna have to take some of your blood to give to him. I need at the least a pint, maybe two. Since your accident it might leave you a little light-headed. Can ya do it?"

"Ya can have all ya need to save him. That's all I care about. Just save him."

Within an hour, it was all over with.

Chad was given antibiotics and over a pint of blood. He was bandaged and covered up on the couch. I was in the recliner next to him and the doctor was right, I was a little light-headed.

They all stayed throughout the night and every time Chad moved or moaned, I was at his side. Floy made me a bed of sorts on the floor right beside him as I held his cold, still hand and finally fell to sleep with my head on the couch.

Some time in the night, I was awakened when the doctor was checkin' his blood pressure again.

"Is he alright?" I whispered.

"He's better. He's stable. I believe, barring complications, he'll be fine."

Smilin', I put my head back down only to be awakened later by fingers runnin' lightly through my hair. I looked up into sleepy blue eyes and a crooked little grin.

"You okay?" Chad whispered.

I didn't quite know what to say. "Yes darlin', I'm fine. How do you feel?" He bit his bottom lip and winked at me and fell back to sleep.

I sat there and looked at him for the longest time. He was sleepin' so peaceful. He looked like a little boy with his bangs in his eyes and his mouth slightly opened. His chest rose and fell with his breathin' and I thought how close I'd come to losin' him. He was the greatest gift God ever gave me and I'd do anything it took to protect him and make him happy.

By mornin', he was wide awake, runnin' a fever and in a huge amount of pain. Doctor Garron gave him pain medication and finally got him settled back down.

"Now that you're better, I can take that IV out," the doctor said. " You had a close call, son. You need to leave them hatchets alone. Okay?"

Chad smiled and nodded his head as he struggled to stay awake and listen.

"I want ya to come into my office as soon as the weather clears up. I wanna check that wound and your blood pressure again. Morris, will leave ya plenty of antibiotics and some pain pills. You take 'em like directed. Okay?"

Chad nodded again, " Thanks, doc," he mumbled.

"Lilah, keep a close eye on that fever. A little is normal for a few days, but if it gets too high, or you can't bring it down, call me right away."

"I will Doctor Garon, and thank you again." I told him as I gave him a big hug.

Toby took the doctor and Morris back to his place on the tractor and Floy stayed with me and Chad until Toby came back to get her that afternoon. I dozed on and off beside the couch while Chad slept after every pain pill.

"Lilah, go to bed. I'm right here. I'll watch him like a mama," Floy urged.

I finally got up and made my way up to the bedroom. Wrappin' myself in my blanket, I fell straight to sleep. It was reassurin' to know that Floy would take excellent care of my man.

It was after noon when I woke up with a start. I thought I'd heard someone yell for help. I made my way from my room and stumbled down the stairs. I stopped in my tracks. Floy was in the recliner readin' a book and Chad was sittin' propped up on the couch sippin' a hot cup of coffee. I supposed I'd had a nightmare.

"Got an extra one of those for me?" I asked more casually than I felt.

Chad turned and looked at me with a glassy eyed expression.

"Hey, thleepy head," he slurred. "'bout time ya come down to me. I need some sugar."

"But honey, you don't take sugar in your coffee," I reminded him.

He looked a little confused, then said "Aw . . . not that kind of sugar . . . I need a kiss, darlin'."

I was glad to supply him with all of those he could ever need, so I leaned over and kissed him. He had set the coffee cup on the end table and tried to pull me over the back of the couch.

"Come on Chiquita, get in my bed with me."

"Wait. Hold on cowboy . . . I can't get in your bed. Ya have a very serious injury. We can't take a chance of gettin' it started bleedin' again."

"Hell, I don't care . . . I want ya to snuggle with me . . . c'mon . . . please? . . . don't tell me no." He looked so cute and so adorable that it was all I could do to resist. I looked to Floy who sat there with an amused look on her face. She cleared her throat and put down her book.

"I gave him a couple a pain pills and set 'em on the coffee table. Big mistake. While I was in the kitchen he woke up and took another. When I called Doctor Garron, he said it wouldn't hurt him, it would just make him really sleepy and a little disoriented. He told me to feed him coffee. He's really kinda funny now that I know he's not in any danger. I have to admit, Lilah, he's a doll, and so sweet. I think he's a keeper."

"Honey?" Chad slurred "C'mere, I . . . I need to . . . to tell ya somethin'."

"What is it sweetheart?" I asked as I sat down on the floor and took his hand.

He leaned close and whispered "Ya can't tell nobody."

It was as if he was drunker than drunk.

"I . . . I . . . I ain't really me . . . shhh . . . it's a big ole secret." He almost nodded off.

"Ok, baby." I looked at Floy and shook my head. ". . . then who are ya?"

"I'm . . . I . . . I'm . . . I'm the Tiger." He grinned a silly grin and fell back on his pillow and proceeded to snore.

I laughed. " I guess I got me a tiger by the tail."

"Yeah" Floy smiled "I guess ya do."

I was feelin' a lot better by the time Toby come back.

"If it's ok with you Lilah, I brought some clean clothes. I figger me and Floy will stay another night to make sure that ya'll gonna be alright. We can head back sometime tomorrow if everybody's okay."

"Thanks Toby. You and Floy are so good to us."

When it was time for bed, I decided that I couldn't leave him down stairs alone and I knew that Floy was exhausted, so I carefully crawled over behind him on the couch and pulled the blanket over us. The fragrance of his skin and the feverish warmth of his body was intoxicatin'. I stole a kiss from his neck and snuggled up to him and went to sleep.

Four days later the weather had broken and the roads were slushy, but passable. The hardest part was gettin' Chad in the Jeep. Luckily I still had my crutches and once we lengthened 'em, they was perfect. I felt more confident drivin' my Jeep instead of his big ole truck and it was easier for him to get in.

We made our way to Bigby and Doctor Garron's office where Chad was pronounced better. But was cautioned to stay off his leg until the stitches were removed. We made an appointment for two weeks later.

"I guess goin' dancin' ain't on the menu, huh?" Chad asked as we drove past King's.

"Not unless you've learned to one step." I teased him.

"I was thinkin' we could just stand in one spot and, what is it they say, polish belt buckles." he laughed out loud.

"Sorry stud, you're goin' home and straight to bed."

"All right! I'm ready for that, Let's get goin'." He said as he turned in the seat and stared at me.

"What are ya doin'?"

"I'm anticipatin' gettin' home and goin' straight to bed." He grinned. I shook my head.

"Get a grip, Tiger, get a grip. It could be awhile yet. Ya still got lots a stitches."

"That just means I can't go walkin' or dancin'. Why . . . I . . . I should be bedridden and ya don't want me to be there all alone and sad and probably depressed do ya?" He gave me his saddest face.

"Give it a day or two and we'll talk about it, okay?" I tried to compromise.
"Hell, I don't wanna TALK about it!"

Life with Chad was a constant guessin' game. One minute he was every bit the man, the one in control, the caregiver, and the protector. The next minute he was like a kid in a candy store.

He was the only man I ever knew that could even make gatherin' eggs fun.

Chad was very tender hearted. A few days before the accident, when we was in the hen house, he told me that he really felt sorry for the hens. That it must be a terrible thing to have to give birth to an egg every day.

And he was dead serious!

Even back when Roz had her puppies, he was right there to help her. I didn't think she needed help, but he was adamant that no mama should be alone when givin' birth. Chad petted her head and talked sweetly to her. When that first pup come out and Roz cleaned it and it was alive, you'd a thought it was his child.

His eyes teared up and he told me, "We just witnessed one of God's greatest miracles, little girl. The miracle of life, and I'm holdin' it right here in my two hands."

I'd noticed that he was almost always happy and easy goin', and usually hummed or whistled when he was workin'. However, when he was serious or upset . . . he had quite the temper, too. He never got upset with me, just things that happened, and from time to time, he would be gone for a couple of hours and come home very angry. I assumed it had to do with his businesses, but he would never talk about that stuff. He was very personal about his past and his business and often assured me that I had nothin' to worry about. He told me he had it all under control, so I let it be.

Floy and Toby come up to see us several times while he was recoverin'. Chad was hobblin' around pretty good on his crutches and Toby would help him down the steps and they'd go do the chores. I felt like he was glad to get out of the house now and then. The first time they went out, he was hoppin' mad when he come back in.

"Honey?" He yelled.

I ran to the back door.

"What's the matter?"

"I wondered where that tree was." He pointed toward the ground. "I damn near bled to death for that thing and ya let it lay in the yard and die?" He was really hot about it.

"That's exactly why it stayed in the yard!" It was the first time I'd really raised my voice at him. "It has your blood on it, Chad. I couldn't bear to have it in the house. And I threw that damn hatchet in the burn barrel, too!"

As I stomped off through the house, I heard him yell, "Well, what the hell we gonna do for a tree now?"

It was almost supper time when the back door opened and Chad come inside followed by Toby who was carryin' a small Christmas tree in a bucket.

"Where do ya want this?" Toby asked with a big grin.

"It's not very big, but it's really kinda pretty," added Chad. "It's like a miniature of the one we found up on the mountain."

"Where did ya find it?" I asked excitedly.

"On the hill, down by the creek. Ya know, the one where we . . . uh . . . went swimmin' that first time?" Chad said and bit his bottom lip and gave me that little wink.

"Are ya insane? What are ya thinkin' walkin' that far?" I practically yelled.

"Whoa, there firecracker! I might look stupid, but I ain't ." Toby jumped in. "I saddled Pride, put Chad on him and we rode down there, okay?"

It was hard not to laugh. They was like two little boys tryin' to explain what they'd been up to and so proud of that tree that I couldn't really be mad. Toby took the tree into the livin' room and put it in the spot that I'd cleared for the first one. Floy and I spent some time after supper gettin' the decorations down. I didn't have many, mostly what Nanny had left and a few from when I was with Walt. After sortin' through 'em, I decided that I didn't want those even in the house. I bagged 'em up and Floy agreed to trash 'em when she got to town. She and I decorated the little tree, which didn't take long, then Floy surprised me by makin' little arrangements out of what was left and placin' 'em around the livin' room.

"That looks really beautiful, ladies." Chad complimented.

"It does. Ya'll done a real good job." Toby gave his approval.

I turned to Floy, "I didn't know that ya was so talented. I'd never've thought of usin' those leftovers to make all that."

"Aw . . . I knew she could do it. Ya should see our house. It's full of that stuff. It looks like some kinda Christmas store. It's purty as anything I ever seen." Toby bragged.

Floy handed me a small wrapped box.

"I got us one and I thought ya'll needed one, too. Go ahead. Open it." she said excitedly. "It's for both of ya." I sat down by Chad and unwrapped it.

Inside was a shiny red Christmas ball. Written in gold was "Our First Christmas" and when ya wound the little key it played, of all things, "White Christmas." It was so beautiful. I hugged 'em both and we thanked 'em.

I glanced at Chad. ". . . but whatever ya do . . . don't sing 'White Christmas' for us!"

He grinned and Floy and Toby looked bewildered.

Shortly before Christmas, I took Chad into Bigby to get his stitches out. I was happy with the way the wound looked afterward.

"Looks like a plastic surgeon done it. It looks great Doctor Garron." I complimented him.

"Well, you look good and it's healed real nice. Stay away from hatchets and if you have any problems . . . you know where I am," he patted Chad on the back as we left his office.

We decided to do a little Christmas shoppin' while we were in town. I'd done some before Thanksgivin', but I still had to get some things bought and in the mail to Mama and Daddy and the kids. On the way back, we stopped in Mason to have lunch with Floy at Shoemaker's Café.

"Guess who waltzed into the store yesterday?" Floy leaned across the table and whispered.

"I have no idea. Who?" She had me curious.

"Lady Godiva, herself."

"Who the hell's, Lady Godiva?" Chad paused eatin' and asked.

Floy and I looked at each other. "It's the name we gave your friend, Danna. Remember?"

He snickered. "Why?"

" 'Cause she has hair down to her knees and very little clothes on." Teased Floy. ". . . and guess what?"

"What?"

"She's pregnant."

I froze in my chair. I looked at Chad who was in his own world and still eatin'. He noticed the lull in the conversation and looked up.

"What?" He asked.

"She's pregnant, Chad."

He sat there a moment as if in deep thought. Then the reality of the insinuation hit him.

"No! . . . no . . . don't look at me like that. It ain't mine!"

"How do ya know?"

"If I'm not mistaken, it still takes two people havin' sex . . . with each other . . . for that to happen," he said casually.

I leaned over and looked him square in the eye, "And?"

He stared me right back down and answered, "And . . . NO, I did not sleep with that woman. I came to town lookin' for one woman and one woman only. I found her . . . end of story."

"Would ya tell me if ya had?"

"I would. But I didn't," He answered calmly. "She sure got over me fast," he mused. ". . .Moved right along I'd say."

I believed him but, it still made me a little uneasy. She'd been too adamant about how she felt about him. Not that I could blame her for one minute.

I didn't have much to say on the way home and I noticed that Chad was very quiet too. When we got back to the ranch it was gettin' later in the afternoon. He was gettin' around a lot better and didn't require quite as much help, so I went on down to tend to the animals. I always liked to brush Patton and Pride a little before I put their blankets on 'em for the night. It wasn't all that late, so

I took my time. I still had to pen up the chickens, and the cows and the dogs needed their supper. I'd just finished brushin' the horses when the barn door opened. It startled me at first, until I saw that it was Chad.

"Ya 'bout done?"

"I just now got the boys brushed and covered. They needed a good brushin'." I told him. "What are ya doin' down here?"

"I came down to check on you," he said softly as he leaned against the door. "I miss ya. I could almost be a little jealous of them two."

"Well, I'll be done in a little bit and I'll be up to the house. Now get your cute butt back up there and wait for me," I ordered.

"Nag, nag," he mumbled as he made his way out the door.

I went out the back door and called the cows and fed 'em and locked their gate. It made me feel better when they was safely locked in their pen. After all, there was still wolves and bears and big cats that would probably love a good steak. The chickens were finally goin' in to roost, so I shut and locked the coop. Before I headed back to the house, I filled my little bucket with dog food and started up the hill. That was when I noticed a car in front of the house. I hadn't heard it pull in, nor had I heard the dogs. I could see Chad out there talkin' to two men but I just couldn't imagine who it might be. I started that way when I heard him yell.

"If I need ya, I'll call ya. Now get the hell out of here! I'll take care of it next week. Don't EVER come here again! Do ya hear me? Never!" He started to walk away.

I heard one of the men say quite loudly, "Ya know ya can't do this, son". Then Chad turned quickly, pointed his finger and stated with an anger and authority that I'd never imagined he possessed, "Don't ever try to tell me what I can and cannot do! Nobody's ever doin' that to me again! Understand me . . . now get the hell out of here! NOW!!"

The men got into the car and left before I could get to the house.

"Chad? What was all that about?" I'd never seen him like that. "Who was those men?"

He sat down on the front steps. I walked over and sat down beside him. He sat there a minute pettin' Roz.

"I gotta make another trip, baby." He took my hand and turned it palm side up and gently pressed his lips to it.

"Where to?" I asked. "Why?"

"Business," he stated flatly, "back down south."

"Ya mean, the Dominican Republic . . . again?"

"Yep," he answered softly.

"What kind of business?" It was obvious that he was keepin' somethin' from me.

"Just investments," he answered as he leaned on his other hand.

"Chad, it's not nothin' illegal, is it? I mean . . . promise me it's not drugs or anything like that."

He looked at me and smiled, "I think it'd be easier to deal with if it were. It's not. It's just personal business."

"When are ya leavin'?"

I suddenly felt sick to my stomach.

"In the mornin'."

I sat there a moment. "How long?" I wasn't sure that I wanted to hear the answer.

He turned and looked at me with those unforgettable blue eyes and I knew in my heart that it didn't matter how long. I'd wait right there for as long as it took.

"I'll be home for Christmas." he whispered.

I just nodded and looked out across the yard. It was startin' to snow again and the air felt colder than ever.

We went inside and put more wood in the fireplace. Chad went to take a shower. I thought I'd make us some hot chocolate. I'd just sat the cups down on the coffee table and threw some pillows on the floor when he came down the stairs. I turned to him, and again, I found it almost impossible to look away. He had on jeans and nothin' else. He was barefoot and shirtless and had a towel dryin' his hair. As he reached the bottom of the stairs, he wrapped the towel around his neck and his hair fell straight forward framin' his face. When the fire reflected off of him, he looked like a golden god.

"What's the matter?" He asked with a total innocence in his voice.

"You're the matter."

"What'd I do?"

"Ya walked down those stairs half naked, that's what ya done."

He sat down in the floor as best he could with his still tender leg and I handed him his hot chocolate. As he took a sip, he looked up over his cup and raised one eyebrow.

"How'd ya know that I was thinkin' that this would taste pretty good?"

"I guess I just read your mind."

He bit his bottom lip and winked, "Damn, I think I might be in deep trouble then."

He set his cup down and laid back on the pillow.

"What am I thinkin' now?" He half-whispered.

I looked at him for a minute. "Ya should be ashamed of yourself, Chad Barrett." I pretended to be shocked. It didn't take a genius to figger out what he was thinkin'. When he got that certain look in his eye, I could always tell what was on his mind.

"Never, little girl, never. I'd be ashamed to call myself a man if I looked at ya in the firelight and wasn't thinkin' what I'm thinkin'." He pulled me down on the pillow beside him. The feel of his skin was like magic for me.

He reached over and turned on the stereo.

We both liked blues and jazz and we'd left a good tape in.

"Dance for me honey. I love to watch ya move."

"I can't dance like that! Not by myself." I protested.

"Just for a minute, c'mon, little one, please. Just for me?"

I could deny him nothin'. I stood up and just began to move with the music. It was easier in the the soft glow of firelight. I soon found myself imitatin' some of the strippers in the movies. Chad sat watchin' me as if it was the first time he'd ever seen me.

"Take your shirt off, honey." he whispered.

I began to unbutton my shirt very slowly and I could tell it was drivin' him crazy. It took a little while before I finally had all the buttons undone and I began to slide it off my shoulder. When I was down to my bra, I skipped to my jeans. The button ups were my favorite, so I had some fun with 'em. Slowly I unbuttoned the top one then slid my thumbs around the waistband and back. When I went to the second one, I couldn't help noticin' that Chad was startin' to breathe a little heavy. By the time I had 'em unbuttoned, he reached for me.

"No . . . no . . . soldier boy . . . can't touch the dancers."

I began to slide 'em down over my hips, then I stopped and turned shyly away and undid one fastener of my bra and let a strap fall, just like in one of my favorite movies, "Gypsy". Then I went back to the jeans, but I couldn't for the life of me quite figger out how I was gonna dance gracefully out of 'em. Another bra strap dropped and I turned my back as I undid the last fastener and let it fall to the floor. My hands were over my breasts as I sat back in the chair. I raised a pant leg toward Chad's mouth, he caught it with his perfect white teeth and pulled it down. With a sly look, he took the other one in his teeth and pulled them free. I knelt in the floor and crawled toward him as he watched me through half-opened eyes. He looked like a tiger ready to pounce.

The power I felt over him was somethin' I'd never experienced. I gave in to the temptation to see just how far I could go with it. He reached for me again and I pulled away and shook my finger at him. He grinned that sexy little one-sided grin. I took one of his arms and put it above his head and then the other. I straddled over him and kissed his ear lobe and worked my way across his face, his eyelids, his cheeks, almost his lips, then his neck. He didn't resist. I went back to his lips and let my tongue outline his full sensuous mouth. My fingers made their way down to his chest, not overly hairy, but very sexy. He was all man . . . my man. Kissin' his nipples, I then worked my way down to his navel. By this time he was havin' a really difficult time keepin' control. I knew it and I loved it. This was somethin' new for me, this game of tease. It took me a little while to unfasten his jeans. I found that undressin' him was much simpler since he had absolutely nothin' on under those jeans. When I started to pull 'em off, he raised his hips and at the same time he reached and removed my skimpy panties. He pulled me down gently on top of him and slid deep inside.

It caught me by surprise and I gasped.

I loved the way he felt inside of me. I felt complete as the sensations of physical love began to take control. I loved the way he looked up at me and chewed at his bottom lip as I moved slowly up and down. The harder he breathed, the faster I moved.

On a whim, I abruptly stopped.

He gasped for air and as he opened those baby blues, I started to move quickly again. Just as I thought he couldn't take any more, he sat up and rolled me to my back. My need was as great as his and the more intense it became, the more I wondered if I would survive it. He pushed harder and faster until at last we reached that point of ecstasy. That place of total completeness.

Still joined, exhausted, unable and unwillin' to move, we just lay together, side by side, starin' into each other's eyes as the fire crackled and popped. I reached up and touched his cheek then ran my fingers through his lush hair.

"Chad?" I whispered. "How old were you when your hair started to turn white?"

He chuckled, "My daddy's hair turned white real young. Most of his family did. I guess it was just my turn. Mine started turnin' white in my late twenties. I . . . I . . . I colored it for a long time, but that's a lot of trouble and . . . I . . . I just got tired of it. Why? Don't ya like it? I could color it again." He casually suggested.

"NO! I love your hair. It's like silk. It's not all blonde and it's not all white. It's a perfect mix. Do ya have any idea how many women would kill to have your hair?"

He looked down and then back into my eyes. "Yeah. I do . . . I . . . I mean. I been told that a hundred times."

We finished our mostly room-temperature hot chocolate.

I just started to doze off when I felt Chad kissin' on my neck. I opened my eyes and he smiled at me.

Then he gave me a long, deep kiss.

"This time," he whispered in my ear "I get to be the one in control. It's payback time, baby."

And payback time it was. He teased and tormented until I was sure I would lose my mind. We made love until the break of daylight. We were gloriously exhausted.

He picked me up and put me on the couch and went to take another shower. When he came back downstairs he was handsomely dressed, packed, and ready to go.

"Honey?" I asked. "I got to do some more shoppin' while you're gone. I need to know where ya get that cologne ya wear."

He sat down on the edge of the couch. "Why?"

"Well, Floy likes it almost as much as I do and I thought I'd get Toby some for Christmas. Is that okay? I mean, ya wouldn't care if he wore the same fragrance would ya?"

"No, I guess not. We'll be the only two in the world."

"Where do I have to go to find it . . . or do I have to order it . . . I don't have much time."

"Baby, ya can't find it . . . or order it."

"Well, where in the world do I get it?"

"It's kinda like this . . . I used to order it a long time ago. It was called 'Platinum' and it was my favorite. Then the manufacturer quit makin' it. So I bought the formula and had my own people manufacture it exclusively for me. Now it's called, 'Platinum E'." he explained.

"I see . . . You own it?"

"Yes . . . I do."

"What,s the 'E' mean?"

"It was the fifth formula that I really liked. A..B..C..D..E." He explained, "I can pick him up a bottle while I'm gone if ya want me to."

"That would be great." I hugged him. "Thank ya, Honey. And . . . please don't be gone too long. I'll miss ya more than you'll ever imagine."

"I'll miss ya, too . . . Lilah . . . just . . . don't ever forget how much I love ya. Okay?"

"I won't, Chad . . . I'll be right here when ya get back."

"When I come in that door . . . I want ya right there on that couch and naked as a jay bird . . . Okay?"

"Okay," he kissed me softly and looked into my eyes.

"Wait for me, precious, wait for me," And just like that . . . he was gone.

Chapter 11

Just as his truck pulled out, that damn rooster crowed. I guess he wanted to tell me it was time to be up and about even though I didn't want to. What I really wanted was to go back to sleep and stay there until Chad walked back in that door.

I hadn't been alone in a long, long time. It made me feel nervous, isolated, and totally alone . . . again. While I was lyin' there my thoughts wandered back to that day when Scott had shown up. I felt a chill run down my spine and I jumped up and ran to lock the door. It was still on the dark side of mornin' and I decided to go upstairs and lay down until the sun come out and brought the daylight.

Some how I must've fallen asleep again and I awoke to the phone ringin'. I reached to the night stand and picked it up.

It was Floy. It was so good to hear from her. I told her about Chad's trip and the strange men who'd come to the ranch.

"Why don't ya call Dee and see if she can come stay. Ya talked about that once before. I just don't like the idea of ya bein' out there by yourself. It's hard to believe that Chad took off and didn't find someone to stay with ya." She sounded irritated.

"He was pretty upset by havin' to leave, Floy. I don't think he was thinkin' about anything but goin' and gettin' back as soon as he could. Besides, I have to learn to be by myself sometime. I used to be fine with it and I will be again," I told her. "Don't worry, I'm a big girl and you know I can handle my shotgun right well."

"I still wish ya would call Dee. At least think about it. Okay? I gotta run. Toby just drove up. Bye."

She hung up.

I took a shower, and got dressed, and started my day. It'd snowed durin' the night and it was so beautiful . I was excited to have a reason to get out in it, and I did have to go to the barn and take care of my chores.

While I was walkin' back through the snow, the fleetin', but burnin' memory, of the two snow angels we'd left up on the mountain beneath the rock ledge, seared its way through my mind. I smiled to myself as I followed Roz and Boots back to the house.

After lunch I drove into town to see if Floy wanted to go to Bigby and Dover to do some Christmas shoppin'. She was glad to have an excuse to get away from the store.

It didn't take long to get most of my shoppin' done. Floy only did a little.

"What's up with ya?" I asked her, "You're not yourself today."

"I don't know, I'm just not ready for Christmas," she said as she let out a big sigh.

"Hey, it's your first Christmas with your husband. Ya have most of your gifts bought, I know ya do. Ya always do."

She walked away toward the toy department.

"Sweetie, are ya not happy with Toby?"

"No. No, that's not it. I love Toby very much . . . ya know that. It's just . . . that . . . it's just that . . . I think he's really gonna be mad at me."

She walked a little further and stopped.

"What did ya do?" I asked her as I caught her arm.

"Oh, Lilah, I . . . I . . . uh . . . I'm late." She mumbled.

"For what? Did ya have an appointment today or somethin'?"

"No," she snapped. "I'm late!" She said as she turned and picked up a soft pink baby blanket.

It took me a moment for the information to sink in. "Late? Oh . . . late!" I said as I took the blanket and held it. "Ya haven't told Toby yet?"

"No. I'm afraid of what he's gonna say. I don't think he's nowhere near ready for babies, yet."

"I think he'll be so excited. I also think he'll be a wonderful daddy. How late are ya? It could just be all the excitement, the weddin' and the trip. Ya might be worried over nothin'," I tried to reassure her.

"No, I've missed two periods now. I think I might've been pregnant before the weddin'," she whispered.

The excitement of it filled my heart.

"A baby! I'm gonna be an aunt." I started dancin' 'round in joy.

"SHhhh . . . I don't want everbody in town to know before Toby does."

"Ya mean he doesn't have a clue?"

She shook her head 'no'.

I could hardly believe it. First I grabbed up the pink blanket and then a blue one just like it. We had to have pink and blue gowns and some bibs and of course some pink and blue hats.

"Wait," Floy protested "Shouldn't we wait until it gets here?"

"No ma'am, this baby's gonna have everything she, or he, needs. When ya gonna tell Toby?"

"Probably tonight. I can't keep it to myself no longer." She answered in a worried tone.

"Call me as soon as ya tell him. I can hardly wait to hear what he has to say."

I paid for the purchases and we started out the door. We were about to get in the car when I heard someone call my name. I stopped and turned to find Walt right behind me. I turned quickly to walk away.

"Lilah, wait."

"What do ya want, Walt? I have a lot of shoppin' to get done."

"Can we talk for just a minute? Please."

I'd never heard Walt say "please" in all the years that I'd known him. I knew immediately that somethin' must be really wrong. I walked back to where he was standin'.

"What is it?" I asked coldly. He looked around and then down at the ground. For just a second I saw the boy that I'd married. His black hair fallin' carelessly around his face, and his deep black eyes seemed somehow softer. He seemed different, although common sense told me to beware. Walt had always been clever at gettin' people to let their guard down.

"I know that we . . . well, I done ya wrong and I know that I did." He looked me straight in the eyes. I could've counted on one hand, minus four fingers, how many times that'd happened . . . ever.

"Sugar, ya know me better'n anybody in the world. I get to drinkin' and then I get diarhea of the mouth. Hell, I just don't know when to shut my damn mouth and I say mean things. Things I don't intend to say and things I damn sure don't mean. It's been botherin' me ever sense that night of the fight. Ya know, when we all got throwed in jail. I had some time to sober up and think about all that shit I said." He fidgeted with his keys for a moment. "Fact is sugar, I was pissed, and mostly . . . I . . . I was jealous. That's the first time I've ever seen ya with anybody that ya seemed serious about. It's real obvious how he feels about you. It just hit me in the gut to think of ya with anybody else. I just wanted to hurt ya. That's why I said all those things. It was mean and not a truth in it." I sensed that he was bein' more honest than I'd ever known him to be.

"Walt, ya don't have to . . ."

"No. Let me finish. I need to tell ya this. Ya was a wonderful wife. I couldn't a asked for nobody better . . . ever. And as for that other stuff . . . about ya gettin' . . . ya know . . . I'd talked to a doctor back then and he told me . . . most likely . . . well . . . it could be all me . . . 'cause of my drinkin' and all. I'm so sorry sugar, that I embarrassed ya and hurt ya like that. I really am . . . I . . . I just had to tell ya that . . . I'm sorry."

With that he turned and quickly walked away. I was shocked speechless as I just stood there watchin' him walk down the street.

"Lilah, what was that all about?" Floy asked as she came back from the Jeep.

"I'm not sure. But I think . . . that . . . Walt just apologized to me." We both stood there for a minute.

"Lilah?"

"Yes?"

"I think hell just froze over and I expect to see pigs fly over any minute. Let's get in the car before we get caught in the shit storm!" We both burst into laughter and climbed in the Jeep and headed home.

It was an uncomfortable, lonely night and I still felt eerily alone. I'd never felt that house so empty, almost as if the vey life had gone right out of it.

The thought crossed my mind once to call Dee, but I felt like I needed to learn to stand on my own two feet again.

The dogs began to bark in the early mornin' hours, but I turned over and tried to go back to sleep. I told myself that dogs bark, and that no one had been back around since Chad had set those hunters straight. Eventually, I fell asleep and I woke up when that rooster began his mornin' serenade to the sun. I vowed that one day, I would put his carcass in a pot with noodles.

It was easy to keep myself busy wrappin' gifts and puttin' 'em under the tree. I'd mailed off Mama and Daddy's and the kids' gifts earlier and I'd bought groceries when Floy and I'd gone shoppin'.

As far as I could tell, I was ready for Christmas. All I needed was my man to make it complete.

Floy called that evenin' to tell me that she'd broke the news to Toby. She said that he'd just sat there at first and stared at her in disbelief. Then he jumped up and let out a rebel yell that would have scared the socks off General Lee. While I was talkin' to her, he took the phone.

"Can you believe it, Lilah, I'm gonna be a daddy! Hell, I didn't know I had it in me. No! Now that didn't come out right. I mean . . . I just didn't really think it could happen. A baby!" He was beside himself, and to think that Floy had been worried and afraid that he'd be mad. I congratulated him and told him how excited I was.

"Now," he said. "We both talked about it and decided that we want . . . no we'd be honored if you and Chad would be our baby's god parents. What do ya think?"

"I would be thrilled and honored." I told him. "I'm sure that Chad will too, but you'll have to ask him. Okay?"

"You bet. I will as soon as he gets back. Thanks, Lilah," he said just before he hung up.

I spent the night wonderin' if the baby would be a little girl or a little boy, and if it would look more like Toby or like Floy? There were lots of different themes we could use for the nursery, and names . . . we'd have to pick a suitable name for him . . . or her. I took a deep breath, I had to get a grip. It wasn't my baby. This was their baby and I needed to try not to horn in. It'd be hard.

Maybe I could horn in . . . just a little.

It was nice layin' on the couch with the TV on. There was nothin' really to watch 'cause we could still only get two channels. The volume was turned almost off and the stereo was playin' our favorite blues tape nice and low. Relaxin' in front of the fire, I tried not to think about the night before Chad had left, but it was impossible to not recall his muscular, naked body as he was stretched out on the floor.

When the clock chimed, I was startled back to reality and decided it was time to go up stairs and get ready for bed. Everything was locked up and I turned the lights out. About halfway up the stairs, I thought I heard the kitchen door knob turn. I stopped and listened for probably four or five minutes, then decided it was my imagination and went on up.

I crawled in bed, but I knew I wouldn't be able to sleep. I dug out a book I'd been wantin' to read and propped Chad's pillow up behind me and settled in.

An hour passed and I heard the dogs goin' crazy outside. I finally got up and went to the window. This time they was barkin' toward the back of the house. Carefully I loaded my shotgun and sat it by my bed and went back to readin'. I made myself a mental note to ask Chad to put a flood light in the back when he got home. Eventually my eyes grew heavy and I drifted off to sleep.

Chad had been gone for three days, but it seemed like months, and I could hardly wait for him to come back in that door. There was nothin' I wanted more than for everything to be perfect on our first Christmas.

We was invited to Toby and Floy's for Christmas dinner, but Christmas Eve was left in my capable hands. It was only five more days until Christmas Eve and I knew that also meant that Chad would be home .

I sat down and wrapped my last two presents except the one Chad was goin' to pick up for me. I'd gotten Floy a gorgeous 24-karat gold friendship bracelet with her name on the top and 'love lilah' on the back. I wrapped it in shiny red paper and put a big silver bow on the top. For Chad's presents, I'd got him some jeans to replace the ones I'd cut off of him, a couple of new shirts, two new jazz eight track tapes, and a pair of white doe skin gloves. His main present was gonna be delivered tomorrow and I was so excited I could hardly wait. Back in November, I'd called Mr. Colonel and asked him to pick me out a young Arabian stud for Chad. One he could break and train himself and I told him it had to be beautiful and flawless. He was due to arrive tomorrow. Before he left, I'd wondered how I was goin' to hide it from him, but this trip had worked out perfect. It'd cost me a small fortune, but I could hardly wait to see the look in Chad's eyes. I wrote a short note and put it in a card. In it I told him that he was the best part of everything good that'd ever found a place in my heart. He brought me fresh air in the summer and warmth in the winter and I wanted him to know that I'd love him even to my last breath. I wanted to give him somethin' special, and he'd find it in the stall between Patton and Pride. I called him Prince, 'cause he was fit for a King and that's what he, Chad, was . . . the king of my heart and I signed it with eternal love and went to bed so excited I could hardly sleep.

Sometime in the night I remembered hearin' them dogs barkin' again and turnin' over and puttin' Chad's pillow over my head. His scent still lingered on the pillow case. I held it close and felt safe as I drifted into dreamland where my Chad was there beside me, breathin' softly in my ear. His fingers were lightly carressin' my face and I felt his lips so lightly on mine. I called out his name.

I must've been sound asleep, 'cause the next thing I realized was an abrupt yank of my hair and then a sudden blow to my face. Then, nothin' but darkness. Later, when I tried to open my eyes, I heard myself moan. Somethin' struck me again and all I could see was glitterin' lights among the sinkin' blackness.

I began to try to open my eyes again. I could tell they were swollen and the throbbin' in my head was horrible. For a confused moment, I thought that I might've actually gone blind.

As I felt myself bein' dragged along the ground, I tried to reason what was happenin'. I began to realize that I was in a bag or wrapped in some kind of blanket. Someone was pullin' one end of it as I bumped roughly over what felt like steps and rocks. When I tried to part the bag or blanket, I became aware that my hands were tied behind me. It felt like my feet were too! I started to cry out, but there was somethin' across my mouth as well. There was a sudden jolt as my head struck somethin'. Then there was the metallic taste of blood, then a deep, cavern of black enfolded me once again.

The next time I tried to open my eyes, I heard no movement. Everything was pitch black and totally silent.

Yes! It was all comin' back to me! At last . . . it was all beginnin' to make some kind of disoriented sense. I was rememberin'.

I listened closely, but there was no sound. Only the actual sound of my heart thumpin' in my achin' head. It was an eerie, unreal silence. For a brief moment the thought crossed my mind that perhaps I really was dead. Just maybe that was what it felt like to be dead . . . complete darkness . . . not able to move at all, and total silence. Quietly I prayed that if it was true and I was dead, that this part wouldn't last much longer. I laid there and waited for the white light that I'd always heard about. The one that my Nanny would be waitin' in to help me to cross over.

It was hard to tell how long I laid there. Maybe it was only minutes, but it felt like hours. Perhaps it'd been hours, there was no way to tell. I must've drifted in and out of consciousness, 'cause I woke up again. Nothin' had changed. Still no sound and no light. Not even a little. Even through the horrific pain inside my head, I started to realize that somethin' was coverin' it. Whatever it was touched my cheek, my eyelashes, and my lips. It was like a sheet or maybe . . . a pillowcase. When I took a deep breath, the scent of Chad became painfully noticeable. I knew then that I'd been right about it most likely bein' a pillowcase. I was sure it was the one off Chad's pillow, but that didn't explain how it got over my head or why.

This had to be just one of those horrific nightmares that ya have sometimes. The ones ya can't seem to get out of 'til ya are almost hysterical, and I wasn't far from that point. While I laid there, I tried to will myself to wake up. It seemed that the harder I tried to wake up, the more aware I became that I wasn't asleep.

Why would someone do this? Who would be so angry at me? Maybe they had me mixed up with someone else. I tried to think clearly. My first thought was Walter. He was a mean cuss but I just couldn't believe he'd do somethin' like this. Next I had to consider Danna. She was really furious when Chad had chosen me instead of her. A woman could be pretty ruthless when it come to her pride. I didn't know her, but she seemed to have a natural mean streak. What about Scott? He'd be the most likely, I rationalized. But the last we'd heard, he was spotted in Florida and they was searchin' for him down there. They'd been sure that they'd catch up with him in a matter of days.

I lay there in the dark and tried to think. Who? Why? And how was I gonna get out of here, and where in the hell was here?

After what seemed like an eternity, I don't know how, but I must've drifted off to sleep again. I don't know how long I slept, but I knew right away that the reason I woke up again was 'cause I needed to use the bathroom. I moaned out loud. There was a slight echo and nothing more. I tried to scream but there was nothin' . . . nothin' but a deep growl that came up from my chest and throat. Maybe I could try to roll over. It wasn't hard to do, but I couldn't tell where I was rollin' to. I didn't get very far before I came to another realization. Somethin' cold and hard was fastened around my bad ankle. Since my feet was tied together, I couldn't use my other foot to explore the object. I yanked both feet and I heard the distinct rattle of chains. I yanked as hard as I could, but I found that the chain was fastened to somethin' that seemed quite sturdy.

Time continued to drag on.

I couldn't get my hands moved enough to even tell what they was tied with.

Maybe I'd left one explanation unexplored. Those men that Chad was arguin' with the night before he left seemed really upset with him and he was definitely upset with them. I'd heard stories about drug people and how they turn on each other.

No! Chad wouldn't lie like that and he surely wouldn't leave me there to face 'em alone. Perhaps they wanted him to do somethin' he didn't want to do and they was holdin' me hostage! Maybe they wanted to hurt him and they was usin' me for bait. I didn't know how I was gonna warn him. I didn't even know who'd taken me or how. The only thing I knew for sure, was that if someone didn't let me go to the bathroom, I couldn't hold it much longer.

I thought once or twice that I'd heard a scurry of some sort. Maybe a mouse? Then, even that stopped.

After what seemed like forever, I heard someone at a good distance. It was hard to hear and I couldn't be sure, but they sounded very upset. Then, I heard scratchin' and maybe growlin' My heart stopped and I froze where I lay. I knew that sound and it wasn't a someone, it was a somethin'! That was a bear!

I was sure of it. It sounded a good way off but I sure didn't want it to hear me. I tried to breathe shallow and not move a muscle.

Where in the hell could I be?

After a couple of minutes I heard the bear growl again. This time it sounded a lot further away. I knew that was a good thing, but what if it come back? There was no way to defend myself. Fear come upon me and I could feel myself leap to the edge of uncontrolled panic. My heart was poundin' and I broke into a suffocatin' sweat. It was important that I get hold of myself. I had to think clearly and find a way out of this mess.

I finally reached the point where I had to make a decision. There was so much pain from not bein' able to go to the bathroom that I knew it was only a matter of time before I'd have to go right where I lay. It was a sickenin' thought but I was runnin' out of time to think about it. I waited and listened and watched for some sort of light, but there was nothin'. Time continued to stand still.

Why hadn't somebody come to at least tell me why? Panic started to creep back in and I felt the tears of frustration and pain begin to run down my face. I couldn't wait no longer. In complete humiliation I finally relaxed and let the urine flow freely. The relief was so great that I soon forgot the embarrassment of it. It was startin' to look like I may have been left there to die anyway. The thought of lyin' there without food or water and eventually dyin' was horrifyin'.

What would Chad think when he come home and found that I was gone?

What would Floy and Toby think? They were about to have their first baby.

I thought about Mama and Daddy and the kids. They'd never know what happened to me . . . or why.

I didn't know where I was, but I was sure it wasn't someplace anybody would think to look. It was obvious that I wasn't meant to be found. My mind was reelin' with thoughts and fears and my imagination was goin' crazy with visons of death and how it would end. I thought about Chad. I knew without a doubt that he loved me very much. Would he think that I'd found some one else and had left with 'em? My mind wandered to our little tree and what all that tree had caused. I thought about my favorite ornament, the red one that Floy and Toby'd given us to mark our first Christmas together.

Our first Christmas!

I didn't even know what day it was.

I was very thirsty and I was hungry, too. The cold of the ground had seeped into my very bones and I needed warmth.

Was it possible that Chad was already home.

Was it Christmas Eve, or Christmas Day?

How long had I been there? I'd started to cry again. I must've cried myself to sleep 'cause sometime later I woke up. There's nothin' in the world like total nothingness to help you search your heart and soul for everything you've ever said or done to those who matter most. My one comfort was the scent of Chad on that pillowcase. It kept remindin' me that I had a reason to get through this and that I had to find a way out. I moved around a little, just to find another rough spot on the floor. It felt like the ground 'cause I could feel some of the rocks beneath me. I searched for the biggest, roughest, and hopefully the sharpest rock and started workin' my hands up and down on it hopin' it would cut the bindin' apart. If I could get 'em free, then the rest would be easy.

It was hard to know how long I worked at it, but after a while I could feel the rock through the coverin'. I knew that I'd at least been able to cut a hole in it. It inspired me to the point that I was workin' so feverishly that I soon felt the warmth of my own blood runnin' into my palms. My hands were so numb that I couldn't tell if I was cuttin' the bindin' or just my hands. It was about that time that I heard a noise and froze for fear it was the bear comin' back. I prayed he wouldn't pick up the scent of my blood or my urine. I could hear it gettin' closer and I lay motionless. It was a strange noise. It sounded different from before and I thought for a moment that I heard footsteps and draggin'. It came closer. It could be the bear with a fresh kill. I wasn't even thinkin' that bears was hybernatin' and not out huntin'.

Suddenly it sounded right beside me. Without warnin', a sharp jolt to my side brought terrible pain and I moaned out loud before I thought.

I heard an evil laugh and my blood seemed to stop flowin' right there in my veins! There was all kinds of movement and noises. At one point I heard chains and I thought that they was gonna put more chains on me. Sometimes I'd hear a grunt or mutterin' and I had to wonder what these people was doin'. What'd they have planned for me?

It became very quiet again. I lay there listenin'. Somehow I sensed that I wasn't alone. Maybe they was still there and was playin' games with me. I didn't move and I pretended to be unconscious.

"Just as well, you'll need all your strength tomorrow, your *highness*!" Someone mumbled in a weird little high-pitched voice. I tried to place it, but nothin' come to mind. What did that voice mean when it said I would need all my strength? I became more than afraid. I was terrified! It wasn't long before I smelled smoke. It frightened me at first until I realized it was just a campfire. The warmth of it was nice and I had to admit it felt good. Although I was horribly thirsty, I was too afraid to be hungry. After awhile, I heard someone snore. It was definitely a man. I didn't hear anyone else breathin', so I felt reassured that maybe there was only one other person.

Given the opportunity, I was sure that I could find a way to get the best of him, whoever he was, as long as he was the only one.

Chapter 12

I was awakened when the blanket was ripped off of me and I felt the damp chill in the air. Rough hands pulled me up into a sittin' position. In a swift movement, the pillowcase was ripped off my head. I blinked, but I couldn't focus on anything. I blinked a few more times and began to focus slightly. It was very dim light from the coals of the fire. At first I couldn't see anyone, until a shadow stepped out from behind what looked like a large table. I tried to focus on him, but I could barely see as my swollen eyes tried to adjust to the light. He walked closer and stood in front of me. He was dressed all in black and had a black hood over his face with two eye holes and a mouth hole cut in it. There was nothin' that seemed the least bit familiar about him. I decided that it definitely had to have somethin' to do with Chads' business. Maybe they were tryin' to get ransom for me. I knew that I'd never seen this creap before in my life.

"Mornin', *highness*!" he sounded like a freak.

He walked closer then stopped. Suddenly, he started to squeal like some kind of demented animal.

"You peed! Damn you! You peed yourself! God how disgusting!!!!" He ran to another area and came back with a bucket.

"Get up! Get up!" He squealed.

I couldn't!

Was he so stupid that he couldn't see that I was tied up. I just sat there and looked at him. He finally came close enough to cut the duct tape that held my feet together and yanked me to a stumblin' upright positon and motioned for me to turn around. I was afraid to turn my back on him but I didn't have no choice.

He cut the tape on my hands and I turned back around. I reached for the tape on my mouth and he slapped me before I knew what'd happened.

"No!!" he screamed. I heard it echo.

I glanced around now that my eyes had adjusted better. We were in a damn cave. For a minute I wondered if it could possibly be the cave that Chad and I had found. But who was this, and how would he know about it?

In that weird little voice he instructed.

"Get outa them pissy clothes." I stood there without movin'.

"Now!" He squealed.

He moved a little closer with the knife. I started to unbutton my gown, but I guess I wasn't movin' fast enough. Before I could blink, he stepped forward and swiftly cut the little straps that held it up. It fell to the ground and I tried to cover my breasts with my hands.

"Get the rest off!" he yelled as he indicated with the knife.

I dropped my underwear to the ground and tried to cover myself with only my hands.

With another quick move he threw a bucket of ice cold water on me. It took my breath as I fell against the cave wall. In seconds he'd gone over to the other side and was back with another bucket and drenched me again. Shakin' uncontrollably, I reached for the tape across my mouth again. There were things I wanted to know! That time he hit my hand and jaw with the bucket.

"No! No! No!" He repeated in that psycho little voice.

He motioned with the knife as he told me to get further from him. This time I did as I was told.

He stepped over and removed a cover from what appeared to be a stack of boxes, but when the cloth was gone I could see a low built table.

"Get up there!"

I shook my head no and was asked again by a fist. Dazed and groggy, I sat on the table. He pushed me backward and grabbed my left wrist. He still had the knife, so there really wasn't anything that I could do to stop him. I had a horrible, sick feelin' in the pit of my stomach, that quickly became a deep dread like nothin' I'd ever felt before. From somewhere he produced a strap and buckled my wrist above my head. Although I tried to keep away from him, my ankle was still shackeled to the cave wall. He grabbed my free wrist and buckeled it above my head, too. He grabbed my one free foot and strapped it to the table leavin' me shamelessly spread-eagled and totally at the mercy of this madman. He came close now as he took the tip of the knife and ran it down my cheek and across my throat. He ran it down my chest and around each nipple. I felt his hand slide up the inside of my thigh.

I shuddered with a mixture of disgust and nausea.

"No!" he squealed. He sounded like the pigs when Nanny had to butcher 'em. That alone made my blood chill!

"He said don't touch it ! Don't touch it! He'll be here and take care of that. No! . . . No! No!"

It seemed as if he was scoldin' hisself ! I watched as he stomped around talkin' and cussin' whoever it was that'd told him "no"!

Scared, I watched in confusion. Never had I seen anybody, not even Walt, so out of control.

He finally went over and curled up in a corner and leaned against the wall. I don't know how long I lay there, naked and cold, and ever so thirsty.

He hadn't even built the fire up. It became quite dark as the coals burned down to almost nothin'. I didn't think there was any way I could rest, but somehow, hours later I must have dozed 'cause when I woke up there was a small fire burnin' and a paper cup of water on the table beside me. One hand had been freed and there was two slices of bread left within reach.

I looked around for the man in black, but I didn't hear or see anyone. It was eerily quiet as I reached up and pulled the tape from my mouth. I started to scream for help, but then I remembered the bear and I decided against it. As terrified as I was, I was desperate enough to take the bread and eat it and drink the water. That little bit of nourishment made me feel slightly better.

I lay there and prayed that the bear would not come back. Maybe that was their whole plan . . . to let it eat me alive!

Desperately I tried to free my other hand, but I knew it was hopeless and I felt more humiliated and helpless by the minute. Screamin' wasn't an option 'cause I knew that if this was the cave that Chad and I'd found, there was nobody for probably thirty miles in any direction.

I looked around to see if there was anything that I could use in the event that I should get loose. There was several chains on the wall and what I assumed was another table that was covered. I took my loose hand and went to work on the strapped hand again. The leather band was so tight that it cut into my wrist. As my fingers worked around it, I located a small lock and I knew without a doubt that it was no use to try. I frantically tried to reach my ankle, but that was equally impossible.

There was some bobby-pins in my hair and I searched until I found one and tried to straighten it with my one hand. I reached as far as I could and did my best to work the bobby-pin into the lock.

I was sure that I'd heard a noise. Maybe it was the bear or it could be that . . . that . . . whatever it was, comin' back. Quickly I replaced the pin in my hair and pretended that I was asleep.

"You awake girlie?" he asked in that unbelievably high-pitched voice. "He's coming! He's coming to see you." he said as he danced around like some kind of derranged idiot. The really scary part was . . . I was sure that was exactly what he was.

He took a dark cloth and covered me. I was thankful for that and I told him so. It didn't seem to matter to him or that I'd removed the tape from my mouth.

Who was "he", and what might happen when "he" got there?

I was more and more sure that these were the two men that had argued with Chad.

The weirdo took off toward what I assumed was the entrance.

Shortly afterward, I could hear the footsteps of someone comin' back to where I was. He too was dressed all in black and had a hood over his head. Instead of scurryin' around like a rodent, the way the other one did, he strutted like he thought he was some kinda royalty or somethin'. I watched through barely-opened eyes. When he got almost to the table, I closed them completely.

He gently took my free hand, raised it above my head, and strapped it down. Then he reached in his pocket and took out a tiny flashlight. He looked in my ears and then in my nose. By this time I couldn't pretend any longer and I opened my mouth to speak but he put his hand over it. At that time he caught my chin and forced it down and opened my mouth. He checked my teeth and my throat. Then checked under my arms and moved down to my breasts.

He examined 'em like a doctor would 've. I cringed with each touch of his cold hand. It was really strange when he took out a stethoscope and actually listened to my heart, my stomach, and lungs. When he moved to my ankle, the one that'd been broken, he checked it very carefully. The same when he checked my leg that'd been broken. How would he know that I'd been hurt? The only one who could've told him was Chad. I became very nervous when he moved up to the private areas. He draped the cloth like a doctor would and pulled a stool up close. There was a large, bright flashlight came on where he was seated. I was beginnin' to shake with fear and apprehension. I ventured to open my mouth and asked.

"Who are you? What do you want from me?" The answer I got was a sharp slap on my outer thigh and a "Shhhh". I didn't say anything for a while and just waited in dreaded anticipation.

I couldn't tell just what he was doin' . . . however I did hear some very strange, suspicious sounds. I didn't dare allow my mind wander there. All I felt was just the warmth of that light and nothin' more. He never touched me.

After several minutes he stood up and paced back and forth. He rubbed his chin as if in deep thought and paced again.

"Why are you doin' this? I don't understand!"

It was as if he didn't even hear me.

"You have the wrong person!" I screamed.

Before I could think, he slapped me across the face several times so hard that my ears began to ring. He took another piece of tape and slapped it across my mouth. He leaned forward so that his nose was almost touchin' mine.

"Shut up." He whispered in a evil, deep, growlin' voice.

Goin' to the opposite side of the cave, he sat down on a stool and leaned back against the wall. I could feel him glarin' at me through the very small holes in the hood. It frightened me to think what horrible things he might be thinkin' or plannin'. At least the one I'd started to think of as the rat-man had huddled up and gone to sleep. This one just sat and stared. It was so quiet that I could actually hear him breathin'.

From time to time I heard the scurry of mice or bugs and once I thought I heard footsteps. After what seemed like forever, he got to his feet and strutted into the dark. I assumed that he was leavin' . . . until I heard voices.

"Can I have it . . . can I . . . huh?" It was the rat-man's high-pitched squealin' voice.

"No!" boomed a loud, deep, angry voice.

I could hear whispers and mumblin'. I wasn't sure but what there might even be a third person. I waited for the rat-man to come back in, but after hours of listenin', waitin' and wonderin' what would happen next, I either passed out or dozed again.

I felt somewhat rested but no less terrified when I woke up. I reasoned that I must have slept a long time. The stress and tension had exhausted me to the point that I didn't even recall dreamin'. My head seemed a little clearer and I felt like I could think a little better. It was very cold and damp, but I thought there had to be a few coals left from the fire 'cause I could still see a faint glow on the ceilin'.

It was so hard to judge time. There was no outside light to be able to separate day from night. I didn't even know what day it was or how long I'd been there. I was hungry and thirsty and I desperately needed to go to the bathroom, again. Time passed slowly and still no one came. The table was hard and my arms had long since gone numb. The coals must've started to die out 'cause the cave was becomin' darker and colder. I felt somethin' scurry beside my leg and I froze as I wondered what it was.

Had one of 'em slipped in and I didn't hear 'em? It moved again and came toward my upper body. I could tell that it was somethin' furry and very quick. I began to twist my body as best I could and I must 've knocked it off the table 'cause I didn't feel it again . . . but I was sure that it was a mouse or a rat. Usually I wasn't afraid of 'em, but then I wasn't usually at their mercy either. There was no way to protect myself from 'em and I felt a new kind of panic begin. Finally, I heard distinct footsteps and saw a light. I dared to hope against hope that maybe it was someone to rescue me. Maybe it would be Chad or Toby or anybody!

"Hey girlie!" My heart sank when I realized it was that little rat-man.

He almost put me in mind of the hunchback from the old scary movies. This time he brought a lantern.

"Bet ya missed me, huh girlie?"

He had a bag that appeared to be full and I prayed it was food and maybe some clothes. I was half right. He had food. He placed a thrown together sandwich and a cup of water on the table and unlocked my one arm. I went straight for the tape and then the water.

". . . bathroom . . . please?" I begged.

He looked at me as if he was shocked.

"Please!"

He ran out of the cave and I was concerned that I'd gotten no response. It wasn't long before he was back. He brought a bucket and sat it down a ways from the foot of the table. With a key he stepped toward me, pulled out his knife, and held it in one hand while the other opened the lock and freed my foot. He moved back and came near my face.

In that same eery little voice he squealed "Don't try it . . . I'll cut you up in tiny pieces, girlie!" I nodded and he unlocked my other hand.

He motioned for me to go to the bucket, so I carefully slid off the table and made my way to the bucket. The relief was wonderful. Just bein' able to move about, although I was still chained to the wall, was even more so. When I'd finished, he motioned for me to get back on the table.

"Can I just sit and eat my food?" He jumped toward me with the knife. I thought for sure he was gonna cut me.

"Down!" he squealed. I laid back down and he fastened one hand and then my free foot

It wasn't easy, but I managed to eat the sandwich and finish the water. I laid back down to wait for whatever sadistic surprises they had in store for me. The cave had an old, moldy, wet smell as if it'd been closed up for many years.

I wondered who'd brought all the barrels and boxes in, but I figgered it'd probably been those two.

My mind went to Chad and what he must be thinkin'. He was home by now and I imagined him walkin' in the door and expectin' me to be there to greet him. He'd said that he wanted me to be butt naked and on the couch when he came back. Well, I was butt naked, but where I was just wasn't exactly clear to me. I allowed myself to remember the taste of his kisses and the smell of his warm flesh when we made love. His arms were so strong and yet he was so gentle. I thought about the day he was out back choppin' the wood and how wonderful he'd looked in the early mornin' sun. The way the muscles had rippled in his tanned back and the way that I felt just watchin' him. Even then, lyin' on that table, I felt that familiar ache deep inside and the yearnin' that only Chad had brought into my life. With my eyes closed, I could picture the way his clear blue eyes sparkled when he looked at me and that crooked little grin that was so uniquely his. I pictured the way he bit his bottom lip and winked at me when he was secretly remindin' me of one of our intimate moments. Without realizin' it, the tears were flowin' down my face and I was unable to control 'em.

"Stop it!" a gravelly whisper ordered as I was slapped back into reality.

I hadn't heard anyone come in, but I couldn't seem to stop the tears. There was another, harsh slap and I lost my temper.

"You son-of-a-bitch, when Chad finds you, he'll kill you! He'll kill you!!" I screamed and then broke into more sobs. Before I knew what'd happened, a fist belted me across the jaw, then another, and maybe another as I sank into the bitter-sweet darkness of unconsciousness.

With little desire to do so, I regained consciousness. I'd been flipped face down on the table. He was sittin' on a barrel starin' at me again. I raised my head and he moved closer, grabbed my hair, and forced my head against the cold table, then leaned near and bellowed into my ear. "CHAD! CHAD!" Then in that low gravelly whisper.

"He can't help you! He can't even help himself!"

"Go to hell, you bastard!!" I screamed in his face.

He stepped back and whispered so softly, "You'll learn how to speak to me and that you only speak when told to do so."

He walked to the other table and uncovered it. I couldn't see everythin', but I saw enough to tell that it held things I didn't understand . . . nor did I want to. He picked up somethin' and came toward me.

"I think your mama didn't teach you very good manners. Too many kids . . . one slipped through the cracks. But I'm here to save you . . . it'll hurt me worse than you!" he whispered in that rough gravelly voice and then went into an insane cackle.

He had what appeared to be a leather strap and before I could think, it came down with unbelievable force across the back of my thighs. I screamed in pain, but before I could catch my breath he lashed me again and yet again, but this time he moved up to my hips. It was hard to know how many times he struck me. I was hysterical with pain. After a bit, the pain turned into numbness and I just laid there as my body jumped involuntarily with each blow. Finally he stopped and leaned close.

"Chad didn't help you this time and he won't help you next time! Forget about him!" he whispered hoarsely.

He left and I cried 'til I just didn't have anymore tears left. I lay there sobbin' as the feelin' began to return to my lower half. From my knees to my waist it felt like I was on fire. It was pure agony. I began to feel the warmth of my blood as it oozed down the sides of my legs. In my heart of hearts, I knew that I couldn't take much more. Yet I felt the torture had only begun. I tried to remove myself from the reality of what was happenin', but I was forced back into full alertness when a bucket of ice cold water was thrown over me. As I caught my breath, another one followed. Someone began dryin' me off, surprisingly, very gently, with a towel. I didn't know who it was, so I just laid there and said nothin'. Carefull hands gently put a salve of some kind on my legs and hips that stung at first, but I felt better after a while. I listened as whoever it was walked out toward the cave entrance. It had to be the rat-man 'cause the other one was too cruel to be so gentle. My face and neck, as well as my lower half, was in such horrific pain that I just prayed for unconsciousness. I lay there in misery and waited!

Time continued to drag by, but it didn't matter so much no more. It was certain and sure that I was goin' to die right there in that time-forgotten cave at the hands of those mad-men. Somehow, I thought, it wouldn't be quite so bad if I at least knew who they were or why I'd been taken. I only knew that I was runnin' low on courage and I was sure that I'd never see Chad again.

What seemed like hours later, the vicious one returned.

He bent down and whispered in my face "Did ya learn anything? Do I get some respect now?"

His breath smelled of cigarettes and unbrushed teeth. It made me nauseated. I turned my face away from him and tried to ignore him. That was when he grabbed me by the hair again and roughly turned my face back toward him. He pinned my head down with his palm and leaned very close. His lips crushed against mine and his tongue searched for the back of my throat, but it was when he licked from my lips up my jaw to my temple, I cringed with pure disgust. He made my skin crawl. I felt sure I was goin' to vomit.

I tried again to turn my head but he slammed it against the table.

"Don't turn from me again!" He ordered in a sharp, growlin' whisper.

"I need . . . water," I told him in a ragged voice. He moved away and I thought that he was goin' to actually get me a drink. Instead he turned and walked out of the cave. I heard mumblin' off in the distance. I figgered he was talkin' to the rat-man. It wasn't but a few minutes and the little rat came scurryin' in to mercifully give me food and water. When I was finished, he motioned to the bucket.

"Yes." I mumbled.

He had the knife in his hand while he unlocked me and let me go to the toilet. I was in pain from head to toe . Movement was slow and I was very wobbly on my feet. I finished and he motioned for me to stand by the wall. I wasn't sure what he was goin' to do but I knew it couldn't be anythin' that I'd like.

He grabbed one arm and pulled it straight out and locked it in a cuff. I wanted to kick him, hit him, anything to keep him from chainin' me to that damn wall, but I was terrified of that knife. In a matter of seconds he had me chained securely. I leaned back against the wall. It was cold and rough against my skin. My arms were too high for me to be able to sit down and my legs already felt weak.

"Now what?" I dared to ask.

The rat-man seemed excited about whatever was goin' on.

"You'll see, girlie! Just wait . . . big surprise!" he squeeled. "Big . . . big surprise."

He turned and scurried out the same way he'd come in. I was thankful that at least he'd taken the time to build the fire up seein' as how I didn't even have a blanket around me. The fire felt good and I'd begun to stop shiverin'. It seemed like I stood up against that wall and in the shadows for an eternity. I wondered if they intended to leave me there . . . I didn't know if it was day or night. How in the name of heaven was I gonna manage to stand for an unknown length of time?

I looked around the place and told myself that I needed to make mental notes of where things were and what might be available to use if I should get the chance to escape. There was a large number of crates or boxes stacked along the back of the cave and some chairs and a table or two. I was certain that if I could get to that one table where he'd taken the strap from, I could find somethin' of use. There was a supply of firewood against one wall and I thought if I could just get hold of one of those logs, I could do some damage to one or both of 'em.

My legs began to tremble and I felt very weak. Maybe I could just hang from my arms for a moment and let my legs rest. My legs felt better, but my injured shoulder soon began to throb and my still-tender wrist was shootin' pains up to my elbow. Finally, I had no choice but to stand up and give 'em a break. I tried bracin' my legs and proppin' my butt against the wall, but it was much too tender.

At last I heard footsteps comin' through the cave. I prayed that they'd at least get me a chair. It was the vicious one and he seemed agitated. He turned up the lantern and walked over to where I stood. My skin crawled as he slowly looked me up and down. He came so close that I could feel his clothes brush against my flesh. I was as close to that wall as I could get and still he came closer. Raisin' his hand, I braced for another blow. Instead he grasped my chin and lifted my face as he crushed my lips with his nasty mouth. I jerked away.

The taste of him was vile and I was repulsed.

He banged my head against the wall "I told you to never turn away from me again! You be nice...I'll be nice!" His gravelly whisper was in my ear.

"I'd rather kiss a snake than you! Leave . . . me . . . alone! When Chad finds you . . . you'll die a slow painful death!" I hissed and spat into his face.

Without warnin', he grabbed my throat and began to squeeze.

"Chad! I 'm sick of hearing about him! I'll show you how tough your precious Chad is!" He growled.

He held my throat like that until I began to feel myself goin' limp. Just as suddenly he let me go and grabbed my hair. He pulled until I was on my tiptoes. I hadn't a doubt that my hair was bound to peel loose from my head. I felt his other hand roughly grasp my breast and squeeze so hard I could hardly endure it. He took the nipple between his thumb and finger and twisted until I was sure that it was bleedin'.

Finally I cried out "No! Please don't . . . you're hurtin' me!"

I felt his hand release and go roughly between my legs. He pushed his fingers deep inside and jammed as hard as he could. I screamed in pain.

"Ya like that, huh . . . I've wondered what you would feel like! Is that how he touches you? Does he make you scream like that? " His whisper became husky as if he was really enjoyin' it.

He quickly backed away and stepped into the dark. I heard him unzip his pants and I could tell that he was relievin' himself.

It was then that I threw up.

He left me there, shackeled to the wall. I don't know how long he'd been gone when the little rat come back. He let my hands go, threw me a blanket and left. I knew that it was only gonna get worse from here on out. I felt even sicker at the thought of what was to come. Even if I should get away, Chad would never get over all the vile things that'd already been done to me. He'd never feel the same again.

I painfully wrapped up in the blanket and cried myself to sleep.

Chapter 13

I woke up when I heard a big commotion farther toward the entrance of the cave. I was terrified to think it, but it sounded like the bear had come back to check out his den and was very angry that the scent of people was still so strong. He growled and bellowed for several minutes before he went on his way. I assumed that he had left since I didn't hear any more out of him. A long time passed before I dozed off again, only to be awakened by the sound of someone stumblin' or draggin' somethin' through the cave. I seriously prayed it wasn't the bear bringin' his kill to the back.

It wasn't, it was the viscious one, again. He was draggin' a large bag that seemed to be full of somethin'.

"Get up!" He ordered in his rough whisper. I sat up as he came over to me and grabbed my arm to pull me up to the shackle.

"Brought you a little somethin' I'm sure you might enjoy." He turned up the lantern light and I rubbed my eyes with my grungy free hand. He walked over to the bag and kicked it and I heard a slight noise. He bent down and grabbed the foot of it and looked up at me and laughed an evil, hideous, little laugh that made the hair on the back of my neck stand up. With that, he dumped out the contents of the bag.

At first it was impossible to tell what it was. He'd rolled it into the dark and I thought from the looks of it that it could possibly be a small animal that he'd killed. Maybe bait to lure the big bear to the back of the cave. I strained my eyes to see into the dark and I suddenly felt my heart stop and my mind rebel. I refused to accept what I saw. It was impossible! This was without a doubt the worst possible nightmare I could ever have.

The bastard stepped closer, still laughin' under his breath, took the toe of his boot and rolled the limp form over. As one arm uncoiled and its head flopped back, I saw a thatch of silver blonde hair and a blood spattered face. It was the face of the man who owned my very heart and soul.

Thoughts raced through my mind and my heart pounded in my ears. I stood in shocked disbelief as my stomach began to churn.

Who were these men and how did they manage to capture him? I'd seen him in action and I didn't see how any one could've taken him. Why? Why were they doing this to us? Dear God in heaven, please don't let him be dead! I just couldn't bear it! I didn't want to live without him. This was my silent prayer and I strained my eyes to see if I could tell if he was breathin'. It was too dark where he was lyin' and all I could see was his hair and part of his face.

"What do you think? Is this your stud that's going to kill me?" the Vicious One whispered in that evil voice. He grabbed Chad's arm and roughly dragged him to the opposite wall. There he chained his feet and threw a blanket over his body and left the cave.

"Chad?" I whispered to him.

He didn't move and I wasn't so sure that he was really breathin'. I told myself that he had to be alive or they wouldn't have chained him.

"Chad?" I called a little louder.

Nothin'.

I heard the scurryin' of the rat man. He came straight to me.

"Shut up!" He squealed. Then he took out that ominous-lookin' knife and put it to my face.

"Bathroom?"

I nodded and he unlocked my hand and one foot so I could reach the bucket easily. After I had finished, I stood up and started back to my spot but made a sudden lunge for Chad. I managed to touch his bloody face and it was enough to tell that he was still warm. At least I knew he wasn't dead. The rat-man grabbed me by the hair and yanked me back across to the other side. When he threw me against the wall, it knocked the breath out of me, and by the time I could breathe normally, he'd shackled my feet again. I could tell he was furious with me.

"I only wanted to be sure he was still alive." I tried to explain.

He answered me with a slap across the face. I fell back against the wall and sat in silence.

Sometime later he brought me food and water and waited until I was done. He still looked very upset with me as he took more chains and chained my hands to the wall. This time they were long enough to allow me to sit down. He came back and brought tape and taped my mouth. I looked at him with questionin' eyes. Why were they tapin' my mouth again? It was obvious that there was no body around to help us. He turned the lantern down low and built the fire back up. As he started toward the cave entrance he stopped and put a black hood over my head. I couldn't see anything at all and soon I heard him leave. I wanted to call out to Chad, but all I could do was make gruntin' noises and flail my feet around. I listened closely and I was pretty sure that I could hear Chad breathin'. I heard a soft moan from across the floor and my hopes soared as I waited, hopin' that he would wake up, but I didn't hear anything else. Hours passed with only the sound of occasional scurryin' little feet. I waited and prayed and listened until I drifted off to sleep again.

I dreamed about the day we went for the walk to find the Christmas tree. The snow was so beautiful. It was like a paintin' in a book. The dream was so real that I thought I could hear the crunch of the snow beneath my feet. Chad was there and we were laughin' as we threw snowballs at each other. He took me in his arms and kissed me so sweetly and as I leaned back to look into those incredible blue eyes, my heart became even more filled with love. When he ever so gently handed me a bundle, I uncovered it and found our baby, a beautiful baby boy with eyes the exact color of Chad's. I began to cry. I cried tears of joy. Tears of complete happiness.

He dropped his head and began to moan and I couldn't reach him. The harder I tried, the further he was away from me. I begged him to wait, but he only shook his head, sighed, and faded further away.

I suddenly awakened, but I couldn't see anything. I quietly listened for a few minutes. There was nothin' but the occasional drip of water and the crackle of the fire. I tried to call out but it was only a muffled moan. At last I heard a slight movement and a moan of pain. I tried again to make enough noise that he'd know that I was there. Finally, I heard him mumble somethin', and then the slight rattle of the chains . . . the chains rattled again.

"Wh . . . What the . . . hell?" I heard his beautiful voice at last and I knew that he would find us a way out.

I made another noise and shuffled around.

"Hello?" He waited for a reply. "I . . . I . . . uh . . . who are you? Where are we?"

All I could manage was more moanin' and gruntin'.

" Are . . . are you okay?"

I shook my head no. The scurry of feet told me that the rat-man was comin'. I sat there quietly and waited. I could hear Chad move and I assumed he'd sat up.

"Who the hell are you? And why am I here?" I heard him ask.

"Shhhh . . . he don't like it when we talk." The squealy voice answered him.

I heard him come near to me, "Mornin' girlie! Did ya see? I told ya . . . big surprise!!" He seemed unusually excited and it brought a deep dread into my heart. I could hear him buildin' up the fire again. The rat-man was so happy he was hummin' to hisself. I could only imagine what horrible torture they'd dreamed up while they was away. I needed to see Chad and talk to him. It went without sayin' that he had no idea that it was me.

It was only a short time and the rat-man scurried down the way and out of the cave.

"Hey! Hey you!" I heard Chad call after him. "Son-of-a-bitch . . . hey, are ya alright? Why won't ya answer me?"

I shook my head in every direction hopin' that he'd understand that I couldn't answer him.

"Why do they have that hood over your head? I . . . uh . . . I . . . Seems everybody has a damn hood!" he mumbled angrily.

He jerked at the chains several more times then finally gave up and was quiet. It was a long time later that I heard the other one march in. It'd taken a while, but I'd finally learned to tell the footsteps apart. It always gave me a sick feelin' in the pit of my stomach when I heard him comin'. He was a dangerous man and I feared he would thoroughly enjoy killin' us both!

I heard Chad. "That's just great, another damn hooded figure! Who the hell are you?"

There was a thud and a groan. I knew that he'd hit or kicked Chad and I hadn't even been able to warn him.

"You! Don't talk unless you're told," he growled in that deep, husky whisper.

"What . . . what do ya want with me? Who are you?" Chad was persistant.

There was another blow, then another and another. My heart was breakin'! I tried to scream but nothin' came out other than noises. I thrashed about as hard as I could hopin' that it would distract him from Chad. I could hear chains rattle and a lot of gruntin' and movin'. There was an unexpected silence and then footsteps came my way. The hood was jerked off my head and the bastard was right in my face. The stench of him turned my stomach!

"Now, you can watch as Mr. Wonderful learns the same tough lessons that you had to learn." he whispered in a low menacin' growl.

I wasn't sure what he meant until he stood up and moved. Chad's barely conscious body was hangin' from the wall by chains above his head. He was facin' the wall and his shirt was ripped half way off of him. Vicious had gone over to the table and picked up the strap he'd beaten me with before. It was no secret to me what was comin', and I went crazy tryin' to scream. Desperately I tried to warn Chad, but he wasn't able to hear or understand. I watched as he leaned into Chad's ear and whispered, "When I say don't talk . . . don't talk. You only do what I say . . . when I say."

He stepped back and struck him across the back with all the power he had. I saw Chad convulse in agony. He drew back and struck him again. I could see the marks begin to welt and turn red with tricklin' blood. He struck him again, and again, and yet again.

I tried with everythin' in me to scream! It had been easier to take the beatin' myself than to watch what I knew Chad was sufferin' through.

Finally I closed my eyes unable to watch any longer. There were many more lashes, but never so much as another groan from Chad. I prayed that he'd been unconscious . I vowed then that if I ever got loose, I'd kill that bastard. Whoever, whatever he was, he was a walkin' dead man.

After what seemed like an eternity, it ended. I listened as the bastard left and I dared to open my eyes. He'd left Chad hangin' helplessly on the wall, but as desperately as I wanted to help him, all I could do was watch and sob. Obviously he had passed out and I thanked God. His beautiful head hung down and his muscular arms strained from the weight of his limp beaten body as rivulets of blood ran down his back. It was by far a worse beatin' than I had suffered.

I heard the rat-man shuffle back in. He stopped and looked at Chad from every angle. He turned and looked at me and pointed to Chad like he wanted to be sure that I'd seen what'd happened. He unchained Chad's hands and let his limp body fall to the rough cave floor as if he was just a hangin' piece of meat.

He came toward me, "Eat?"

I shook my head no.

I had no appetite after what'd just happened.

"Bathroom?" He asked in that high-pitched voice.

I couldn't deny that I did need to use the toilet.

He took the chains off so that I could go to the bucket. When I was done I reached for the tape over my mouth. He raised the knife to my throat and I put my hand down. I managed to cover myself with the blanket before he chained my hands back to the wall and left. I sat for what must have been hours and watched for any movement from Chad. Emotionally and physically exhausted, I managed to lay down for awhile. The pain I felt in my heart was worse than anything the Vicious one could ever do to me

I closed my eyes and tried to rest, but the fear and pain I felt just wouldn't allow me to relax, not even for a moment. It was then that I heard a faint movement from Chad. He was facin' the wall but I could see him move his head. After some time, he finally tried to sit up but fell back. I wanted desperately to go to him and help him. I wanted to make it all better, hold him and tend to his wounds, but I was helpless to do anything except sit and watch.

I sat up and tried again, to no avail, to call out to him. He rolled to his back where, fortunately, a blanket was beneath him. He lay there for a good while as if he were tryin' to get his strength back. Finally, he raised himself up on his elbow and attempted to sit up again. As he started to lean against the wall, the surge of pain forced him to lay back down on his side. His eyes were closed, but I could see that one was horribly swollen and black. There was bruises and blood all over his face and upper body. His beautiful lips were swollen and blood trickled down the corner of his mouth. The depth of the anger inside me was somethin' I'd never felt before. I'd never wanted to hurt anybody the way I wanted to hurt that animal. My Nanny once told me that no one could be cruel and vicious without it comin' back to 'em tenfold. I prayed that I'd live to witness that occasion.

Eventually Chad raised himself up on his elbow again, wiped the hair out of his eyes, and looked up. His eyes locked with mine and my tears began to flow again. Workin' to focus in the dim light, I finally saw recognition register in his face. He sat up and leaned toward me as if he couldn't believe what he was seein'. I felt myself flush as I became aware of what I must look like. I hadn't had a bath in days, maybe weeks. My hair was a nasty, tangled mess, and I was totally naked. For all I knew I probably didn't look any better than he did.

"L . . . L . . . Lilah?" he whispered in total shock.

All I could do was nod frantically. I broke into deep sobs and I could hardly get my breath.

"It's . . . I . . . uh . . . is it really you?" his voice broke.

I nodded again.

He sat there in stunned silence. "How? Who . . . "

I heard the rat-man comin' back and I turned my head and looked Chad's way and shook my head as if to say *Hush . . . he's comin'*!

Chad must've got the point 'cause he went silent and laid back down. When the rat-man came in, he stopped and looked at Chad again and cackled evily under his breath.

He shuffled over to me "Eat?"

I cautiously nodded my head.

He brought me water and bread with cheese. As he unlocked my hands, I reached for the tape then stopped and looked to him to see if it was okay.

"You're learnin' girlie!" he squealed in delight and nodded "okay."

Carefully, I removed the tape. It felt like it'd taken half my skin with it. I was careful not to draw attention to Chad, so I never even glanced his way.

I ate, drank, and quietly laid back down hopin' that he would forget about the tape. He shuffled about in the back of the cave. I carefully pulled the blanket up over me and closed my eyes. I opened them once and cautiously glanced across the way at Chad. He was starin' straight at me. We silently shared a moment of understandin', then we closed our eyes and pretended to be asleep.

It was a while before the rat-man built the fire up and shuffled his way outside. I couldn't believe that he'd actually forgotten the tape and to lock my hands back.

"Lilah?" I heard Chad's anxious whisper.

"Shhhh . . . " I cautioned.

I didn't trust the rat-man. He could be waitin' just around the bend. It was a long time before I felt safe enough and cleared my throat.

"Chad?" I whispered. "Are ya alright?"

"I will be, baby. What the hell's goin' on?"

"I . . . I . . . I don't know. I think that they're two of those guys ya argued with just before ya left."

"No! Those guys are very good friends of mine. I trust 'em with my very life. Besides, I saw 'em on my trip." he sounded confused.

"Then who are they and what do they want?" I was even more confused than I had been.

I'd thought that I had it figured out, but this information put me back to square one. There was a long, silent pause.

"Chad?"

"Yeah?"

"I was sure it was someone ya knew."

There was another long silent pause.

"How long have ya been here, honey?" He asked me in a voice filled with disbelief.

"Since the night before Christmas Eve. What day is it now?"

"The last day I remember was the eighth of January."

I sat in stunned silence.

I 'd missed Christmas and New Years.

"We've been searchin' . . . " he started and then hushed when we heard footsteps headed our way.

We both laid back down and pretended sleep.

I could tell by the sound of his steps that it was the vicious one, again. He walked past us and went to the back. I could hear him mumblin' to hisself and then he come back and stood beside where I lay. He pushed me with his boot toe.

"Get up bitch!" he ordered in that gruff whisper.

I didn't dare look toward Chad as I sat up and pulled the blanket around my nude body.

"Stand up and turn around!" he yelled in his deep gravelly voice.

"I can't, my feet are chained." I told him softly so that I wouldn't set his temper off again.

He grabbed my arm and yanked me up and fastened one arm over my head and to the side. Then he unchained one foot and turned me around and chained the other arm. My blanket had fallen to the ground and I heard Chad catch his breath as he realized that I was totally naked. I knew he could see the bruises on my legs and hips and I hoped he wouldn't say anything that would turn that animal on him again. While I stood there facin' the wall and wonderin' what he'd do now, I began to shiver, partly from the cold damp air, but mostly from pure fear. I felt his gross hands in my hair and then on my shoulders.

"So beautiful . . . " he growled.

Then his hands moved around to my breasts as he began to squeeze and rub them.

"Please. Don't." I begged him.

"Hush shsh . . . sh . . . " he growled in that deep whispery voice that I so loathed.

His hands moved down to my waist and then to my hips. I tried to move away, but he moved up close behind me and pushed his pelvis firmly against me. I squirmed to move away.

"I knew you would like it." He whispered as he began to breathe harder.

I could feel his arousal and it made me sick to think that Chad was lyin' there havin' to watch my total humiliation. It was when he ran his hand up my inner thigh again and began to touch and caress me that I lost any shred of control. With one leg unchained, I managed to turn enough to catch him directly in the groin with the fullest force of my knee. What he might do to me later on didn't matter, the satisfaction of bein' able to give him as much pain as I possibly could was worth anything. He stumbled back and fell to the floor in agony and grabbed his crotch. He rolled around for a few minutes and I thought for sure that he was gonna throw up, but he laid there breathin' hard and not movin'. Although I knew he wasn't, I prayed that he was dead. I glanced over my shoulder at Chad who was up in a crouched position even with his legs still chained. There was a look on his face that I'd never seen. He was beyond furious and I knew that he was goin' to get us in worse trouble than I'd already gotten into. I shook my head at him but he was in a blind fury. Vicious crawled to the back of the cave and curled up in a fetal position and lay still. I dared to whisper to Chad.

"Please don't, Chad. He might kill you! Please, I beg of you . . . just lay back down and be quiet. Please!" I could barely see him out of the corner of my eye. I had no idea if he listened to me or if he could even hear me. When vicious was able to get up, he carefully made his way to where I stood, but well out of reach of my knee.

"You . . . You'll pay . . . dearly!" he whispered and staggered from the cave.

Several hours later, I was really startin' to feel the strain of my predicament. My shoulder was achin', my hands were numb and my arms were hurtin' so bad I wanted to cry. I felt around with my free foot until I found a rock. It wasn't very big but it was enough that when I stood on it I could get a little relief for my arms. I wondered if Chad had gone to sleep since I hadn't heard a word out of him in what I thought was several hours.

"Chad?"

"Yeah?" he answered after a very long pause.

"I . . . I just wanted to know if you're okay?"

There was a longer pause and I thought he wasn't goin' to answer me. Then finally.

"What the hell do ya think? I . . . uh . . . I want to know what they been doin' to ya all this time? Tell me everything!" he demanded. I took a deep breath and managed to choke the ugly story out.

"Chad . . . I just don't understand . . . why are they doin' this to us?" I began to cry again.

I didn't think that I had any tears left in my body, but from somewhere deep inside they came and flowed like tiny rivers from my swollen eyes.

"We'll get out of this honey . . . somehow . . . I will get ya out of here. Then I'm gonna kill those son-of-a-bitches!"

I don't know how long I hung there. We had no water, no food, and the fire went out. It became very cold. I began to wonder if they'd decided to let us die right where we were. It'd become pitch black and I couldn't see nothin' at all. Chad and I whispered back and forth from time to time, but thirst had begun to take its toll on our voices. I was sure that I heard the bear again and I cautioned Chad to lay still and pretend to be dead if it should come back into the cave.

"Bear? What bear? What the hell . . ."

It growled and made a lot of noise and then it seemed to leave or at least, I thought it did. Not too long after that we heard sounds of someone or somethin' comin' toward us.

"If it's the bear . . . no matter what it does . . . don't move and don't make a sound." I cautioned.

We could smell it long before it came into our area. It was gruntin' and huffin' and makin' all kinds of angry sounds. With the fire out I supposed it was no longer afraid to come back into the cave. It stopped and I was sure it had caught our scent. It let out a huge roar, but we both stayed very still. I heard it knock over some things and then my heart froze in mid-beat. The bear's cold nose touched my thigh, then it sniffed at my private areas and licked at my hip. I tried to prepare myself for it to take a huge bite out of me as I hung there and didn't move. There was a sudden horrific pain as it's claws slashed across my back and I bit my lips as hard as I could to keep from makin' a sound. The blow had knocked me against the wall so hard that I wasn't sure I'd ever breathe again. Nanny had always told me that if a bear should ever get ya cornered that ya should roll up in a ball and play dead. It'd be the only thing that could save ya. I hung there like a limp rag doll as I felt the distinct warmth of blood runnin' down my side and hip. I could hear it knockin' Chad around to see if he was alive. When it was satisfied that nothin' back there was worth foolin' with,

I heard him lumberin' toward the entrance as he grunted and growled. I hung there shakin' as tears of pain streamed down my face.

"Honey? . . . are ya ok, baby girl?" I heard Chad whisper.

I managed to get enough strength together to answer.

"I think . . . so . . . but I . . ."

"Ya what? Talk to me Chica . . . but what?"

"I . . . I think I'm bleedin'".

"What did it do? Did it bite ya?"

"No, it . . . it hit me with . . . its claws".

He started cursin' and yankin' on the chains and I knew that he was at his wits end. I must've been bleedin' pretty good 'cause I began to feel weak and whether from pain or exhaustion, I suppose I passed out. When I came to, I heard the rat-man squeal like he'd been stuck with somethin'. Chad told me later that he'd come in and lit the fire and the lantern. When he came to see about us and saw what'd happened to me, he screamed like an hysterical woman and ran out. It was only a few minutes and he was back and unlocked my chains and picked me up and laid me on the table. After he flipped me over and chained my hands and feet, he ran out of the cave still squealin'. That must've been when I started to wake up because I heard vicious comin'. I braced myself for whatever he brought with him. He didn't seem surprised about anything as he took his time examinin' my wounds.

"Tetanus shot up to date?" he growled.

I pretended to still be unconscious so I wouldn't have to talk to him. He fumbled around and then a sharp pain in my hip told me he'd decided to update my vaccination. He growled to himself and I could hear him doin' somethin' in the back. After a few minutes, I learned what he was doin' as he started to give me injections in many different parts of my back and side. I bit my lip as hard as I could to keep from screamin', and eventually, I couldn't feel any of it and relaxed a little as I felt him cleanin' out the wounds. He seemed very precise as if he knew exactly what he was doin'. He began to put in stitches and I could feel the push of the needle and the slide of the thread as he quickly tugged, tied, and clipped it, and moved on to the next one. This wasn't his first time to suture wounds. I didn't understand why he wanted to torture me one moment and gently tend to my wounds the next. He finished with the bandages and I felt another stick. I assumed that he'd given me an antibiotic of some type. Suprisingly he put a blanket over me and left me to rest. It felt wonderful to lie down, even on a hard table and I had little to no pain for the first time in days.

I listened to see if there was any sound from vicious. It was hard to know if he'd left the cave or if he was just sittin' there lookin' at me again. I was terrified to open my eyes so I held my breath and strained my ears to hear anything at all. Nothin'. After a few more minutes of silence I moved slightly and moaned as if I were just comin' to. Barely openin' one eye, I peeked carefully around. I saw no one.

"Honey?" I heard Chad call softly.

"Hmm?"

"He's gone . . . are ya alright, baby?"

I raised my head and looked his way.

"Yes, I think I'm better. When did he leave?"

"Right after he stitched ya up. That bear must 've done a number on ya. He put a lot of stitches in ya. I have to tell ya this . . . he knew what he was doin'!"

"I know . . . I was awake the whole time."

We heard footsteps and fell silent. It was the rat-man! He scurried in and took water and food to Chad. I was glad, he'd had nothin' since they'd brought him there. Thinkin' he was asleep, he unlocked one of his hands. I was terrified that Chad would try somethin' and bring down the rath of the devil on hisself but he quietly laid there. The rat-man took some more blankets and made a bed where I'd been chained. I was willin' to bet that he was goin' to carry me back over and lay me down. That meant that he'd have to unchain me from the table and that would be my best opportunity to gain control. It'd be my first time to be completely unchained. My mind was reelin' as I tried to plan the best way to overpower him. The best I could hope for was to get to that rock that I'd been standin' on and bash his head with it. He went to the back area, turned his back, and was doin' somethin' I couldn't see. He turned around with another needle in his hand. I guessed it was another antibiotic . . . I guessed wrong. The needle went in and I went out. It must've been a very strong sedative 'cause I never knew when he picked me up off the table. I woke up much later and found myself neatly chained by my feet and one hand and tucked nicely in a cozy warm bed while the fire was blazin' and keepin' us warm and toasty. I must've moaned a little when I tried to stretch.

"Lilah?" I heard a soft whisper.

I opened my eyes and was immediately met with a vivid blue gaze from across the floor.

"Yeah." I answered with a yawn.

"How do ya feel, honey?"

"I don't know yet. How are you?"

"Aw . . . I . . . I'm just great. I'm chained up in a cave in God only knows where. My girl's chained and naked on the other side of the damn place and some bastard keeps puttin' his damn hands all over her. Hell . . . I'm just great!" I stared in disbelief.

It was the first time he'd ever called me his girl.

"How'd they take ya, baby?" he asked me after a long pause.

"I don't really know. I finished wrappin' my gifts and locked up and turned out the lights and went to bed. I remember hearin' the dogs bark . . . then I recall somebody pullin' my hair and . . . then . . . yeah. Somebody hit me in the jaw. The next thing I knew I was here. When did ya get home and how in hell did they get you?" He sat there for a little while then he sat back as best he could and told me about his homecomin'.

"I came straight home from the airport. It was earlier than I'd expected and I thought ya would be really excited that I got home sooner than ya thought I would. I drove up and somethin' just didn't seem right. I couldn't quite put my finger on it, but I knew somethin' was wrong. First of all . . . the dogs didn't come out to greet me. I can go into Mason for somethin' and be back in a hour and they act like I was gone for months. They were no where in sight." He sat there a minute and looked at the ground. "When I got out of the truck, I heard 'em barkin' in the barn so I went down to see if you were there. I wanted to surprise ya. When I went in, the dogs was locked in one of the stalls. I couldn't figure out why, but when I opened it they flew out of there and straight to a dry water bucket. I ran 'em some water and they drank 'til I thought they'd drown. The horses didn't look like they'd been fed, so I fed and watered 'em.

That was when I found a new addition to the family. I didn't figure that out 'til later. Anyhow . . . I went into the house. It was cold, dark and I noticed that I didn't have to use my key to get in. I stood in the livin' room for awhile . . . everything in me screamed that somethin' just wasn't right! I called out to ya 'cause I was sure ya was home. Your car was still parked outside. I went all over the downstairs and then I went upstairs. When I went in our bedroom . . . the only thing that seemed wrong was that our blanket was gone and for some reason one of the pillows didn't have a case on it. Everything else looked normal. I went out back and called out the back door but there was nothin'. Then I sat down for a minute and tried to think it out. Floy and Toby would know where ya were. That was one thing I thought I knew for sure. I picked up the phone and called 'em but Floy said she'd been callin' ya all day and ya hadn't called her back." He stopped for a minute.

"Chad, I'm so sorry. I can only imagine how ya felt." I could tell that he'd probably been through hell.

"I searched everywhere . . . even up to the little cabin, but there was no sign of ya. The dogs were goin' nuts, but I guess the snow had killed the scent. They'd head one way and then the other. They was as confused as I was, so I called the Sheriff. Stan came out and they did a search and asked me to sleep downstairs and not to touch nothin'. They were callin' it a crime scene, honey. I . . . uh . . . I thought I'd lose my mind. By daylight there was cops everywhere, even though it was Christmas Day. Floy and Toby came out and a bunch of people I didn't even know. They organized some search parties and spent days lookin' everywhere. I went and stayed with Toby 'cause I just couldn't stay in that house and not know what'd happened. One mornin', when I got up to head for the search, it was still dark and I started to get in the truck . . . that's the last thing I remember until I came to in this mad house.

He looked toward the fire and took a deep breath. "Ya know, they even questioned me. Like maybe I'd done somethin' to ya and . . . but Stan and Toby stood by me. Stan just told me not to leave town. Now they're gonna think I skipped out and they'll feel for sure that I knew somethin' I wouldn't tell 'em." He looked straight at me with a deep sadness in his eyes.

"I guess they just don't know how much I . . . I . . . uh . . . I love ya. I could never, ever hurt you. I'm a damn sorry excuse for a protector. This is killin' me baby. I'm powerless to do anything for ya! I'm so sorry."

"Don't!" I told him. "Maybe this is exactly what they wanted. Maybe I'm just bait to catch ya." He sat there a moment in deep thought.

"I don't think so. I . . . I . . . I think there's a lot more to it. I been watchin' 'em. I do know one thing for sure . . . we gotta find a way outta here. Besides them . . . there's that damn bear to deal with!"

"Chad?" I whispered. "I have bobby pins in my hair."

He looked at me for a moment in complete confusion.

"Bobby . . . okay . . . how many?"

"Two that I'm sure of."

"Can you toss one over here?" he asked me with a note of uncertainty in his voice.

"I can try . . . but I'm right-handed and they have my right hand chained . . . besides . . . the free hand is on the side the bear attacked and the feelin' is really startin' to come back. It hurts like hell."

"Okay . . . okay . . . don't even try honey. It'll be too painful for ya right now. We'll wait until the right time. Why don't ya lay back down and try to get some rest." He paused a moment "Do ya have any idea how much I just want to hold ya? How much I need to hold ya? I thought I'd lost ya forever!"

"Yes." I answered. "I know exactly how ya feel. I need so badly to be held by you."

I laid down and a second later he did too. We laid there watchin' each other in the firelight until we fell asleep.

Chapter 14

I awoke to the sounds of someone comin' through the cave. I wasn't awake enough to tell which one it was. As he suddenly snapped handcuffs on both of Chad's wrists and yanked him to the chain on the wall, I could see that it was the vicious one. He'd waited 'til Chad was asleep and then snuck up on him and cuffed his hands. He knew that if Chad had gotten hold of him he would've killed him with his bare hands. Chad was tryin' to wake up as he was bein' secured. In confusion, he looked over at me through the silver blonde hair that covered his eyes. Vicious turned toward me. I had no doubt that he was still very angry with me for what I'd done the day before.

The thought of apologizin' crossed my mind, but I decided that I would not say I was sorry for doin' somethin' that I wasn't sorry for. The only thing that I was sorry about was that it didn't kill him. I struggled to sit up in my bed and wait for whatever he had planned for the day.

"Get the hell up!" he growled in an angry whisper. I barely managed to stand while still holdin' my blanket. I was so sore and stiff from my injuries that it took some doin' for me to find my way to my feet. From nowhere his fist caught me in the jaw and I staggered and fell backwards.

"You son-of-a-bitch! Touch her again and I'll kill ya, So help me God!!!" Chad growled in a deep furious voice.

Unexpectedly, there was another blow to the other side of my face and I saw stars. That was followed by a solid backhanded slap right in my mouth. My lip split and I could taste the saltiness of my own blood. I tried to be strong and not show any weakness, but my legs grew weak and just as I was sinkin' to the ground, I heard Chad yell.

"Cowardly son-of-a-bitches beat women! Why don't ya undo me and fight like a real man? Maybe you're too scared a gettin' a little of your own blood on ya!"

Vicious turned abruptly, took two steps and buried his fist in Chad's mid section. That was the last thing I heard or saw before I sank into total darkness.

I was awakened again with a cold bucket of water thrown into my face. When I opened the one eye that I could see out of, the rat-man was bringin' another bucket of water. I gasped as he threw it on my naked body. I looked around and saw Chad hangin' from the chains. His head was down and he was limp.

"Get up!" He squealed to me as he threw me a towel. "He wants you clean, girlie."

Then he snickered and left.

I dried off as much as I could with my cold shakin' hands. My blanket was wet, so I wrapped the damp towel around me and quietly called to Chad.

"Chad? . . . sweetheart? Can ya hear me ?" He moved a little and finally managed to raise his head. I couldn't believe what I saw. Both of his beautiful eyes were blackened and his brow was bleedin'. His lip had been busted again and his face was black and blue.

"Oh God! I just can't take any more of this!" I cried as I accepted the reality that if we didn't get outta there they would kill us both and I knew I couldn't stand to watch him beat Chad to death before my eyes. My external wounds were nothin' compared to the ache that continued to grow in my heart.

"Shhhhh . . . Don't . . . please don't cry like that . . . I . . . I . . . I always look . . . like . . . like this . . . when I wake up." he tried to smile, but winced with pain instead.

"You forget that I've woke up with you more than once . . . and . . . you've never looked like that. It's no time to joke darlin'. They're gonna kill us."

"Honey," His southern drawl was thick "We're all gonna die sometime . . . we're dyin' from the minute we're born, some of us just do it faster than others." He semi-chuckled.

"Chad . . . stop it!"

We heard the footsteps that were so pronounced that I knew who was comin'. I knew in the very depths of my soul that I was at a breakin' point and I wasn't sure but what Chad was already there.

"I told you that you'd pay, didn't I?' Vicious hissed.

"Leave her the hell alone!" Chad warned through gritted teeth.

Vicious turned to look at him. "You're just asking for another ass whooping aren't you boy!"

I was startled!

Somethin' in that voice was familiar. I couldn't quite place it . . . but there was somethin' there. Chad's face turned a dark red beneath the blood and bruises. The muscles in his jaw clenched and pulsated. Chad stared straight at that monster and told him. "You touch her again and I swear on my Mama's grave . . . this planet ain't big enough for you to get away from me!" His voice was low and filled with venom.

"And how are you going to manage that, pretty boy? I'd say you've been neutralized!" Vicious cackled.

Chad yanked violently at the chains again and again.

"I'm not warnin' ya . . . I'm promisin' ya!" Chad gruffly whispered.

"Well, BOY, I intend on doing a lot more than touch her! Now let your imagination chew on that for a while!"

He turned and strutted toward the cave entrance. As he walked by Chad, he saluted smartly and left.

"Chad...stop tauntin' him! He's gonna hurt ya again!"

"That ain't nothin', honey, there's nothin' they can do to me that can hurt me half as bad as it hurts ever time he touches you!" He said as he bit his bottom lip and winced in pain.

It wasn't long before the rat-man came through offerin' food and water and a bathroom break. I was allowed to sit on the bucket but I figgered rat-man was afraid of Chad so he only got one hand freed and the bucket set near him. Rat-man had that knife right to his throat to make sure that he didn't try nothin'.

When he left, he left my hands free, but only one of Chad's.

"Lilah? Did ya notice anything odd . . . about . . . those two?" He whispered in a pain-wracked voice.

"Like what?" I managed to ask.

"I been thinkin' . . . about this for awhile. I think . . . there's only one of 'em! They're never . . . in here together. I been watchin' . . . they wear the same identical clothes and shoes. Ever time. I think this person has a . . . what do they call it . . . like a split personality or somthin'. He's a Dr. Jekyl and Mr. Hyde!"

"Chad . . . a minute ago I almost felt like I recognized that voice. Ya made him so mad that he forgot to whisper. I've heard that voice before."

He looked at me in surprise.

"Who did ya think it was?"

I shook my head in confusion. "I just can't place it yet."

We fell quiet for awhile and I tried to concentrate on what it was that sounded so familiar. I couldn't even remember if it was what he'd said or if it was just the way he said it. Maybe . . . it could have been someone from the bar. There was somethin' hauntin' me that I just couldn't put my finger on. I have always hated that feelin'. It's like when somebody asks ya who played in a certain movie and ya know the name is just on the back of your tongue but ya can't seem to cough it up. I knew that . . . in time . . . I'd remember who that voice belonged to.

I looked over at Chad. He stood leaned against the wall, lookin' down at the floor and chewin' on the knuckle of his free hand. I didn't say anything 'cause I hoped he was hatchin' a plan to get us out of there.

Later, vicious came struttin' back in and I found myself watchin' his every move and mannerism. The closer attention I paid, the more I began to notice. Chad was right. Both of 'em had to be the same man. They just seemed to change personalities, voices, and the manner in which they walked. I couldn't believe that after all this time I'd never noticed it.

Okay, so we had figgered out one mystery. Now . . . who in the hell is he and why is he doin' this? Vicious paced back and forth between us for a while. Chad sat there and refused to acknowledge him. I pretended not to look but I watched him out of the corner of my eye. As I turned to massage my ankles where the chains had begun to rub them raw, I was grabbed from behind.

Vicious quickly fastened handcuffs on me and pushed me down on the damp blanket. He pulled my hands above my head and fastened 'em with the chain.

I was really gettin' tired of bein' chained . . . and man-handled . . . and naked!

He stood up . . . and took my towel. I laid there exposed to his leacherous, filthy stare. He knelt down and leaned over and tried to kiss me. I turned my head away. He grabbed my hair.

"What did I teach you about turning away from me?" he whispered gruffly "Don't piss me off, beautiful!"

There it was again. Somethin' about his voice! Why couldn't I place it?

He roughly grabbed my chin and turned my face to his. He ground his lips to mine in a frantic show of superiority, but as soon as I could, I jerked my face away. My reward was another smack across the face.

"You bastard!" I heard Chad growl. " Leave her the hell alone!" He began frantically yankin' on the chains.

Vicious laughed out loud. "Go ahead, cuss and yell all you want to. You threaten and act like the macho man . . . but you aren't goning stop what's about to happen . . . right here in front of your very eyes!!"

My heart began to pound in fear. I didn't know if he was gonna kill, rape, or just beat me again!

When his hands began, once again, to explore my body, I knew where it was headed and I couldn't stand the thought of it happenin' right there for Chad to have to witness.

"Please, don't," I begged. Why do ya want somebody who doesn't want nothin' to do with you. How could ya enjoy that?"

"Oh, but beautiful, I will enjoy it. You have no idea how much I will enjoy it. I've dreamed of it! I've fantasized about it. I have lived for it! I will not wait any longer. I could tell by the way you kissed me that you want it as bad as I do."

My blood ran cold with true terror and my heart forgot how to beat. This was worse than any nightmare I could ever have imagined. I turned my head to look at Chad. He was still yankin' on the chains that held him captive to the wall.

Vicious leaned over me and began to kiss me and like some kind of animal, he began to lick my entire body.

"You like that a lot don't you?"

"No! I don't! I hate it!" I screamed. "Stop it!"

He was kissin' me up the inside of my legs. I tried to roll him away with my body.

"Yeah baby, that's it . . . go ahead and squirm. I know you love it!" He panted.

He began bitin' me all over and I started to feel sick, very sick .

It was then that he stood up and took his pants down.

"Please don't do this, SCOTT! I'm beggin' ya, don't do this!"

I heard Chad gasp in shock and it was then that I heard him go crazy. "Nooo!" he screamed like a mad man.

Scott knelt between my legs and forced my knees apart. I was totally helpless . . . again!

"Scott? If you ever felt anything for me . . . please don't!" I begged.

"Oh, Beautiful girl! It's because of what I feel for you that I must. I've been waiting so long. So damn Long!" he squealed. " I have to have you. You know you want it too!! Say it! Say it! Tell me you want me inside you. Tell me you want us to be one!! Tell me!!"

It was the breakin' point for me. I couldn't endure anymore. Not now! Not with Chad to witness this disgusting act. I felt like a trapped animal that had no hope left .

"NOOOOOO!!!!! Chad!!! Help me! Don't let him do this! Oh God . . . please Chad!!!!"

Scott dropped on top of me and viciously plunged deep inside. I could feel my flesh tear as he slowly began to move in and out and then to a more frantic rhythm. He grunted and squealed like the deranged maniac that he was.

I laid there and cried helplessly.

Somewhere I could hear Chad yellin' and jerkin' on those chains. Those damn chains. I wanted to wrap them around Scott's neck and strangle him. I wanted to kill the son-of-a-bitch!

As he continued the brutal act of rape . . . I felt that he was killin' us. Killin' me and Chad. What we had. What we were. It would . . . could never be the same. Scott had taken what was ours and murdered it!

I went numb and removed myself from what was happenin'. I didn't feel, I didn't think, and I couldn't cry anymore.

At some point Scott jumped up in frustration and ran into the dark. I knew what he was doin'. He couldn't complete what he'd started, so once again, he had to finish it himself. It didn't matter. I didn't care. The damage was done . . . feelin' cheap and dirty and defiled, I only wanted to die. It would be so much easier if I could simply hold my breath and cease to be.

From somewhere in the distance I heard Chad make one final massive jerk on the chain and as it slipped from the bolt in the wall, he fell face first to the floor of the cave. He stretched himself as far as he could but he still couldn't reach me.

"Honey!" he cried, "baby, look at me . . . Lilah? "

I could hear him as if he were somewhere far, far away, but I couldn't bring my self to look at him. I knew I would see nothin' but pure disgust in his eyes. I felt like I was somewhere above and beyond it all. Nothin' mattered. Nothin'! There was an eternity, it seemed, of silence . . . just sweet silence!

From out of the darkness there came a horrific growl and a roar that vibrated through the cave! A horrific, agonized, ear shatterin', scream split the air. There was another scream mixed with growls and more growls and roars and an endless, eternal screamin'.

Then it stopped. As suddenly as it'd started it was done. I think I remember some hideous sounds that eventually ended too.

I heard Chad from somewhere far away tellin' me to play dead.

"Don't move, baby! Just play dead. It's the bear . . . he's back!"

Why would I have to play, I couldn't have moved if I wanted to. I was sick, exhausted and paralyzed with endless fear. It was only a few moments and I could hear the stumblin' gait of the angry violent creature.

He went to Chad first and sniffed and pushed his limp body around and then he came to me. I laid there on my back as he sniffed my entire body and nudged me with his massive nose. Then he looked square into my eyes and I unblinkingly stared right back.

I broke the cardinal rule that you never stare an animal in the eye. It's like a challenge. I saw the fresh blood and flesh that covered his face and neck! The sight burned into my mind, but I was powerless to react. He must've saw the complete surrender there because he snorted a couple of times and went toward the entrance. I laid there and watched the dim light of the lantern as it cast shadows across the ceilin. It was like watchin' ancient warriors move about in some mystical dance of surrender or death. Again that black empty hole of silence seemed to grow with every passin' moment.

Chad was waitin' to make sure the bear was actually gone. Myself, I felt like I was a prisoner in my own skin. There didn't seem to be any way out . . . it held me as immobile as the very chains that chewed into my wrists and ankles.

"Lilah? Baby girl? Talk to me . . . please! Ya gotta be strong. I know that ya are. I've seen it! We gotta get outa here before that beast comes back. Just look at me baby!" he pleaded.

Humiliated, I turned my head the other way.

"Honey? I need you. I can't do this by myself."

I laid there and prayed to die. I couldn't tell if I went to sleep or just allowed myself to drift into oblivion. What did it really matter?

Then Scott was there and he kept hittin' me and touchin' me and finally he was on top of me. I suddenly came up screamin' and I just couldn't stop.

"Lilah!!" Chad yelled at me.

It startled me and I turned to look over at him.

"Darlin', ya gotta be quiet or that damn bear is gonna hear ya! Honey, listen to me . . . I need one of them bobby pins."

I laid back and continued lookin' at him and thinkin' that we'd had the most precious moments between us, destroyed. I opened my mouth to speak but nothin' would come out. His beautiful blue eyes were pleadin' with me and the whole time my heart was just broken. It was impossible to tolerate his gaze any longer and I closed my eyes. It was quiet for a very long time. It felt like that wonderful quiet after a bad storm.

From somewhere far away, I thought that I heard someone hummin' and it was nice . . . it was soothin', even to my broken spirit. I could hear soft sweet words that reached and touched my heart and soul. I looked back at Chad and he'd raised himself up on his crossed forearms. He was singin' softly to me and I saw a tear trickle down his cheek. I didn't know the song but the words were so beautiful . . . "Please don't stop . . . lovin' me. You were born to be . . . loved by me."

He had the most incredible voice I'd ever heard. He sang like an angel and I knew that only God could give him that incredible gift!

His eyes pleaded with me and begged me to love him and be strong enough to help him.

Somewhere deep inside he touched a part of me that only he could reach. Forever seemed to pass before I could manage to open my mouth.

"Chad?" I finally managed to whisper when he finished the song. "I could never . . . stop . . . lovin' you. When I take my last breath in . . . this world . . . it's your face, your eyes, your lips that'll be my final memories and God willin' . . . I'll take 'em . . . to the next."

He lowered his head to rest on his arms and I heard him release a shaky sigh.

"I'm so sorry, little one. I'm sorry I didn't protect ya . . . that I couldn't . . . stop him . . . " he paused for several minutes then continued, "I . . . I . . . I've had so much, but all I ever really wanted in my life was to be loved the way you love me now. There's been so many . . . so many people that . . . wanted to be a part of . . . that I thought loved me. Ya love me without even knowin' . . . with no . . . for no other reason but love. I . . .I . . . uh . . . I done some wrong things in my life but it . . it was outta control . . . all of it! I do love ya, Lilah Marie, I . . . I love ya from somewhere inside . . . that I didn't even know existed."

"But Scott . . . he killed it all for us." I mumbled. " He took what I gave to ya and destroyed it . . . It's done, it's over." I sighed and felt myself drift back into hopelessness.

"No!" he shouted and stared dead into my eyes. " It'll never be over between us!

You own a part of me that no one else has ever touched . . . and I . . . I have your very blood flowin' in my veins. He might have tried, but he only stole a moment . . . nothin', and I mean nothin', can touch what we have together! Nothin'!"

As he continued to talk to me, I felt the fog begin to lift a little. Anger started to boil inside and a new determination started to emerge. If nothin' else . . . I had to help Chad outta this mess. I was the one who had brought it all down on us and I knew I had to try and fix it!

I stretched as hard as I could to try to reach those pins but my hands were too far above my head. I tried yankin' on the chains the way Chad had done, but I couldn't pull hard enough. The stitches in my back were still too tender and the wound was extremely sore. My entire body begged for rest and a long, hot bath, but I didn't think I was anywhere near as bad off as Chad. He'd been beaten so bad I still wondered how he had the strength to pull those chains loose. The pure frustration caused me to start to cry again.

"I can't get 'em Chad!" I cried out. "I can't do anything."

"Stop it! We'll just have to come up with another idea." He sat up and started to yank on the chains that held his feet.

"I need a . . . a damn rock! All I got over here are some that aren't much more than gravel."

I remembered the rock that I'd stood on earlier. My feet were a little looser than my hands, so I tried to feel around and locate it. At last I found it and pulled it away from the wall with my bare toes. After I pushed as far as I could with the right foot, the left foot took over. With great difficulty I'd worked it a good distance but eventually I pushed it out of foot range.

"What now?" I looked at him desperately.

"Let me think a minute." He glanced around. "I have nothin' over here but this nasty blanket."

"That's it!" he sounded excited. "Honey? See if ya can pull that rock back to ya just a little."

I stretched with everything in me, but I couldn't seem to get a toe hold on it.

"I can't Chad. I can't reach it any more!"

"Okay. It's Okay . . . just rest a minute. We'll try again in a little while."

I relaxed and tried to think of another way, but it seemed impossible. If I at least had one arm free, it would be so simple. I remembered all the times the rat-man had left one and sometimes both arms free. The rat-man . . . all that time it'd been Scott. I assumed that he was dead then. What a horrible way to die. Nobody I ever knew deserved it more, no . . . not even Walter. It was still hard to believe that I didn't have a clue that it was really Scott the whole time. He was sicker than I could ever have imagined. I should've listened to my first instinct. Enough!! It was time to try and find a way to get us free. I yanked on the chains above my head and pulled with every ounce of strength I had left. The only thing that I managed to pull loose . . . felt like some of the stitches in my back. It didn't matter and I didn't care . . . I had to help get us out. Once more I pulled as hard as I could so that I could maybe get just a little closer to that rock with my feet. Whatever I did, it gave me another fraction of an inch.

As I stretched harder I was able to tip the top of the rock and it rolled back maybe an inch or more. With that I could get a better hold with my toes and moved it even closer.

"I got it! I got it closer. Now what?"

"Good . . . baby . . . good. I'm gonna try to throw this blanket close enough that ya can roll the rock back onto it and hopefully I can drag it back over here. Honey?"

"Yeah?"

"Ya can start prayin' any time!"

I saw him raise up on his knees and pull the chains attached to him as tight as he could. Then he took the blanket, rolled it up, held one corner, and flung it across the cave floor. It fell short by a good foot. My heart sank. He pulled it back to him and rolled it up again. I closed my eyes and prayed with all my heart. He flung it again. It was still short. Again, he patiently pulled it back to him.

"I need another foot or more of blanket!" he sounded irritated at that point. We were both quiet for a little while so that he could think it out. I heard him rustlin' around.

"What are ya doin'? "

"Hell, I'm tryin' to figure out how to get out of these damn pants. In all my life . . . I never had a problem gettin' out of my pants!" he growled.

Then I heard material being ripped. I didn't have a clue what he was doin' but I guessed he had an idea. Before long he was back on his knees and I was surprised to see that he was as butt-naked as I was. It seemed he'd torn his pants off and then tied them into a loop, which he fastened to the end of the blanket. I thought it was an insane idea, but it was better than anything I'd been able to come up with.

"Start your prayers, honey."

He threw the contraption toward the rock, but it landed way on the far side of it. He pulled it back again, rolled it up, and tried several more times, but his aim was off.

"Chad . . . just get it as close as ya can and I'll try to roll it into the loop."

He flung it again. This time it was really close. I took my foot and pushed the rock toward the loop. It was tortuous. I could only move it a fraction at a time. It was almost on the edge of it, but my strength was fadin'. I had to rest for just a minute. That was when we heard what we were most terrified of hearin. It sounded like the bear was back. We could hear him snortin', gruntin', and makin' all kinds of gastly noises. Chad hunkered down against the wall of the cave. I laid there motionless. I began to pray harder than I'd ever prayed in my entire life. We could hear it comin' closer.

"Shhhh", I heard Chad say as we both fell dead silent.

I didn't know how it was possible, but that beast smelled even worse than before. This time he came to me first and smelled around. I heard it go over to Chad. It sounded like he might have smacked him around a little. I heard a loud snort and a hard thud. My heart sank at the thought that he might've done serious harm to him. It'd be impossible for me to get to him if he was badly hurt.

With a great roar It lumbered out toward the entrance again. I jumped when it stopped near the front and let out another bellow that vibrated all the way to the back of the cave. I shuddered inside. It was silent for a long time before I felt comfortable enough to move.

"Chad?" I dared to whisper. I heard nothin' at first. Then a faint "Yeah?"
"Chad?"

I called again. There was a long agonizin' minute of silence.
"Yeah?"
"What are ya doin'? Are ya alright?'

His head popped up "I'm Okay! I was givin' thanks to God Almighty!" He was grinnin' from ear to battered ear.

"What's goin' on?" I asked him as I thought that maybe that bear had damaged his brain. He raised his hand and waved it at me. In it he had the rock we'd been tryin' to get to him for hours.

"How?" I asked in amazement.

"That damn goofy bear knocked it over here! Can ya believe that? See! God does listen to our prayers!"

He waited a little while before he started to pound on the chains to make sure that the bear was gone.

"I think he just thinks of this place like his private pantry." Chad told me. "He comes back ever so often to make sure that nothin' has disturbed his food supply! I just don't understand why he ain't hibernatin'."

He began to beat on the chains with the rock. It went on for several hours and the headache I already had was reachin' epic proportions.

"Got it!" he called. He held up one foot with a nasty red ring around the ankle, but it was free.

"Just one more baby!" and he began to beat on the other one. I felt relaxed listenin' to the continuous poundin'. The poundin' that signaled freedom with every blow.

The minutes and hours had turned into days, weeks, and probably even months by now and I was just too tired to even think about it any more. Poundin', poundin', poundin' . . . it became more and more distant as I sank into a deep sleep of pure exhaustion.

Gently, I felt fingers strokin' my hair. Then lips gently touched my forehead. I drifted deeper into that wonderful world of slumber. The first real sleep I'd had since the night I'd been taken.

When I finaly opened my eyes, I was shocked to see a large fire closer toward the entrance of the cave and I found that I was under a warm blanket. I turned my head and was face-to-face with my sleepin' angel. Chad lay there beside me and before I realized it, I reached up and touched his face.

I was free!

My hands and feet were all free.

I didn't know how he'd done it without wakin' me up, but he had!

My handsome prince had rescued me yet again. I thought it was surely another dream...and if it was, then I wanted to follow that dream just as far as it would take me! I cuddled up to him and fell blissfully back to sleep.

I don't know how long we slept, but it was the best rest we'd had in such a long time.

"Mornin', baby girl." I heard him whisper.

I opened my eyes to meet that crystal blue gaze that always amazed me with the ability to take my breath away. Even in these horrid conditions.

"Mornin'." I whispered. "You did it. You got us free."

"Free as a bird in a tree!" he grinned.

"How?" I whispered. "I didn't feel anything."

"Yours was easiest . . . I used the keys they left on the table over there."

He kissed me gently on the forehead and sat up.

"We still have some huge problems to over-come though."

"Like what?" I yawned.

"Like . . . food and a way out . . . and clothes!" He bit his lip and winked at me and my heart, once again, skipped a beat.

"Why can't we just leave?"

"'cause I'm sure we're bein' watched."

"By who?" I wanted to know. "If someone's been watchin' us and did nothin' to help...."

"No." He stopped me. "Not someone . . . something. That bear! I went a ways toward the front earlier and when I got close enough to see daylight . . . I could smell the nasty beast. He's guardin' his kill."

"What do ya mean 'his kill'. Are ya talkin' about . . . Scott?"

He nodded his head and looked down for a minute.

"I found what was left of him and drug it back up this way and covered it with a blanket from the back. That's why I moved the fire. I think that was the only thing that was keepin' it away before. If we keep it built up good . . . I think it'll leave us alone. At least 'til we can maybe figure another way to get outta here."

"Do ya have a plan?"

"Nope."

We both sat there thoughtfully.

"I think we should look in the back here and take stock of what we have." He suggested.

I nodded.

"Maybe there's a little food in some of those bags they brought in."

Chad got up and wrapped the blanket around hisself.

"Wait a minute," he said as he went back to the back.

In a moment he returned with another blanket and a knife. It was the same knife the rat-man had used to scare me half to death. He carefully cut a strip off one side of the blanket and then cut a slit in the center.

"Stand up." He said as he offered me his hand. "It's not a mink, but maybe it'll keep you warm."

He said proudly.

He slipped it over my head so that the slit was the neck opening and then he tied the strip around my waist. It felt so good to be wearing clothin' again. Primitive . . . yes . . . but I knew it was made with pure love.

We went to the back. It was the first time I'd been able to move around freely since the day before my capture. My legs was wobbly and I was weak, but I'd never before appreciated my freedom so much. In the bags we found two more blankets, some medical supplies, a bottle of tequila, some candles, and a whip with several leather straps with metal balls at the end of each one.

Chad picked it up "I bet this was for me!"

"It was probably for both of us. Which ever one pissed him off first."

"The sorry bastard," He cursed under his breath..

Further investigation revealed some bread, cheese and a roll of summer sausage. We sat down, ate a little and had some water. Chad picked up the bottle and poured us each a shot of tequila. It warmed us up and relaxed our nerves.

"What are all these boxes?" Chad asked as he looked around.

"How would I know? I don't even know where we are."

"Okay . . . you're right . . . let's look and see."

The boxes were wooden so we knew that between what Scott had stored in there for firewood and these that we'd have plenty of fuel to keep that bear out. The boxes were huge but weren't very heavy. They were stacked all the way to the ceiling and appeared to be at least eight to twelve deep, as well as all the way across the back. We pulled one box out and used the knife to pry the boards apart. While Chad was takin' 'em apart, I was neatly stackin' 'em over by the firewood. The first several were empty. They were only good for firewood. We found a couple that were filled with what appeared to be what was once woolen blankets. They must've been very old 'cause the moths and other bugs had left very little to identify. We finally took a break and leaned against the boxes.

"Got a plan yet?" Chad asked me.

"I didn't know I was supposed to be makin' one," I told him. "How about you?"

"Nope." He answered simply. "Ya know . . . there was a time in my life that I swore I'd never wear denim again . . . but I tell ya what . . . I sure wish I hadn't tore up them jeans. I'd give a brand new dollar for another pair." He shook his head and chuckled as he walked over to put more wood on the fire.

"I hope someone is lookin' after my animals," I said thoughtfully.

"I'm sure that Toby is takin' great care of 'em. Ya know, he's a good friend to you. Him and Floy both are the kind of friends ya want to have around forever. I know from experience that there ain't many like that. Real friends, the ones that really love ya, are few and very far between."

I sat there and thought about what he had said. I missed Floy so much. We'd been through so much in our lives.

Then I remembered "Did they tell ya that they're gonna have a baby?" I asked him. He looked shocked.

"No! I'll be damned. That's great . . . they'll make great parents." he smiled and looked into the fire.

After a very long pause, "I was married once." he mumbled.

I was stunned. He'd never talked about it in all that time.

"I had a baby girl . . . she was beautiful . . . but . . . "

"But what?" I whispered. I didn't want to spoil the moment.

He'd kept his life very private.

He suddenly stood up and the mood completely changed.

" . . . but that was another time and another place. This is now and a totally different world."

I was afraid to pursue the topic. Deep inside I was afraid that somethin' horrific had happened to 'em and he wasn't ready to tell me about it. I let it drop.

We kept openin' boxes for a while. As we worked our way back, we decided to see how deep the boxes went. At last we found the back wall of the cave.

"Honey! Come back here and look at this!" Chad called.

I worked my way to the back of the boxes. There was just enough space between the stack of boxes and the rock wall for one person to walk comfortably. Chad stood blockin' the path.

"What is it?"

He stepped back to reveal a very large door embedded in the cave wall. I just couldn't believe what I was seein'.

"A door?"

He bit his lip, nodded and winked. "A door!"

I walked up to it and started to reach for the door knob. I looked at Chad in confusion.

"I know, I noticed that."

There was no doorknob.

"What do ya think it is?" I asked.

He looked thoughtful then grinned.

"A door!" he laughed.

"Smart ass! Where do ya think it goes to?"

"I don't know, but anywhere's better than here. Let's see if we can find somethin' to break it down with."

We began frantically to open boxes. We weren't thinkin' about organization any more. This could be the answer to our prayers. I got the knife and brought it to Chad. He worked for some time tryin' to wedge it open.

"I think the door's too thick. We gotta come up with somethin' else," he sighed.

I went back out to open more boxes in hopes of finding a better tool. I heard him call out again. I rushed to the back to see what was happenin'. I can only describe the look on his face as total confusion.

"I moved a couple a these boxes to give me a little more room and I found a hole in the middle."

I looked and sure enough there was an openin' into the stack of boxes. I took the lantern Chad handed me and stepped inside. It was a small frame room with a small table and a chair. I sat the lantern down and turned to him.

"What do ya think this is?" I asked.

"Hell if I know."

We discovered several dozen boxes stacked in a corner, only they weren't wood, these were metal. One of 'em appeared to have been opened while the others were padlocked. Chad knelt down and opened it up. We both stood speechless. Glowin' in the lantern light were a large number perfect bars of what appeared to be pure gold! We looked at each other.

"No way, man!" he shouted as he picked one up. "Damn, I think this might be real!"

"You're kiddin' me, right? " I asked. " Do ya think it was Scott's?"

"No, I don't think he ever got back this far. There's too much crap stacked in front of it."

"Chad?"

"Yeah?"

"Chad? Will this help us any?" I handed him a long metal bar that'd been layin' against the far wall.

"Aw Man . . . this just keeps gettin' better and better!" he was so excited.

He took the bar and went to work on the door.

A huge growl stopped us in our tracks.

"Sounds like somebody's not too happy with us." Chad whispered.

"Is the fire still goin'?"I asked.

"I'll check." he said as he went out the end. He was back in a short while. "It's okay. I put some more wood on it to make sure. We gotta keep an eye on it. It's the only thing keepin' him back. I think he came back for supper." I shuddered at the thought.

Chad went back to work on the door and I continued to rummage in the boxes outside. I could hear him bangin' on the door and mumblin' a few choice words from time to time. Most of the boxes were blankets. Then I found a box of what looked like very old military gloves. The leather was pretty much rotten but I figgered it would burn, too. Next I opened a box that I thought was well worth the effort. It was full of pistols wrapped in oil cloth. I was certain that if there's pistols then there's bound to be some ammo. I had to open three more boxes before I found it and I prayed that it was the right ammo for that gun. I took a box of the shells and one of the guns to Chad to see what he thought.

"I hope I got somethin' useful here!" I told him as I hurried behind the boxes.

"Where'd ya get these? This is a real antique." He was elated.

"Boxes," I said. "Is it the right ammo for the gun?"

"You bet it is little girl. Now let that bear come back and see what he gets. I just wished I'd had it when I first got here. None of it would have happened. None of it."

He looked at the gun and then back up at me as if to say he wished he could make it all go away. I nodded and sat down on the chair and watched him work at the door for a long time. I didn't feel so good and I was unusually cold and beginin' to shiver. As bad as I felt, I knew Chad would need all the help I could give him. He needed all his strength. I went out and got him some water and food and brought it back to him.

"Thanks, baby. How'd ya know that I was startin' to need that?" He smiled at me. "You Okay?" he asked as he took a drink. "Why ain't ya eatin' too?"

"I'm not really hungry. I'm just really tired."

He finished his food and drink and went out for a minute.

"Come on, I made ya a place to lay down and sleep for a little while. It's been a long day...or maybe night."

He stepped back so I could get out of the tunnel. He'd made me a bed just next to the entrance to the hidden tunnel behind the boxes.

"I thought ya might want to be closer."

"I do. Thank you." I laid down and he covered me up and went back to work.

A long day . . . he was right, he had no idea if it was day or night and neither did I . . . I just knew that I was very tired. It seemed that every time Chad was workin' to get us free . . . all I could do was fall asleep.

When I woke up, sometime later, I could still hear Chad workin' on that door. I got up and made my way back there.

"How's it goin'?"

"Come here a minute," he said. "I got it loose, but I can't get it to open. Can ya help me a little?"

We both pushed on the door as hard as we could. Finally we heard somethin' move. We looked at each other in excitement.

Out of nowhere, all hell broke loose as we heard what sounded like boxes crashin' and that bear roarin'! He sounded frighteningly close.

Chad took the gun he'd already loaded. "I pray this still works."

"It'll take several shots...he's really big!" I warned him as he slipped silently down the tunnel.

He turned back to me, "Stay here. No matter what . . . promise me . . . STAY!"

I nodded, but he was nuts if he thought I was gonna stay back and not be out there to help him. As he cleared the tunnel I was right behind him. It was pretty dark out there although I hadn't noticed it before. I guess we'd let the fire burn down too low 'cause there was only the embers to give enough light to see. If I'd been awake I would've noticed and added more wood.

The furious bear came chargin' in and Chad fell to one knee and took aim. The bear rose on his hind legs and stood to his full heigth.

My first thought was David and Goliath.

Chad opened fire. He hit him in the head with the first bullet, but it only seemed to make the bear angrier.

"The neck, Chad. Aim for the neck!" I screamed.

The giant of a bear began to charge at him.

The next shot hit the neck dead on. He fired three more times into the bear,s neck and chest. It let out a horrific roar and fell over. My heart was racin' and I was shakin' all over. The cave was filled with smoke and dust. The rancid smellin' beast was still breathin' and movin' its feet when Chad walked over and carefully aimed for its heart and shot.

In seconds the animal lay motionless.

I came up beside Chad. We stood and watched as the life drained out of the bear. We sat down on the ground and stared in bittersweet silence at the animal that'd probably saved our lives.

Chapter 15

After we pulled ourselves together, Chad ventured closer to it and nudged it with his foot. Its huge head rolled to one side and its mouth fell open. I shivered to think that it was those teeth that had taken a life in this very place.

"Damn, look at the size of those teeth!" Chad said as he knelt down beside it. He took the barrel of the gun and pushed its jaw open wider.

"Well, I just solved another mystery. At least now I know why he wasn't hibernatin'."

"What'd you find?"

"Come here and look at this" he called. He pushed its lips back and I could easily see a huge abscess on its swollen red gum.

"Oh sheez!" I stepped back. "How much pain must that've caused? I can't help but feel a little sorry for it."

Chad looked at me, "That's another thing I love about ya, it was gonna have us for supper and ya feel sorry for it. Ya amaze me girl." He smiled.

We went to the back and sat down on my blankets.

"I'm not a heavy drinkin' man, but I believe I need another shot of that tequila." Chad said as he went over and got the bottle. He turned it up and took a good swallow, and then offered it to me. I gratefully accepted and downed a couple of good swallows.

"I thought my life before was a three-ring circus. But I have to tell ya, honey . . . life with you has been just one huge adventure after another," He laughed softly.

I nodded. "So what do we do now? We can go right outta the front if we want to. There's nothin' to stop us. We can go home."

"Yeah, but there's one thing we gotta do first." he told me.

"What's that?" I questioned.

"I gotta know where that door leads to. We almost had it. Do ya feel like tryin' it again?"

To be honest, I really didn't. I felt sick, nauseated, and very dizzy. I didn't say anything, I just got up and headed to the door.

Together we pushed and pushed, and each time we could feel it move a little more.

"I think there's somethin' against it." I told him.

"Yeah, but it's startin' to move," he answered as he gave it another hard shove.

There was finally enough of an openin' that he could wedge his shoulder in. We shoved again and he squeezed his way through.

"I'll be damned!" I heard him say. "I'll just be damned. Honey, ya ain't gonna believe what I just found. C'mon. You gotta see this! It just beats everything I ever saw!"

I squeezed myself through. Even though the pain in my back was almost unbearable, I stood in amazement, shock, and total disbelief. I knew this place so well. Hell, I owned this place!

We stood smack dab in the middle of the small cabin. I turned around in complete awe of where we were . It was the giant armoire that'd been blockin' the door.

"It's a secret entrance." I mumbled .

We looked at each other for a moment and then burst into a border line hysterical laughter.

"We've been in our own back yard the whole time!" Chad shook his head.

He became very serious.

"The whole time," he spoke softly, " we searched and looked and I wondered and prayed, and ya was just on the other side of this wall. So close and yet . . . I couldn't find ya."

"But ya didn't know. I didn't even know. Once, I did wonder if this could've been the cave we found that day, but I was sure that it wasn't possible."

He stood there a moment and then he turned and ran out through the secret passage.

"I'll be right back!" I heard him holler as he left.

I went and laid across the bed, a real bed, and relaxed for the first time in what seemed like an entire lifetime. He couldn't stand it and had gone to see if it was our cave. He was gone for quite a long time, or at least it seemed that way. I really didn't feel good at all. I closed my eyes for just a brief moment.

"It is!" he yelled as he came burstin' back in. "It's our cave. I saw the tree that we didn't cut down. It must circle around and come out way around there. It's a really deep cave!" He stopped short. "What's wrong?" He asked as he came to the bed.

"I'm just really tired and I . . . I feel like I'm gonna be sick."

He touched my head with his cool hand. It felt so good.

"You're burnin' up, little girl!"

"My back hurts . . . so . . . bad." I finally confessed.

He rolled me over to my side and untied the string around my make-shift dress and pulled it up over my shoulders.

"Jesus! What the hell? How long's this been hurtin'? Why didn't ya say somethin' baby?"

"Since the day it happened . . . I just didn't want ya to worry. Ya had enough on your mind as it was."

"It looks bad infected. I'm not a doctor but I've studied a lot about medications. I'll be back." He said as he disappeared behind the armoire again.

He came back with the case that Scott had brought in when he did the stitches.

"I don't know what any of this crap is. He's wrote stuff on here that I can't read."

He turned and left again. This time he brought back the tequila bottle.

"I don't think I need another drink," I told him.

"This time it's not for drinkin'. It's for cleanin'," He told me. "Lay real still and let me clean this a little."

He went to the armoire and looked inside to see if there was anything that he could use to clean my wounds. Surprisingly he found an old tablecloth neatly folded in a drawer. He unfolded it and laid it between me and the bed and poured the alcohol freely over the area. I bit my hand as it sat fire to the skin across my side and back.

"Honey . . . we gotta get a doctor. This is more than I can handle."

He ran his fingers through his hair as he went over and looked out the window.

"What the . . . ?" he said under his breath.

"What is it ?"

"I'm not sure, but it don't look good. There's still cop cars at the house. It looks like some news media, too." He sounded worried.

"I . . . I don't understand Chad."

"I'm sure they think that I knew what happened to ya. When I . . . I disappeared too . . . I know that made me look guilty as hell."

"But when they see us and we tell 'em what happened . . . they'll know ya didn't do nothin' to me and it'll be fine."

"Naw . . . I . . . I . . . ya don't understand. I can't . . . uh . . . " he began to pace like a trapped animal.

"Chad, what's wrong?"

" . . . Uh . . . I . . . I . . . hell they tried to tell me . . . they warned me . . . but naw . . . I . . . I . . . uh . . . just give me a minute to think." He looked pale and he'd begun to sweat.

I stumbled from the bed and went to him. When I touched his shoulder, he jerked away. I'd never seen him like that, he was almost frantic and he was scarin' the hell outta me.

I was so dizzy that I could hardly see him and my stomach churned. I began to see stars flicker in the darkness that was wrappin' around me.

"Chad?" I heard myself ask as I slipped into that darkness.

When I opened my eyes, we were back in the cave. For a moment I was overcome with the horrific thought that gettin' out had all been another bizarre dream. Chad was there with a wet cloth and a concerned look on his face.

"What . . . happened . . . did I fall?"

"No baby . . . I let ya down. I wasn't takin' care of ya. I'm so sorry, honey. I should a been lookin' out for you instead of myself. Do ya feel any better?"

I looked into those concerned baby blues and wanted to lie just to make him feel better.

"No, not really." I whispered. "It hurts so bad . . . worse than ever." I admitted. "Why are we back in the cave?"

"I couldn't risk the light bein' in the cabin so I had to bring ya back in here. I'll try to explain later . . . but . . . right now . . . I gotta find some help. I need ya to stay right here. I got a fire built and I won't be gone long. Will ya stay here?"

I nodded.

"No, ya did that last time. Promise me . . . you'll stay here."

I promised. This time I knew I'd stick with it 'cause I was too weak to go anywhere.

He left quietly and was gone for what seemed like several hours.

I fell asleep waitin' and thinkin' about how the cave was startin' to smell really bad. I don't know what I was dreamin' or if I was dreamin' at all, but somewhere in the recesses of my brain I heard somebody comin' from the cave entrance. That was impossible because nobody knew that we were in there. Chad would've come through the cabin. Somewhere in my fevered brain I began to think that maybe it was the rat-man. Maybe Scott wasn't by himself. The rat-man was comin' back to get me. He might have that knife back and be after me again. I looked up and saw two figures come runnin' out of the dark.

I screamed with everything that was in me. I buried my face in the blanket and sceamed for Chad.

Someone grabbed my shoulders and gently lifted me into his arms. I screamed hysterically and swung my fists at him. Then I heard that sweet gentle; southern drawl.

"Honey, honey it's me. Wake up and talk to me . . . it's Chad. I opened my eyes and was met with sparklin' blue ones and I knew that I was safe in his arms.

"Look who's here little girl. I brought Toby."

I was stunned.

I started to cry, "Toby? Toby!" I managed to grab him around the neck and sobbed on his shoulder.

"It's okay, Lilah . . . aw sweetie don't cry. Me and Chad's right here. They ain't nobody ever gonna hurt ya again. We can guarantee ya that."

He held me in his arms for a long time and when I'd settled down, he laid me gently back onto the blanket.

"Let me look at that back, sugar." he said as he rolled me over. "Shit! We gotta get Doc out here. How'd this happen Chad?"

"Damn bear over there," Chad explained as he pointed to it.

"I don't understand. How'd she get stitched up? Did you do this?" He asked Chad in total confusion. ". . . and why ya hidin' up here instead of comin' down to the house?"

"Toby, I can't explain it all right now. The most important thing is to get her some care. I can't trust nobody but you."

"What do ya mean 'ya can't trust nobody' ? Everybody in this whole area thinks the world of ya."

"It's not the people in the area that I worry about. It's the ones from out of town that I have to avoid. I saw national news media trucks down there and . . . I . . . I . . . uh . . . I can't risk 'em seein' me."

"Why?" I asked weakly.

"We'll talk later, honey. Just trust me."

With no more questions, Chad and Toby worked out a plan to get some medicine without anyone bein' suspicious. Toby was to go get Floy to go to her cousin Morris, the pharmacist, and tell him that Toby had cut his self on a saw. It was badly infected and she needed some antibiotics to get him over it. Afterward, Toby and Floy would come back to the cave.

Toby'd left and I must've got worse, 'cause I began to throw up and shiver somethin' terrible. I had never in my life been so cold. Chad laid down beside me and wrapped his arms and legs around me and held me 'til I quieted down and drifted off.

I woke up again. We were still wrapped in each other's arms and Chad was sound asleep. My stomach felt better, but I was burnin' up and the chills were startin' up again. I moved slightly and Chad came awake instantly.

"What is it honey? What ya need?"

"Just some cool air and a little water."

"Water I can do . . . but ya don't need no cool air."

He got me a cup of water and let me sip it slowly, then he began to blot my face with a cold rag.

"That better, honey?" he asked softly. I nodded my head and cuddled back against him.

"Lilah? Lilah! Oh thank God! You're alive! " Floy broke into a river of tears when she came runnin' through the cave.

I opened my eyes and tried to focus on her, but the best I could manage was a weak smile.

"Chad! Damn it! I want to know everything! " she yelled.

"Did ya get some medicine?" he asked calmly.

Floy stopped in mid-rant and handed him a package.

"I got everything that I could get my hands on. Morris gave me antibiotics and instructions. Now, tell me what this is all about! Where the hell have ya been? They been scourin' the country for you two!!"

"Darlin', let's get Lilah fixed up before we go attackin' Chad, okay? We need to take care of our girl here. Don't ya think?" Toby added.

"Yes . . . yes . . . well of course we do. I'm sorry Chad . . . I've just been sick with worry. I didn't know what had happened to either one of ya. Now listen, Morris fixed up a shot of antibiotic, but he fixed it for Toby and Toby's a lot bigger than Lilah . . . so I wouldn't give her all of it . . . okay?"

"Yeah, you're right . . . I'm thinkin' about a little more than half. What do you think?" Chad asked her.

"I agree. He gave me some pills too. I got disinfectant and antibiotic ointment and some bandages, all kinds of stuff!"

"Ya done good Floy. You're a wonderful friend. Lilah is blessed to have ya." I heard Chad tell her.

After a shot and a gentle cleansin', some medicine and bandages, I didn't know if I felt any better, but I was more comfortable. Besides, I had my best friends in the world and the man that I loved more than life right there beside me. What more could I ever want or need?

Floy had brought food and drink. It was almost like old times with the four of us together in front of the fire. Chad was fillin' 'em in on the events when I drifted off again. I was glad it was before the part about the sexual attack. I wanted, with all my heart to forget about that bastard ever touchin' me.

It was a couple of days before I felt well enough to sit up and talk for any length of time. Chad had just come out from behind the boxes and sat down beside me.

"I got a surprise for ya." he whispered.

I noticed that he'd bathed and washed his hair and even had real clothes on. He looked and smelled wonderful. He was still pretty bruised up, but he was beginnin' to look like hisself again.

"When did ya get clothes? How . . . "

"Toby and Floy . . . do ya feel like a nice shower? And maybe some real clothes?" he nibbled his lip and gave me that adorable little wink.

"Oh yes. Yes. Yes. Yes." I was elated at the thought. "But honey, I gotta tell ya one thing . . . we gotta do somethin' about our livin' arrangements. I can't stand the odors anymore. It's makin' me sick to my stomach again."

"I know," he answered. "We got a plan to get that taken care of . . . real soon. Now . . . come on . . . let's get ya to the shower."

We moved carefully through the passage and into the house. It was daylight so there was no need to turn on any lights.

"It's been so long since I've been in the sun. Doesn't it look wonderful out there?"

He didn't answer me.

We went into the new bathroom and he started a shower for me. I untied the string that held my makeshift dress on and Chad slipped it up over my head. He took off the bandages.

"Man, that looks so much better than it did the other day. It looks like those stitches are past ready to come out."

I stepped into the wonderful warm water and simply let it run down my body.

"I started to run you a bubble bath, but I didn't think that ya needed to soak in a tub yet. We'll save that for later." He smiled as he poured shampoo into my long, matted hair.

I'd never had the luxury of havin' a man shampoo my hair. His hands were strong, but gentle, and I could feel the love in his touch. Two shampoos and a cream rinse later, I already began to feel like a new woman. He took a wash cloth and soap and carefully washed my face and neck. He gently turned me around and ever so carefully washed my back. It felt so unbelievably good that tears began to well up in my eyes. After every inch of my body was gently washed and rinsed, he helped me out and wrapped me in a large white towel that I assumed Floy had brought. He put his arms around me and pulled me close.

"Ya okay, little girl?" He whispered into my ear. I nodded my head and cuddled gratefully into his arms. We walked slowly over to the bed.

"I want ya to lay down here until we get things straightened out. Okay? Toby and Floy will be here in a little bit and we'll all sit down and make our plans."

I looked straight into his eyes. "I love you, Chad."

He started to say somethin' but Toby come through the passage, followed closely by Floy. It was the first time that I'd really felt like I'd been able to see 'em clearly. Floy was startin' to show her pregnancy and she looked so cute that I almost cried again.

"Look at you. I think you're in a family way."

"It's about time ya started talkin' and actin' like your old self. I've missed ya so much." She laughed as she sat on the bed and we hugged each other.

"So what's the plan, my brother?" Toby turned to Chad.

"Well, first . . . we gotta get Lilah outta that damn cave..."

"Yeah," interrupted Toby. "That place smells horrific! But how we gonna explain that dead body and that dead bear? And how did we find Lilah?"

"I . . . I . . . I been thinkin' about it. We'll pretty much tell the truth. The bear killed Scott and when it left, Lilah managed to build a fire to keep it away. She found a gun that Scott had left and when the bear charged through, she shot it. She was bad hurt and was too weak to get out . . . but she found some medicine in Scott's bag and started takin' it. Let's see . . . then . . . "

"Then I crawled outta the cave and made my way back to the house!" I added.

Everyone sat there and stared at me. "What ? Is that a bad idea?"

"Chad! I just realized . . . ya shouldn't a cleaned her up. Nobody's gonna believe that she was held in a cave, went through all she did, dragged herself halfway around a mountain, and come out lookin' like a little angel."

Toby made a valid point. We all sat there in deep thought.

"I didn't think of that . . . I . . . I just knew how bad she had been wantin' a bath . . . I . . . uh . . . I just wanted to make her happy." Chad looked down at his feet like a kid who'd done somethin' wrong.

"It's not that big of a deal," I offered " I still have my blanket dress and it still smells like hell. There's still dirt in the cave and bad as I hate to think it . . . a dead bear that stinks to high heaven. I say . . . wait . . . wait a minute. I don't understand somethin' . . . why don't we just walk out and say 'Here we are!' I mean we act like we're hidin' somethin'. We didn't do nothin' wrong. Scott held US prisoners . . . not the other way around!"

I was suddenly very perplexed.

Chad looked at Toby and Floy and then back at me. He sat down in a chair near the bed, leaned forward and buried his face in his hands.

"Guys, can I talk to Lilah alone for a minute . . . Please."

Floy and Toby left and went back into the cave. I looked at him in deep confusion.

"Chad? What's goin' on? I feel like I walked in on the middle of a movie."

He sat there and just stared at the floor.

I waited.

He looked up, bit his bottom lip, and shook his head.

"I . . . I . . . aw . . . I . . . I don't know how to explain it."

"What sweetheart?" I pushed.

"There's already so much news media out there . . . I . . . uh . . . I know that when ya come out . . . there'll be a whole lot more media coverage . . . " he mumbled.

"What difference does that make, Chad? They'll just be so glad that we're alright! I'm confused. What's the problem?"

"I . . . I . . . I can't risk the cameras and stuff. Ya know . . . my life is private and I don't want a bunch of nosey reporters askin' a bunch of questions."

"Why? Is there somethin' that you're hidin'? Are ya wanted for somethin'?"

He slid from his chair and knelt beside the bed.

"It's not what you're thinkin', honey." He spoke softly in that sweet southern drawl, "I . . . I just need a little more time . . . that's all. Can ya just trust me? No questions . . . just have a little faith in me. Please?"

I stared into those bedroom blue eyes and I asked myself; *'How could any woman alive refuse him anything he asked when he looked at 'em like that?'* I nodded.

"What does Toby and Floy know?"

"The same thing I told you . . . I just want my privacy, okay?"

"Okay," I whispered and we sealed it with a soft, gentle kiss.

It didn't take long to undo all the nice cleanliness that I'd enjoyed for such a short time. Floy helped mat my hair and we found plenty of dirt in the cave to cover any sign of clean. Soot from the old fire did wonders toward my cave-woman look. I reluctantly rubbed my hair and hands in the wretched fur of that bloated bear and slipped my blanket dress back on.

The plan was that Toby and Floy were goin' to go 'round to the house to tend the horses and animals. That's when they'd find me stumblin' out of the woods. They'd go to great lengths to cover all the footprints. The only ones would be mine.

"Okay." I said. "But what about you, Chad? Where will you be?"

"We'll close the door to the cabin. I'm gonna stay in the little room in the boxes. Toby'll seal 'em back against the wall and you can tell 'em that this is your property and this is a bunch of stuff ya had stored in here. Just don't give 'em permission to go through any of it. Okay? I'll stay there and in the little cabin until it all dies down."

"Then it's a plan . . . let's do it," added Toby.

Chad and Toby helped me outta the cave and down to the distant edge of the forest. It was a long treacherous hike that seemed like it took forever. They made their way back to the truck, erasin' footprints as they went. It took 'em a long time to drive back 'round the mountain to the house. I stood there almost knee deep in the snow, but it felt so good to be outside. The fresh air was wonderful even though my feet were freezin'. Waitin' behind some trees, I started to think about the whole situation. I couldn't for the life of me understand what was up with Chad. He'd lived here for months and had come to know everyone in Mason and a lot of people in Bigby and Dover. Everybody liked him so much. Now he acted as if he was hidin' from somebody. What could he possibly have done that could be all that bad. I just couldn't begin to imagine. He was the kindest, gentlest, most generous man I'd ever known. He loved kids and dogs and horses . . . and me.

I had a sick, nervous feelin' in the pit of my stomach.

Snow began to fall lightly as I saw Floy and Toby drive up. There were some other cars and trucks and vans parked in front of my home. I didn't know why but I guessed I was about to find out.

After a good five to ten minutes I saw 'em walk out. Floy stood on the porch while Toby made his way toward the barn. A man in a suit was talkin' to Floy as she watched Toby trudge through the snow. I hoped that someone would look my way soon before I got frost-bite of the toes.

Toby looked back toward the house, then back at me and yelled at Floy. He started runnin' across the clearin' as I stumbled out of the woods. I didn't have to pretend much since my feet and legs was so cold that I could hardly move 'em. Before I could get very far, I was surrounded by police and reporters.

I collapsed conveniently into Toby's arms and he carried me up to the big cabin. As we got near, my Boots and Roz went nuts. They almost knocked us down before we could get through the back door.

Aw, I thought. *My home! At last, I'm home!*

It's strange how a home develops it's own scents. When you're gone for a while and ya come back, the first thing ya notice is the distinct smell of "home."

Toby carried me in and laid me carefully down on the couch. He covered me up with the blanket that was on it . . . the first thing I noticed was that it still smelled exactly like Chad. Floy and Toby did a great job of pretendin' that it was the first time they'd seen me in weeks. I went through the whole story just like we'd planned. Toby was askin' just the right questions when I left somethin' out and Floy was fussin' over me like a old mama hen. It took forever for the police to get through with their questions and then some of the news media managed to get in and started in with their endless questions. Stanley was there and I was so relieved to see a couple of other faces that I knew.

"Lilah, do ya need a doctor?" he asked me. "Not now. What I need right now is a good long bath. I'll see the doctor tomorrow."

"Can ya find your way back to the cave, Ma'am?" someone asked.

"Yes, I can. I didn't know it 'til I got out, but I own that cave . . . it's where my family has stored old stuff for years. I just didn't know where I was at the time."

They wanted me to take 'em there the first thing the next mornin'. I agreed and finally Stanley got 'em out of the house and told reporters that we'd hold a news conference sometime the next day. That seemed to satisfy 'em and they finally left. Late that evenin' the Sheriff left, too. When I was sure that everybody was gone, I turned to Toby.

"How'd I do?" I asked.

"Ya done real good. Ya even had me upset all over again, thinkin' that ya had to kill that bear all by yourself. Then ya had to stay there alone with the bear's body and Scot's mutilated body 'til ya got enough strength to stumble back home. You're a tough cookie! Ya really are ya know . . . I don't know how ya survived it."

"Go get Chad, Toby. I don't like him up there by hisself. Go out the back and work your way through the shadows. Be careful."

He left quietly.

"Floy? I'm scared." I told my best friend.

"Of what sweetie?"

"I don't know. Somethin's up with Chad. I've never seen him act like that."

It was a long time before I heard the back door open. I sat up on the couch and turned to look, but I was shocked to see only Toby standin' there.

"Where's Chad?"

Lookin' intently at his face, I knew before he answered that somethin' was bad wrong.

"Toby?" he just stood there, then looked at the floor.

He took his hat off and licked his lips as if he was stallin' for time. Time I wasn't willin' to give him.

"Toby!"

"He . . . a . . . I . . . well, it's like this, sweetie . . . he ain't there." He looked worried. "I don't know where he went. There's nothin' there to show he was ever even there. Lilah, there ain't even no footprints to show which way he went."

I couldn't believe what I was hearin'. Where'd he go? Why'd he go? Could it be that easy for him to just walk away and leave me? I sat there in stunned silence.

Chapter 16

The damn rooster reminded us that mornin' was comin'. I hadn't been able to sleep for worryin' about Chad and where he could possibly have gone.

"We're stayin' here for awhile," Floy said. "At least 'til they get this all settled."

"Ya already spent last night here. The doc should be here any time to check me over. You don't have to stay. I know ya have things to do to get ready for that little baby."

"Sweetie, right now I'm more concerned about you. I've never seen ya this worried and depressed. Don't ya at least want to talk about it? Scream about it? Somethin'?" she asked.

"No."

I felt like my world had cracked and I was slippin' into a bottomless pit. How could my life go on without him? How could things continue as if he'd never existed? In my mind I could hear his voice. It was pure southern on black satin. I could remember his arms around me at night and my heart wouldn't let me go any further.

I laid back down on the couch and pulled the blanket that I cherished up around my neck and closed my eyes.

It was just after breakfast when the doctor finally got there.

"I'll tell you what young lady. . . if it's not one thing with you, it's another," he smiled sadly when he came in the door. "I've been out here more times this year than I have in the last thirty."

He sat down on the couch beside me.

"Are ya doin' alright sugar? You've had a lot of trauma lately. I want to check ya out and make sure you're alright physically, first. After that, we'll talk."

He gave me a good goin' over and finally removed those stitches from my back and side. It felt so good to get 'em out. They'd really started to itch and it was all I could do to keep from scratchin' the heck out of 'em

"Who put these stitches in? Was it O'Grady? I have to tell ya, I already heard about everything you went through. God love your heart. I met that son-of-a-bitch O'Grady a couple of times. I didn't like him from the git-go. He had a strange streak about him that I just didn't care for. It was a horrible way to die, but, God forgive me, it served him well enough!"

I just nodded my head and avoided the subject. Although I was listenin', my mind was elsewhere and I knew it'd only be a little while before I'd have to go back to that cave with the police. It was the last thing I ever wanted to do.

We were supposed to go first thing, but they decided I should get checked over first. I wasn't sure how I was gonna handle seein' that place again, especially since I knew that what was left of Scott's body was still there. Chad had been thoughtful enough to cover it. I'd never seen it. The bear had to be a decayin' mess by then. They had no idea how I hated that smell. I wasn't sure I could manage it.

Doc tried to get me to discuss it all, but I was so afraid that I would let somethin' slip about Chad that I figgered it was better to just not say anymore than I had to.

"It's not that I don't appreciate the concern Doc. It's just that, I guess I ain't ready to talk about it any more than I absolutely have to. Please try to understand."

"Of course I do." He was very compassionate. "And when ya get ready to talk . . . ya know where I am. Okay?"

Doc had been gone about an hour when Stanley and some of the investigators got there.

"Lilah, do ya feel like takin' us on up there?"

"Sure."

I went upstairs and found some good warm clothes, socks, and boots

Toby'd come to the house from the barn.

"If ya tell me how to get there . . . I can take 'em up and ya won't have to get out," He offered.

"No, I can do it. It's just not gonna be a very pleasant mornin' is all."

I could've driven 'round the same way Floy and Toby'd been comin' up, but I felt like a nice long walk would do us all some good. We took off across the yard. Floy stayed behind 'cause Toby and I didn't think that she needed to be trekin' through the snow. It was a very long walk.

It was hard rememberin' havin' taken the same walk with Chad when we was lookin' for our Christmas tree. Somehow it just didn't seem as cold back then.

We passed the rock ledge. I couldn't help but recall some vivid memories of snow angels.

Eventually we came to the entrance of the cave. We could smell the horrible smell long before we entered it. I held back for a few minutes tryin' to decide if I'd vomit now or when I got inside. I wasn't at all sure that I could control it.

Some of the investigators and policemen had drawn their weapons and were bein' very cautious. I supposed it was because I'd told 'em that for so long I'd thought there was two of 'em. Maybe they thought there was the offhand chance that I was wrong and there could be another lunatic inside. They all had flashlights that made it easier to see where we were at as we all tried to make our way through the dark, rancid cave.

We got to the fire site, which was nothin' but a pile of ashes by then. It wasn't far 'til they found the remains of the bear. It was a bloated, god-awful sight.

Not far from there was the blanket-covered remains of Scott O'Grady. When they pulled the covers back I saw what was left of his face and the horrified expression on it. I began to feel myself spiral into darkness as I passed out cold. It was only a minute or two before I was comin' out of it. Stanley and Toby were tryin' to give me a drink out of someone's coffee mug. It tasted terrible and I turned my head away. When I was able to get up, the chief investigator asked me if I could identify the body as the one who'd kidnapped and raped me.

"Yes," I said without much expression. "That's Scott O'Grady, and he's the one who did all of that."

They took pictures of everything. I dared to glance slyly toward the boxes at the back. They'd been moved to cover any sign of entrance to the back of the cave. The investigators took notes as I explained the table with the straps and the table with the torture tools that he'd set up. It wasn't long before they asked me about the different sets of chains on the walls.

"I don't know what he had planned. Sometimes he'd chain me to one side and other times he'd chain me to the wall on the other side. If I fought him or didn't cooperate, he'd chain me to the table and beat me. That happened several times.

He came and went as two different people, but I finally figgered out that they was both him." The chief walked around for a minute.

"How'd ya get loose, Lilah?" he aked

"I was chained on that side over there." I stated as I walked to the side Chad'd been chained on, "After he was dead and the bear was gone, I found a large rock and I beat the chains off with my one free hand that he'd forgot to chain back. He done that sometimes."

I looked down and there on the ground was the rock that Chad had used. As I bent to pick it up, I felt an unexplainable tug at my heart and held it to my chest.

"That was remarkable thinkin', Lilah. I just don't know how you did it with the injuries you had." I looked him square in the eyes.

"I think it's called 'survival' Chief. A sheer will to survive."

I explained about the supplies that Scott'd brought in and that I'd found the gun in the bag. It was loaded and thank God it worked when I'd had to use it.

They took everything that was in there except the boxes.

"What's in those boxes? Do you know?" the Chief investigator asked.

"Just a bunch of junk my Nanny and some of the other relatives stored in here. It always seemed like a good place to put it, but I need to get it cleaned up right away and get this all cleared out. It's been here as long as I can remember. We used to play all over here when we was little kids."

"Well, I think we got everything that we need. If ya decide to use it as a storage, ya might want to seal up that entrance with a door or somethin'. Ya sure don't want to come up here an find another bear!" Stanley advised.

We made the long journey down 'round the mountain and back to the cabin. I was still a little dizzy and I was surprised to find that my strength wasn't all that I'd expected.

Once we got back, I went straight to the couch and laid down. I can't begin to explain how wonderful it felt to lay down with my blanket in front of the fire and finally relax. I was relieved that it was over.

Of course, the police weren't content to just leave me alone. They came back to the cabin, too. There was still a thousand questions that they had for me. I just stayed focused and answered 'em as best I could, but in the back of my mind I couldn't quit thinkin' about Chad. My heart needed to know if he was alright. Was he comin' back? Where in the world had he gone?

I soon learned that the press conference was to be held at three o'clock that afternoon, on my own front porch. I was none too happy 'bout that 'cause I just wanted to be left alone. Of course the authorities hung around all day until the rest of the news media arrived. We went through almost everything again, however, the police answered most of the questions. They accepted my explanation pretty much without hesitation. I just stood in the back ground and listened. There was very little I was asked directly. Within two hours it was over and done. Everyone had left except Stanley.

"Lilah, can I ask ya a couple a more questions? I mean . . . off the record ?"

"Sure Stan. What is it ya wanna know?"

"What ever happened to that Barrett guy? He was here while we was all searchin' and he seemed genuinely upset. Then all of a sudden he just disappeared! It seemed odd . . . and it made me really suspicious of him. I would've almost bet he had somethin' to do with your disappearance. If ya hadn't come back when ya did . . . we was gonna issue an all points bulletin to have him brought in."

I sat there for what seemed like an eternity 'cause I wasn't sure what to tell him. There was no way I could betray Chad by tellin' him the whole truth . . .

but now I was gonna have to come up with somethin'. Stan had been my friend for many years and I knew that he was the most honorable officer anyone could ever hope to have in their town. I also knew that he was officer first, and friend second. Besides, I couldn't very well say that Chad didn't want to be on television, even though he was the one who'd saved me. Finally I took a deep breath and looked him right in his eyes.

"Stan, Chad and me was callin' it quits a long time before I disappeared. He was goin' back to wherever he'd come from. He probably just decided to go on since nobody was havin' any luck findin' me. He had no reason what-so-ever to stick around."

He chewed on his toothpick a little more and seemed to ponder my explanation.

"Well, that's too bad, honey. We all liked him. He seemed like a genuine good guy Maybe he'll think it over and come to realize that he just left the best thing he could ever hope to find."

"Thank ya Stan. But it's okay. It really is."

Floy and Toby stayed a couple more days 'til I finally told 'em that it was okay for 'em to go back home. I was doin' fine . . . most of the time.

It was really difficult when I finally talked to my Mama and Daddy. Mama felt sure that it was all her fault 'cause she'd asked Scott to come check on me in the first place. I tried to reassure her that it'd probably have happened either way. He had his mind set on what he was gonna do and he'd have found me sooner or later. It took a long time to get her calmed down, but Daddy was takin' care of her and I knew that he'd help her work it out.

When everyone'd gone and the phone calls had dropped to a bare minimum, I went out and sat on the porch in the cold. Just me and my two dogs.

It almost seemed like it was the way it used to be before I even heard of Chad Barrett.

The moon was full and the fresh snow was covered in silver moonbeams. I stood up to go in and glanced up. It reminded me how Nanny told me once that Mr. Moon could see everything and I knew that he knew exactly where Chad was at that very minute and what he was doin'. For a moment I caught myself becomin' a little jealous of that all-knowin' old moon, but I thought a moment longer, and decided that if it was meant for me to know, then I'd most surely come to know.

As time passed, I found myself bein' more and more depressed. Even after that damn rooster woke me up, I had to make myself get up in the mornin's. The last thing I wanted to do was tend to the ranch. I wanted merely to sleep 'til it was dark so I'd have an excuse to go to bed and sleep some more.

Food became scarce since I had no appetite. I found that all I wanted was my iced tea. I'd got to the point that I only took a bath when I could no longer live with myself. I quickly grew to avoid the telephone. It took too much energy to talk, so I just let it ring. Most times I simply sat and looked at it 'til it quit ringin'.

Maybe I'd hire someone to take care of the ranch and I'd just supervise. I thought I'd even try to hire Dee back, if for nothin' more than just the company, but I didn't really want any company.

Many was the times I'd go up and lock myself in the bedroom.

I hadn't been to church in . . . well . . . I couldn't remember how long. Sometimes I even locked the doors and pretended I wasn't home. There were only a few visitors, mostly people from the church and sometimes Floy and Toby. Durin' most of those times I hid the jeep in the barn so no one'd know that I was really there.

Tuesday mornin' came and I decided to go down-stairs and maybe find somethin' to eat. I went into the kitchen just as the phone rang . . . again.

I ignored it . . . again.

Just as I sat down with a piece of toast and a cup of coffee and stared out the back window, the snow began to lightly fall. I didn't know how long I'd been sittin' there but I was sure it was at least three or more cups of coffee long. The front door opened and Toby and Floy come rushin' in. I'd forgotten that Floy had her own key.

"Where have ya been?" Toby demanded. He had a wild look in his eyes. "We've been callin' ya for three days or more!"

Floy sat down beside me and just stared at me.

"What?" I finally asked her.

"Sweetie have ya looked in the mirror lately?"

I simply looked at her and then turned to look back outside.

"You still haven't heard from Chad, have ya?"

"Did ya look 'round to see if he left any kind of explanation?" Toby asked as he poured himself a cup of coffee.

"There was nothin' left in the cave." I answered him flatly.

"Did ya look in the little cabin?"

I sat there a good long time and thought about it. It'd never occurred to me and I hadn't been back to the little cabin since that day.

"No." I sighed.

Toby finished his coffee and started to the back door.

"Where ya goin'?" questioned Floy.

"To the little cabin! He might've left a note or somethin'."

"Wait!" I told him as I got up and slipped on my boots and coat. "I'm comin' too!"

Floy waddled to the door, but decided she'd wait there. In her condition she didn't need to be trekin' across the back yard and takin' a chance at fallin'.

We made our way down the back steps and through the back gate. It was beginnin' to get slippery since the snow was comin' down heavier. It took us a little bit to get up to the other cabin. We were both out of breath from the climb in the ice and snow mixture.

The door wasn't locked. It never had been.

There was a very uncomfortable feelin' about the cabin now. I'd never felt that way before, 'cause it'd always had a cozy feel about it.

It was impossible to tell that there was a secret entrance to the cave. The armoire had been put back in place and the whole cabin was in order. Even the supplies that Floy and Toby had brought us was missin'.

"Toby, help me move this," I asked as I took hold of the armoire.

"Why?"

"I just thought about somethin'," I said as we pulled the big chest forward.

As it moved, it pulled the heavy door to the cave open and the tiny room was immediately open to view. I lit a lamp and the two of us walked in.

"I saw this, but I don't think I ever even walked in here." Toby mumbled.

The table and chair were still there. Even the metal bar was leaned against the wall. I looked at the other wall and immediately felt a huge wave of nausea over take me. It was as if the air had all gone out of the room and I dropped to my knees and covered my face with my hands.

"No!" I cried. "No! I'm such a fool."

"What's the matter with ya baby?" Toby came rushin' to my side.

I began to sob without control and everything that'd happened came pourin' out with a mixture of tears. Sweet Toby simply sat and held me while I cried 'til there was nothin' left but weak sobs. He thought that it was just a sort of breakdown over everything, but when I finally pulled myself somewhat together, I began to try to explain.

"It's gone, Toby."

"What's gone?"

"When we first found this room there was several boxes in here. One was open but the rest was still locked."

Toby looked puzzled and finally asked, "What was in 'em?"

"It was pure gold bars. The family money I suppose. I don't know where they got it, but I'm sure it was a fortune. Everything indicated that the old story about the captured gold shipment must have been true. Chad had to have taken it."

We sat and stared at each other for several minutes.

"I don't think that he'd do that, Lilah."

"He's the only one besides me that knew it was there. All he wanted was money! That's probably why he came here. I bought those horses and he was there. He saw me pay for 'em in cash and he figgered I was just some little bumpkin and a easy mark. I guess he figgered right. All it took was some sweet words with a sexy southern accent, a couple a hot kisses, and I crumbled right into his hands. He got everything he wanted and then some."

Toby got up and walked around for awhile.

"I can't believe that. I don't think he's that kind a man. Besides, he had his own money. Remember when ya'll fixed up our house?"

"Toby, how do I know he had the money to pay for that? He might've bought it on credit knowin' that when we got married . . . he'd have plenty of money."

"Should we report it to the police?"

"What good would it do? There's nothin' here to show he was ever even here. There's nothin' at the house either. It's all gone." I pointed out.

"Well, I helped him move all that to our place when the cops pretty much sealed up the place. They searched through everything he had before he could take it. We thought it was pretty odd too when he disappeared and only took what he was wearin' and his truck. He probably went back to the house and got his stuff while we were all here with you. I ain't checked yet." Toby sounded upset.

"The cops would just think I'm havin' some kinda breakdown, Toby. Ya know that's what they'd think. I'm just such an idiot! First Walt, then Scott, and now Chad. I'm battin' a thousand ain't I Toby?"

I broke into tears again. I'd never felt so betrayed and so abandoned. An idiot, yes, I'd bought into it hook, line, and sinker. I supposed that he was laughin' all the way to the bank . . . yeah . . . Laughin'? A sudden remembrance jumped out of nowhere to catch me off guard . . . how I had loved to hear him laugh. I'd loved to hear him talk and I'd even loved to hear him breathe. I'd just loved Chad, period.

Well, I hoped he'd enjoy it. That it fulfilled his every dream and fantasy. If he'd have listened, I could've told him that money wasn't everything it was cracked up to be. I'd had it for quite awhile and yet the only thing that fulfilled my every dream . . . was him.

We put the armoire back into place and waded back out into the cold. It seemed like winter was dead set on bein' with us for awhile. It didn't matter . . . it was no colder than my heart had just become.

We went in the back door and Floy met us with steamin' hot cups of coffee.

"You must've found somethin' up there! You was gone a long time," she said.

I sipped my coffee and looked out into the snow. "It's more what we didn't find that told us the whole story. He's gone and he won't be comin' back. He got what he wanted and he's gone . . . just like that."

Toby sat there in confirmin' silence.

"I still can't believe it," said Floy after we told her the whole story. "I'm not that bad a judge of character. I know he loves you. It was written all over his face. Ever time he looked at ya his eyes just glowed with it."

"Yeah, they glowed alright. Glowed with dollar signs," I snarled. "If ya'll will excuse me for a little bit . . . I'm gonna go up and take a shower. Just make yourselves at home. I'll be back."

I stepped into the hot shower and began to wash away the sweat, the stress, and the tears that I began to shed once more. These were tears for all the "what ifs" and "could haves" in my life. Maybe I just wasn't the type of woman that men cherished. Maybe I was just a giver who always attracted the takers. I wept for my babies. Those that I'd never have. Those that I'd never hold and cuddle. I cried for all the times that I couldn't. The sobs finally began to subside. I knew that it was over. It'd all washed down the drain with the soap and shampoo and the last of my tears.

By the time I'd done my hair and my body was squeaky clean, a new woman emerged from that shower. I dressed, toweled my hair, brushed it out and I went down the stairs with a new attitude and a completely different way of lookin' at the world.

Toby and Floy could see it from the moment that I come back into the kitchen.

"I'm hungry. What ya'll want to eat?" I asked as I began to dig out the last of the refrigerator's contents.

"I'm not really that hungry." Floy answered.

"Boy I am! Nothin' like the snow to get my appetite in a tiz." offered Toby.

"Your appetite stays in a tiz, Toby, the damn snow ain't got nothin' to do with it." Floy teased.

I fried bacon, made homemade pancakes, and homestyle fried taters with gravy. Me and Toby ate like there wasn't gonna be no food tomorrow. Floy ate a little, but was true to her word. Afterwards, I didn't know 'bout Toby, but I absolutely felt sick to my stomach. I knew that I'd way over-done it, especially since I'd hardly eaten anything in weeks.

Later that mornin' they left for home. I busied myself with cleanin' the kitchen. When I was done, every room in the downstairs area was dusted, mopped, polished, and scrubbed. I thought about goin' upstairs and gettin' started, but decided it would be better if I saved that for the next day.

Later that afternoon, I decided to go to the barn early and spend some time with the animals. It'd been a long time since I'd taken time to brush and spoil 'em. I didn't even know the new colt. In fact it dawned on me that I hadn't even seen him yet.

I bounced down the front steps and was joined by Boots and Roz. They seemed particularly glad to see me. I began to feel a little of the old determination try to sneak in on me.

It'd been so long since I'd been in the barn. Pride and Patton were watchin' the corral gate when I opened it and they both nickered and began to paw and prance with excitement. I gave 'em each a pat and a hug then went around to the new baby. It was a shock when I saw him. He was one of the most beautiful colts I'd ever laid eyes on.

A young Arabian.

He was sleek, well-built, shined like coal, and had the most adorable face in the world. His eyes were sparklin' with his youth, his curiosity, and his excitement of just bein' alive. I took a handful of oats and held my hand out to him. He was cautious, but very curious, as to what I was offerin' him. He looked straight into my eyes as if tryin' to decide if he should trust me.

"Come little boy . . . it's okay." I spoke softly.

He nickered again while noddin' his head up and down. I must've passed inspection 'cause he began to step cautiously toward me. As I opened my hand, he nibbled shyly at the oats while I reached with the other hand and petted him gently.

He'd been Chad's Christmas present. I was a little surprised he didn't make room for him when he made his dash to freedom. After all, he had cost me a small fortune.

He nuzzled my empty hand and looked hopefully at me. I gave him a little more of the oats and stroked his neck as he nibbled.

"I'll never walk away from ya, little fella. I'll give ya a great home, pastures to roam, and all the love ya could ever want. That's my promise to ya. I'll be your best friend...always." I stood there a moment "That's it . . . your new name is 'Promise' That's a beautiful name for a beautiful little guy. I have Patton, Pride, and Promise. My boys."

They followed me into the barn where I brushed and fed 'em. I made my way back to the cabin. It was gettin' dark and I was startin' to get tired. It seemed like I still had a ways to go before I'd have all my strength back.

After I ate and sat down, I fell asleep on the couch, covered with the blanket that still reeked of Chad's cologne.

On Saturday Floy and Toby came out. I was glad to see 'em. I thought they seemed surprised to find me still clean and dressed, and my house was spotless. Floy was a little over five months but I guessed that bein' such a short little thing made her look like she was much further along. Toby was the ever adorin', lovin', husband and father–to–be.

"Ya look so much better, Lilah. Look at ya. I like the new hair do. Did ya go into town and get a cut?" Floy asked.

"No . . . don't laugh . . . I cut it myself."

"Why for heaven's sake?"

"'Cause I never get it cut like I want it . . . so I read in a book how the 'Gypsy shag' was just a lopped off pony tail. I put a loose pony tail on top of my head and . . . lopped it off."

"It looks great. In fact, ya just look cute as a kitten in a mitten."

Toby and I both looked at her.

"A kitten in a mitten?" Toby asked in an amused little voice.

Floy busted out laughin' "Yeah. I been practicin' my bedtime stories for the baby and I guess some of them phrases are just startin' to stick." We laughed as we went into the kitchen in search of a another cup of coffee.

"So what are you guys doin' out here?"

"We came to get ya." Toby offered.

"Me?"

"Yes ma'am." Floy added as she sat down with her coffee.

"For what?"

"I need a little help."

"Sure. With what?"

"I'm beggin' up a dancin' partner for my man. I need someone who is worthy and TRUSTworthy. I can't dance that much and he so loves to dance. Would ya please be my husbands temporary dance partner?"

I looked at 'em both as if they'd lost their minds.

"When's this dancin' takin' place?"

"Tonight," Floy said slyly.

"Tonight?" I don't know if I can even dance anymore. It's been a very long time."

"Please?" she begged.

"Pretty, please?" pleaded Toby as he flirted with his soft grey eyes.

It was somethin' I thought about for a little bit. I didn't know if I could go back out there. Everyone in the county knew what'd happened to me. Besides . . . I was afraid that the memories would be more than I could handle. I finally made up my mind that I wasn't gonna cave in to gossip and old memories, especially the ones I was workin' so hard on forgettin'.

"Yeah, I guess I might as well get my feet wet and get back out into public. I've hid out here long enough."

I got some clothes together and my make-up, and all the usual stash of goodies that a girl needs when she is going with her best friends to get ready to go out.

"Ride with us. We'll bring ya back home afterward," Toby offered.

We loaded up in his truck and went back to their house. We fixed somethin' to eat before we got ready to go. Floy looked so cute in her jeans and little maternity western shirt. Deep inside I envied her more than she could ever begin to imagine. She had a wonderful husband and a baby on the way. What wasn't to envy?

Then there was Toby . . . with his tight-fitted jeans, bright red shirt, and black Stetson hat. He was just a hot lookin' little cowboy. Myself, I was wearin' my best-fittin' pair of jeans with a purple and black shirt that looked almost like a vest with long sleeves. My belt was very stylish with my name on the back and a pair of lace-up boots to match. I'd decided to have a good time come hell or high water, but by the time we pulled up at King's I'd started to become very nervous. My stomach was churnin' and my hands was gettin' sweaty.

"Floy?" I said shakily "I don't know if I'm really ready to do this."

"Listen to me . . . you're about the bravest one person I've ever known. Ya lived through a hell of an ordeal includin' bein' attacked by a sure enough bear. I promise ya . . . there ain't no bears in there. I ain't gonna let nobody bother ya. Now, ya got my word on that, darlin'," Toby vowed.

I nodded. We got out and made our way to the door. The parkin' lot was full, but there was a short line . We reached the door and I found myself grabbed in a bear hug. *Maybe that was a bad choice of words!* Then I recognized Tony, the door man.

"Lilah Marie! God love your heart girl! I'm so glad to see ya back out here. How the hell ya been? Heard about what happened and if that S.O.B. wasn't dead . . . I'd a killed him myself . . . me and four dozen others. Ya look beautiful Sugar . . . just beautiful!" He gave me another hug and a little kiss and refused my money.

Tony didn't seem the least bit repulsed by me and he didn't seem to hold it against me in any way. I followed Toby and Floy in and let 'em find a table. It was more comfortable for me to remain in the background as much as possible. The table they found was back away from the dance floor, just a tad secluded. It was a comfortable place to sit and watch the dancers for a while.

"Ya ready to dance?" Toby asked me.

"Do ya mind if we wait just a little bit, Toby. I need to feel a little more comfortable. Okay?"

"Sure. Take your time . . . I'm gonna go get a brew," he hesitated and looked at Floy." . . . and a water! Do ya want somethin' to drink?"

"Yeah I do. Make it somethin' strong!" I told him as I winked at him.

Me and Floy was watchin' the dancers and admirin' some of the outfits when a familiar voice spoke up from behind me, "Ya like to dance?" I looked up and to my pleasant surprise it was Jamie. "How ya doin,' Lilah? I sure have missed ya out here. Want to scoot a boot?"

I hesitated then stood up.

"Sure . . . I believe I do."

He gently led me out to the dance floor, where we began a comfortable two-step. As we made our way around the floor, I had several people tell me how good it was to see me again and how glad they was that I was alright.

Alright?

I wasn't sure that I'd ever be alright again . . . but I was damn sure workin' on it.

Jamie and I danced for a while, then he walked me back to my table.

"Can I ask ya to dance again?"

"Yeah, I'd love to."

He was such a nice guy. Why couldn't I just feel a little bit of attraction to him?

Nope! I told myself . . . we ain't lookin' for no damned "attraction". Maybe a friend. Maybe a dance partner.

That was it . . . Never again!

I danced with Toby most of the night and a few others includin' Jamie.

We were glidin' 'round the floor when the DJ called out a get acquainted mixer. It made me uncomfortable as I remembered the last time I'd danced to one of these. It was the first time I'd danced with Chad. For some reason, every time we had to switch partners I kept hopin' that the next one might be . . . Chad.

There was a lot of old friends out there . . . even some of the newer ones. I had danced with both Jamie, and Toby, but the last one was very gentle and a very good dancer. He had his hat so low down that the shadow covered his face. He looked vaguely familiar, but I just couldn't see him that well. The dance went directly into a beautiful slow song. He gently held me as we continued to dance. Somethin' inside told me that I knew that man. It took me awhile before I finally got up the nerve to reach up and push his hat back. I was stunned, to say the very least, when I discovered who lurked beneath that hat.

"Who are ya hidin' from?" I asked him.

"Nobody, for a change" he answered. "How are ya Lilah? Ya know . . . I was sure worried sick about ya. I searched and searched for days. Me and a lot a other folks 'bout tore that countryside apart! When I heard that ya was found . . . I got on . . . well . . . I did, I got on my knees and thanked God."

"Why?" I asked in total confusion.

"'Cause ya was always the best thing in my world. I never deserved ya. But that don't mean that I won't always love ya." Walt answered.

"How much have ya had to drink tonight?" I asked him as we continued to dance.

"One beer" he answered. "That's my limit from now on."

"What happened?" I wanted to know.

"I reckon I realized how short and un . . . unpre . . . what a surprise life can be."

"Why couldn't ya have figgered that out all those years ago."

"I reckon, it was just the beast in me, honey!" He grinned and shook his head.

"Walt . . . I . . . I just don't know what to say."

For the first time in years we laughed and continued to dance. When the song ended, Walt stood there a minute just holdin' my hand.

"Could I maybe have another dance . . . later?"

"Maybe," I answered as I walked back to my table.

Toby had just walked Floy back.

"Whew . . . I'm gettin' too big for that. I thought that was never gonna end." She sighed. "Who was that last guy you was dancin' with?"

"Ya wouldn't believe me if I told ya."

"Try me, ya'll danced pretty good together."

"We should . . . we been dancin' together for years!" I said.

Her jaw dropped. It was about that time Toby came back with beers and water.

"What's the matter baby? You feelin' okay?" He looked at me as he handed me a beer.

"She just went catatonic when I told her that I was dancin' with Walt . . . 'cause it didn't end up in a free for all." Toby looked like somebody smacked him with a dead cat.

"What are ya thinkin', Lilah?" Floy all but yelled at me.

"It wasn't on purpose. He just happened to be the next one in line on the mixer. He was surprisin'ly nice. We actually had a good time."

"Don't ya even think about it, Lilah Marie. I'll grab ya up and bust your ass!" Toby threatened.

"Oh, don't ya worry Toby, I ain't gettin' involved with nobody again . . . ever!!"

I drank my beer and tried to relax some.

Even though I knew there wasn't a chance, I caught myself searchin' every crook and cranny of that club. It was as though my eyes had a mind of their own. I was sure I never wanted to see Chad Barrett again . . . but my eyes couldn't quit lookin' for him. Once, I thought I saw him and I was surprised to find that my heart had literally skipped a beat. I found myself comparin' every cowboy I looked at with him.

I swear I could almost see him standin' over there against the bar. His ostrich boots and very tight fittin' jeans along with that black western shirt left open at the neck to show his gold rope necklace, the black belt with the gold medallions on it and the black Stetson hat. He was always the most beautiful thing I could ever imagine. In my mind's eye I could see that thick silver blonde hair, and when I imagined him lookin' back at me, those vivid blue eyes still took my breath away.

Someone walked in front of me, blocked my imaginary view, and I snapped back to reality, angry with myself for allowin' my heart to have control to that extent.

I turned the bottle up and downed the contents. As the waitress came by, I ordered another. Floy and Toby were visitin' with some friends so they never noticed how many beers I actually managed to consume in a very short period of time.

"Would ya dance with me?" I looked up to find Walt there with his hand held out.

"Hell yeah!" I said as I jumped up and headed to the dance floor with him.

As we danced, I noticed that he'd really cleaned up. He had a nice hair cut and was clean-shaven. Walt'd always been a real knock-out with his black hair and liquid black eyes, and that dark complexion. It gave him such an exotic look. He had a Hollywood smile that had always made every woman he looked at blush. He had pretty lips, perfect teeth, and a cute little dimple in his chin.

Walt was tall and extremely well built, but he'd always been such a smart ass and a rumbler that most people stayed clear of him for fear of gettin' into a fight . . . or worse . . . jail.

We danced the two-step, then a nice slow song. Walt pulled me close, but surprised me when he treated me with more respect than I could ever remember before. He was unusually gentle. I didn't even remember him bein' that way back when we first got together. The song ended and we walked back over to the table.

"It was good to see ya again, Lilah. You take care a you. okay?" Then he turned and walked away.

I could hardly believe that it was really Walt.

"I think he's been possessed," declared Floy. " I ain't never seen him that respectful in all the years I known him. What ya reckon he's up to, Toby?"

"I don't know but I want no part of it. Whatever it is it'll be trouble . . . guaranteed! And as for you Missy . . . " he pointed his finger at me, "You will stay far . . . far . . . away from that . . . man!" He leaned in close, " . . . or you'll answer to me."

"Yes sir!" I answered as I delivered a very loud and unexpected hiccup.

"Lilah . . . are you toasted?" laughed Floy.

"Maybe . . . just a little . . . bit." I whispered so no one else would know.

I danced some more with Toby and then with Jamie, as well as a few men I didn' t even know. How much more I drank was anybodys guess. I was feelin' no pain whatsoever. In fact, I was feelin' extremely good, better than I'd felt in a long, long time. Somewhere along the way, I found myself dancin' with Nicky.

"I'm sure glad to see ya back out here, sweetheart. Ya know, damn near this whole place was out searchin' for ya. I have to say this . . . I was surprised as hell that Walter was out there, clean, sober, and frantic to find ya. He wasn't the only one though. Ya remember that cat ya met out here? The kind a blonde guy? I kinda thought he was gonna have a break down or somethin'. They had to drag him in out of the dark at night and he was the first one out there ever mornin'. Then one mornin' . . . he just wasn't there no more. Never did come back. Have ya heard anything from him? I liked him . . . he was a pretty cool cat."

"No, I haven't heard anything from him. I guess he had other fish to fry," I answered him as indifferent as I could.

"That sure does surprise me. He sure acted like a man in deep love . . . or lust!" he laughed.

I laughed with him. Mostly to keep from cryin'. I'd also thought that he was in deep love.

Sometimes there's just not enough laughter to cover all them tears. Nicky was a great guy, but I was glad when the song was over and I could escape back to my table. No one was there when I reached it, so with the help of several more drinks, I had ample time to pull myself together before they got back.

Finally, they called last dance and last call so we decided to go ahead and leave. We wanted to beat the rush to the cars and trucks. It'd been a long day and I was glad we were goin'. I'd had enough of socializin' and I wasn't feelin' none to well at that moment.

We'd only gone a couple of miles when I begged Toby to pull over and stop. The moment he did, I bailed out of the truck, but when I stepped down, I found nothin' but air under my feet . The steep downward slope caught me off guard and I found myself rollin' helplessly down into the ditch to lay in a heap at the bottom.

In shock, I just laid there.

It'd scared me so bad, I'd forgotten about bein' sick. I noticed how cool the dirt was on my flushed face and for a moment I was almost sure I could hear the earth's heartbeat. I eventually realized it was only the sound of Toby's boots hittin' the hard ground as he hurried toward me.

"Ya alright, sweetie?" He asked as he sat me up. I looked up at him and started to answer, but nothin' would come out of my mouth. Those damned uncontrollable tears started and I was helpless to stop 'em. The one thing I should've remembered was that alcohol doesn't remedy anything. All it does is bring your defenses down to the point that ya can no longer keep 'em in check. He knelt there and held me while I cried. From somewhere unexpected, I turned and wrapped my arms around his neck and kissed him. I kissed him like a drownin' woman would embrace air. It shocked him, but for one second he kissed me back then jerked his head away. We just sat there lookin' at each other in total horror.

"Oh, God, Toby! I'm so sorry . . . I never meant to . . . I'm so, so, sorry."

"No, I'm sorry, that shouldn't never a happened. I . . . I . . . there's no excuse." He stammered.

"It wasn't your fault, Toby. It was all me. I guess for a minute . . . I . . . I wanted so bad for ya to be Chad! I miss him so much, Toby. I just miss him so much." I sobbed.

"It's okay. It never happened. Okay? It just never happened. Come on... let,s get ya to your feet and see if we can climb back up where we come from."

We stumbled back up to the truck and Floy was outside standin' beside it.

"Ya'll okay? Ya scared me to death. What if there'd been water down there?" She said as she put her arms around me and held me like a sister.

"Did ya get sick? Poor baby."

I was sick alright. I was sicker than I'd ever been in my entire life. Floy and Toby were family to me. How could I have done such a horrible thing? Why did I do that? Toby would never be able to look at me the same. It'd just never be the same between us.

They tried to get me to stay the night at their place, but after what'd happened, I just couldn't do it. I wanted to go home, hide my face under the blanket and die of shame.

When we got to my cabin, I hugged Floy and told her good night. To my surprise, Toby got out and helped me take my stuff inside.

"I'm gonna wait in the truck. Ya make sure everything is okay inside the house before we leave, honey. Get her settled in. I'll call ya tomorrow, Lilah," she called out.

We went inside and Toby put my stuff on the couch and went straight to check the back door lock. He went upstairs and checked out the rooms up there. When he came back down stairs, I could hardly make myself look at him. He stopped and reached for my hand. I looked up and met with his soft grey eyes.

"Lilah, I meant what I said back there. That kiss should never a happened, but I do understand what ya was feelin'. I really do. I don't want this to affect our friendship, sweetie. You're like a sister to me and Floy both and I'll wade through a field of rattlers to keep it from comin' between us all. I'm sorry for any part I was responsible for and I hope you'll accept my deepest apology."

"I meant what I said, too. You've nothin' to apologize for, Toby. All I could do all evenin' was look for Chad and think about Chad and after I drank too much... well... that's the only excuse I got. I guess I just needed to be kissed... maybe to take the pain away. I don't know. But again... I'm so sorry."

"Let's just forget it happened, please?" He begged.

"Done." I said.

When I walked him to the door and thanked him for checkin' things out, I waved to Floy and they left. I shut the door and bolted it. It was then that I walked toward the couch and completely broke down as I wrapped Chad's blanket around myself.

The sweet scent of his cologne surrounded me and I dreamed about him that night. Beautiful dreams of love, babies, and forever happiness. A beautiful fantasy!

Chapter 17

Eventually I drug myself up the stairs and into my bed. Never in my entire life had I felt so alone. I'd been content before I met Chad and I was happy with my life just the way it had been . Why did I let him have my heart, let alone my very soul? I wondered where all my determination and courage had gone. Earlier in the day I'd pulled myself together and was on a new road. Yet there I lay, right in the middle of despair again. I figgered I could thank that countless number of beers that I'd downed for all I was feelin' right then.

After I tossed and turned for no tellin' how many hours, I finally got up and went to the bathroom. I came out, sat in the rocker by the window, and looked across the moonlit yard. The dogs would go out toward the barn and then come back to the house. There was a couple of raccoons sneakin' 'round the yard too. Everything in the world seemed so bleak and empty. For the life of me . . . I didn't know how I was goin' to get over it all.

While I was sittin' there, I became aware of what appeared to be someone standin' by the big tree behind the corral. I leaned forward and wiped at my eyes. The vague image appeared to be wearin' all black. It was really hard to focus in the darkness of the night even with fresh fallen snow on the ground. Just as quick as it seemed to be there . . . it was gone . . . just like that. It was all I could do to keep myself from goin' out there and confrontin' whoever it might be. Just the way Chad had done!

For a brief moment, I wondered if that could possibly have been Walt. He'd been like a different person that night. But ya never could tell with Walt 'cause he was an expert at playin' the part of whatever he thought ya wanted him to be. There'd been a time when I really thought I'd been in love with him and I was sure that he was in love with me. Then I found out about all the other women and not only was my heart broken, but I guessed my ego had been broken, too. I'd always told myself that there was somethin' about me that'd made Walt choose me over all the other girls in school who chased after him. He'd been the typical, irresistable rebel. Handsome as the devil, Mama used to say about him, and always prone to get in some sort of trouble. He'd had a hard childhood and in order to make hisself feel better 'bout things, he'd played the adorable bad boy. I guess I wanted to save him . . . turn him into what I thought he could be. It didn't take long 'til I learned that ya can't fix anybody. Nanny was right . . . what ya see is what ya get. If there's any changin' goin' to happen, it's up to that person to want to change themselves. I'd always believed that if we could've had a baby, maybe that would've been enough to make him want to make that change. It just didn't seem to be in the cards for us. I reckoned later on that it was probably for the best in the long run. Most likely I would've just been left with a little one to raise on my own.

It was four in the mornin' when I finally crawled back in my bed. I woke up later that mornin' with the worst headache I'd had in my entire life. It seemed like it took forever to get to the bottom of the stairs. Every step I took, felt like the earth moved and tilted.

Eventually I got the coffee made and found the aspirin. I stood by the back door and looked out across my land. There'd been another light snow durin' the night and it seemed like winter was determined to last forever this year. The cold and the overcast skies just seemed to add to the gloom that seemed dead set on devourin' my very bein'.

After I ate a light breakfast, I got dressed, grabbed another cup of coffee, and went out to sit in the cold mornin' air of the front porch. Boots and Roz were quickly at my feet.

Edgar had taken two of Roz's puppies home with him when he took her back to his farm. It didn't matter, Roz found her way back to Boots everytime we turned around. Finally Edgar told me to just let her be. She'd been there ever since.

The mornin' was quiet and peaceful until I heard the sound of a car comin' up through the grove.

It was Floy.

I was suddenly very nervous about seein' her. I'd tried to put what happened the night before out of my mind, but the instant I saw her little truck I felt sick again. How I would've loved to suddenly develop the ability to vanish into thin air.

She pulled up in front of the house and got out of her truck. I thought how adorably cute she was as she waddled up the steps. I wasn't sure what to say. We'd never had secrets from each other and I didn't know how I was gonna manage this one.

"Hi Sweetie. How ya feelin' this mornin'?" she smiled her sweet smile as she gave me a hug. "Ya look like hell," she teased.

"That's pretty much how I feel, too. Do ya want some coffee? I just made it a few minutes ago."

"Sure, I'm always ready for your coffee, but do we have to drink it out here in the cold?"

"No . . . I was just tryin' to clear my head." I told her as we went back inside the cabin.

I poured her a cup and we sat at the table. What I really wanted was to crawl under it, but I did my best to act as normal as I could.

"How are you feelin'?" I asked her.

"I'm good." She said as she took a drink and stared into her cup. We sat for a moment in an uncomfortable silence that made me think that maybe she suspected somethin'.

"Ya know . . . we still want ya to be the baby's godmother. We really wanted Chad to be the godfather . . . but now . . . I . . . I . . . I don't know."

Without any warnin', I burst into a torrent of guilty tears. I'd never felt so low and shameful in my whole life. Floy moved to the chair beside me and put her arm around me.

"I know honey and I do understand. But I'm here to help ya get through all this. It's beyond me what Chad could be thinkin'. I don't believe he had no idea how deeply ya loved him. Maybe we was all fooled and he wasn't half the man we thought he was. Maybe he just didn't care who he hurt. I'm just so sorry it was you, Lilah. What can I do to make ya feel better?" I looked into her eyes and found that there were no words in my mouth. The tears started again and I cried so hard that I thought for sure that I was goin' to throw up.

"It's not . . . it's not just that . . . I . . . I don't deserve no better. I deserve whatever . . . whatever I get. I'm just a low life. Maybe . . . maybe I always have been."

"Don't say that. That's not true. You're the kindest, most decent person I've ever known. I've known ya all my life and I could never hope to know a better person nor have a dearer, more precious friend. Now I just won't stand for no more of that kind of talk."

The more she said the worse I felt. How could I have betrayed her trust like that. I didn't even want to kiss Toby. Yes, he was very attractive, but my heart was owned by only one man. Why I'd initiated that kiss was somethin' I'd never understand. I didn't even remember how I got in the ditch or what happened that caused me to do what I did. I jumped up from the table and ran into the livin' area and curled up on the couch. Floy came in and sat down beside me.

"Look at me," she ordered. "Lilah Marie, look at me."

It was all I could do to make eye contact with her. She gently took my hands and pulled them to her.

"We been friends as long as I can remember. We been through some terrible times and some great times. We've watched the sun go down and the sun come up and we shared laughter and we shared tears. I plan on doin' all that again and again until we sit on the front porch and try to remember what we was talkin' about. Lilah, I know that part of what ya are so upset about is because of what happened with you and Toby last night."

I almost passed out. I went numb from head to toe! I couldn't believe what I was hearin'.

"Oh, Floy . . . it wasn't what your thinkin'! It was my fault. I . . . I never . . . "

"Shhhh . . . " She said. "Toby told me about it as soon as we got home. He said he hadn't planned on mentionin' it 'cause it was somethin' that needed to just be forgot. It was then that he got to thinkin' about how we'd agreed that we would never keep secrets from each other. So he told me."

I buried my face in the blanket and sobbed again.

"It's okay, Lilah. I understand. Honest, I really do. It wasn't Toby ya was kissin'. It was Chad. I saw ya lookin' in every corner of that club last night and my heart was just breakin' for ya. Me and Toby was thinkin' that if we got ya to go out that maybe ya would start to move on with your life. At first I thought that Jamie might be a great help, but then we both got scared when we saw ya dancin' so much with Walt. I do understand and we are okay. Me, you and Toby . . . we're okay."

I threw my arms around her neck "Just say ya can forgive me, Floy!" I begged.

"There's nothin' to forgive, sweetie. It's done and forgotten. You're my best friend and I love ya so very much."

"I love ya too. I don't deserve such a friend."

After some time of talkin' about it all, we agreed that it was not to come up again.

"C'mon in the kitchen and we'll find somethin' to eat." I offered.

"I'm ready for that." Floy agreed and we headed for the kitchen.

I felt so much better. It was like I could breathe again.

"Can ya believe it snowed again?" Floy asked "I wonder if we're gonna celebrate Easter in the snow."

"I know, I 'm so ready for some spring weather. This year I want to plant some flowers and brighten this place up."

It was so good to change the subject.

We sat down to eat some pancakes. "Ya know . . . the strangest thing happened after I got home. It was impossible to sleep, so I got up and was sittin' in the rocker by the window. It was snowin' and I was watchin' animals wander around the yard when I thought I saw somethin' back in the trees behind the corral."

"What did it look like?" Floy wanted to know.

"It looked like a man leanin' against a tree. He was all in black."

"How could ya see him if he was in black?"

"Well, it sounds funny but I guess with the snow . . . well . . . he was blacker than the shadows. Then I blinked and there was nothin' there. I wondered if I'd just dozed off in the rocker. That's probably all it was."

Floy nodded and we finished our breakfast and sat back and enjoyed our last cup of coffee.

After she left, I felt so much better. I now felt like I had a new lease on life.

I went down to the barn and let the animals out. The horses still needed their blankets, but they were happy to go run in the pasture. The cows were also ready to get out into the big pasture and even the chickens seemed glad to be out. Maybe they knew that spring wasn't too far off.

I was feelin' pretty good 'til I started back to the cabin and happened to glance up the mountain at the little cabin. It felt like an arrow had pierced my heart. It felt like, if I just ran up there and rushed in, that I'd find him there. Perhaps layin' on the bed or just gettin' outta the shower. It wasn't gonna be that way. It was never gonna be that way. I turned back toward my cabin and found that my feet had suddenly grown heavier as I made my way across the yard. How could money be that important to anyone? I'd have given it all to him if he would've just said that he needed or even just wanted it. I had enough in the bank to last me two life times.

Walkin' in the house, it suddenly struck me that . . . it was almost the first of February and I still had my Christmas tree up, the poor little dead thing and it still held all the decorations. Chad and I'd never even opened our presents. We probably never would. I'd never given Floy and Toby theirs either. Chad hadn't forgotten to pick up Toby's cologne. He'd even wrapped it and put it under the tree.

There'd been just too much happenin' too fast.

I took their gifts and put 'em on the table and decided I'd take 'em to 'em some time that week. It was difficult to be sure about the rest of it. I didn't think I could deal with it right then, so I went to the linen closet and got a sheet and wrapped it carefully around the tree and gifts and vowed to take care of the matter another day.

I soon decided to go back to the nursin' home and try and pick up where I'd left off. It should've been a day that I'd remember as the first day of gettin' back to life. I hadn't been there ten minutes when I learned that dear, sweet, Mae Baron had passed away in her sleep just the night before. I hadn't known her that well nor had I known her that long. It didn't matter 'cause she was one of those rare people that you're just plain lucky to meet. Five minutes after ya met her, ya felt like ya'd known her all your life. I'd looked forward to spendin' a lot of time with her. I felt from the beginin' that she had a lot to share and just needed someone to share it with.

When I walked past the room that she'd lived in for ten years, I felt another emptiness deep inside. I paused for a moment and thought about some of the things she'd told me in the short time we'd visited. She'd shared with me about her son, Jonny, and what a bottomless hole his death had left in her heart.

She told me how her husband had grieved hisself to death over it. I recalled her tellin' me about how her family had all passed, one by one. She was the only one left and she was pretty sure that God had just plum forgot about her. I'd told her that He hadn't forgotten her, He was just waitin' until after I got to spend some time with her 'cause He knew we'd be great friends. That was when she laughed and told me how her family had always said she was the tardiest person they'd ever known. Her Aunt Gladys had told her once that she would be late to her own funeral. She smiled sweetly and told me how she figgered they'd all be lined up at the river when it came her time to cross. They would let her know how long they'd been waitin' on her 'cause she was stayin' true to her course, right up to the very end.

One of the housekeepers was cleanin' Mae's room while I was standin' there.

"It's good to see ya back, Lilah. Are ya doin' alright?" she asked with true concern in her voice.

"Yes, thank ya for askin,' I was doin' pretty good 'til I heard about Miss. Mae. I still can't believe it. She was such a sweet lady."

"We're all gonna miss that wonderful lady. She was one of a kind. I don't think that there's a single one of us that didn't go to Miss Mae at some time or other for advice. Ya know, she didn't know ya all that well, but when she heard about what happened to ya . . . Lilah . . . she prayed for hours on end for ya. She said that ya was a special young lady."

Tears began to trickle down my cheeks as I stood there. I could just picture her sittin' in her chair by the window as though she was waitin' or watchin' for someone in particular.

"Lilah, come here a second."

I walked hesitantly into the room.

"Ya know that Miss Mae didn't have nobody. From what I heard all her stuff here is gonna be donated. There's a couple a things that I just don't think should be donated. I think she might want ya to have 'em."

She opened a box on the little dresser and took out a simple weddin' ring.

"She wore this up 'til her little hands swoll up so much that she couldn't. It was her weddin' ring."

She took out a chain necklace with a gold heart locket on it.

"This here was give to her by her son, Jon, he put his picture in it for her to look at 'till he come home from the war. I just don't feel right about anybody donatin' this kind of stuff. I think . . . no . . . I know she'd be so happy for ya to have 'em."

"But, don't she have nobody that was close to her at all? I only visited with her a couple a times."

"No. Just a few friends . . . but she thought an awful lot of you . . . right off the bat. She really liked ya."

She was so insistent that I finally took the ring and necklace and vowed to cherish 'em always.

"Now, it'd be best if ya don't say nothin' about this. Somebody might get the wrong idea and make a stink about it. I just believe she would want it this way." She whispered.

"Okay . . . if you're sure." I told her.

I looked at a picture of Miss Mae that was sittin' on the chest. She was beamin' with happiness. What a message, I thought to myself. She had no one and yet she was just a ray of sunshine and I decided that would be my life lesson from her. I wanted to always feel that I was someone's ray of sunshine.

The day was long and sad as everyone I visited with wanted to talk about the loss of Miss Mae.

It was later on in the day before I stopped by to see Lamar for a few minutes. I didn't know if he'd remember me or not since it'd been so long since I'd been there.

I knocked and he invited me in. Before I could say a word he smiled and said "C'mon in, Lilah, I was wonderin' when I'd get to see ya again."

"How did ya know it was me, Lamar?" I asked him. I was amazed at his ability.

"Two things, my dear, the way ya knock on my door and the smell of your hair."

"Are ya serious?" I asked in surprise.

"Oh yes, that and the fact that I heard one of the orderlies say that it was good to see ya again, 'Lilah'!"

"Mr. Lamar, I never know when ya are serious and when you're just messin' with me! How've ya been?"

"I was doin' real good up 'til this mornin' when I heard about my sweet Mae. It's sad for me and all us still waitin', but I'm so very happy for her. Ya know what she told me just yesterday?"

"I have no idea, Lamar."

"We was sittin' out in the sun room and she said, just out of the blue, 'Lamar, I miss my Mama. It's been so many years and I just long so to see her face and hear her voice.' Then she sighed the weariest sigh and said, 'I'm so ready to go home now.' Then she just smiled the sweetest smile and went back to rockin'. Ain't that somethin'! Now today . . . she's gone on home!" I saw a couple a tears rolled out from under his dark glasses.

"Yeah, it's somethin' . . . I agree . . . she's at rest, Lamar."

We talked for a while longer rememberin' Miss Mae. Before I knew, it was time to start home. I gave him a hug and told him I'd be back in a couple of days, and we'd talk more.

Sadly, I headed home with a heavy heart. It was so hard to even imagine what it must've been like to have absolutely nobody. Of course, she did have a lot of friends. I wish I'd gotten there sooner. I would've liked for her to know that I certainly thought an awful lot of her, too. In fact, I wished that she knew how many people were so saddened by her passin'.

 I was very deep in my own thoughts as I drove home. The sun was just beginnin' its descent when I pulled out of the tree grove and toward the house. If I hurried, I could get everything fed and tended before dark. I didn't like to be outside alone after nightfall. It didn't used to bother me, but with all the prowlers and Scott and the bear . . . I'd just become very skittish. It was nice to be safely locked inside when the night shadows fell. It didn't take long to get my chores done, but Boots and Roz seemed to be in hot persuit of somethin up at the little cabin. They ignored me when I called 'em and they just continued their silly barkin'. I decided to leave their food on the porch, even though both Toby and Chad had warned me not to do that 'cause it might draw wild animals up to the house in search of the dog food. At last I got into the house and had the doors locked. Food was my first order of business. I was really hungry for the first time in . . . I couldn't remember when. I soon had my plate fixed and parked myself in front of the television set, and tried to find somethin' to watch.

 Mornin' was introduced by that damn rooster who was so close to becomin' a pot of dumplin's that it wasn't funny. I turned over and pulled the pillow over my head and went back to sleep. When I awoke, several hours later, it was to the sound of a horn blowin' insistently in my front yard. Who in their right mind was up here honkin' like that at the break of daylight? I crawled out of bed, looked at the clock and discovered that it was ten o'clock in the mornin'. I didn't know the last time I'd slept in like that.

 The horn blasted again as I went to the window and looked down at the driveway. There was a strange van that was parked there and of course Boots and Roz had whoever it was, well-treed. I put my robe and house-shoes on and hurried downstairs so the dogs wouldn't give whoever it was a heart attack. Cautiously, I unlocked the door and stepped out on the porch. The dogs came to my side immediately and placed themselves at guard, one on each side of me. The door to the passenger side of the van opened and a young man of about twenty peeped out.

 "Is it okay for me to get out?" He asked in a shaky little voice.

"Sure, they'll be good as long as you don't try to come near me."

He started climbin' out of the van with a large vase of red roses. I'd never seen anything so beautiful. There must've been at least four dozen in that vase. I signed for 'em and he left in a big hurry. I took the flowers inside and sat 'em on the table. The smell was intoxicatin'.

Who could've sent 'em? Of course my first thought was of Walt, or maybe, Jamie. I wasn't sure, anymore than I was sure of exactly what the occasion was. The card that was with 'em was tucked neatly inside. I opened it and I immediately searched for a place to sit down.

I read it once, then I caught my breath and read it again.

My head was spinnin'. I couldn't begin to think clearly. I laid it down and found myself another cup of coffee. As I drank it, I paced from the back door to the front door, lookin' at it again each time I went by. This can't be for real. This has to be some kind of sick joke. I went back to the kitchen table and sat down. I picked up the note and read it again, very slowly, and very carefully.

"HAPPY VALENTINE'S DAY," it read, and underneath was scrawled a simple hand written note. 'Hope to see ya soon! Love and miss ya, TCB.'

Why would anyone play such a cruel joke. There was no humor in it whatsoever. This had to be somethin' that Walt had thought up. I should've known that he was up to somethin' because this was just the kind of thing that he'd find quite funny.

I picked up the phone and called him. It was the first time that I'd called him since I'd thrown him out of our house.

"Hello?"

"I got the flowers! Thank you! Did ya think it was funny? I saw no humor in it at all. I just want to ask ya why ya always want to be so cruel? Ya almost had me fooled into thinkin' that ya had changed!"

"Lilah?" he asked. "Lilah, I hate to say this but, what flowers are ya talkin' about?"

"The roses ya sent me this mornin'!" I practically yelled at him.

"Lilah."

I continued to rant and rave.

"Lilah, will ya just hush and listen to me for a minute. I got no idea what ya are talkin' about. I didn't send no flowers. I wish I had . . . but I just didn't have the money right now."

His words fell abruptly on my rage-filled ears.

"You . . . what?"

"I never sent ya no flowers. Right now I couldn't afford free wildflowers."

I stood there speechless. Talk about gettin' the wind knocked outta your sails. Then if not Walt . . . who else would do such a hateful thing? When I thought about it for a moment, I knew Walt would've admitted to it. He always liked to hear people's reactions to his sick little pranks. It wouldn't be like him to not take credit for it.

"I'm sorry, Walt. I just assumed that it was you."

"It's okay. Usually when I get accused of somethin', hell, I'm guilty as charged, but this time I didn't do it. Whatever it is . . . it sure upset ya. I'm sorry . . . but it's not me," he reassured. "I'm through with that sort of stuff. It's time to grow up and start bein' at least a halfway decent human bein'."

There was no way that those flowers actually come from Chad. I hadn't heard from him in... weeks...months...I couldn't remember. He'd just left. He had the gold so why would he want to contact me again. I spent several hours tryin' to unravel the mystery before I gave up and called Floy.

"I need to talk to ya."

"Sure, what's wrong, sweetie?"

"I got some Valentine flowers delivered this mornin'." I told her. "Four dozen red roses."

"Wow! From who?"

I read her the card.

Silence.

"Floy, are ya there?"

"Yeah, I just don't know what to say." She sounded as shocked as I was.

I told her I'd called Walt and what he'd said.

"I believe him." I told her. "Ya know he's always ready to take credit for any little prank that he pulls. He said he didn't do it."

"So who do ya think did? Ya don't suppose that witch Danna would've done somethin' like that do ya?" She asked.

"No. I don't think it would be her . . . she has a baby due any time and I'm sure she's much too busy to think about somethin' like that." I just couldn't imagine who it could be.

"What about Jamie? Maybe he was jealous of Chad and . . . well . . . that wouldn't make a lick of sense now would it?" She offered. "I'm stumped! Maybe it really was Chad. After all this time, I just figgered he was gone for good."

I sat there and thought about what she'd said for a moment, but I just couldn't even let myself think that they really came from him.

"Well, whoever sent 'em, I appreciate it. They're just beautiful, and I haven't gotten flowers in years. Whatever the reason, it's their problem. I'll just enjoy 'em and forget the rest."

I knew deep in my heart that I was lyin' through my natural teeth and I wouldn't be able to let go of it 'til I knew for sure who'd sent those flowers.

Chapter 18

On Saturday afternoon, Floy and Toby came out and we fixed supper, sat in front of the fire and played cards and dominoes 'til late. Floy was the best at dominoes, but Toby was the master at cards. The last time we'd played was when Chad was there. He'd beat us all at just about anything we played. We had threatened to lock him in the closet next time.

"Who wants some hot chocolate?" I asked.

Of course everyone did, so I went into the kitchen and made us each a cup. As I started out, I noticed the Christmas presents sittin' on the bureau. I picked 'em up and took 'em into the livin' area. While we were all sippin' our drinks, I handed Toby his and Floy hers.

"What's this?" Toby asked.

"The Christmas presents that ya never got. With everything happenin', I just plum forgot 'em. I'm sorry and I'd love for ya to open 'em now."

When Floy opened hers, she started to cry. I supposed it was a pregnancy thing since everything lately seemed to bring on the waterworks. It was the gold bracelet that I'd gotten when Chad and I had went shoppin'.

"Thank you Lilah, I love it."

"I'm glad ya like it. It's a 'best friends' bracelet."

Toby opened his. "What's this?" he asked as he unboxed the cologne.

"Platinum 'E'", he read as he opened the bottle and sprayed some on his hands and rubbed them together. The fragrance was almost more than I could handle. It was as if Chad had just walked in the room. We all looked at each other in silence. I knew we were all thinkin' the same thing.

"I'm not sure what to say," Toby said as he looked from me to Floy. "I always did like whatever it was that Chad wore. It was an unmistakable fragrance. I never dreamed that I'd end up with my own bottle. I've never seen this stuff anywhere. Thank ya so much, Lilah."

"It's private stock, Toby. Chad got it for ya on that last trip."

"Ya know . . . if it's gonna upset ya for me to wear it . . . I won't."

"No! I'll get used to it. It was just one of the many significant things that was Chad and Chad alone."

"Lilah? Your gifts are still at the house. We just didn't know when the appropriate time to give 'em to ya would be." Floy told me.

"I'm not worried about it, Floy. I just found these on the cabinet in the kitchen and wanted ya to have 'em."

They seemed genuinely pleased with their presents and I was happy that they liked 'em. I was disappointed that it hadn't been the way I'd planned. Chad and I were supposed to exchange gifts with 'em on Christmas Day and celebrate our first Christmas together.

It wasn't long and they decided to head home before it got much later It'd been a bitter-sweet evenin' and I was kinda glad when they left. I made another cup of hot chocolate and took it to the front porch. It was peaceful and I was beginin' to love it out there at night, as long as my dogs were right with me! The more time I spent out there the more secure I was becomin'. This was my home and I was determined that I would not be afraid inside or out.

It wasn't quite as cold that night as it'd been lately. The stars were so bright and the moon was almost like a street light. Boots and Roz had found their spot by my feet. It was really nice 'cause the heat from their bodies kept my feet toasty. I sat and thought about the roses I'd gotten. They was still so beautiful and the entire house smelled like fresh roses, even Toby'd noticed. Floy had sat down and looked at the note that came with 'em.

"I don't recall ever seein' Chad's handwrittin'. Maybe he did send 'em." She had said.

"I just can't let myself believe that. I can't." I'd told her. "He has enough gold to consider hisself a very rich man. What on earth would he want to come back for? There's nothin' left for him to take!" I was totally lost in my thoughts, when suddenly Roz and Boots jumped up at the same time. They was lookin' up the mountain toward the little cabin. As they ran to the edge of the porch, they began to bark and the hair on their backs began to stand straight up. I immediately became very nervous. Perhaps I should've given a second thought to leavin' that dog food out on the porch. What if a bear had decided to come down for a snack. I walked cautiously toward the end of the porch. When I looked up toward the little cabin, I was surprised to see what appeared to be a flashlight flicker about inside it. It was then that Boots and Roz bolted off the porch and headed up there in a dead run. They could go ahead as far as I was concerned, I was goin' inside to lock and bolt the doors. I'd go investigate in the mornin'.

When I got snuggled in my bed, I began to feel a little better. I just couldn't imagine who'd been up there. It was a good walk up to the cabin. Maybe it was some hunters just takin' shelter for the night. Nothin' like that'd happened since Chad had put a stop to that nonsense. I sure hoped it wasn't startin' up again 'cause I didn't like the idea of strangers roamin' around at all hours of the night.

It all made me very restless and I couldn't fall asleep while somebody was apparently prowlin' around up at the cabin. Quietly, I crawled out of the bed and went to the back bedroom window and looked back up the mountain. I could see the little cabin clearly. The light snow on the ground reflected the moonlight to the point of darn near daylight. For over an hour I watched, but there wasn't any more sign of anyone up there. Maybe the lights were just playin' tricks on my eyes. I didn't see or hear the dogs and there was no sign of no flashlights. After watchin' for another half hour, I decided that there was nothin' to it. I'd go and check it all out in the mornin'. I was always braver in the daylight.

I crawled back into my bed and soon fell sound asleep.

The usual alarm crowin' from the corral fence post woke me bright and early. That damn rooster'd woke me up every mornin' for years. Somehow he had gotten next to my heart. I guess I did sorta love the stupid thing!

I got dressed and went downstairs to have a quick breakfast. I had several things that I needed to look into. Reachin' under my bed, I got the shotgun, and headed toward the little cabin as fast as I could with Boots and Roz right behind me. We were three on a mission, and I'd had enough. I was determined to take back control of my life and my ranch!

When we got there I opened the door and charged in. There was nothin' to find. Everything was the same as it'd been the last time I was up there. We checked the bathroom and the whole of the cabin, but there was nothin'. It was a big relief that I hadn't had to deal with a confrontation, but I knew that I would've if I'd had to. I wasn't sure what I'd thought to find, but I was glad for what I didn't find.

I walked over to the bed and sat down. It was easy to imagine Chad standin' there the way he was when I last saw him. The sun streamed in through the windows, and brought a soft early morning glow to the entire room. Still it felt cold and empty, just like my heart and just like my life. The time I'd spent with him had been magical. It'd been like a fantasy come true, and somethin' I'd never expected to happen in my lifetime. As a young girl, I'd dreamed of a love that'd capture my heart and soul. Every girl I'd ever known had those fantasys, but I was one of the rare ones that got to experience the whole dream. I sat there a long while before I realized I was just buryin' myself in painful memories . . . memories that I was better off to let go of. I'd almost let my guard down as that old familiar ache tried to creep back into every part of my bein'. There was no tellin' how long I'd sat there, dreamin', rememberin', and hatin' him for what he'd done, yet longin' with everything in me to see him just once more. I stood up determinedly and went back outside and softly closed the door.

Me and my dogs made our way back to the big cabin. They wanted to play, so I picked up a stick and threw it and they raced to retrieve it. They were funny as they slipped and tumbled on the snow then made their way back, each holdin' an end of the prize. Even though I was still upset . . . they made me smile. As we came through the back yard, I paused as I noticed the logs where Chad had been choppin' wood, and the place where he'd trimmed the branches off the Christmas tree. Some of the dead branches still lay on the ground. For a moment I felt a lump rise in my throat as I remembered all that had happened on that day.

I started for the back steps, and stopped dead in my tracks as the definite smell of fryin' bacon, toast, and coffee drifted from the kitchen to my nose. I knew that I hadn't started breakfast and no-one was at the house . . . so . . . what the hell?

I leaned to peek in the window just as the door swung open. The shotgun fell to the ground as I felt the blood drain from my face. My heart skipped at least two beats and my lungs failed me miserably.

He was standin' there in jeans and a black tee shirt. His silver blonde hair was hangin' casually over his forehead and almost into those beautiful, crystal blue eyes. They sparkled as his full pouty lips spread into a gorgeous smile. I couldn't move. I just stood there not sure what to do or say.

"Hi, honey," He almost whispered.

All I could do was stand there, paralyzed. I knew that I had to be dreamin. I'd imagined him comin' back so many times over the last many weeks. This just couldn't be for real.

"I . . . uh . . . I . . . I'm sorry it took me so long to get back. I ran into . . . uh . . . some problems and it took me a little longer than I expected."

Still, l just stood there. Maybe in shock, I didn't know how to react.

Before I could think, I found myself in his arms when he stepped out on the porch and pulled me to him. His lips covered mine in a desperate kiss, a kiss of so much passion and desire that I felt myself melt into his arms and return that kiss with equal need. He released me long enough to pull me into the house and shut the door.

"I . . . uh . . . I . . . God I missed ya, baby girl," he breathed into my ear as he began to kiss my neck. I finally snapped to my senses.

"Stop!" I yelled. "What the hell are ya doin'? Where have you been? Why? Why did ya leave me like that?" Before I realized what I'd done, I slapped him across the face with every ounce of strength I possessed and began to beat hysterically on his chest.

He just stood strong and took it. I was cryin' so hard I couldn't see and when I managed to look up at him and saw the bright red welt across his face and the pain in his eyes, I cried even harder.

"Why didn't ya call? Why? How could ya just leave me like that?"

He grabbed me up and carried me into the livin' area, and sat me on the couch. I cried so hard I couldn't breathe . . . then finally . . . I just sat there with my face in my arms.

"Uh . . . I . . . are ya . . . are ya 'bout done now?"

I sat for a long time and tried to pull myself together. It wasn't easy after agonizin' over him for all that time. My lips still tingled from his kiss. I'd never thought that I'd feel those lips again. Yet there he was, beautiful as ever. It was hard, but I finally looked up at him again.

"Can we talk now?" he asked me in a soft, patient voice. It took a while before I trusted my voice to let me say anything.

"Chad," I choked out, "I don't think we have anything left to talk about."

He looked puzzled. "What exactly is that supposed to mean?" he asked. "I . . . I . . . uh . . . I know I left kinda sudden like, but I couldn't get to ya to explain."

"Explain what?"

"To explain why I had to leave."

"Why ya HAD to leave? And can ya tell me why ya couldn't pick up the damn phone and call, or write a damn letter and let me know?"

"I was afraid that ya wasn't alone. I couldn't call from where I was, and I couldn't be sure that you'd be the only one to get a letter."

"And what difference does any of that make? So what if I wasn't alone? You said that ya would be there at the little cabin. Instead ya packed up everything and snuck away. What? Did ya run outta money so quick that ya had to come back and try to get more?"

Chad looked completly shocked and confused by everything that I'd just said.

" . . . and what exactly do ya mean by that?" He asked with a hint of real anger in his voice.

"I mean the damn gold ya took. Why in hell didn't ya just tell me it was money ya wanted? Hell, I would've given it to ya! Ya didn't have to steal it, Chad. I would've give ya anything ya wanted," I yelled hatefully.

"That's what you're so damn mad about? I thought if ya found it gone, ya would understand. I thought ya could figure it out! Damn Lilah . . . do ya think that little of me?" He stepped back with a cold, devastated look. "I been accused of a lotta things in my life . . . but I ain't never been accused of takin' anything that didn't belong to me."

He stood up and walked toward the front door. He opened it and just stood there with his hands braced on each side of the door frame and stared out across the yard. Somethin' told me that there might be more that I needed to know about all that'd happened. I just wasn't sure what I should say or do. I'd been so sure that I had it figgered out. It'd all seemed to make sense at the time . . . but now?

Chad leaned against the door sill as he continued to search across the yard. Finally I got up and walked over to him.

"Chad?" I whispered.

He didn't move, nor did he speak. I reached out and touched his arm. He jerked away and continued to stare out the door.

"Chad? Tell me about it." He turned and looked at me as if he didn't know who I was.

The hurt that I saw in his eyes tore at my heart and the red mark on his face filled me with shame.

"I want to listen . . . I want ya to tell me that I was wrong. I need to know that I was wrong. Please Chad . . . make me know that it wasn't the way I thought it was!" I pleaded and the tears began again.

At last he wrapped his arms around me and held me close. It seemed like a lifetime since I'd felt that safety, that glorious feelin' that told me that I was where I belonged. We held each other for a long time before either of us spoke. We walked over to the couch and sat there lookin' at each other. Finally he spoke . . . so softly at first that I could barely hear him.

"Why would ya think I would steal from you?"

I thought about it for a couple of minutes, "You were supposed to hide in the little room for a while. Ya didn't. Ya took everthing ya had and the gold and ya left. What would you have thought?" I asked him.

He thought for a moment and then dropped his head.

"You're right, I didn't have time to think it out. When I realized what the authorities would do if they found that gold, I knew that I had to get it out of there."

"I don't understand. What could they do with my family's gold.?"

"Take it." He said. "Do ya have any proof that it was yours? Where did ya get it? Got any proof of that?" I began to see the point.

"I don't even know where it came from. I didn't have any idea that it was even in there. I think that it was just somethin' that'd been forgotten about."

"How do ya know that it belonged to your family?"

"Well, Nana had always told us that . . . "

"Yeah, . . . Nana had always told ya! Did Nana have any written proof that it was hers?"

I sat there in stunned silence.

"Not that I know of," I answered him meekly.

"Lilah, nobody that I know of owns pure gold bars! I never knew anybody that had gold and kept it in a cave! Do ya think the law would believe ya? I only knew that if ya was gonna be able to keep what was yours, then I had to get it out of there and away from the ranch. So I took it and slipped out before they brought you back to the cave." He explained. I nodded and thought about it for a moment.

"Where is it now?"

He sat there a few minutes and looked at the floor.

"I took it out of the country."

"Ya mean ya took it to the city?"

He grinned and shook his head.

"No, I took it to another country."

"I don't understand . . . why?"

"It's a long, complicated story. I'll make it short and sweet. I took it to another country and a friend of mine helped me to exchange it for cash. U.S. cash, which is a lot easier to explain than gold bars."

"Then what'd ya do?"

"I brought it back here as soon as I felt it was safe and put it back in the hidden room. C'mon, I'll show ya. I want ya to see it for yourself."

He took my hand and we grabbed our coats as we hurried out the back door. It didn't take us long to get to the cabin. Once we were inside, he produced a flashlight and, we moved the armoire and slipped behind it and into the hidden room. There were all the large metal boxes, plus several more, on the floor. Chad knelt down and unlocked each one. When he opened the lids, I gasped. I'd never seen so much money in my life.

"How much?"

He turned and looked up at me, bit his bottom lip, winked, and whispered. "Millions, baby, Millions!"

I couldn't believe it. "Are ya sure?"

"It would've been more, but the dollar just ain't what it used to be. I made sure it was a fair deal though." He stood up. "That's what I been doin' the whole time I was gone. Except for the time I had to wait on my friend and his contacts. Then I had to wait until I was sure ya wasn't bein' watched."

"I had no idea, Chad. I thought ya just took the gold and cleared out. I didn't think I would ever see ya again and my heart was just broken. You . . . you're like a giant puzzle with half the pieces missin'. When I think I've found one . . . it just doesn't fit."

He stood there and looked at me with the same icy stare from earlier.

"Yeah, well, didn't look too heartbroken the other night out at Kings!" He said through gritted teeth.

I looked up, "What do ya mean by that?"

"I mean I saw ya all hugged up with that Jamie cat, again. I also noticed that you and Walt was pretty chummy too."

I was speechless "You were there? Ya didn't say a word and ya was right there?"

"I was gonna dance with ya and let ya know that I was back . . . but ya looked like ya was pretty busy, so I left."

" That WAS you that I saw! I thought my imagination was playin' tricks on me . . . but it was really you."

He took a deep, ragged breath, "Yeah", he whispered and turned away.

I wasn't sure what to say at that point. It must've looked just as bad on my part as it had on his.

"Chad? I thought I was betrayed. I was tryin' to get past it."

"By turnin' to another man? How's that gonna fix anything?"

"I wasn't turnin' to nobody. I was just dancin'. Tryin' to have some-what of a good time. Instead I ended up drunk on my butt and Toby had to literally carry me home. Why do ya think that was? If I was havin' such a great time with another man . . . wouldn't he have carried me home?" I saw the muscles in his jaw flinch and his eyes shot blue fire.

"I better never hear of you with another man. I couldn't take it! I just couldn't!"

Then I was in his arms and his kisses were like fire on my lips, my face, my neck.

The next thing I knew we were on the bed. We couldn't seem to get rid of clothes fast enough. His white hot kisses covered my body. I ached for him like I'd never ached for anyone but him. When at last we were one, I felt my nails dig into his beautiful, muscular back as I pulled him deeper inside. I just couldn't get enough of him. At one point he stopped and raised up, I opened my eyes and looked into his. He held my eyes captive as he began to move slowly, sensuously, like a dance with no music but our own. The pace quickened until at last we blended into one on that glorious crest of ecstasy.

Afterward, we lay there in each others arms. The scent of that wonderful cologne found its way to my nose. The wonderful fragrance that was his and his alone. This was a feelin' that I liked and I didn't ever want to move from that very spot.

"I'm sorry." I heard him whisper.

"For what?"

"That I made ya doubt me and that it hurt ya so bad. I . . . I . . . I never meant for any of that to happen."

"I know . . . I do understand."

He turned and looked at me. His eyes reflected so much stress and somethin' else that I just couldn't quite put my finger on.

"But you're home to stay and everything'll work out fine."

I saw him flinch when I said that. I wasn't sure why, but I felt like I'd struck a nerve somewhere. He started to say somethin', but I blocked it with a kiss. When he tried to say somethin' again, I kissed the words right outta his mouth . . . again, and again, and again. At last he seemed to forget what he was gonna say and there was no more talkin'.

It was a while later, as we dozed in each other's arms, that Chad suddenly jumped straight up in the bed. It scared me so bad, I choked.

"What is it? Did ya hear somethin'?"

"NO! . . . I left breakfast cookin'!!" We looked down toward the big cabin and smoke was boilin' out the back door that we'd left open.

We tried to hurry and get dressed. It might have been easier if we hadn't thrown clothes to the four corners. At one point I had Chad's shirt on and he had my socks. We finally sorted it out and were dressed and frantically runnin' to the house.

When we got inside we found the bacon'd turned to charcoal and so had the toast, the coffee was boiled dry, and the house was full of smoke. Chad carried the burnt offerin's outside and I opened up the doors and windows as fast as I could. It wasn't so bad upstairs, but the downstairs was a mess. I went outside with Chad and we climbed up and sat on a couple of logs and stared at the smoke-ridden abode. He looked at me with huge blue eyes as if he was expectin' a good chewin' out.

I gave him a stern look and then smiled.

"Welcome home, Honey! See . . . ya just set everything ya touch on fire!" I laughed. He looked relieved and then he started to laugh with me.

"I thought you was down at the barn and I meant to surprise ya with breakfast." He explained.

"Oh . . . ya surprised me alright." He shrugged his shoulders as we wrapped our arms around each other and waited while the house aired out.

We went back up to the little cabin to shut and lock the door.

"Why are we lockin' ourselves inside?"

"'Cause we're goin' out the way I come in. I gotta get my truck."

We slipped out behind the armoire and pulled it shut. The little tunnel was open through the boxes that led the way into the cave. Chad closed it back as we left. He shined the flashlight around the cave for a second.

"I'd never planned to come in here again," I told him.

"Me either, but it seemed the safest way to get the money back where it went."

We looked around the place for a moment.

"Man, them cats took everything in sight. How come they didn't move those crates?"

"I told 'em that they'd been there since the beginnin' of time and that they was private property, just like ya told me to tell 'em. They left 'em alone."

"Ya done good, darlin'. If they'd found that entrance, ya could bet it would've been all over town the next day . . . this way . . . everything is safe and only four of us know about it. Man, it looks like they scraped the floor and walls and took every thing they could haul out. What'd they do with that bear?"

"I have no idea. They had some people come in and take it out. They sent Scott's remains back down to Arkansas."

"They should've just tossed his sorry ass in the river and let the scavengers have him." he growled.

"I can still smell that horrid smell in here. Let's get the hell out. We'll close it up so nobody can get in here. I'll try to get that done this week."

It felt so good for him to be makin' plans for things he wanted to do around the ranch.

We made our way to the entrance and came out beside the little tree that we hadn't chosen for our Christmas tree. His truck was parked just down the hill. We climbed in and headed back toward the cabin. I looked at the sun shinin' through the trees and thought to myself that, in my world, it just didn't get any better than that.

As we came in the back door, the phone was ringin'. I answered and it was Floy.

"Why weren't ya in church this mornin'? You're gettin' a pretty bad habit of not bein' there!"

Chad came up behind me and slipped his arms around me while I was talkin' to her.

"Oh, I had one or two things to tend to and I just lost track of time." I said as I snuggled against him.

"What kind of things were so important? . . . Lilah? . . . Are you ok?"

With Chad standin' behind me and pullin' me up close against him, it was very hard to concentrate on a telephone converstation.

"Well, there was just a couple a things that came up." I tried to sound casual, but Chad's hand slipped under my blouse as the other held me tight against him.

"I think somethin' just come up again," he whispered in my ear.

I giggled before I remembered I was on the phone.

"Lilah! What's goin' on over there?" Floy demanded.

"Well . . . Ya'll come over for supper at six thirty. I'll be expectin' ya. Damn . . . I gotta go."

I hung up the phone and ended the call very abruptly. I turned quickly and pulled Chad to the floor.

"Okay, damn you . . . put up or shut up," and I kissed him soundly on those luscious pouty lips of his. He laughed out loud as he began to unbutton my shirt. I was way ahead of him as I took and ripped it open. It wasn't so easy with his tee shirt. We wrestled and rolled around the kitchen floor and laughed and kissed until we were both completely naked.

Again, we made unbelievably passionate love andI was discoverin' an entirely different side of myself. A side that wasn't so afraid to ask for what I wanted and I had a man that was more than willin' to comply. Chad was a shy lover, but he could be gentle and sweet as well as strong and demandin'. He gave every bit as good as he got and I knew in my heart that there'd never be another like him. After him . . . I could never settle for anyone else.

Somehow we ended up on the couch under the blanket that still held his scent. We'd fallen asleep after exhaustin' ourselves in each other's arms. When I woke up and opened my eyes, I found a pair of remarkably tender blue ones lookin' deep into mine.

"Hey." He whispered.

I smiled at him.

"Ya know . . . we could do this all day . . . but somebody invited some company for supper. Don't ya think we might ought to get dressed and decide what we're gonna feed that company?" he gave me that sweet crooked little smile. I stretched lazily and pulled him to me.

"I suppose you're right . . . but I have all afternoon to fix supper. Right now . . . I'm starvin' to death. How about you? Could ya eat a bite?"

"I sure could . . . ya are talkin' about food ain't ya?" he chuckled.

"Yes, I am. At least for now. I have no strength left."

"Then let's search that kitchen. I don't think I burned up everything." We pulled on shirts and underclothes and made our way into the kitchen to rummage.

Chapter 19

Chicken and dumplins were simmerin' and everything was just about ready. Chad and I'd taken an hour long shower and were dressed and ready for our company. He was settin' the table when I heard 'em comin' up the steps. I hurried to the door and flung it open.

"Hello, hello." I greeted 'em. They both just stood in the doorway. "Well, come on in!"

"Sweetie, what's up? You look like the cat that ate the canary," Floy said as she stared me down.

"You look wonderful. Better than ya have in months. What happened?" Toby stepped inside with her. "Are ya feelin' alright sis? Ya ain't been drinkin' again have ya?" I was stunned that he'd think so.

"Not hardly! I have a great . . ."

That was as far as I got.

"Honey? Are we outta butter?" Chad called as he stepped out of the kitchen. "Hey guys! Damn it's great to see ya. How ya doin'?"

Floy and Toby stood there with the shocked looks on their faces that somebody would have if a ghost suddenly appeared for supper.

"I . . . I . . . Chad? When did ya git back?" Toby asked in disbelief.

" A couple a days ago."

Toby turned and looked at me. "Did ya know about that?"

"Not 'til this mornin'."

"Where the hell was ya? Do ya have any idea what ya put this girl through? Why the hell didn't ya call her? Man, I thought we was friends. Ya don't lie to friends and sneak out on 'em like that." Toby was right in Chad's face.

I jumped between 'em.

"Wait! Hold it Toby. It's not what we thought at all. Chad will tell ya about it and you'll understand. Please Toby, just calm down."

Floy walked up about that time. She looked at me for a full minute then she turned to Chad and put her arms around him.

"We're so glad to see ya, Chad. We all missed ya so much. Welcome home." She said with true sincerity in her voice. The tension immediately started to ease and we all settled down.

Chad looked Floy up and down, "Ya ain't plannin' on havin' that baby tonight are ya?" he grinned.

"No, I got a ways to go yet." She smiled.

"Maybe it's twins. That'd be really special. Ya know twins got a bond that ain't like no other. Even if one lives and the other don't . . . the one always knows that there's a major part of himself missin'." Chad turned very serious for a moment.

"I wouldn't know what to do with twins, man, I ain't sure I'll know what to do with one." Added Toby.

He'd calmed down and was becomin' excited to see Chad as much as we were. After supper Chad explained it all to Toby and Floy and the warmth of our previous friendship began to return. Once again we sat in front of the fire, sipped hot chocolate and played dominoes 'til it became late.

"We gotta get goin'. I gotta work tomorrow and Floy needs her rest." Toby said as he got up and found their coats. He helped Floy into hers and sweetly buttoned her up like she was a little child. Then he turned to Chad.

"Man, I'm sorry. I never should've doubted ya. But . . . ya looked so guilty, buddy. I don't know what else to say, 'cept I really am sorry."

He held his hand out to Chad.

"I know . . . it's okay." Chad answered as he took Toby's hand. "And I realize now that I could have handled it all a lot better, but once the thought hit me . . . I just panicked. I was just thankful that I had seen where O'Grady had hid my truck when he hauled me up there. I never would've got all that out on foot."

"But why did ya take everything you had stored at our house?" Toby questioned.

"Hell, I didn't have any idea how long I would have to be gone or what I might need."

"You sure threw us for a loop! I'm just glad we was wrong and you're back." Toby said with a friendly smile.

Floy gave us big hugs and she and Toby left for their home. We stood in the doorway and waved 'til we couldn't see 'em any more. Nanny'd always done that whenever any one left from a visit. Ya could always look back in the mirror and see her wavin' 'til ya got into the grove. Chad turned and looked at me.

"I got a question, little one."

"Yeah?"

"What the hell is that white thing in the livin' room? It looks like you're decorated for Halloween already."

I couldn't help but laugh. "It's an old friend."

"What'd he do . . . come by and die?"

"Pretty much . . . yeah . . . you're pretty much right." He stood there for a minute and tilted his head to one side.

"You're kiddin' me . . . right?"

"Not at all." I said, "Come on and I'll introduce the two of ya."

We went inside and I seated Chad on the couch. Carefully I unwrapped the sheet from that poor dead tree.

"You . . . I . . . I can't believe what I'm seein'. Ya haven't thrown that out yet?"

"We haven't had Christmas yet. I just couldn't find it in my heart to take it down."

He stood up, came over and took me into his arms.

"It's just like it was the night I came home and found ya gone."

"No," I told him "I gave Floy and Toby their gifts the other night. They loved 'em."

"Did ya open yours?" he whispered in my ear.

I looked at him and thought for a moment.

"I didn't know that I had any to open. Ya still have several to open yourself. I know that ya saw your main one. I've been callin' him "Promise". Ya can rename him if ya want to."

He stood there and thought about it for a minute.

"No. I think Promise is a good name. I like it."

He took my hand and pulled me to the floor.

"This is the way we always did it when I was a kid. Everybody sittin' in the floor passin' out gifts." He smiled. I handed him one of his, and he surprised me by fishin' out a pretty pink one and handing it to me. I'd never noticed it before.

"You first." He instructed.

I opened the beautiful box and inside was the most gorgeous pink sweater I'd ever seen. It was pink cashmere with a white fur collar and pearl buttons.

"Oh Chad! This is just beautiful. I've never seen anything like it." I gave him a hug and a big kiss as I took it out of its box. It was the softest thing I'd ever felt.

He opened the jeans and then his shirts and last of all . . . his white gloves.

"Now how do ya expect me to get any work done with white gloves?" He teased as he thanked me and gave me hugs and kisses.

"I don't, those are just for lookin' good. That's somethin' ya do very well," I flirted.

Then he reached into the tree and pulled out another, smaller box and handed it to me. I opened it and took out a bottle of cologne. I turned it around and the label read Platinum "E" la femme. I looked at him.

"It's Platinum "E" for my lady. It's the very first bottle and I had it made just for you. It'll never be made for anyone else. It's a lighter version of what I wear."

I took the heart shaped glass stopper out and smelled. It left me speechless. It was the most special thing I could ever have imagined.

"Thank you, Sweetheart," I told him and gave him another big kiss.

"Ya have one more here," he said as he searched in the tree.

I'd never thought about hidin' presents in the tree. This one was a smaller box yet. I opened it and sat there in awe. Chad took the delicate little necklace out, kissed my palm, and laid it in my hand.

"These are my initials, and this.." he said, "Well, do ya remember I told ya that the first time I saw ya in Lexington that I felt like I'd been hit by a bolt of lightnin'? This here is the lightnin' bolt. I had it filled in with yellow diamonds. Each one, I hope, tells ya how much I love you. How much I will always love you!" he fastened it around my neck and gently kissed my shoulder.

"I'll wear it forever." I whispered.

I stood up, took his hand and pulled him to his feet. I handed him his jacket and got mine and led him outside.

"Where we goin'?"

"To visit you're number one present."

We walked down to the barn and went in. The horses began to get excited. I guessed they probably thought we was goin' for a ride. We walked over to Promise and he came right to me.

"Looks like my present likes his giver more than he does his receiver." Chad laughed.

"It's just 'cause I've been with him more. As soon as he gets to know ya, he'll be fine."

He reached out to Promise. The colt nuzzled him. I put a little sweet feed in Chad's hand and the little guy instantly became his best friend.

"He's beautiful, honey. I . . . I . . . uh . . . I loved him the minute I saw him . . . just like I did when I first saw his giver." he said as he bit that lip and gave me that adorable wink.

We went back to the house and Chad read the card I'd written him. He finished it and sat there and looked intently at me.

"I'd like to spend the rest of my life right here on this mountain with you. But honey, I can't promise that I'll be able to do that. Let's just take one day at a time and consider that's one more day that God has blessed us with."

I was confused by that statement but decided to let it go 'til another time. This time, this night was such a night . . . a night like I'd never known and I didn't want to take a chance on tarnishin' it in any way. I smiled at him and nodded.

"Ya ready to go up to bed?" I asked him. He nodded and we started toward the stairs.

"This is one of the very best Christmases I've ever had, Chica. Thank you for everything . . . I love you, honey." He half-whispered as he took my hands. "Merry Christmas."

"Merry Christmas to you too my love."
And with that we went up to bed.

Monday mornin' come bright and early when the damn rooster began to serenade us at daybreak. I laid there for a minute or so and I wondered if the last twenty four hours had really happened or if it was just another of those vivid dreams that I'd been havin' ever since Chad had left. I prayed, please God, let it be real. Let him be there when I turn over. Don't let my heart break again.

I dared to slide my foot over behind me. I soon reached the edge of the bed and there was obviously no one else in my bed. I turned over and found myself alone....still. Tears began to run down my face as I rolled over on the other pillow. This was without a doubt the cruelest dream I'd ever had. Why was my mind doin' this to me? The scent of him was so strong that I buried my face in his pillow and sobbed.

"Hey? Honey? What's wrong?" I heard that oh so familiar whisper as a hand touched my head. I quickly raised up to find him there, on my bed and I clung to him desperately.

"It's you! It's really you! I . . . thought I'd dreamed it all. Oh Chad . . . don't ever leave me again. I couldn't deal with it. I just couldn't." I buried my face in his chest as my tears ran down to his stomach.

"I'm right here baby. I'm right here. It was no dream . . . it was very real." He whispered as he rocked me gently back and forth.

"Shhhh, little girl. I got ya right here." He laid down beside me and pulled me as close as we could get and I fell back to sleep in those wonderful arms.

Later in the mornin', I turned over and opened my eyes. His beautiful face was the first thing I saw. I barely recalled the early mornin' panic as I watched him sleep. I still couldn't imagine how a man like him hadn't been caught up a long time ago. Of course he'd told me that he'd been married once . . . and I thought he'd also said that he had a daughter. I wondered where they were and who they were. I wondered what kind of woman could possibly live after lettin' this man go. How could any woman love a man, especially this man, enough to bear his child and then just let him go? He smiled in his sleep and the corner of his lip curled up so cute that it was all I could do not reach up and touch 'em. He slept so peaceful, so at ease with himself as his chest rose and fell with a steady rythym and I could hear his heart beat, strong and regular. I wanted to live within it for all time. Those full, sensuous lips started that familiar cravin' deep inside me. I pushed it aside, 'cause he slept so quietly that I wasn't goin' to disturb him. His long, softly-curled eyelashes lay gently on his cheeks. His hair was coverin' his forehead. He'd let it grow quite long since the last time I'd seen him. It was well below his ears and almost to his shoulders, but it was beautiful, like silk. It was then that I noticed somethin' I hadn't before. He'd shaved his beard. He had left a little moustache and long sideburns and I was amazed at how much younger he looked. He looked a lot like someone I'd seen before . . . but I hadn't the slightest clue who it was. It didn't really matter. He looked exactly like Chad. My beautiful, sexy Chad.

His eyes fluttered slightly and began to open. He blinked and then focused on mine.

"Mornin' sleepy-head." I whispered.

"Mmm . . . mornin'. I guess we fell back asleep. What time is it?"

"Almost time for me to go to work. Do ya wanna go with me?"

"Work? When did ya start workin'?"

"Sometime back . . . I volunteer at the nursin' home in Bigby. I visit with the residents and help 'em with whatever they need done. Sometimes I read to 'em and write letters for 'em. Whatever they need."

"That's great. Yeah, I think I'd like to go with ya."

We got up and dressed, ate breakfast and headed to Bigby.

On the way I told him about Miss Mae and how upset I'd been at losin' her. I told him about her son, the locket, the little weddin' band that she'd worn thin, and how I'd ended up with 'em.

"It's a pretty sad story . . . but beautiful . Can ya imagine the joy . . . the happiness that filled heaven when she was reunited with her husband, son, and her Mama and Daddy. Some day I'll see my Mama again . . . and my brother." He told me.

I didn't know ya had a brother. What happened?"

"Yeah. I . . . I . . . uh . . . I never knew him. He was stillborn. I reckon it 'bout killed my Mama. Maybe that's why she spoiled me so bad." He chuckled.

"I wish I could've met her. She sounds like a very special lady."

"She was . . . she was my livin' angel and I loved her more than life. I wish ya could've known her too. She would've loved you. The same as I do." He grew quiet then.

It wasn't long before we pulled up at the home.

"Do I need to check in or anything?" He asked.

"I don't think so, but we can ask, just to be sure."

I found the receptionist at her desk. "Junie, this is my . . . friend, Chad Barrett. He's gonna go with me to visit the residents today. Does he need a pass or to sign in?"

She looked up and froze.

"Junie?" I asked.

She looked at Chad as if she'd seen a ghost.

"Junie?"

Finally she shook her head and looked at me.

"Yes . . . I mean no. He doesn't." She stared at him again.

I knew he was handsome, but she was bein' ridiculous.

"You . . . you look like . . . like somebody I should know." Junie mumbled.

"I . . . uh . . . I . . . I hear that a lot. I guess I just have one of those faces," Chad laughed as he bit his lip and winked at her.

I could literally see her melt. He had that way about him and I have to admit that I felt a big bite from that green-eyed montster . . . the one called jealousy.

Grabbin' his hand, I pulled him forcefully away from the desk. As we went down the hall, we passed Miss Mae's old room. It was painfully obvious that someone was already settled in and I was surprised at the effect it had on me. We went on down to Lamar's room. I knocked.

"C'mon in Lilah! Bring your friend with ya."

"Now, Lamar, who told ya that I had a friend with me?"

"Why, nobody . . . I just knew that ya didn't have four feet." I thought about it and had to giggle.

"No, Lamar, you're right. This is my friend Chad Barrett, Chad . . . this is my dear friend Lamar."

They shook hands and Lamar held Chad's hand for a moment. He raised his head as if to look into Chad's eyes.

"Ya know Chad, ya can tell a lot about a person by his hands."

"Is that right, sir? I….I never paid much attention to that."

He nodded. "Yes, that's right. For instance, I can tell that you're a very sensitive young man. Ya like physical work, but it's not what ya do for a livin'."

"What else, Sir?"

"Well, I believe you're a warm outgoin' sort. But sometimes ya come across a little shy."

Lamar turned Chad's hand over and traced the lines in his palm. Then he felt his fingertips and the backs of his hand.

"Hmm..I sense some confusion on your lifeline. You sir, are a very generous man with a gentle heart . . . you play the guitar some…" Lamar laughed. "And you're very much in love with my dear friend, Lilah, here. That'll be two dollars for the readin'," and Lamar slapped his knee and burst out laughin' again.

Chad smiled, but I thought that it unnerved him a little that Lamar was able to tell so much just from touch. We visited with him for a long time and he managed to set Chad at ease enough that they were talkin' like best friends by the time we left.

"It was a pleasure to meet you, sir." Chad told him.

"No, the pleasure is all mine. I'm honored to know ya. I'll be prayin' that everything works out for ya." Lamar said.

We started down the hall.

"What was that all about?" I asked him.

"What . . . uh . . . was what all about?"

"You know, when he said that he'd be prayin' for ya?"

Chad studied on it. "Ya know how old folks are . . . they're always prayin' for somebody. Ya can never have too many people prayin' for ya!" he teased.

We visited with several others before we left. I was pleased at how easily he gained their confidence and how they seemed flattered to meet him. We finally got to the Jeep and headed home.

"Do ya wanna stop by King's and have somethin' to drink?" I asked him.

"Naw, I'd rather go by Shoemaker's to eat and maybe go by and see Toby and Floy for a minute. How does that sound to ya?"

"Fine with me."

Toby answered the door, "Hey guys, what ya'll doin' out this late? C'mon in and sit down. Floy's layin' down. Let me go tell her you alls here."

"Is she feelin' bad? We can come back another time." I told him.

"Oh no you won't," said Floy from the door. "Get in here and sit! It's been a long time since ya'll been over here. Where ya been?"

"I went to work and took Chad with me. He about gave the receptionist a stroke! She couldn't quit what do ya say . . . oglin' him!"

Toby looked confused.

"Doin' what to him? Damn, buddy that don't sound like no fun at all!" he teased.

"She was flirtin' with him, Toby," said Floy. "Did ya have fun meetin' all the old timers, Chad?"

"Yeah, I did. Ya know, it takes a lot of courage to grow old. I don't know if I have what it takes or not."

"What do ya mean by that?' Toby asked.

"You know, the aches and pains, losin' your memory, your sight, your hearin'. Just sittin' all day in a room with nothin' but strangers come to visit. I just don't know if I'm that brave!"

I thought Toby would laugh, but I think that the reality of what Chad had said was a bit of a shock to us all. I'd never given it much thought before.

"Well," Toby said. "Ya know . . . I don't think we have much choice in the matter. I suppose the best thing is to just suck it up and take it one day at a time."

"I look forward to gettin' old, myself," chimed in Floy. "Maybe I'll have lots of words of wisdom for the young."

"Shoot, with my luck," laughed Toby "none of 'em won't listen any better'n we do!"

"If I had my choice, I think I'd rather check it in before it gets to all the fallin' apart stuff." Chad added as he got up and walked over to the window.

"Well, I vote we stop talkin' about death and play some dominoe's. You guys ready to get you're butts kicked by the ladies?" asked Floy.

"That will sure nuff be the day" teased Toby as he started to scatter the dominoes on the table.

It was late when we finally got home. It'd been a long time since we'd spent such a great evenin' with our best friends. We'd hardly walked in the door, when the phone began to ring. We looked at each other in surprise.

"Who would be callin' this late?" Chad asked.

I was afraid that somethin' had happened in Arkansas.

"Hello?" I answered in a panic. "Hello?" The line was open, but no one was answerin'. After a couple a minutes, I hung up.

"I guess it was a wrong number."

Chad was lockin' up and turnin' out lights and I'd just turned to go up the stairs when the phone started to ring again.

"I'll get it!" Chad sounded irritated. "Hello? . . . Yeah . . . what did I tell ya about callin' here? I don't care! Well . . . take care of it. That's your job! Then tell 'em so and don't call me about it. I won't tell ya again!"

There was a tone in his voice that I didn't recognize. I'd never heard him speak that way to anyone.

"Who was it honey?" I asked after he hung up.

"It was just some of my business people. I get tired of 'em always expectin' me to know the answer. That's what I pay 'em for. To be takin' care of my business."

"Why do ya always say not to call here or come here? I don't mind if your business partners come out or call here."

"This is not a place to talk about business. This is your place and it's our space to spend time together. I wish they'd all just go the hell away!"

I was a little shocked. I just didn't see why it was such a big deal. He acted like we were havin' a secret affair and he seemed to be really agitated 'bout the whole thing. I decided to add that to the ever- growin' list of "things we needed to talk about later."

Several days passed. We were involved with the new colt and makin' plans for the spring. We'd gotten closer than ever. We spent every spare minute either in each other's arms or in the bed. We'd gone into Bigby a few times to the home, but mostly we just wanted to stay home and spend time together.

It was on a Saturday when Toby called and wanted to know if we wanted to go out to King's. He said it would probably be Floy's last chance to go out and maybe dance a little before the baby came. We hadn't been out there in forever.

"Sure," Chad told 'em. "We'll pick ya'll up on the way and we'll go eat somewhere and then go on out."

We picked 'em up about six and went to the little cafe in Dover.

Floy was really showin' and deep inside I envied her more with each day that passed.

"I tell ya, dear . . . you're gonna have twins . . . or maybe triplets," I teased.

"Naw," said Toby, "I told her I think it might be a whole damn litter!"

"Toby! If ya don't quit tellin' people that, I swear, I'm gonna plant my size six shoe in your 'you-know-what!" threatened Floy.

Chad had let us out and went to park the truck. I sat watchin' him through the window as he came across the parkin' lot. He was wearin' the baby blue shirt that I liked so much. It was the one with the initials on it. I loved the way he rolled his sleeves almost up to his elbows and had his hat sittin' on the back of his head.

When he walked in the door, I couldn't help but notice every woman in there turn and watch him come inside. It seemed that no matter where he went everyone was watchin' him. I guessed I was the worst of 'em all. I could hardly take my eyes off him. What with that blue shirt . . . his eyes were such a beautiful bright shade of blue. It made me so proud when he came to our table, leaned over, and gave me a sweet little kiss before he sat down. I felt like that was his subtle way of lettin' everybody in there know that he was taken and so was I. No matter where we went, I was always so proud to be with him. He was always such a gentleman, so kind and polite to everyone.

We ate, then headed for King's.

"I think everybody,s gonna be glad to see ya again, Chad." Toby told him.

"I don't know about that, Toby. I can think of a few that probably won't be too happy."

We walked in and it was less than two minutes before Nicky had come up to us.

"Hey partner? I'm sure glad to see ya again. I was worried about ya. Ya just kinda disappeared on us there." Nick said and patted him on the back. " I'm sure glad to see ya two out here again."

"Thanks Nick, it's good to be back," answered Chad.

They visited for a few minutes before Chad sat down and Nicky went back to work at the bar. Toby and Floy went straight to the dance floor. It was a nice slow song, so it seemed that everyone wanted to be out there .

"Ya wanna dance?" Chad asked as I stood up and let him lead me to the floor.

He twirled me around and brought me close against him, then took my hand and held it across his heart while we danced. The song was a Willie Nelson tune, "You were always on my mind." It was one of my favorites. It was a pleasant surprise when Chad began to sing it softly to me. I didn't get to hear him sing very often. He mostly whistled or hummed, but I loved it when he sang. He had the most beautiful voice I'd ever heard. He sounded like a combination of Marty Robbins and Elvis. I told him that once and he started laughin' so hard he almost choked. I think he thought I was teasin' him, but when the song ended, some of the people dancin' near us even began to applaud him. He was so embarrassed that he took my hand and drug me back to the table. There was several people still starin' and makin' comments. Some of 'em even came by the table and told him how much they'd enjoyed it. One guy asked him if he'd get on stage and sing.

"I . . . uh . . . naw . . . I . . . I don't sing. I . . . I'm not an entertainer . . . I was just kinda singin' to my girl. Thank ya though, thank ya very much for askin'." Then he got up and quickly made his way to the bathroom.

Some people I knew came up and asked me who he was and where I'd met him.

I was relieved when Toby and Floy came back and joined me.

"What's all the fuss about?" Toby asked.

"Well, Chad was singin' to me and a lot of folks was impressed and wanted him to sing on stage." I told him.

"You're kiddin' me! Where's he at?"

"He made a run for the bathroom. I think they scared him the way he lit outta here."

"I better go see about him," Toby said as he stood up and headed in that direction.

"I wish I'd been here. I've never heard Chad sing, is he good?" Floy wanted to know.

"Yeah. He's very good. In fact he's damn well amazin'. But I'm tellin' ya . . . don't ever ask him to sing 'White Christmas'!" I snickered as she gave me that confused look.

Before long the guys were back with beers and water. Of course Toby was still teasin' Chad about the singin'. He started callin' him, "Hollywood". Chad just shook his head and gave him that little half smile.

We was havin' a great time 'til the get acquainted dance. It started off just fine. I'd danced with several guys and then I ended up with Jamie. He appeared to have had way too much to drink and was not too sure on his feet. That was really unusual for him 'cause he was one of the best dancers I'd ever known.

"Hey Lilah, girl," He slurred. We danced for a minute. "I see you're out here with that old fart again?" I was shocked. He'd never been so rude in all the times I'd danced and talked with him.

"That was uncalled for, Jamie."

"Maybe, maybe not. I been waitin' to see ya again and here ya come with that old geezer. What ya see in him anyhow? What's he got that I ain't?" He was really wasted.

"Ya wanna know the truth, Jamie?"

"Hell yeah, I just don't get it?"

"It's really simple . . . what he has . . . is my heart. I'm very much in love with him."

"That's bull shit!" he burst out. He was holdin' me really tight and he was beginnin' to hurt my hand.

"You asked me and I just told ya the truth. Plain and simple . . . I love him. Why are ya bein' like this? You and I hardly know each other, Jamie."

"That ain't my fault. Ya just act like you're too high and mighty for me. I heard what happened to ya. Ya ain't no better'n anybody else. I heard that old boy got what he wanted before that bear got to him. Is that true, Lilah? Did that old doctor get in your pants? Seems to me ya shouldn't be so uppity, now!" I stopped dead in my tracks and before I could think, I'd slapped the whiskers off of him.

Once he regained his balance, he looked me straight in the eye and slapped me as hard as he could. It almost knocked me off my feet, but I'd vowed that no man would ever hit me again and get away with it. Instinct took over and I doubled up my fist and punched him square in the nose. I heard it break and saw the blood begin to pour. He started toward me with pure vengeance in his eyes. I was ready for him. I had my foot ready to nail him right where I knew it would hurt him most. That was when "Gallahad" appeared out of nowhere. He took one look at my bruised face and I saw fire shoot from those blue eyes. I knew in my heart that he'd kill Jamie. I grabbed his arm.

"He's drunk, Chad! Just let it go."

He already had Jamie on the ground with his arms twisted behind his back. That was when Nicky and his crew of bouncers showed up. Nicky put his hand on Chad's shoulder.

"Let him go, Chad. We'll take care of it. He's drunk and outta line."

"Nick . . .he hit her . . . I ain't gonna let him get away with that!" He said between gritted teeth as he jerked Jamie's arms up higher.

"He ain't. I'll call the Sheriff's office and they'll take care of him. Okay? Just let him go before ya get yourself in trouble." Nick reasoned. Chad sat there astraddle Jamie's back. I could see that he was havin' a very hard time lettin' go. I realized that after everythin' that had happened with Scott, the last thing he was prepared to do was to sit back again and helplessly watch another man abuse me.

"Honey, come on. He ain't worth it," I whispered in his ear. He looked up at me, the muscles were twitchin' in his jaw and he was so angry that he couldn't even talk. He leaned over Jamie and said in a quiet, very threatenin' voice, "Ya ever come near her again, and they'll take ya home in a box!" Jamie nodded that he understood and Chad forced himself to get up.

"Ya should a killed the bastard!" Someone in the gatherin' crowd yelled.

"Yeah, let us have him for a little while, Nick!" Someone else yelled. They were workin' themselves into a frenzy.

"Ya wanna hit somebody . . . try me! We don't hold with hittin' no women 'round here!" Someone else chimed in.

Nick held up his hand as his bouncers began to take a stance with bats in hand.

"I'm the damn owner of this place! I'm callin' the Sheriff and this'll be handled like it ought to! Now calm down and go back to your partyin' before the Sheriff gets here and decides to haul ya all off for public drunkedness!"

That seemed to put a little of the fire out. Almost everyone headed back to their tables or the dance floor. The bouncers took Jamie to the back office as Nick turned to us.

"I swear Lilah Marie, you seem to stir up more shit in here than I can handle." He laughed.

"But I wasn't doin' anything, Nicky."

"I know. It seems like trouble just follows beautiful women. Ain't that right Chad?" He teased. "How's your face honey? Do ya need anything for it? Ice?" asked Nicky.

"No, I'm fine."

We went back to our table with Toby and Floy.

"You're sure 'nuff a scrappy little thing! I thought ya was gonna whoop that old boy's butt. Probably would have if Chad hadn't showed up." Toby teased me.

"I wouldn't have thought that Jamie was like that. He always seemed so sweet." Added Floy.

Chad sat there lookin' into his beer and said nothin'.

"Ya alright?" I asked as I snuggled closer.

"I just ain't used to lettin' somethin' like that go. I still think I should've beat the hell out of him."

"Then ya would go to jail, too. That would've put a real damper on the night."

He reached up and gently touched my face.

"You okay little girl?"

"Yes, I'm fine."

"Hey, it's late. Ya'll wanna go? The mood kinda sucks right now." asked Toby.

We all agreed that it was better to leave and try another night. We finished our drinks and started for the door. Several people along the way asked us to stay and not let it ruin our night and some of 'em even teased me about signin' me up for a boxing match.

We'd just stepped outside when the Sheriff and several Deputies arrived.

"Let's go back inside folks. I don't want anyone to leave 'til after I find out what all happened." The Sheriff said.

He sent us back into the club along with a few others who were headed to the parkin' lot. It wasn't long before we was in the back office with the Sheriff, Nicky, and Jamie. Of course they wanted to know what all had happened. I told 'em and for a moment I was worried that I was gonna get in trouble 'cause I'd struck first. However, when I told 'em that he was hurtin' me and wouldn't let go, they seemed to understand.

"Yeah, and if he ever comes near her or lays another hand on her, I'll kick his ass!" said Chad.

It's hard to recall for sure what happened after that, except that Jamie, even though he was handcuffed, lowered his head, and made a hard run at Chad.

Not realizin' that Floy was right behind him, Chad stepped out of Jamie's way and thought that Jamie would just run into the wall. Instead he smashed straight into Floy, slammed her to the floor, and landed right on top of her, knockin' her unconscious. The Sheriff smacked Jamie over the head with his bat and the Deputies took him out.

Chapter 20

We were all on the floor with Floy.

"Call an ambulance!" I screamed.

We had cold rags on her face and tried to make her as comfortable as possible. It seemed like it was hours before we heard the siren pull into the parkin' lot.

Toby was beside himself with worry.

It seemed like forever before we arrived at the hospital. We were all seated in the waitin' area hopin' to hear some news. Chad stood at the far end with his head down.

"She'll be alright," I tried to console him.

"It's my damn fault. If I hadn't stepped out of his way, he wouldn't have hit her. If anything happens to her or that little baby . . . I . . . I'll . . . "

"No. It's not your fault. It was Jamie,s for bein' such an ignorant ass," I told him.

Toby came over then, "Chad, ya can't blame yourself. It was just somethin' that happened. They'll be okay. I know they will. Lots of babies are born early and do just fine. Now quit blamin' yourself and just think good thoughts. Give up one a them prayers you do so good," He patted Chad on the back and went back to his seat.

A nurse stepped in and asked Toby to go with her. She didn't say where or why, but I feared the worst. Several hours went by and we'd heard nothin'. There'd been no one else come in and I began to think that maybe they had forgotten that we were waitin' out here.

When the door finally opened, it was Mr. and Mrs. Felton, Floy's parents. I introduced them to Chad and of course they wanted to know what'd happened and if we'd heard anything. I told 'em generally what'd happened and then we all sat there waitin'.

"Well, no news is good news, isn't that right?" asked Mrs. Felton.

"That's what I've always heard." I tried to reassure her.

It was about thirty minutes later when the door opened and Toby came in. He was in a daze and my heart sank with fear. I looked at Chad and I could read the sick fear that was written all over his face. Toby didn't say anything. He just leaned against the wall as tears ran down his cheeks. Mr. and Mrs. Felton stood up and waited in dreaded anticipation. I walked over to him.

"Toby?" I asked softly. "Toby, what happened?"

"I . . . I . . . " he sobbed.

"You what?" I asked him as my heart began to ache.

" I just . . . I just held my baby daughter! She's so beautiful."

"Is she okay?" I pressured him. "How's Floy?"

"She's . . . asleep . . . in recovery."

"And the baby?"

"They put her in the incubator . . . but they said she looks great. Lilah, Chad? I got me a baby girl!"

He started to come out of the shocked state that he'd been in when he first came in. As the reality began to sink in, he became so excited that he could hardly contain himself. We were all so relieved and so deliriously happy.

"So everyone's alright?" Chad could hardly believe the good news.

"Yeah . . . everbody's great. She's so beautiful! I never seen anything so beautiful!" He went to Mrs. Felton and gave her a hug and spun her around.

"Ya got yourself a granddaughter!"

It was awhile before they'd let us go in to see Floy, so we all huddled at the nursery window to get a peek at the new addition to our crew. When they finally opened the curtain and rolled the incubator over to the window, we all fell silent in amazement. She was tiny at four pounds and seven ounces. She had such a perfect little head and a nose so tiny that I wondered how she got enough air to survive. Floy's Daddy had tears rollin' down his cheeks as he admired his first grandbaby. It was about a half hour before we could see Floy and she was so groggy that I wasn't sure she really knew what'd happened.

After I was reassured that she and the baby were well, Chad and I decided to go on home.

"We'll be back tomorrow and give ya a ride home, Toby."

"Oh, don't worry, Lilah," said Mrs. Felton. "We'll take him home whenever he wants to go."

That was really a shock since Toby and his in-laws had never really gotten along too well. Maybe the baby would be the beginnin' of a new relationship for 'em. I knew that it'd troubled Floy for some time and it would bring her a lot of relief.

Chad and I didn't say much on the ride home. I felt like he had a lot to think about and so did I. We were gonna be godparents and I could only imagine how wonderful it was gonna be. Floy and I'd always thought of each other as sisters, so I was determined that I was gonna be the best aunt that any little girl had ever had. It was most probable that she was gonna be the only baby that'd bring me as close to being a mama as I'd ever see.

It was late when we finally crawled in bed. I cuddled up close to Chad and wrapped my arm around him.

"What ya thinkin' 'bout?" I questioned.

"Well, I . . . uh . . . I can't quit thinkin' about how I would've never forgive myself if anything had happened to either one of 'em. It just happened so damn fast. I didn't have time to even think." He was still very upset about the whole incident.

"Honey, don't dwell on that part. Just think about how well everything turned out and be thankful. Did ya ever see such a precious baby girl?"

He laid there quietly for a long moment.

"Yeah,......once." He mumbled. I looked at him a little surprised.

"Do what?"

"I saw one just as beautiful once. She was mine and I thought she was the prettiest thing I ever seen. She was so tiny and perfect and the first thing I thought when I saw her was that I just wished that my Mama had been there to see her. I know that she would've been so proud. She didn't live long enough to see her only granddaughter." His voice began to break and I felt so bad that I'd even asked.

"Where is she now?"

"With her mother."

"Where's that?"

"Out west. I'd rather just drop the subject, Honey. That's not somethin' that I'm fond of talkin' about."

"Okay." I told him, "I understand."

I turned over and he cuddled up behind me and wrapped his arm around me. It wasn't long before I heard him snorin' very lightly. I laid there awake for a long time and wondered what his daughter must look like. Did she look anything like him? Did he ever go see her? I couldn't begin to imagine havin' a baby with Chad. The idea of his child growin' inside me was . . . was too gloriously painful to dwell on. Somethin' so deep inside ached at the very thought. Not to mention the emptiness that welled up at the knowledge that it'd never happen. I didn't care what Walt had said. I'd been with Chad so many times that if I was gonna get pregnant, it would've already happened. I wanted to cry at the absolute realization that the two of us would never share a child. We'd never experience what Floy and Toby were sharin' at that very moment.

I don't know when I finally fell asleep, but the dreams were more like nightmares. In my dream, I sat up in my bed. There was a blue light shinnin' in my open closet and I could hear Chad singin'. It seemed to be comin' from somewhere inside the closet. I walked toward it and peered inside. I couldn't imagine why Chad would be inside my closet. His singin' was beautiful, but seemed so very distant. Then his hand reached out of the dark as if to invite me to take it and go with him. I was surprised at the number of rings with fabulous jewels, as well as the one he always wore with his initials on it, that adorned his beautiful hand. His jacket sleeve was as white as pure snow. I wanted to go to him with all my heart as his voice lured me and his hand beckoned me . . . but I was so afraid. I was terrified to enter the unknown darkness that surrounded him and held shadows and figures that seem to lurk on ever' side of him. Suddenly I awakened in a cold sweat. That was about the time the damn rooster began to crow.

Chad continued to sleep. I raised up on one elbow and watched him in the early morning light. He slept like an innocent child. So peaceful, so beautiful, with his hands folded across his chest and his head tilted slightly to one side. There was a great sadness come over me as the thought creeped into my mind that I should cherish every second with him and love him with every ounce of my bein'. Somethin' in my gut told me that this wasn't, nor could it ever be, a forever thing. I felt that the time might be near that I'd have to give him up. My throat tightened with the sobs I refused to shed. From out of nowhere, a panic washed over me like I'd never experienced in my life. I slid silently from the bed and made my way down the stairs with my robe in hand. I wanted to run screamin' into the yard and go as fast and as far as I could. Sanity kept tellin' me that I had an over-active imagination that needed to be reined in.

I went into the kitchen and put on a pot of coffee and sat down at the table. Try as I did, I couldn't shake that terrible uneasiness that held me captive. I finally took my coffee and wandered down to the barn. The horses always cheered me up. As soon as I opened the door, they began to act up with excitement. I petted everyone and shared my good mornin's with 'em. When I came to Promise, however, that horrid feelin' of panic reared its very ugly head. Promise looked deep into my eyes as if to ask me what was wrong.

I stroked his head "I don't know little boy, there's just a bad feelin' in the air. I feel like I could cry at the drop of a hat, scream at the top of my lungs, and would terribly enjoy breakin' somethin' to pieces."

He snorted softly and began to nod his head up and down as if to tell me that he knew somethin' too. It was barely daylight and the air was still very cool with the light breeze that swayed the door. I sat down in the stack of hay that was against the wall and sipped my mug of coffee. There was always somethin' so peaceful about bein' out there with my boys. The way they nickered and and the smell of the hay and the leather mixed with the scent of the earth as it thawed from the winter cold. It promised to be a time of renewal and rebirth. This was a time when everything sprang back to life and the world would share in its abundance. It was such a wonderful time . . . so why'd I feel so damn lousy? I had just about everything a woman could possibly want.

Nanny used to tell me that God gave woman the sixth sense 'cause man would never slow down and take time to listen to it. Well, I was wishin' that I wasn't hearin' it right then. Maybe it was just that I was still very uneasy about the fact that Floy had delivered the baby so early. Even though she was perfect and the doctor had said that both of 'em were in great condition, I was still uneasy.

The barn door opened just then, Chad stood there in his jeans, a tee shirt and his jacket on.

He looked angry, "Why are ya down here?" his tone was short.

"I woke up and you was sleepin' so good that I didn't want to wake ya up."

"Ya scared the hell outa me!" He growled. "I woke up and couldn't find ya nowhere. The coffee was made and you were gone."

I could tell that he was really upset.

"I'm sorry honey. I didn't think about ya wakin' up so early."

He came over and sat down beside me, ran his fingers through his hair, rubbed his forehead, and turned to look at me with worried blue eyes.

"Please, don't do that again," He sighed as he put his arms around me.

He held me for a long moment.

I offered him some of my coffee.

He took it. "Ya know, I have nightmares about ya disappearin' again. Sometimes I dream about that idiot and that damn bear and I just wake up in a sweat! If you're gonna get up and go out . . . just tell me . . . okay?"

"I will, I promise."

We finished the coffee and laid back in the haystack, and watched the horses. Chad nodded toward Promise, "He's a beautiful creature ain't he?"

I was still lookin' at Chad.

"Yes," I answered, "he most certainly is!"

We lay there and talked for a long time. I guess we'd just gotten up too early and before long we fell asleep in each other's arms. Totally content at last, I slept better than I had in a long time.

We stopped in town to eat lunch before we went to the hospital to see the new baby. We had a quiet lunch at Shoemaker's café, but I couldn't help but notice several people starin' when we went in. It seemed that for whatever reason, we were the subject of several people's conversations. Just as we was about finished, a couple came up to our table.

"Hi . . . we were out at King's last night. We heard ya singin' and . . . man, you was great. We was wonderin' . . . uh . . . what your name is and where ya sing at?"

Chad looked startled and looked down at the floor.

"I . . . I . . . uh . . . I don't sing nowhere. Thank ya . . . for the compliment . . . but . . . uh . . . I . . . I only sing for my girl here. I wasn't tryin' to entertain nobody. I . . . I was just singin' to her. Excuse me." He muttered as he got up and went to the washroom.

I wasn't sure what to say.

"He's really shy . . . I think ya embarrassed him."

"We didn't mean to upset him . . . it's just that he sounds so familiar and he kinda looks like . . . "

"Shut up Sissy! People's gonna think your're nuts!"

The guy said as he grabbed her arm and rushed her outta the café.

Chad came back and was in a big hurry to get out of there.

We left and went to do some shoppin' and then straight to the hospital. We was loaded down with gifts for the baby and a vase of flowers for the new mama. The baby was in the room with Floy and Toby when we got there.

"Hello new mommy and daddy!" I called as we came in the room.

Floy was nursin' the baby. Toby was sittin' in the rocker.

"Oops," said Chad as he did an about-face at the sight of Floy's exposed breast.

"It's okay." Toby said as he got up and draped a baby blanket across Floy and the baby.

Chad was still turned toward the wall.

"Honey, ya can turn around now. They're covered."

He peeked over his shoulder and finally turned around. He was actually blushin.

We stayed for awhile and watched Floy open the gifts that we'd brought. When Toby laid that sweet baby in my arms, I thought I'd cry for sure. She was so tiny and delicate. I'd held Mama's babies, but they were always big babies, even the twins. This was almost just a sample of a baby. I held her for a long time before I walked over and put her in Chad's arms. He looked at her so sweetly and held her as though she would shatter.

"She's beautiful," he said. "I think she's a keeper. What we gonna call her?"

"We can't make up our minds. We thought we still had a couple a months yet," Floy said.

"I told her that I guessed we could call her 'Jamie' since he's the idiot that caused all this to start so early," teased Toby.

"Toby . . . I'm gonna stick your head in dishwater if ya even think about that again." I warned him. Of course he was jokin' . . . and we laughed . . . but it was still a sore subject.

It was gettin' late when we left for home and we still had chores to do before we settled in for the night. On the ride home, we talked at length about the baby and how cute she was.

"She looks a lot like Toby." Chad said.

"I don't know, I kinda see more of Floy in her, but you can sure tell that Toby is her daddy."

"Yeah, they can't neither one of 'em deny her, that's for sure."

"Ya sure caused a stir at the café." I commented. "I guess there was a lot of people that were really impressed last night. You do have a beautiful voice and I love it when ya sing for me."

"I'm glad . . . I just wasn't thinkin' that people was payin' attention to us."

"Well, if they wasn't . . . they sure are now," I teased him.

He didn't laugh and he looked quite serious.

"Did I say somethin' wrong?"

"Naw . . . you didn't say nothin' wrong, honey. I . . . uh . . . I just don't like all that attention. I never should a done that."

"Don't worry about it . . . they'll forget all about it in a week or two." I tried to assure him.

I didn't want him to think that every time we went out that people were goin' to try to maul him. I actually thought it was kinda cool how everbody was so impressed with him.

We rode the rest of the way home quietly thinkin' our own thoughts.

Four days later the doctor released Floy and the new baby. We waited until they had time to get home and get settled in before we paid a visit. Mrs. Felton had gone over to stay with 'em for a couple of weeks. I knew that Toby was just thrilled with that, but it was just part of married life. Floy was gettin' around really well and in fact, she was the one who answered the door. Toby was holdin' the baby. Her mom was in the shower.

"Come in," she greeted. I gave her a big hug.

"Ya look so good. I'm glad you're home. I don't like seein' anybody in the hospital."

"Chad, how are ya?" she asked as she gave him a big hug too.

"I'm real good. Where's that little princess?"

"Right there with her daddy," She motioned.

Chad knelt down beside Toby's chair and admired the tiny girl. He looked up at Toby.

"Does she have a name yet?" he grinned.

"Yes she does." Toby announced. "Aunt Lilah, Uncle Chad . . . I'd like ya to meet Miss Laurell Marie Ellis. She's named Laurell after Floy's aunt and Marie after you, Lilah. Sorry Chad, we just couldn't fit any of your names into it. However, we still expect that you'll be her godfather."

"I wouldn't have it any other way. I have a little welcome home present for her," Chad said as he slipped his hand into his jacket pocket.

I'd been to town with him when he bought the present, so I was thrilled that he'd taken it upon himself to present it to her. He pulled out a small pink satin box. He opened it and inside was a tiny golden ring. The top had two little hearts with a perfect diamond nestled between 'em. He gently took her small delicate pink hand and slipped the ring on her ever-so-tiny finger, fastened the little safety chain and lovingly placed a kiss upon it.

"My prayer for ya little angel, is that ya will always have reason to smile at the sun and sing to the stars." With that he kissed her sweet head and backed away.

I could see tears in his eyes and I knew that he was thinkin' about his own baby girl. Floy went to him.

"Chad, you're a wonderful godfather and we do love ya so much."

"Thank ya buddy, hell, your gonna make me haul off and bawl. That was about the nicest thing I ever heard anybody say." Toby muttered in a choked up voice.

"I think it's time for a glass of tea. What do ya'll think?" Floy asked as she headed toward the kitchen.

We stayed for awhile and visited. It was the first time we'd been able to really talk since the baby was born. It seemed like there was always someone in the room or leavin' the room, or callin' every minute that we were at the hospital. We sat and talked about the night Laurell was born and what all had happened.

"I was shocked at the way Jamie acted!" sighed Floy. "I know he was drunk . . . but he acted as nuts as Scott did."

"I guess it just goes to show that ya never really know people. Ya think ya do and then somethin' like that happens and ya realize that they're just not at all who ya thought they was. But . . . no . . . he still couldn't hold a candle to Scott," I pointed out.

"That's for sure. I always thought Jamie was a kinda nice fella. Honest truth, I think he had a thing for ya Lilah and he just couldn't handle seein' ya with Chad. He got drunk and just made a fool outta himself!" reasoned Toby.

"Maybe so, but the fact is he almost seriously injured my best friend and my new little neice. I hope I never have to lay eyes on him again." I was adamant.

It was still too vivid in my mind the way he'd charged at Chad and smashed into Floy.

It wasn't long before the baby woke up and was ready to be fed, so Chad and I left and headed for home. Once again my thoughts returned to how wonderful it'd be to have our own baby. Maybe a little boy, since he already had a little girl. The thought of bein' Mrs. Thomas Chadwick Barrett gave me a slight case of goose bumps.. He 'd told me a million times how much he loved me . . . but not once had he mentioned the word marriage. Neither had he mentioned havin' our own baby and I wondered if he'd ever even let the thought cross his mind.

Before we could turn around twice it was the weekend again.

"Honey! Honey?" Chad called through the house.

"What?" I called back from the kitchen.

He came slidin' through the door in his sock feet.

"I know we always go with Floy and Toby . . . but do ya want to go dancin' for a little while tonight?"

I thought about it for a moment.

"What if Jamie is back out there?" The thought made me very nervous.

"I think I could handle Jamie just fine, but I doubt he will be anywhere in sight." He bit his lip and winked at me. "Besides . . . ya gotta trust me."

"Well, it's fine with me if that's what ya wanna do."

"Then you're sayin' that you'll go out on a date with just me?"

"Yes, Mr. Barrett, I suppose that I am."

"Then I'll pick ya up at seven."

"Ummm . . . okay . . . I'll be ready."

I took extra time with my shower and took more time with my hair and makeup than I usually did. I wanted to look special for him. I wore my best pressed jeans, my red silk shirt, my red boots and matchin' belt. I topped it off with a good dose of my exclusive perfume.

I was surprised when I heard someone knock on the door. I didn't know where Chad had gotten off to, so I hurried down the stairs and answered it. I was even more surprised when I found the most gorgeous man in the world standin' at my door. I didn't have a clue where he'd come up with it, but he had on a bright red western shirt, perfectly pressed jeans and a western jacket that was as white as pure fallin' snow. His black hat against his silver blonde hair was like a crownin' touch.

He asked politely if I was ready to go. I grabbed my purse and jacket, locked the house, and followed him to his truck. If possible, he was even more handsome than ever, and I was so proud to be out with him.

"Where did ya get that jacket?"

"At the gittin' place! " He teased.

"Well, ya look awful handsome in it."

"And you, my love, are unbelievably beautiful. I'm honored once again to get to be your date." He bit his bottom lip lightly and winked.

We drove for a good hour and a half or more to one of the biggest cities in the area. I couldn't recall ever bein' there before. When we turned up the drive, I became very uneasy.

"Chad, I'm not dressed for this. I thought we was just goin' to Dover or somethin'. This place is way fancy for how I'm dressed."

"Ya look great and you'll fit right in. Ya worry too much."

But when we pulled up and there was a valet to park the truck, I nearly had a panic attack. Chad opened the door for me and we walked up the steps where a doorman opened the main door. I was shocked when we stepped down into the main dinin' area. It was all done in a country and western theme with bandana tablecloths and the cutest waitresses in jeans and bandana tops. Oddly enough the place was called, Bandana's. They had a live band on stage and an area sectioned off for dancin'. I was very impressed. Chad must've made reservations 'cause we were seated right away. I'd never seen any place like it.

"This is wonderful, Chad. There are so many people here."

"I heard about it and I thought ya might like it."

Our supper was the best and I was surprised at . . . well. . . . how pretty it was. Ya know how ya order stuff sometimes and when ya get it . . . it looks like somebody sat on it or just threw it at the plate.? This meal was just picture perfect. We had a great table that was a little toward the wall, but sort of close to the dance floor. It was more private than a lot of 'em.

"That was really a great supper, Chad."

He stared directly into my eyes.

"I'm glad ya liked it . . . uh . . . would ya like to dance? I hope so . . . cause I'd really love to be holdin' ya right now."

How could anybody resist such an invitation? I stood up as he took my hand and we made our way to the floor. The music was slow and pretty and he pulled me full against him and wrapped his arms around me.

"I been wantin' to hold ya like this since we got in the truck. You take my breath tonight." He whispered in my ear. I couldn't help but giggle a little.

"It's the cologne . . . it does it to me every time you wear it, too."

"Hmmm. I'm wearin' it now. So . . . what ya think'll happen ?" he whispered as he kissed my ear and neck.

Chills ran through my entire body.

"I don't know, but if ya don't slow down . . . we might get arrested!" I whispered back.

"For what? There's no law for dancin' close."

"No. But there's one for gettin' naked in public and if ya don't stop kissin' my neck . . . that's just what might happen!"

He busted out laughin'.

I loved to hear him laugh. It was the way his voice kinda broke when he really got tickled. There were a lot of people dancin' but I don't think that any of 'em were havin' as much fun as we were. We stayed and danced until the crowd began to thin out.

"Ya 'bout ready to go, baby?" he asked sweetly.

"Yeah, I think I am."

"Let's go home and . . . get naked!" He teased as we went to the door. He gave the valet our parkin' ticket and we were waitin' on the porch of the restraunt for the truck when a young man came runnin' up to us with several other people.

"See! I told ya . . . It's him. I know It's him!"

Cameras started flashin' and people began to gather 'round us. I didn't know what the heck was goin' on, but I was frightened by all the confusion. Chad turned his back to 'em and wrapped his arms around me as if to protect me from 'em.

Just then our truck pulled up and we pushed our way through and got in. Chad squealed the tires as we pulled out onto the street. I looked at him in total panic.

"What was that all about? Who were those people and why did they attack us like that?"

Chad looked upset but ya couldn't tell it by his voice.

"They must've had us mixed up with someone else. I never saw any of those people before."

He reached over and pulled me up under his arm.

"I wonder who they thought ya was?"

He sat there a minute, "I don't know but I sure feel sorry for whoever it is . . . he must have a hard time takin' his girl out."

When we finally pulled up in front of the house, I realized I'd forgotten to leave the porch light on. It was pitch black in our yard. We pulled up and parked and Chad turned to me.

"This is kinda like high school. Remember when everbody went parkin' after a date? I guess we could just make out in the truck like teenagers."

"I hate to tell ya this, but I much prefer the softness of our own bed."

"Yep, that does sound pretty good," He said as he got out and found his way around the truck in the dark. He opened the door and the blue interior light switched on. I froze as his hand reached out of the dark to take mine. The white jacket and his beautiful hand with his initial ring was exactly like the dream I'd had. The only difference was the number of rings that he was wearin'. I sat there for a moment. It was as if the dream had just come to life.

"Honey?" His sweet southern drawl brought me back. "C'mon. Let's go get in our bed. Now!" he teased.

The moment left me uneasy and apprehensive. It just seemed too odd to be a coincidence. I got out of the truck and Chad scooped me into his arms and carried me up to the door. He had to put me down to find his keys, but he picked me up again and hurried into the house and up the stairs. Although our love makin' was very tender and very passionate, I almost felt that Chad was afraid of not lovin' me enough that night. I still had that very strong sense that our time was limited. I didn't know why I felt that way, but the uneasiness continued to grow. For whatever reason . . . I sensed that he felt the same.

The next week Chad decided to take care of a chore that he'd been avoidin' for long enough. That was the day he was gonna close in the cave entrance so that no one, nor no bear, would be prowlin' around in there.

"Do ya wanna go with me?" He asked. "We could take some sandwiches and stuff and make a picnic out of it."

"Sure," I answered as I went to change clothes and get a few things together. When I came back downstairs I found Chad in the kitchen gettin' a lunch together. We took off on foot with a pack of supplies and a lunch basket.

I'd forgotten how far it was up there.

At last we came to the cave. I suddenly felt a nausea sweep over me. I wasn't sure that I could go back in there.

"How are ya gonna seal it?"

"I don't know yet. I need to be sure that there's nothin' in there before I start."

I headed toward the openin' with him, but then I had to tell him that I just couldn't do it.

"It's okay, honey. I can do it," He said as he took his flashlight and stepped inside.

I waited for a long time before he came back out.

"What took ya so long?"

"Just makin' sure there wasn't nobody hidin' in there or that we didn't have another bear in there. I also looked around to see what options we have for closin' it in."

"What did ya find?"

"Well, there's a big boulder in there that, if I could get it to move, would probably cause a cave in."

"That sounds too dangerous." I told him. "What's plan B?"

"We could gather rocks and move some of the smaller boulders and close it in….then we could plant a few bushes and trees to secure it."

"I like plan B better. Wait! Look up there. I see some big boulders that'd probably be easier to roll down the mountain than it'd be to try and push 'em to the mountain." I suggested.

"Now that's what I call a damn good idea. You're pretty smart . . . for a girl!" He teased.

We both climbed up the steep edge to where two very large boulders perched. Behind 'em were several more large ones and a whole bunch of smaller rocks.

"How we gonna make sure that the boulders will go the right direction, Chad? If they get off course…we'll never get 'em moved."

He looked around for a minute and I could tell by that slight frown, that he was hatchin' a plan.

"Okay. Here's what I think we'll do." He explained his idea. I agreed.

We started to clear a path from the boulders down to the mouth of the cave. Chad took a small shovel he'd brought and deepened the path by several inches.

"Okay . . . we've gotta be careful now. I have to clear under the boulders so we can get 'em started."

He took a fair-sized rock and put it in front of the one boulder.

"We'll try it one at a time and see how it works or if we need to make some adjustments. We're only gonna get one try with each one."

I could see that if it worked like we had planned, it should drop the boulders right in front of the cave.

"Wait Chad. We need to put somethin' down there to make sure they don't roll too far."

"You're right, Chica . . . c'mon."

We went down to the cave entrance and searched around. We found some large limbs and pulled 'em to the entrance and then we pulled rocks that we rolled onto the tarp we'd brought.

"We built a kind of a corral for boulders." I bragged.

Chad climbed up and dug away at the top of the entrance in hopes the boulders would just drop straight off.

"What do ya think?" He asked.

"Looks good to me."

He was standin' straddle-legged across the top of the entrance when I heard somethin' crack. Behind him I saw the huge boulder move.

"Chad run!!"

"What?"

The boulder began to move forward. I pointed and he turned to look just in time to jump and roll. He missed the so-called corral and rolled to my feet. All hell broke loose as the boulder knocked the other one loose and the entire mess came barrelin' down the mountain. We turned and ran to the side and up the edge. The dust and debris was so thick we couldn't see or breathe. We laid on the ground coverin' our heads with our jackets.

It finally got quiet. We looked up at each other. I'm sure that my eyes were as wide as his. An avalanche was the last thing that we'd expected to create. We stood up and went to see what we'd done. We both stood there in total shock and amazement. The two huge boulders had fallen directly in front of the cave and everything else had filled in on top. Chad dusted off his shoulders and sleeves and ran his fingers through his hair.

"Yep, just the way I planned it!"

I looked at him and shook my head.

"The way you planned it, my hind leg. You barely got outta that one alive!"

He turned toward me, "Who, me?" He asked as he grabbed his chest and wilted to the ground.

I sat down with him as he lay laughin' on the grass.

"I sorta thought I was a goner. Ya know what they say about your life flashin' before your eyes just before ya die?"

"Yeah."

"It ain't true . . . all I saw was a place to jump and a chance to grab you and run like hell."

"It couldn't have worked any better. It just looks like a natural landslide." I commented. "We don't have to try and plant no trees either."

"Well, it didn't take as long as I thought it would. I'm hungry . . . let's eat." he said as he went for the supplies we'd brought.

"What'd ya fix?" I was pretty hungry myself after all the excitement.

It was a good feelin' to know that I never had to worry about that cave again. The only way in or out was through the little cabin and there were only four of us that knew about it.

Chad handed me a cup of hot chocolate as I sat down.

"I wasn't sure what to fix, so I just used what was handy."

"That's fine, ya know I'm not picky." I assured him.

He opened the pack and began to lay out what he'd brought. I'd never seen such a combination in my life.

"Chad? Honey? Do ya really plan to eat tomatoes and onions with this sandwich?"

"Yeah, why?"

"I just never had that with a peanut butter and banana sandwich. But . . . that's okay. I'll give it a try."

"You'll like it . . . ya really will." He tried to convince me.

I did eat it, but I secretly vowed to never let Chad be in charge of packin' a picnic again.

We packed everything up and started back toward the cabin. Chad suddenly grabbed my arm and stopped me.

"Look honey. Remember last winter when we were up here? That's the ledge where we . . . well, ya know . . . made snow angels.

I turned to look over at the ledge and the memories came floodin' back.

"Yeah, I do remember that. It was a wonderful day 'til somebody got careless with the hatchet."

"I don't want to remember it that way. I want to remember how romantic it was before that." He whispered as he dropped the gear and slid his arms around me. His lips burned against my neck and I melted against him. I was like butter in the sun when he touched me. Sometimes, all it took was just lookin' into those blue eyes and I was his. He knew that kisses on my neck could guarantee a quick and passionate response.

He stopped long enough to take the tarp and place it under the ledge. He turned and looked at me as he chewed his bottom lip. With his finger he motioned for me to come to him. The way he stood there, so sexy, so confident, and so very irresistible, he knew I wouldn't hesitate. I walked slowly to him. It was almost like the first time. Somethin' deep inside told me that this time would be different. Maybe it was the way he looked at me or maybe it was the place, but I couldn't remember ever wantin' him any more than I did at that moment.

He pulled me to the ground with him. He was leanin' on his elbow and I was flat on my back as we stared into each other's eyes. He leaned over and kissed me so softly and so sweetly. His lips touched my neck and then down to my chest. My breathin' was comin' faster as my heart began to race. His fingers expertly undid the buttons on my shirt and he slid his warm hand up my side and across my stomach. I felt the muscles convulse from the sheer magic of his touch. He pulled me gently up and slid my shirt off my shoulders and removed my bra. Leanin' down, he kissed the breast that he held so gently in his hand. It was like electricity shootin' through every vein in my body.

I raised my hand and began to unbutton his shirt. I ran it across his warm hairy chest and I felt the same shiver run through his body. I moved my head closer and let my tongue circle his nipple, first one and then the other.

I heard his breath catch in his throat.

I slipped his shirt off his broad, muscular shoulders and pulled him to me so that I could feel my naked breasts against his chest. His lips covered mine in a kiss so passionate I could hardly breathe. His tongue explored my mouth as mine did his. The taste of his lips and tongue were so sweet and I knew that I could never get enough of him.

I felt his hand unbutton my jeans and then the zipper. I loved the way his heavy breathin' increased at my touch. It wasn't long before we lay together . . . naked.

We'd made love so many times and each time had been magical, but this was different somehow. He ran his warm hand down my leg to my ankle and slowly up the inside of my thigh. I quivered on the inside as he gently moved his hand between my thighs. His eyes were locked with mine and I couldn't seem to break the gaze. Somehow the look in his eyes held me captive in a way I'd never known before. It wasn't just a look of passion or desire. It was also a look of surrender and complete commitment. As we held that gaze, he pushed my legs apart and caressed the inside of my thighs with both hands. Then he leaned over me without ever lookin' away. I felt him begin to push inside and I raised slightly to accept him fully. This time was like no other. Our direct eye contact while makin' love was the most intense experience I could ever imagine. I searched the deep blue of his gaze as he began to move slowly. I watched every expression of pleasure as it sparkled in his eyes. His movements gradually became faster and more intense. My eyes wanted to close, but the sheer wonder of watchin' our pleasure reflect in his was somethin' I didn't want to miss a moment of. We moved together in perfect, passionate harmony. Suddenly he stopped. I looked at him questioningly. Then he pushed inside..deeper...and Deeper . . . slowly . . . and held. I could feel him throb inside. His crystal blue gaze was intent as we lay there motionless and lived in that moment.

He began to move again with slow rythymic movements that took me higher and closer to that sensuous brink. I could see the moment in his eyes as it came near and I knew that he had to see it in mine. It was as if we were joined in our souls, as well as our bodies. I wanted to keep that visual connection until that very moment and I wanted to watch it in his eyes. Then it was there, explosive, passionate, all consumin', and I still couldn't look away. I'd never experienced anything like it. It was like nothin' I'd ever known . . . not even with Chad. There was a deeper satisfaction than I could ever have imagined. At last I was able to close my eyes, yet even then I saw his beautiful, passion-lit gaze. He relaxed on top of me and into my arms. If it'd been humanly possible, I'd have simply absorbed him into my very bein'.

We lay there for awhile before he rolled over to his side and pulled me near him.

"Aw . . . girl . . . you're killin' me." He sighed.

I smiled at him.

We laid there quietly in each other's arms.

Chad broke the silence. "Ya gotta know how I feel about ya, Lilah. I just never thought that I . . . uh . . . that I could find anything like this again. I mean . . . Yeah, I loved my wife . . . ex-wife. I always will. We're still very close friends. But I . . . well . . . I thought ya could only feel that way maybe once in your whole life. I never dreamed that . . . I . . . I could feel this way again. Lilah, you're so sweet and kind and . . . aw . . . hell girl, I just love ya so much. Sometimes it just hurts on the inside . . . honestly . . . it just scares the hell outta me."

"Scares you? Why? Chad I'd die before I'd ever hurt you or intentionally cause ya any kind of pain." I tried to reassue him.

"I know that. That's exactly what makes me love ya so much. Ya have such a unconditional love. My Mama was the only one who ever loved me like that. It didn't matter what happened or what I did, she always loved me. She would a loved you, too. Almost as much as I do."

"Then just let me love you, too." I told him as I leaned over and kissed him on the tip of his nose.

We eventually got dressed and started our hike back down the mountain to the cabin. It'd clouded up at some point in the day and it began to sprinkle on us as we got near to the little cabin.

"Let's sit on the porch for a little bit. Maybe it'll stop rainin'." Chad suggested.

Just as we stepped up on the first step, it began to pour down.

"Man, I didn't see that comin'," he said. "It's a regular Tennessee frog strangler!"

I had to laugh to myself as I watched him try to dodge the leaks in the rickety roof of the old porch.

"Let's go inside where it's dry." I suggested.

He followed me in. We both stopped as we stepped inside the door. Chad looked at me in confusion, but I had no answers for him.

Chapter 21

"What the hell is this?" He asked in total shock.

"I'm not sure . . . but it looks like someone's been in here." I told him in equal shock.

He looked under the bed and in the bathroom. But no one was anywhere to be found. Chad and I both looked at the armoire at the same time. He stepped over and opened it but there was no one inside. I motioned for him to pull it out and look behind it. We looked outside to make sure that no one was lookin' through the window, then we pulled the huge armoire out from the wall. I kept watch while Chad went inside to check things out. He was only gone a moment and stepped back out and pushed the it back into place.

"Everything's where we left it. But somebody has definitely been in here."

It was obvious from the food containers, gum wrappers, pop cans, newspapers, and even dirty towels that littered the floor. I picked up one of the papers and unfolded it. I gasped when I saw the article.

"Chad! Look at this . . . it's us! We're in the paper."

" What? Where?"

He grabbed the paper and stared at the picture. The title read "IS IT? OR JUST A LOOK ALIKE? YOU BE THE JUDGE!"

Chad went pale as he stood there without movin. I waited for him to say somethin', but he didn't utter a single word. Finally he sat down on the bed.

"Chad, who do ya think brought this up here? Why's our picture in the paper? What's the 'look alike' business? Who do ya think's been stayin' up here? I can't believe that Boots and Roz haven't let us know! They're usually very good watch dogs."

Chad still hadn't said a word.

"Honey? Talk to me! What's wrong?" I pleaded.

He looked up then, with tear-filled eyes and just shook his head. He looked devastated, but I couldn't figure out why and he still wouldn't say a word. He finally stood up and took my hand.

"Let's go to the house." he said in a strained voice.

We ran across the little pasture and then the back yard through the rain. We made it to the cabin at last. Once inside, I grabbed towels to dry off and I handed one to Chad.

"Are you okay?" I asked him.

He looked down for a moment, then he bit his lower lip, and looked up at me. He just shook his head.

"I wanna catch that sneaky son-of-a-bitch. I'm goin' back up there and hide in the cave 'til he comes back!" he snarled through gritted teeth.

"Then I'm goin' with ya."

"No! You're gonna stay right here where it's safe."

I could tell by the tone of his voice that there was no changin' his mind.

He changed into black pants and a black turtle neck sweater, got some water, and started for the door.

"Chad!"

He stopped and turned to me. I ran over and gave him a hug.

"Be careful, Honey. Ya don't know who might be out there." I told him as I ran my fingers through his hair. He closed his eyes for a second then pulled me to him and kissed me sweetly.

"I'll be back. Just stay here."

With that he went out the back door.

It was well into sunset and the clouds made it fairly dark outside. I tried to do what Chad had asked, but he had no idea how impossible it was to do anything when all I could do was walk from window to door and stare up at that cabin. It got quite dark and I'd stood about as much as I could. The decision was difficult, but I went upstairs, changed into black pants and a shirt, tied my hair up, covered my head with a black scarf, and grabbed a dark blanket. Carefully, I went out the front door so that Chad wouldn't see me. I slipped around the house, up into the timber and made my way up toward the little cabin. Carefully, I climbed up the edge of the mountain. I found myself a good-size tree so I could climb up high enough that I could see the porch and through the window into cabin. I wrapped the dark blanket around me and settled down to keep watch.

It was hard to know how long had passed, but it was long enough for my butt to go numb. I was repositionin' myself on the limb, when somethin' caught my eye in the bright moonlight that shown through when the clouds broke for just a minute. Someone was sneakin' up to the big cabin. I could see 'em very clearly as they slipped from window to window peepin' inside. There wasn't a sign of Boots or Roz and I had to wonder where my dogs were. They'd never allow this prowler such free reign. It looked like he decided that we was upstairs 'cause he stood way back and stretched his neck as if to see in the upstairs windows. At that time he turned and headed up toward the wooded area. He moved quietly along the tree line toward the little cabin. I began to get very nervous as he got closer and closer to my hidin' place. When he slipped directly beneath me, I held my breath and prayed that I wouldn't make a sound that'd give me away. He went past and up on the porch as silently as a cat, opened the door, and eased inside. My spot was perfect as I could see clearly in the window and I felt like I had a ring side seat. I didn't know exactly when Chad intended to confront him, but I could hardly wait. The idea that whoever it was felt like he had the right to come onto my property and roam around like he'd somehow been given permission to, was dumbfoundin'. In these parts, that was a good reason for shootin' some body. I wondered who he was and what he thought he was doin'. I was thankful that there only seemed to be one of them.

Time passed as it got later and I could see the man walkin' 'round in the dark of the room. I guessed that he knew better than to turn the light on. It looked like he had a very small flash light for what light he might need. Finally he appeared to lay down across the bed. On our bed! The bed we'd made love in! He definitely had some nerve. I waited and watched and wondered what in the world Chad was waitin' on.

It was later that I saw movement in the cabin. As best that I could tell, the armoire was movin' at last. The light suddenly come on and I had a perfect view. Chad had him by the neck and arm and flipped him over. It looked like they were arguin' about somethin'. Chad sat the man up on the bed and stepped away from him. I saw him shake his head at the intruder and then point his finger in his face. The man jumped up and grabbed the newspaper and showed it to Chad as if he thought he'd never seen it. Then the man shoved it in Chad's face and that was when Chad slugged him. It surprised me and I almost fell from the tree. The man jumped to his feet again and charged at Chad. That was when I saw that kung fu stuff again. I'd only seen it done like that on TV and in some movies, but Chad was awesome and the prowler was out on the floor. I watched as Chad gathered up the papers and crammed 'em into a bag along with some other stuff. He handed the man the bag and shoved him out the door.

"Get the hell outta here, Larry! You and the rest of your so-called paparazzi friends are nothin' but a bunch of leeches. Let it out and I'll make ya look like the fool ya are! Leave me the hell alone and don't ever let me catch ya tryin' to follow me again. Next time ya won't walk away. Ya understand me, son?" he yelled at the man who was rapidly departin'.

It was time that I'd better depart myself before Chad got down to the house and discovered that I'd not listened to him . . . again. I scurried down the tree and quickly through the woods. As fast as I could, I rushed in the front door and up the stairs just as I heard Chad come in the back door. Quickly I dashed into the bathroom and started to run bath water as I stripped and hid my black clothing in the hamper. Just as I settled into the tub, the door opened.

"Honey?" I said in mock surprise. "Ya back already?"

"Yeah." He mumbled as he slipped out of his shirt.

"Did ya see anybody?" I asked innocently.

"Yeah." He sighed. "I took care of it."

He sat down on the edge of the bed and rested his head in his hands. I settled for just a quick rinse and got out and wrapped a towel around myself. It was really obvious that he was still terribly upset. The uneasiness that I'd been dealin' with for several days seemed to intensify. I sat cautiously next to his feet.

"Talk to me, sweetheart. What is it?"

He looked up at me with those beautiful, intense, blue eyes. A single tear rolled unchecked down his cheek.

"Chad, you're scarin' the hell outta me. Tell me what's goin' on! I think I've a right to know!

Somethin' was terribly wrong and I felt the same fear I'd felt in the dream when the dark surrounded a single, white sleeved hand. Finally he spoke.

"Honey, I . . . aw I . . . I uh . . . I love ya so much! I . . . I'm just not sure how to . . . to tell ya this." He took a deep, shakey breath. "There's no easy way to put it."

"Chad," I whispered. "Just say it."

"When . . . when I . . . I first saw ya. It really was like a bolt of lightnin'. I wasn't just sayin' that. It hit me right in the heart and I had to find ya and get to know ya. There was somethin' about ya that . . . that I just couldn't walk away from. When I come out here and saw this place . . . aw man . . . it was like heaven on earth. So quiet, so peaceful, and I fell so hard for ya. I thought . . . I thought . . . I was stupid enough to believe that it was possible that I could live the rest of my life, right here, with you . . . in this . . . this . . . Terra de Gracia!"

"I've heard ya say that before . . . what does it mean?" I was strugglin' to try and stay calm.

"It means . . . this . . . land of grace. It's this place, it's you . . . I wanted more than anything in this world to stay here forever."

"You can, Chad."

"No. No baby." He mumbled softly. "Listen to me . . . I . . . uh . . . I can't explain it . . . but I can't. I have to leave . . . now . . . right now!"

My breath caught in my throat. I couldn't breathe. I wasn't hearin' this.

"I'm so sorry, precious. I never thought this would . . . could happen. They tried to tell me I was bein' a fool. But I . . . I wouldn't listen. I dared to follow a dream that I thought . . . I dared to hope . . . no . . . I prayed would be everything I wanted . . . you wanted . . . that we could . . . " He stood up and walked to the window. "I wish I could explain it all to ya . . . that I could tell ya everything . . . but . . . oh dear God!" He cried out in an agony that I just couldn't understand.

"Why me? It's too much! I just want a normal life!" He dropped to his knees and sobbed.

I rushed to him and cradled him in my arms. The man had just told me he was leavin' me, and my heart was breakin' for us both, and I still didn't know why. I'd never have believed that this strong, confident, bigger than life, man could just fall to pieces before my very eyes. Not knowin' what to say, I just held him and rocked him 'til he gained control. He finally sat up and raised his head. It was a moment before he could look directly at me. The thought that I'd never look into those incredible blue eyes again tore at my very soul. He bit his lip and his chin quivered as he cleared his throat and wiped at his eyes.

"Lilah, will ya just trust me and believe that I can't go into the details. I can only tell ya that I'll love ya with every piece of my broken heart 'till the day I take my last breath!" He whispered in more pain than I'd ever witnessed. "I don't know if I can ever come back . . . but I don't know that I can't either."

He paused for a long devastatin' moment as more tears ran down his cheeks and neck.

"I can only say . . . don't look for me . . . don't expect me . . . but don't be surprised should it happen."

"But where are ya goin'? Take me with ya, Chad . . . please!" I begged as tears streamed down my own face.

"I can't tell ya that either, little one, and I'd never be so cruel as to take ya into the dark insanity that's my world."

"I don't understand, Chad." I sobbed. "I'll never understand how ya can walk away from me again!"

I took a moment to try and pull myself back from the brink of nothingness that threatened to suck me under.

"But . . . I do trust ya and I'll love ya every minute of every day 'til the end of forever. I just want ya to remember this . . . that . . . that never before . . . and never again . . . has anyone loved you . . . this much."

He lifted my chin with his finger tip and kissed me so softly that it could've been the wings of a butterfly. Then he took his suitcases out of the closet and packed everything that belonged to him as quickly as he could.

"You'll take care of Promise for me?"

"Yes," I whispered.

And just like that . . . he was gone.

After Chad left, I spent weeks in a state of depression that I couldn't begin to free myself from. I spent some time in Arkansas with Mama and Daddy, but eventually, I had to go back home. Floy and Toby and the baby did everything they could to try and help me find the strength and confidence I needed so desperately. They didn't really understand any more than I did. But we all knew Chad well enough to know that whoever he might have been, he was a wonderful, gentle man whom we were blessed and lucky enough to get to spend an entire year knowin' and lovin'.

It was April and the daffodils were just beginnin' to bloom when he left, but spring held so little for me to celebrate. The months passed, the weather warmed at last, and still I heard nothin'.

It was then that, I unexpectedly learned that I still had so much to live for.

On a snowy mornin' in the first week of January, I gave birth to Chad's twin sons. Tiny, beautiful, identical, replicas of their Daddy. The first time they handed 'em to me I was spellbound. Just like their Daddy, they took my heart and soul.

The first born I named Eli Aron and the second born I named in honor of Miss Mae's son…Jon Baron. When they finally opened their tiny eyes and looked at their new world, I was thrilled to find that they both had their Daddy's amazin' crystal blue eyes as well as his full pouty lips. I began to fear that for that reason alone . . . just like their Daddy . . . no one in the world would ever be able to deny 'em anything that they might ever want.

The next spring, I decided to go for a short horseback ride on Pride while Dee watched the babies. Before long I found myself by the creek, the same creek where Chad and I'd first made love. I was stunned to find that someone had planted enough red rose bushes to cover the entire area where we'd been.

I don't know who, how, or when, but I think I know why. It was so no one would ever lay there again.

I later found that the ledge on the mountain where I believe to this day is where our boys were conceived, was filled in with bolders the size of Texas. It was completely impassable.

To Floy's huge relief, I finally found a name for my ranch . . . Tierra de Gracia Ranch. She agreed that it was perfect once she knew what it meant.

It was a beautiful, snowy, Christmas Eve, just before the babies first birthday. I had just tucked 'em in for the night, I hoped, and sat down in front of the little tree I had put up for 'em. It was a bitter-sweet time for me. The memories spun in my head like a whirlwind. Some were wonderful and some were heart-breakin'. I still missed Chad with evey beat of my heart, but I'll admit, the boys were such a dream come true that it made it easier. There was a sudden knock on the door.

"Who is it?" I asked before I unlocked the door. After all, it was late and I wasn't expectin' company.

"Special delivery for Lilah Parker." The man on the other side casually answered.

I hesitated for a second and then unlocked and opened the door.

"I'm Lilah Cullwell." I told him.

"Please sign here." He instructed as he handed me a clipboard and a small package.

I signed, thanked him, and closed the door. I couldn't imagine who would send me a package, by special delivery, way up here. I sat down on the couch and opened it. It was a full minute before I could even begin to believe what I held. Beautifully packaged, was a small bottle of Platnum "E" la femme. There was no card . . . but I knew who sent it. I clutched it to my heart and got up to go to my room. I had just started up the stairs when the phone rang.

"Hello . . . hello?" I answered. "Hello?"

There was a huge amount of static on the line.

"Hello? Is anyone there?" I asked.

" . . .static . . . static . . . I . . . uh . . . hi Honey . . . It's me."

About the Author

Linda Holmes Drew grew up in East Texas and later returned to her home state of Oklahoma. Retiring after thirty four years as a barber/stylist and shop owner, she decided to fulfill a lifelong desire to write novels. This is the first book in a two-part series. She and her husband, David, live in central Oklahoma with her Maltese puppy, Chelsea. They have four children and twelve grandchildren.

Made in the USA
Charleston, SC
26 June 2015